Excerpt from Heroes Live Forever:

He came around and kneeled in front of her. He lifted each leg to push the skirt aside, then rocked back on his heels and slid his hands up her calves. Soft pressure behind her knees pulled her to him. She sucked in air as he kissed a path up her thigh.

She grabbed a handful of raven black hair and forced him to look up. Taking as much of his tunic in her fists as she could, she tugged until he stood.

"You are my prisoner." She struggled to hold his wide wrists with one hand while undoing the tunic's toggle fasteners. He crossed his wrists offering a more manageable hold for her smaller hands. It gave her the advantage she needed.

"Hah, victory," she declared and removed the tunic, then continued to undo his breeches. "A lesser woman would've given up. Now, I will know what you desire, milord."

Basil brought his lips to her ear. "I want to make love to you with each of my senses. I want to smell you, inhale your scent," he told her and nuzzled her neck.

Heroes Live Forever

Chris Karlsen

May a hero haunt your dreams—
Chris Karlsen

Books to Go Now Publication

ISBN-13: 978-1493648474

ISBN-10: 1493648470

Other Stories by Chris Karlsen

The Knights in Time Series
Knight Blindness
Journey in Time

The Dark Water Series
Golden Chariot
Byzantine Gold

Prologue

Battle of Poitiers
September 19, 1356

Basil Manneville, Earl of Ashenwyck, lost count of the different banners on the enemy field. Every noble house in France was represented. The English were outnumbered three to one if he had to guess, but if it turned out to be five to one he'd not be surprised.

Behind him, a horse whinnied. Basil turned as his old friend, Guy rode up. Once the battle started, they'd be in the first line of mounted knights leading the charge with Edward of Woodstock, the Black Prince.

Basil and Guy had each kept his own counsel that morning as they made ready. But for the first time in this campaign, Guy had tied several bright colored favors to his armor. The ribbons covered the length of his upper arm and were as different as the ladies who'd offered them.

Guy broke the silence. "Do you think the battle will be as bad as Crecy, or worse?" he asked, as he studied their enemy who continued to form up on the opposite plateau.

"We'll be lucky if it's only as bad as Crecy. I imagine it will be much worse. You shouldn't worry too much," Basil said, eyeing the favors decorating Guy's arm. "Half the ladies at court have lit candles for your safe return."

"I'm not worried, not about the French. I worry about the ladies. When I return, I must pace myself and some are bound to be disappointed." Guy said with a broad grin.

"You're like a fine gardener. You go from flower to flower, cultivating the ladies. I envy you and your garden. At least there'll be one who will weep for you."

"You speak as though there are none who would mourn you."

"Only my brother," Basil said. "I'm not like you. I never saw women as delicate flowers for me to gather. I gave them a rousing tumble or two and then put them from my mind."

A large company of French knights dismounted and handed the reins of their destriers to waiting squires. Horses and men made a muddy mess of the soft soil and wet grass. The knights removed axes and morning stars. They left their long swords in the scabbards on their saddles. Instead, they took arming swords, strapping the baldrics to their waists.

"They're saving the best of the cavalry for the initial charge," Guy said.

Basil nodded. "The rest will fight on foot, ready to rush through our weak spots."

Priests in black robes walked among the English ranks blessing swords and bows before the order to form three columns came. Prince Edward's men lined up on the plateau at the edge of Nouaille Wood. Their position gave them clear view of the French forces which stretched as far as the eye could see.

A battle cry rang out.

Hidden behind a cover of hedges, Edward's archers employed the same strategy his father used ten years earlier, at Crecy. The bowmen had dug a trench in front of the thicket to slow the oncoming cavalry.

The first charge of French men-at-arms and cavalry made for a gap in the hedge. The pounding of the approaching heavy horses thundered in Basil's ears. The ground beneath him shuddered. The roar of men and beasts grew louder as though the earth were being ripped open. His mount, Saladin, stamped and snorted in anticipation. Basil murmured an order and tapped the horse's flank with a golden spur. The warhorse ceased his prance and held steady.

English archers rained arrows down. Wounded horses squealed and reared, throwing their riders, while others fled, panicked, their massive hooves trampling on friend and foe. Men screamed and cried out in fear, in pain, dying. Metal clanged against metal. The deafening roar raged on, carnage and chaos ensued, the slaughtered piling up but a couple of lengths in front of the prince's column.

Still the French came on in fierce hand-to-hand combat. Behind Edward, sword in hand, Basil spurred Saladin and leaped the hedge. Too late he saw the glint from the enemy ax hack into his destrier's chest. The great mount's front legs collapsed as he landed and rolled to one side, trapping Basil.

The French knight struck swiftly. Basil parried the blow, and then slashed upward, burying his sword in the man's groin. Saladin pawed at the air as he struggled to rise, the movement crushed Basil's leg into the ground. Blinded with pain, he didn't see his enemy's blade. One instant, then two, passed before he felt the searing pain. The force of the strike cut through his chain mail and into his neck.

Warm blood filled his mouth and spurted through his lips. The blood choking him, he turned his head and tried to spit. As he did, he saw Guy on his grey

Percheron, fighting to reach him. Basil raised his sword and waved with all the strength he had left. He struggled to call out, to tell Guy to leave him. It was futile. He couldn't be heard over the melee.

Surrounded and pulled from his horse, Guy fell from Basil's sight. Only the flashes of steel stayed in view, rising and falling, again and again.

A heavy boot came down on Basil's chest, pinning him. As he arced his sword toward his enemy's leg, he felt the Frenchman's blade slice deep across his throat.

Then he felt nothing.

Chapter One

Badger Hollow Manor
Norfolk, England-1980

Elinor stood in the kitchen head cocked, and listened for another...scream? The sound cut off midstream. All was quiet upstairs.

"Nora, Nora, Nora!" Her friend, Lucy, hurried down the stairs and skidded to a halt in the doorway. Hand to her chest and wild-eyed, she gasped to catch her breath. "I've just seen a ghost!" Arms stretched out, she repeated, "Ghost!" Wild flipping hand motions accompanied the declaration, as if the gesture helped define the word.

"I suppose you think that's funny, screaming like that. I was about to run upstairs. I thought you'd hurt yourself."

"I'm not trying to be funny. I did see a ghost, a knight-like ghost...a Galahad-Lancelot ghost. Cross my heart and hope to die, if you'll pardon the expression. At least it looked like a ghost." She peered warily over her shoulder. "Oh, I don't know. It happened so fast."

Elinor looked too and saw nothing unusual. "Show me."

She followed Lucy up the dark oak staircase. Lucy twitched with every creak of the steps as they went. At the top, she paused. Elinor urged her forward and both women moved to the center of the small hallway.

"Where was this ghost, because, I don't see a thing," Elinor asked. Under her breath, she said, "never do," as

Lucy went to the door of the master bedroom and stopped.

She huddled next to Elinor in the doorway and peered around.

"Go on, I'm right here," Elinor told her.

Lucy took a few tentative steps into room. She stood by the window which gave her a view of the bathroom too.

Elinor leaned against the doorjamb. "Well? Seems like a big nothing so far, no cold spots, no weird lights, no ectoplasmic figures."

As far back as she could remember Elinor was fascinated by spirits and karma. How many places had she stayed hoping to see a ghost and didn't? The Mermaid Inn in Rye, the Angel and Royal Hotel in Grantham, the Witchery in Edinburgh, all disappointed her. And now, her avowed non-believer friend claimed one appeared to her in Elinor's own home.

"I don't know," Lucy said at last and glanced around the room again. "I'm not sure what I saw."

"Did you see a ghost or not?" Elinor asked, unsure if she wanted Lucy, the cynic, to say yes.

A gust of wind ruffled the sheer curtain behind Lucy, the hem brushing her elbow. She screamed and bolted past Elinor, down the stairs.

"It's only the breeze," Elinor called after her, but Lucy continued her dash for the kitchen.

Unafraid, Elinor walked around the bedroom. She dragged her hands over the newly plastered walls as she circled the room. It had needed a brighter and fresher look. The paint and repair work on the house was one of the first things she did after inheriting the manor.

Elinor checked the bathroom and second bedroom. Like her bedroom, everything seemed normal.

At the top of the stairs, goose bumps suddenly dotted her skin and the hair on her arms stood end. Weird. She glanced back, but didn't see anything strange, or more to the point, Lucy's ghost. She shrugged and continued down.

Chapter Two

"What the devil are you playing at?" Basil snapped.

"I was experimenting," Guy said, casually.

"Experimenting?"

"Yes. I thought our ghostly presence might be more acceptable to your Elinor if she had a glimpse or two of us first. Soften her up for the main event, as they say nowadays." Guy strode past Basil, not sparing him a second glance. "Revealing ourselves to her is your idea. I figured I'd contribute something too."

"How does scaring the life out of her friend soften her up?"

"It doesn't. I expected Elinor to come upstairs, not her friend," Guy added, in the same nonchalant tone. "I guessed wrong." He scrutinized Basil. "Since we're on the subject, I never asked your reasons for us befriending Theresa. It seemed harmless enough, she being an old widow, but why her granddaughter?"

Basil had anticipated the question when he'd approached Guy about making their presence known to Elinor's grandmother. Their previous experiences with mortals left them bitter. The women asked them to spy on their husbands or lovers. The men were worse. Driven by greed and lust for power, some wanted the knights to injure rivals, even commit murder on occasion and became belligerent when he and Guy refused. They avoided mortals for centuries as a result.

"I understood why you empathized with the loss of her son. He reminded you of Grevill," Guy said.

"Yes. When Clarence limped in and removed the metal brace from his leg, yes, I thought of my brother." Basil recalled the pain her son hid from Theresa. The nights Clarence lay in bed doubled over from the cancer destroying his bones. "He must have known, or at least suspected, he was dying."

"Maybe...probably."

"I think, deep down, Theresa knew something was terribly wrong, that his illness was worse than he said. She may have even guessed he'd come home to die."

"Her mind might've acknowledged the possibility, but not her heart. What parent can bear the thought of losing a child?"

Basil nodded. "She started to fade after Clarence died."

Her desolation became Basil's and her loneliness his. A lonely ghost, God's teeth! He'd questioned how such a crazy phenomena could happen to him?

Basil gazed out from Elinor's bedroom window at the ruin of Castle Ashenwyck, his home in life. The remains of the former fortress lay not far in the distance. He focused on the sight and tried to find a way to describe the emptiness that filled him at the time.

"Over the years, did you ever miss human contact, the warmth mortals are capable of?"

When Guy didn't answer, Basil turned around. After a long pause, Guy finally admitted, "Yes, on rare occasions. Although, I never thought I would."

Basil shared the sentiment. "After so many centuries of self-imposed isolation, I grew tired of being a shadow. I longed for mortal companionship. It felt good to ease Theresa's solitude."

"And Elinor? Why pursue her friendship? At her age, I doubt she's lonely."

Basil didn't have a firm answer to explain the attraction Elinor held for him. "I enjoyed Theresa's company. I know you did too. I believe there's a lot of her in Elinor."

"Go on."

"I appreciate her kindness. She'd come upon Theresa, alone, or so it must have appeared, engrossed in an odd one-sided conversation. When in truth, she was chatting with us. Elinor never mocked her for talking to herself or acting strange. She accepted her as she was." Basil smiled as he remembered more about the encounters. "Sometimes, Elinor looked our way, and I swear she could see us, at least sense our presence."

Guy didn't look convinced. "You think engaging her friendship will be as pleasant as Theresa's?"

"I hope so. I dread having to remove ourselves into the shadows again."

Basil drifted out of the room, Guy right behind him.

"If you'd bothered to ask, before frightening the wits out of that Lucy woman, I'd have told you I already planned how to reveal ourselves." Basil tipped his head toward the stairs. "Shall we? Hopefully, we won't find Elinor's Lucy in hysterics," Basil said, as they descended.

Chapter Three

Basil stood by the kitchen door and Guy sat opposite Lucy at the table. The ladies were in the midst of a discussion about the existence of ghosts. Intrigued, Basil moved closer to Elinor, particularly interested in her inclination. It might make a difference in their plan.

Theresa talked to her plants in the garden, drank whiskey straight from a china teacup and to the knight's amusement, cheated at solitaire. She was eccentric enough to appreciate them and welcomed their company. If Elinor wasn't at all receptive, then they'd withdraw and leave her alone. A sharp pang of disappointment shot through him at the prospect.

"Tell me again, what this apparition looked like?" Elinor asked with poorly disguised skepticism.

"I'm not sure I saw a ghost. I thought I did. You can stop smirking. I don't think you appreciate how hard this is for me. You know I don't believe in paranormal nonsense."

"Describe him again."

"He was dishy. Like I said, he looked like a knight."

"Hmm, better a knight than a bandy-legged Hun, I guess."

Lucy lifted her shoulders in a what do you want me to say gesture. "Maybe I imagined him. I do know this," she added with a mischievous smile, "If a ghost who looks like the very shaggable Sean Connery wafts into the room, I'll become a believer with lightning speed."

"A ghost who looks like Sean Connery, wouldn't that be convenient?"

Elinor stepped onto a footstool in front of a glass doored cupboard. She began arranging dishes from a box on the counter on the shelves. "In all the years I've known you, you've always maintained there's a scientific reason for everything. Now you come over, supposedly to help unpack." Elinor arched an accusatory brow at Lucy over her shoulder. "I've seen none of this help, by the way. Time to declare, Lucille, after today will you at least acknowledge the unscientific possibility of ghosts?"

Lucy angled her head to one side and took a few seconds before she answered. "Maybe. I have to think about it some more. The Yeoman Warders say Anne Boleyn haunts the Tower of London. She's a perfect example of why I've never wanted to see a ghost. Who wants to see the specter of some old, dead queen?" Lucy shuddered.

"I see," said Elinor. "So for you, the line between belief and disbelief is based on the appeal of the specter."

"No, but if they exist, I'd rather not see a scary one. What about you, Miss Paranormal, Miss Show Me an apparition and make me happy? What do you think you'd do if you ran into a ghost? It's a distinct possibility now, right here, under your roof."

"I've asked myself the same thing. You know, I'm ashamed to say it, but I'm not certain. I'd like to think I possess some courage. My biggest fear is that my reaction would be like one of those nightmares you have, where you scream and freeze, or worse, try to scream and nothing comes out.

"I admit, I'd be pretty frightened if I got locked up in someplace like the Tower overnight," Elinor said with conviction. "I've read there are a lot more ghosts hovering about those grounds than just Anne. What if they look bloody and mangled from being tortured? Think of all those people killed there, often innocent folks. I'd bet some have unfinished business still holding them to the place."

Basil winced at the observation. He hated when the living talked that rubbish. Unfinished business was an assumption made by mortals to explain the supernatural. There wasn't any unfinished business. What if some poor ghost hasn't a clue why he's here?

Elinor continued, "But, if I were locked in the Tower and heard chains rattling, say from the Armory, I'd never go and investigate. I've watched every cheap horror film made and learned one absolute rule. If you hear a creepy sound, never, ever investigate. Downstairs or upstairs, it's always the same. The downstairs invariably leads to the crypts. The upstairs is worse. It always overflows with secret chambers and usually headless apparitions."

He rolled his eyes at her take on typical ghost behavior. In his six hundred years, he'd yet to meet one who enjoyed hanging around crypts. As to spirits walking around headless, well, of course, a few did, but not all the time. Out of boredom, some of the spirits frightened mortals that way as a joke. He'd considered the same once or twice, when certain people aggravated him. Mortals never seemed to find it funny.

Basil moved a bit closer to Elinor.

She rubbed her arms several times and checked the counter around her. She stepped down and pivoted in a slow circle. "Do you see a bug on me?"

"No, why?" Lucy asked.

"I had this ticklish feeling, like something was on me."

Guy brought his open palm close to Lucy's neck and grinned at Basil.

"Ugh." Lucy brushed at the back of her neck with her hands. "Now, you've got me feeling the creepy-crawlies."

Guy moved his hand away.

Lucy stopped swiping at her neck. "Maybe your grandma is haunting you, invisibly tickling you," she whispered in a spooky voice along with fey finger movements.

"Don't be an idiot. My gran isn't haunting me. Although, I still walk into a room sometimes and expect to hear her talking to herself." Elinor looked thoughtful for a moment and smiled. "She'd be jabbering away and in quite colorful language too. At times her chatter was so animated it sounded like one side of an actual conversation."

Elinor leaned against the sink. "Back to your dishy ghost, I hate to break it to you Luce, but I seriously doubt Galahad's ghost is anywhere nearby. I doubt many look like Sean Connery either. If only."

Lucy looked over the kitchen. "This is such a big place. I know you loved Theresa. But because she left you the house doesn't mean you have to keep it. Have you considered selling?"

"No." Elinor gazed out the kitchen window. "I'll never sell. I love this house. I love my view of Ashenwyck Castle, or what's left of it anyway. When I was little, I fantasized I lived in a castle where knights walked, and jousted, and rode huge destriers." She turned back to Lucy. "I want to raise my children here. I want to marry a man who loves the area as much as I do. I want my little girl to look out at the castle and dream of gallant knights too, just like I did."

Lucy gave an unladylike snort of derision. "You're such a die-hard romantic."

"So? There are worse things to be, and when did you become such a pessimist about love?"

"When I started dating. I think it's incurable," Lucy said, drawing a heart pattern on the table with her finger.

Elinor nodded. "Dating does have that effect. I give men the chocolate cake test. I ask myself, would I rather be at home in my robe with chocolate cake and the telly, or making small talk with this guy? The cake wins ninety percent of the time."

"I'm convinced dating is the Black Plague of the twentieth century. If you're done, can we go?" Lucy stood. "All this talk about romance or more specifically lack thereof is making me hungry. I'm ready for lunch."

Elinor grabbed her purse. "Sounds good to me. I'm famished. Since the pub doesn't carry Ghost Food Cake, for dessert I'm ordering Angel Food Cake with strawberries."

"He didn't look angelic. That was part of the attraction. He was devilishly handsome," Lucy said.

"Of course, silly me. Who wants a sweet-faced ghost?" Elinor asked, as they walked out the door.

Chapter Four

Basil waited until the women drove away, and then drifted with Guy into the drawing room.

"Did you hear? The Lucy woman called me, 'devilishly handsome,'" Guy said.

"Her assessment is clearly impaired by the fact she only got a glimpse of you," Basil said.

They busied themselves examining unpacked boxes. An open one contained vacation photos of Elinor. Guy removed one of her in a hot pink bathing suit and tipped it so Basil could see.

Unlike most women he'd known, Elinor's complexion was sun darkened, at least in the picture. "It's pleasant, this color on her face. I wouldn't have thought so, if I hadn't seen for myself. The exposed skin is another boon." He began his own search of the box it came from. "Have you ever heard of this Sean Connery?"

"Scottish fellow as I recall." Guy wrinkled his nose. "An actor, I think."

"Scottish," Basil grunted in disapproval, "a savage lot."

Guy leaned back on his heels, arms resting on his knees. "Before he joined my knights, Stephen first squired with a knight who lived near Carlisle. The incessant reiving on the part of their Scots neighbors presented never-ending problems. He used to say it wasn't a Scots fault there were Scots, no more than it's the fox's fault he's a fox. He claimed the problem lay with the Romans."

"The Romans?"

"According to him, they should have built their wall higher." Guy moved to a pile of albums stacked by the stereo. "So, what's this plan of yours? Personally, I don't see why we can't just pop in the kitchen like we did with Theresa."

"Not much put Theresa off. She took most anything, including us, in stride. The last thing I want is to frighten Elinor. I've decided on a different plan from my original, and it came from the lady herself. When she's alone and gone to bed, we'll make our entrance." Basil couldn't resist a smile at his own cleverness. "You heard her. Mounted knights in shining armor, jousts, chivalry, childhood fantasies she still holds onto. We can be her dream knights come true."

"When?"

"Tonight."

Chapter Five

Basil kept an eye on the stairs watching for Elinor. She'd returned from lunch that afternoon and finished emptying all the boxes in the kitchen. Afterward, she'd gone upstairs but left the lights on in the drawing room. He hoped she'd return to unpack the boxes in there.

Elinor didn't disappoint him. He looked up as she came down and went straight to the stereo. He joined her as she rifled through the stack of albums and pulled one out.

"She's playing that plague music again," Basil said to Guy. "The one about Saturday night fevers."

The knights leaned over to get a better look at the cover. A man in a white suit posed on colored boxes, while a mirrored ball appeared ready to drop onto his head. Elinor lingered over the picture before removing the black disc.

"Surely, she can't find this skinny fellow handsome. He's so—common," Basil said.

"Probably French," Guy said with a measure of disgust.

The record dropped down and as the first notes played, Elinor began to hum and sway. The white man's shirt she wore covered all the essential spots, as long as she stayed moderately still. She danced over to one box, opened it, and then moved to another. The shirttail flipped back and forth as she sorted through their contents. Flashes of lacey panties popped into Basil's view where the garment rode high.

Guy's gaze slid from Elinor back to Basil. "Do you think it odd we find ourselves, *such as we are*, so drawn to some mortals? I'd have thought that sort of feminine attraction might have ended or have no validity for us now."

"Elinor has joyousness, a generosity of spirit, a kind nature. That's in and of itself, a strong enticement." Basil followed her as she worked, moving nearer as she sorted through the boxes. "There's a pleasing grace about her."

Elinor removed two large paintings from their containers and set them against the sofa. She picked off the fragments of packing material stuck to them.

Basil studied the artwork. The first was a beautiful woman in a long white gown. A dark-haired man in chain mail and surcoat knelt before her. The lady held a sword to his shoulder as though knighting him. It was titled, *The Accolade.*

"Interesting paintings, don't you think?" Basil asked, curious how Guy would interpret Elinor's choice.

"I think I'd rather bed the wench than be dubbed by her." Guy peered over to where Elinor was dusting the frames. "Though, I'd not mind having her dub me."

"You are confusing dubbing with tupping." Basil joked back and went to the sofa. "In my experience, women and swords are a bad combination."

The second picture, called *Godspeed*, showed a company of knights passing through a castle portcullis. One knight on horseback was stopped. A young woman with reddish gold hair bent to tie a fringed silk favor to his mailed arm.

Basil tilted his head and critically appraised the works. "This is her ideal of what knights were like. This is the vision she is enamored with and has stamped on her heart." A pensive sadness touched his eyes as he studied the art. Basil's gaze lifted to Elinor. "Oh milady, sometimes it was this lovely, but more often, it wasn't."

Long legs and more of the frilly panties revealed themselves as Elinor bent and picked up the empty picture boxes. Basil's attention fixed on her. He took his time letting his eyes travel downward from her bottom, the length of her thigh, over her firm calves then back up in slow appreciation.

Elinor half-hummed, half-sang along to another song.

"Rhiannon," Guy said and smiled over at Basil. "I went to Wales once, on king's business, to sort out a problem on the border. One of the loveliest ladies I ever bedded was a Welsh maid I met there named Rhiannon."

Basil was fascinated as Elinor's hips rolled to the rhythm of the music. Primitive in his opinion, and boldly sexual, he wanted the dance and song to go on and more. He wanted to slide his hand over every place his gaze touched. He wanted to know if her flesh was as smooth and warm as he imagined. He wanted to make her heart race with his caress. *He wanted.* The resurrected sensation astonished him.

Elinor danced over to the table and gathered her hammer, nails and a pencil then danced back without missing a beat. She laid the hammer and nails down and held the pencil in her mouth.

She stepped onto the sofa and raised the first picture to the wall. She struggled, staggering a bit in the soft cushions with the unwieldy painting's weight. She positioned the picture and pencil marked a spot on the wall and then lowered the painting. Elinor hammered a nail in and with a small grunt lifted the painting up. She rocked back and forth on the cushion, barely managing to maintain her footing.

Basil laid a palm under the bottom of the frame while Elinor hooked the wire over the nail.

"Well, that was easier than I thought," she said, and then shuddered. "Ooh." She brushed the back of her legs vigorously and inspected the sofa.

She sidestepped across the sofa, squinted to gauge the distance between the pictures. She marked another spot and then hoisted the second painting.

Guy positioned himself behind Elinor on the left, while Basil stood on her right. Each took a corner of the frame and lifted as she raised the picture.

"I must be getting used to the weight," she muttered. She lowered the picture long enough to hammer a nail into place. Once again, the knights lifted the corners. Elinor hung the piece with ease.

The knights lingered close to her.

"Ugh, spiders!" Elinor cried in a strangled voice as she swatted, rubbed and shook her head repeatedly. She jerked back hard, lost her balance and tumbled backwards.

Chapter Six

Strong arms caught her. *Strong arms?* Before that curious thought formed in her confused brain, she found herself upright.

Elinor blinked several times, trying to get her bearings.

"I didn't feel that. I'll look behind me and see no one is there," she reassured herself not wholly convinced. Prepared for flight over fight, she spun around.

A man stood a few feet away. At least what was visible looked like a man. He appeared to be a knight, similar to the one in her painting, except semi-transparent. She gasped, momentarily more stunned than afraid. The knight seemed as disconcerted as she was shocked. Two ebony eyebrows slashed downward into a harsh frown as he stared back. He composed himself. The fleeting moment where he looked rattled, gone.

He wore mail and a dark blue surcoat with a leopard embroidered on it in bronze silk. The metal links gleamed and the tunic appeared fresh pressed. Tall, with shoulder length hair, in the soft lamplight, his eyes were as black as his hair. He had a hawkish nose. A bump at the bridge and slightly crooked, it looked like it had been broken and not properly set. The flaw suited the harsh jaw line and high cheekbones. She smiled to herself. Her mother often teased her about her attraction to men with large noses. The distracting thought was short lived and she focused on the strange figure.

"Milady." The corners of his mouth tipped in weak smile. "I would've liked us to have met under better circumstances."

He'd spoken with an English accent she couldn't place a region to. There was a rich, old world quality to it like strong imported coffee. The exact voice she'd have associated with the knights in her paintings.

A sinking feeling grew stronger as she began to put two and two together. The paintings, the ones she loved were the last things she saw before falling.

"Oh, my God, I'm dead!"

Elinor searched the area around her. Her words came in a breathless running commentary. "Where's my body? People who've had near death experiences say they floated above their bodies. Shouldn't I see my body too?"

"You're not dead. You're fine," the knight said.

"I didn't think I'd go this young."

"Elinor—"

She slid her hand tentatively over the back of her neck.

"Did I break my neck?"

"Elinor--"

The sinking feeling faded as she struggled to accept her death with dignity. "My poor mom, first my grandmother, now me-"

"God's teeth, woman. Will you listen?"

"This will devastate her."

"You're not dead!"

His raised voice grabbed her attention. No longer semi-transparent, the knight appeared solid now. "My God..." She backed up until her calves touched the sofa. "What...who...are you," she stammered. "How do you know my name?"

"You're not dead," he said. "Why would you think that?"

"I fell off the sofa. Clearly, I'm dead and seeing angels or...I'm in a coma, that's it."

She'd always believed angels were androgynous and...blonde. Masculine and rugged looking with his inky eyes and hair, the angel before her walked out of a fanciful daydream.

"Why else would a figure from my favorite painting come to life? Quite honestly, I'd say it's very thoughtful to send me an angel dressed like a knight. I guess you felt I wouldn't be scared this way." She sighed. "At least my death was painless."

Elinor thought for a moment then pointed an accusing finger. "You swore. Angels aren't supposed to swear or raise their voices."

"I can assure you of two things. I'm no angel, and you aren't dead or in a coma, whatever that may be. You're very much alive and I'm very much a ghost."

She analyzed what he told her. Her body wasn't lying on the floor, so she probably wasn't dead. There were no fuzzy edges to her vision, like she imagined accompanied a coma. This was a hoax, she concluded.

"Lucy put you up to this, didn't she? Well, I don't appreciate the fact you broke into my house to play this stupid trick." She pointed to the door but kept her eyes on the man. "Get out. Go. Now, before I call the police."

He shook his head. "Lucy didn't put me up to anything, Elinor. I'm telling you the truth. I'm a ghost."

"How do you know my name, if she didn't tell you?"

"I've always known your name."

It was late. Her patience was exhausted. And, this bloody actor was in her house. He had to leave or she'd have no choice but to call a constable. "Out!"

"This is not going well." Another voice, invisible, whispered loud enough for her to hear.

"Appear for her."

"Who are you talking to?" Elinor considered the intruder with wary curiosity.

A brown-haired knight in mail appeared. A fraction shorter, he was handsome in the traditional sense, the way the first knight wasn't. His surcoat was scarlet and charcoal grey with a swan embroidered on the front.

"Oh. My. God. In the movies, this is where the heroine faints." She wasn't that fragile. Elinor lowered her head, and as unobtrusively as possible, measured the distance between her and the front door. Her heart beat triple time against her ribs. She wondered if her feet could move that fast.

The first knight smiled. "You said you wanted to meet a ghost and voila, twice as many as you hoped for."

The second knight winked at her.

If they weren't sent by Lucy, and if she wasn't dead, they were either truly ghosts or none of this was real. She went with the logical answer. "I banged my head when I fell, and I'm hallucinating." Something the first knight said clicked in her mind. "When did you hear me say I wanted to meet a ghost?"

"I overheard you speaking with your friend. I figured you'd be happy we weren't headless apparitions."

"You said Lucy wasn't involved."

"She isn't."

Elinor racked her brain and couldn't think of an explanation for the second knight's materializing out of midair. Professional magicians make things appear and disappear all the time. This was no rigged stage. This was her drawing room. No way could Lucy arrange such a sophisticated trick.

Elinor closed her eyes and pressed her fingertips against the lids. "Maybe this is a dream. When I open my eyes they'll be gone. I'll find that I fell asleep on the sofa." She opened her eyes a crack and peeked out through the narrow slits. "You're still here. Great, I've lost my mind."

The back of her neck started to ache with the beginnings of a migraine. Migraine: an innocuous word that lacked the intensity to describe the giant Japanese drums pounding in her brain.

"You'd rather condemn yourself as crazy than accept we are ghosts? Yet, you were willing to believe when you visited all those supposedly haunted places? Why?" The first knight asked, "Why is it more plausible to see a ghost in someone else's house?"

"For one thing, they were seen by a number of people at different times. Not by me. Never by me," she told him. "They were also brief sightings. Not up close and personal encounters, like this. If you really were ghosts."

Enough talk. Elinor walked to the door. "The point's moot. We're done here. Time for you two nutballs in tin cans to leave."

The knights didn't move.

Guy leaned close to Basil and whispered, "What did she call us?"

Elinor heard him. "I called you nutballs in tin cans. You're done up in chain mail, and whoever, or whatever you are, you sound like nutters to me." She glared at Basil.

Basil approached the door. "Would you at least let us try and prove ourselves? Mayhaps, if I walked through the door, you would believe?"

"Good idea. I'd like that very much, Lancelot. Mayhaps you could walk through the door and straight to the road. And take," Elinor jerked her chin in Guy's direction, "Galahad with you."

Guy's mouth fell open and he shot an incredulous glance at Basil. "No woman has ever spoken to me so disrespectfully. Women like me," he said, challenging Elinor with a harsh look.

She returned it, hands on hips, in battle-ready pose. Widening his stance, Guy crossed his arms over his chest. Basil stepped between them and turned to her.

"Watch me." He passed through the door and immediately came back, holding his helm and banner. The banner mimicked the emblem on his surcoat. At his side he wore his sword with a leopard claw pommel. "This is my family's heraldic symbol."

At a loss for words, Elinor retreated a few feet, unsure if her eyes deceived her.

"I can remove my mail and sword if it puts you more at ease."

Instantly, he appeared in a hunter's green velvet tunic and hose. Close fitting black leather boots came to mid-thigh, and his sword vanished. His legs looked large and strong in the mail. The boots and hose revealed how well-defined his thighs and calves actually were. Impressed more with that than the door trick, she was tempted to find out if he was as rock solid as he seemed.

The one she called Galahad stepped forward. Guarded, she followed his every move. Those Japanese drums thundered in her ears. With an abbreviated flick of his wrist, a lit torch appeared on the wall.

Elinor gasped. Grinning with self-satisfaction, the man changed and outfitted himself in similar fashion as Lancelot. In the crook of his elbow a helm materialized. In his hand, he held a banner. The standard copied his surcoat.

His powerful build was also evident through the rich clothing. On one hand, he wore a large gold ring with a red cabochon, which she supposed was a ruby. Inlaid in the stone was a carved swan.

Fascinated, she hesitantly reached to touch his helm and then swiftly withdrew her hand. She stared, torn between denial and serious consideration of their claim. Between the torches, the walking through doors, and the clothing change, Elinor had to believe the men.

The black-haired knight stepped towards her. "Ghost or not, stay right where you are, Lancelot." She tightened her grip on the hammer still in her hand and gave it a menacing little shake. "You too, Galahad," she ordered.

"We're not here to hurt you and we're not Arthurian knights," Lancelot said, with a small head shake. "Those are foolish romantic tales sung by bards."

"Why would you think us such?" Galahad asked. "It's silly."

"How dare you question me? My house. I get to ask the questions."

She shifted her attention to the impudent knight. She appraised him with a superior and critical eye, up and down.

He responded but not the way she expected. His exploration of her was bold and brazen. Scrutiny she met with bored disdain, refusing to feed the ego of any smoothie from any century.

Lancelot mimicked her. His unhurried perusal lingered on her lips, her collarbone, and the hollow of her throat.

She'd been ogled before by men, but this was no street corner ogling. This was different. A slow caress. No warm hand touched her, but it couldn't have been more real. Elinor enjoyed it. A lot. He cut a dashing figure, better than the fairy tale Lancelot. To her chagrin, the more he looked, the more she smiled. Time for a reality check. *This is bad, very bad. I'm flirting with a ghost.*

"Please, Elinor. We mean you no harm." Lancelot said and lifted a hand palm up in a sign of peace. "I'm Basil Manneville." He turned toward the other knight, "This is Guy Guiscard. I was liege lord here and the Earl of Ashenwyck. In my time, this land your house is on belonged to my family." Gesturing to a chair, he suggested. "Would you like to sit and we can talk?"

"I'm not sure I believe any of this," she said and dropped onto an overstuffed chair.

Basil sat across from her. "The circumstances of our introduction didn't proceed as I had planned. It was never our intention to scare you."

Elinor choked out a half-laugh. How ironic. She'd spent hundreds of pounds staying at allegedly haunted inns. Only to find out there are two living...she shook her head at that misnomer, two, what? Two ghosts residing in her house. Who would've guessed?

"I'm still not sure this isn't a dream...a very realistic dream." She took a deep breath and told the one called Basil, "Let's talk. You first.

Chapter Seven

Elinor perched on the edge of the chair, not ready to relax yet.

"We were friends of your grandmother," Basil said with a smile.

She'd heard enough. He was talking nonsense. Her grandmother didn't have ghost friends. They were playing her for a fool.

Elinor waved a dismissive hand in his general direction. "If you're going to stick to that story, then we've nothing more to discuss and you can leave. Because, *if* you're ghosts, and *if* my grandmother knew about you, why wouldn't she tell me?"

"I can't speak for Theresa. I know she was lonely," Basil told her.

The hint of his Middle English inflection came through in the words as he spoke, articulating each, enriching them. It explained why she hadn't been able to put a region to his accent. The inference her grandmother was neglected stung to hear, in spite of his pretty manner of speech.

Before Elinor could protest, Guy added, "Maybe, she was afraid you'd think her dotty. We're right in front of you and yet you doubt what you see, what we are. Why would she assume you'd believe her?"

"If she was worried about that, why didn't she tell you to appear for me? Why isn't she here?" Elinor challenged back, irritated by the logic of his observation.

"I don't know why some are compelled to remain here and others are not."

There was a brief bitterness in Basil's tone before he continued in a gentler voice. Elinor found the change curious.

"With your grandfather and her son long dead and most of her friends gone too, maybe she wanted friends of her own again."

"You're wrong. Oh, maybe she wanted friends again, but she'd have told me about you. I loved her. She would've trusted me with the truth," she said, defensively.

Guilt knotted in Elinor's chest as she remembered the days she promised to visit and didn't. All the time, her grandmother suggested she come by for tea and Elinor begged off, saying she was too busy. Maybe if she'd come more often, her gran would've shared her secret.

Their story had the ring of truth and she chose to believe them, at least temporarily. Not to mention, this was the experience of a lifetime. For the moment, she'd take advantage of the situation. She'd finally encountered ghosts and had a bazillion questions on the tip of her tongue.

"Go on," she said.

Basil began his story. "My family's been on this land since William the Conqueror. Originally the area given them was much larger than the ruin of Ashenwyck you see at present. The castle stood for five hundred years before Cromwell ordered it destroyed. His cannons fired in waves. They brought down the towers, then the curtain walls, and finally the great Keep."

She envisioned the ruin that fueled so many childhood fantasies. As he spoke, in her imagination, she saw the castle as it once was, grand and full of life. The home Basil had grown up in and loved.

Nothing in his matter-of-fact description of Ashenwyck's destruction betrayed anger or sorrow, but she felt it. She felt his loss.

"How devastating to watch your heritage ravaged stone by stone. Does one ever get over something like that?"

"You don't, but you learn to go on."

Elinor nodded in understanding. The early summer nights still held some chill. She shivered and shifted, curling up with her legs underneath her for added body heat. "Please continue."

"I inherited the holding and the Earldom in 1354."

She relaxed and studied Basil more. She'd never met anyone with such dark eyes. Black pupils melded with black irises giving them a mysterious quality. He hadn't formed laugh lines or crow's feet, and his forehead wasn't wrinkled. She wondered if he died young, or if those imperfections disappear at death. Was it rude to ask?

When he moved a certain way, the tip of a horizontal disfigurement at the base of his throat showed. She couldn't ascertain what exactly since his tunic collar covered most of it.

Her gaze slid over to Guy. He had warm, brown eyes that sparkled in a way Basil's didn't. Few creases etched his face and he looked the same age as Basil. Scars marred both of Guy's hands. An especially vicious one ran from the base of the thumb to the wrist. He moved, and the sleeve of his tunic edged away and exposed another ugly scar. On his other hand, a wide, jagged line from the wrist ran up to what was visible of his forearm. Deep and violent, they were the wounds from warding off heavy blows. Someone had hacked at him. She realized they were the killing blows. Basil's tunic collar hid the same.

She wanted to ask but was embarrassed by her own morbid curiosity. Inquisitiveness won out over propriety. "How old were you when..." she hesitated over the right words. Were there any right words? Is there a socially acceptable way to remind someone of their death? Elinor couched the question as best she could. "Neither of you look old. I mean, minus the last six centuries, you don't seem much older than me."

"I was a score and six at the time of my death," Basil said. "So was Guy."

Even more curious, she asked, "What happened? Were you executed or something?" Neither knight struck her as a traitor, Basil in particular. It was his nature more than his status as a nobleman which made her feel that. He'd seen the loneliness in an old widow her family missed, including herself, and didn't ignore it.

"No, nothing so dastardly," Basil said, answering the impolitic question. "We fell in battle, at Poitiers, serving the Black Prince."

Queasiness washed over her at the grim vision of their deaths filled her imagination. Basil glanced at Guy. Almost imperceptible in its brevity. A remote emotion flickered and disappeared in Basil's expression. Guy remained impassive, offering no additional information regarding their deaths. She sensed Basil had left a piece of the story out. What else? What wasn't he saying, she wanted to ask. The time wasn't right. Elinor opted to change the subject and get some ghost questions answered instead.

"Since you owned this land when you were killed, are you..." She tried to be tactful. "Are you...not condemned, but confined here. Or, can you travel?"

"We can travel but we prefer not to. We stay because we're comfortable here," Basil replied. "For the same reason, we choose to array ourselves in this apparel. We've been to London a number of times. It gets very wearing, too crowded."

Elinor agreed. "Tourist season is a madhouse, the worst, and the traffic is horrible all day long."

"Not crowded with mortals, crowded with our kind milady," Basil said with a low, throaty chuckle. "They're everywhere. Sooner or later, you run into someone you know. More often than not, it's someone you never liked in life. Trust me, death doesn't make them any more likeable."

Guy snorted and muttered a concurrence.

Elinor laughed too. She never considered that possibility. "This is fun," she said, warming to the subject and her uninvited guests and enjoying being addressed as "milady." She looked to each. "What sort of things can you do?"

Basil frowned as though stumped by the question. He turned to Guy, who shrugged looking as confused.

"What do you mean, what else can we do?" Basil asked.

"Obviously you can walk through walls and make torches and things appear, but what else? Can you move stuff, rattle chains? You know, ghostie things."

A simultaneous "Ah!" came from the knights.

"Yes, we can move things." Guy looked baffled and asked, "What do you mean by rattle chains? What sort of chains?"

To Elinor the question was self-explanatory. "I don't know. Don't you know? You're the ghost." She blurted the first thing that came to her mind. "Dungeon chains, I guess. That's what it seemed like."

Their brows lifted high. "You know other ghosts?"

"Certainly not."

Why were they acting so confused? She suspected they were being deliberately obtuse. Or, maybe spirits were like magicians and couldn't discuss their secrets. A ghost *code of silence*. It was a viable possibility.

"Dungeon chains...so you met some of the lads from the Tower, then?" Basil asked.

Exasperated, she said, "I didn't meet any 'lads from the Tower.' Ghosts in movies always rattle chains."

Basil and Guy exchanged a look of shared bewilderment.

"Odd business, I don't know anyone who get up to that sort of thing, other than the Tower chaps. Do you?" Guy said to Basil.

Basil shook his head.

Elinor took a deep breath and waved the topic aside with an impatient hand gesture. "Oh, never mind about the chains. What other stuff can you do?"

"We're capable of quite a bit," Guy said with a certain hauteur. "Was the weight of your paintings not lightened as you placed them?"

"Yes, that was very sweet of you both," she said, pleasantly surprised. "Thank you. I've another question. When I was hanging the paintings, something incredibly light brushed against my legs. A touch that wasn't a touch. You again?"

Basil nodded. "Our presence can be felt in that way."

She stifled a yawn, tired, but too curious to go to bed. "I don't understand how you can move objects or lift things."

"Allow me a moment, while I try to think of the simplest way to explain." Basil paused and his eyes searched the four corners of the room and then settled on the television.

"Once, while watching the telly with your grandmother, we saw a man who could bend spoons with his mind. It's comparable to that. We can compel force within our power in a similar manner. The action requires a great deal of concentration and drains our energy. We're usually unseen during the effort. Only with tremendous exertion can we lift or move heavy objects and stay materialized."

"I always thought that spoon fellow was a charlatan." She laughed softly at the irony of the situation, at herself. Here she sat accusing someone of chicanery while engaged in a conversation with two ghosts. The explanation also clarified his semi-transparent appearance those first few minutes.

"May I?" She reached over to touch the sword at Basil's side. Her finger passed through the weapon. "A manifestation?"

"Yes."

"It looks real, as does the rest of your armor."

"We're able to recreate the appearance of different objects. We can't reproduce them in solid form. We can only alter our appearance with, as I said, great effort."

They'd talked well into the night. Elinor stifled another yawn. Basil and Guy had seen the effort and rose from their chairs. "I believe you might be more comfortable under your blankets."

Basil's suggestion sounded good to her. Elinor scurried upstairs. She didn't need to undress. The white man's dress shirt was her sleepwear. She crawled under the covers, propped herself up on two pillows and waited.

The knights drifted into the room. Each took a side and lay next to her. Medieval bookends. She hadn't anticipated this turn of events, but their actions didn't fluster her either. The little thrill that shot through her when Basil lay down was another story.

In novels a woman can lust over anyone from tortured artists to vampires. Perfectly acceptable—in fiction. In real life, one just didn't get hot over a ghost, even when he turned out better than a fantasy knight from a painting. Weird, way too weird. She decided to ignore the issue.

Basil and Guy went back and forth describing their victories in jousts, their prowess both on and off the battlefield. Several arguments ensued regarding female conquests.

Elinor rolled her eyes at the predictable nature of men, even dead men. Consistent, if nothing else, at least regarding women. Chivalry had changed though. It was sorely lacking in the modern world. Conversely, her medieval bookends had been quite gallant to her grandmother, their old world values evident.

Elinor's sleepy voice interrupted a squabble. "Basil."

"Yes."

"Thank you for being so kind to my grandmother." She dozed off before hearing his answer.

The knights moved off the bed and wandered around the room. One oblong glass bottle caught Basil's eye. *L'interdit* was written across the front in a gold feminine script. French for "The Forbidden." With such a title, he had to know the contents. He unscrewed the top and sniffed the liquid inside. He recognized rose and jasmine, but not the faint essence of spices mixed with them. He sprayed a thin mist of the liquid in the air. He'd never smelled anything like it. He found the unusual fragrance more enticing than the heavy rose perfumes worn by women of his time. It wasn't a scent he'd have associated with Elinor. Now he'd never associate it with anyone else.

A silver-framed photo of Elinor and her grandmother sat on the dresser. He touched a finger to Theresa's image, remembering the day the picture was taken. He missed the old woman.

Elinor's lips parted with a muffled sigh as she rolled over. Guy stood by the side of the bed as she slept. "Were this another time and place, I'd have given the lady a much better reason to rest contented other than decorating."

"Were this another time and place, do you think I wouldn't have vied for the lady's attention also?"

"I'd be disappointed if you didn't."

As Guy amused himself with the clock radio, Basil watched his childhood friend. Always sought after, Guy was adored by all the women, young and old, both the highborn and the servants.

The ladies were mad for him. When they spoke to Basil about Guy, women claimed he was special. "He makes you feel like you're the only woman in the world." The declaration was consistently followed by a dreamy sigh and a nauseating, besotted gaze. Basil always wondered how he was supposed to respond. The temptation to tell them how long it took Guy to perfect that look hovered on the tip of his tongue.

Their feelings were reciprocated. His friend liked all women and charmed them equally. At banquets, he'd dance with the plain ones as often as he danced with the fair ones. Hearts melted when he entered the hall.

For reasons Basil never grasped, Guy enjoyed talking to women about all and sundry subjects. They'd discussed this on occasion. Basil recalled his skepticism. "Engaging women in non-frivolous conversation is silly," he argued. "If it doesn't lead to tupping, what's the point?"

He turned his attention to Elinor and pictured the women he knew, comparing them to the woman asleep before him. She wasn't an incredible beauty like some. But she had a classic elegance to her. *A knight would be proud to carry your favor, milady. In another age, I'd have made certain it was me who garnered that token.*

Chapter Eight

Sunlight poured through the bedroom's leaded window waking Elinor. The events of the previous night came back. She sat up, and scanned the room. No knights. It was only a dream. What did she expect? The realization disheartened her.

She slid out of bed and padded barefoot into the bathroom and paused, hand on the doorknob. "What if it wasn't a dream?_What if, by some strange miracle it's true and they come back_and I'm in the shower?" They could watch and she'd never know. Elinor shook her head at the bizarre scenario she pictured. If, and it's a big if, they were real, why spy on her when they could spy on a gorgeous movie star? The situation was too ludicrous to even think about. She didn't bother to close the door.

Elinor dressed, trudged downstairs, and made a pot of coffee. The pungent smell filled the kitchen as it percolated. Brochures for pre-fab stables sat on the counter unread while visions of the knights invaded her thoughts. Silly as it was, she wished they were real.

Unable to concentrate, she grabbed a mug of coffee, the brochures, and headed for the woods. A damp mist still clung to the ground, cloaking her house and the trees. Here, on the far side of the Fens, it would be another hour before the vaporous haze burned off.

She made herself comfortable at the base of an ash tree and watched a squirrel scamper at the edge of a nearby stream, one of the many mini tributaries of the Nene that riddled the area. The squirrel made several trips to the water and back up a tree on the opposite bank.

“Do you have a nest of babies up there, little one?” She’d remember to bring nuts next time.

Elinor sorted through the brochures and read the more practical ones. She leaned back, sipped the coffee and mentally measured the area needed for Guardian, her thoroughbred. Knees up, mug in hand, she sat lost in thought.

"Your stable should be made of stone."

Elinor jumped, sloshing coffee everywhere.

Basil jerked backwards, "Milady!"

"Basil, are you crazy? You nearly scared me to death!" She held a hand to her chest waiting for her heart to slow.

"Sorry," the apology choked out over his laughter.

“You are real,” She said and stared at him wide eyed. “When I didn’t see you this morning, I...well; I assumed I’d dreamt you.”

“I was often told ladies dreamed of me,” Basil teased.

Guy plopped down on the other side of her. "Jumpy?"

The aside earned him a stern look. "No, not usually. But I don't have much experience with spooks sneaking up on me. You could've called out first."

“Duly noted, milady. As to being the object of ladies dreams, my list of sleeping beauties is legion.” Guy sniffed and bent forward, challenging Basil to comment.

Basil made a rude retort and the witty insults and jibes continued until Elinor finally raised a hand. "Stop. Big, brave knights and you two carry on like a couple of my school girls."

"What have school girls to do with you?" Guy asked.

"I'm a history teacher at Stoneleigh, a private academy for girls in Ely." With immense pride Elinor mentioned the school by name whenever possible. Often referred to as Eton for girls, it was well known throughout England. The median age of a staff member was forty-five and only candidates with impeccable backgrounds were chosen. Elinor had been accepted upon her graduation from Cambridge, a major accomplishment for such a young woman. Her parents were thrilled.

With co-workers, Elinor exercised absolute discretion. Never were her personal beliefs regarding the paranormal discussed. It would be tantamount to career suicide. The administration would take a dim view of any instructor who admitted to the possible existence of ghosts. They'd be labeled "unsound" or worse, for such whimsy.

"Define girl, what age are these girls?" Guy's eyes sparkled with a depraved twinkle.

"They're seventeen and eighteen. Why?"

"Seventeen," he scoffed. "In my time, many young ladies that age were already married with a babe. I should like to see your girls one day. I imagine they're quite lovely."

"Leave my students alone, understand?" Elinor warned in a firm voice. "You're what, six hundred plus years old, way beyond the May-December parameters."

"Aye, but I'm young in spirit," Guy countered with a wink and leaned back on an elbow.

"You're a womanizing rascal."

He lay down, arms behind his head. "Yes, but a handsome one. Do you not think so?"

While she and Guy discussed his lascivious nature, Basil edged closer. They nearly bumped noses when Elinor turned his way. At this proximity Basil's eyes weren't so black but flecked with deep brown. His lashes were short but thick and added a scholarly element to his damaged nose.

Awareness of him as a man flared. "Ummm..." Elinor giggled when she looked Basil in the eye. She twisted away, took a deep breath, composed herself and faced him. "You refer to me as milady. Am I supposed to say my liege since I'm on your land?"

"You may call me Basil. And one day, I will tell you how I'd like you to whisper it," he traced her lips stopping at the vee, his finger suspended in place.

Elinor didn't know how to take his provocative suggestion. He said it with such ease she wasn't sure if he was seriously flirting with her. Everywhere his finger touched, an erotic tingle formed. It muddled her thoughts and made coherent speech difficult. "Yes, one day you should," came out. *Good God! I'm going mad. He's a ghost.*

A bolder woman would be intrigued by the idea. A worldlier woman would dazzle him with a glib retort. Coward that she was, she gathered her things and started to leave, mumbling about more boxes to unpack. She didn't get far. A pair of warhorses stood in her path. "You have horses with you?"

Guy approached one of the immense stallions. "Yes, our favorite mounts." He swung into the saddle of a majestic Percheron, with a steel grey coat and pure white mane and tail. The destrier's coat glistened as though brushed that morning.

"What's his name?" Elinor asked.

"Thor." Guy stroked the animal's neck affectionately.

"The name suits him, and he matches the grey in your banner."

"You're one of the few people who've noticed."

Basil mounted his horse as big as Thor. Completely black, the absence of any light markings gave the stallion a fierce appearance. He might've leapt from the pages of a mythology book. He only needed to sprout wings to complete the picture. Man and horse made an impressive combination.

"What's his name?" Elinor asked.

Basil adjusted himself in the saddle. Sitting arrow straight, he looked every bit the warlord. "Saladin."

"You named him after the Infidel?" She asked with skepticism. "Didn't your ancestors fight in the Crusades?"

Pride tinged his voice. "The Sultan Saladin was a brave and fearsome warrior. This Saladin was also. He served me well, even unto his death."

"Well said. He's magnificent."

"Thank you."

Elinor left for the house. In the kitchen, she poured another cup of coffee and went into the drawing room. She was going through her record albums when Guy came up behind her.

"Elinor."

Her hand flew up to her chest, again. "You have to stop doing that!"

"What?"

"Sneaking up on me," she snapped in a raised voice, more in frustration than irritation.

"I was not sneaking, Lady Elinor," he said, sounding insulted. "I called out as you wished. What would you have me do? Do you desire me to rattle chains?"

"No, please forget the comment. I'm sorry I brought it up yesterday. I need some time to get used to all of this."

Guy smiled. At ease again, he hovered next to her. He pressed closer as she returned to the albums. "Would you show me how this machine works?"

"I'd be delighted."

Once he'd memorized all the parts, Guy crowded Elinor aside as he experimented with all the knobs.

"Since you appear to have a handle on how the stereo works, I'll leave you to it," she said. "I need to tend to some book boxes in the library."

He gave her a low grunt in response.

Basil joined her, and they reminisced about her grandmother as she unpacked.

"Did you know she loved sardine sandwiches and ate the kind with their little heads attached?" Elinor asked, grimacing.

Basil nodded and told her Theresa talked to her plants on a regular basis and cheated at cards.

He went on to discuss the manor and the castle. Not surprisingly, he was a fountain of information about the history of both. "I hesitate to tell you this, but there was once a fine library at Ashenwyck. My family possessed several manuscripts of Welsh Bardic Poetry from the seventh century along with some illuminated bibles."

"Really?" The teacher in Elinor salivated at the revelation. "Where are the books now?"

"Gone. Cromwell and his men burned them."

"Bastards!" Elinor wanted to wail at the loss.

Basil looked a little sheepish. "I can't cast too many stones. I burned a library or two in France trying to keep warm." He went on; his accounts were filled with humorous anecdotes, along with tragic events. The fascinating details wove a tapestry of violence and grandeur, nobility and ignominy. A master storyteller, she was captivated.

When she finished unpacking, Elinor inspected the room with a critical feminine eye. "Plants. The room needs plants to add color. What do you think?"

His brows came together, relaxed, and then knit together again. "What kind of plants?"

"My first choice is a Dwarf Areca Palm. They can be used in decorative ceramic pots." His expression turned blank and he didn't speak for several long seconds. If he'd been a robot she'd assume his battery went dead.

"In the past, I heard talk of a strange plant called a palm that grows on some islands in the Hebrides. I never put much stock in the stories. Palm trees, selkies, faeries, I believe it to be a lot of Scottish balderdash and superstition."

"I see." Elinor wasn't fooled by the diversion of the Scottish slur. "You don't know what a palm is, do you?" she asked, cocking a brow.

"I said I didn't put much stock in their existence. Shall we move on, what's your second choice?"

It was a temptation to ask him to describe a palm and she almost did. From the look on his face he anticipated she would. He watched her like a patient cat watches a noisy bird. Elinor decided not to pursue the palm question. "A lush fern, in a beautiful oriental jardinière."

"Go with the ferns."

"Ferns it is. Well, I'm off." Elinor breezed passed him.

"Where are you dashing off to?"

"To the village to buy some plants. Why?"

"I'd like to accompany you."

Elinor froze. As much as she'd like for him to come along, if he stayed materialized it could prove disastrous. How would she explain the presence of a medieval knight walking next to her? "People will see you." If there was a note of panic in her voice she didn't care.

"Can you only bear my presence within these walls? If so, I prefer your honesty." Basil straightened and folded his arms.

Dismayed he'd misinterpreted her reasons, Elinor reached out to touch him. When her fingers began to tingle, she lowered her hand.

"Basil, I'd be proud to be seen anywhere with you. My concern has nothing to do with being in your company. The way you're dressed, I'm afraid people will think you're an actor. It'd be worse if you wore a sword or surcoat. If they tried to touch your clothes or your body, I might not be able to stop them."

"I'll change into more appropriate attire. You needn't fear. I have experience with mortals and know how to avoid their curious fingers."

"Okay. If you're sure it won't be a problem, let's go." Elinor started towards the door, stopped and turned around. Better to check what he deemed more appropriate attire.

He stood within arm's reach. His hair no longer hung loose, but was drawn back into a ponytail. The tunic was gone. In its place he wore black thigh-hugging breeches tucked into tall riding boots and a silky white shirt with the collar open just enough to show a tuft of dark hair.

Now, he looked like Mr. Darcy after a booster shot of testosterone. She sighed. "No, no way you're walking around like a Jane Austen character either. Jeans and a casual shirt are a good choice. And no boots...especially those Lord of the Manor kind."

She should've specified, "Loose, relax fit jeans," not *best tight butt fitting jeans on the planet.* He changed the shirt from silky white to a classic, white cotton dress shirt. He kept the collar unbuttoned exposing the scar at the base of his throat. His lack of self-consciousness didn't surprise her. She assumed he accepted the wound mark came with the image he manifested. She also knew, no woman in the village would notice the scar considering how fine he looked everywhere else.

Basil tipped his head inquisitively.

"Ahh...sorry, did you say something?" Elinor stammered.

The corners of his mouth twitched, "Do I meet with your approval?"

A hot blush seared its way to her hairline. He'd caught her gaping like a teenager. Nor did he fool her for a minute. The stinker knew exactly how good he looked.

"Oh, yeah, you'll do."

Guy glanced up as they walked through the drawing room. "Where are you going?"

Basil flicked his hand, prompting Elinor forward and out the door. "Do not worry," he said. The little hairs on the back of her neck tickled as he stepped close and urged her on again. "Continue your fiddle with the machine and we'll return soon."

Elinor scowled at him for acting so churlish and refused to budge. "To the village. Do you want to come?"

Behind her Basil groaned with exaggerated impatience.

Guy said he'd love to go, and shut off the stereo. Elinor stayed him as he headed towards the door. "You can't go dressed like that. You'll need to change too.

His appearance altered into an outfit similar to Basil's first one. Guy had chosen buff-colored breeches and a white, loose shirt, also open at the collar. Chocolate brown boots hugged his legs.

"No. You are not going like that. I told him no," she nodded toward Basil, "and I'm telling you no. Wear jeans and a tee shirt or something casual, really casual."

He did as she asked.

"Oh, dear god," Elinor said, looking him over. He'd switched to black jeans and a black tee shirt that hugged his broad chest and biceps. The tee shirt had a large red mouth with the tongue sticking out emblazoned across the front. It was the iconic Rolling Stones logo.

She picked up the last album cover Guy had handled. There, on the back, was Mick Jagger in the same shirt and jeans. *Thank God, at least it wasn't a Kiss album.*

Guy smiled and asked, "What do you think?"

"I think you two are going to be a big problem in town."

Chapter Nine

Basil hurried to the car and sat in the front passenger seat. All the gauges intrigued him. There were quite a few more than the last time he'd ridden in a car.

"We rode with your grandmother in her vehicle, twice." He said to Elinor as she backed out of the drive and onto the road.

"What did you think?"

"I wasn't overly impressed. Saladin, on his worst day could gallop faster." Elinor immediately stepped on the gas as he suspected she would. The scenery streaked by and Basil smiled to himself.

Elinor found a parking space near the High Street shops. Basil and Guy exited the car after she did.

"Oh, jeez." Elinor furtively glanced around.

Puzzled, Basil asked, "What are you watching for?"

"I'm making sure no one saw you get out without opening the doors, apparently no one did," she said, looking relieved.

As soon as they reached the sidewalk, she grew agitated again. "Every female who isn't an old-age pensioner is gawking at you two." She aimed an accusatory glare at Basil. As he was about to defend himself a pretty brunette in tight jeans stared heatedly at Guy as she passed by. Elinor's tense gaze shifted from girl to Guy to Basil. "If she stares any harder he's going to catch fire." Guy returned the girl's stare with a scorching one of his own.

"Stop it!" Elinor hissed the warning under her breath. "Ooh, I'd love to jab you in the ribs right now."

With obvious reluctance Guy faced forward and kept walking. "I was just looking."

"Your expression indicated you were thinking of doing more."

"Aye, would that I could." His eyes glittered under their long lashes.

Elinor watched Guy closely as they walked. Neither noticed Basil had lagged behind in front of the butcher's shop.

The butcher was speaking to a young mother with a baby pram. The attractive woman had the heavy breasts of a nursing mother. Each time she leaned forward and pointed, the butcher's arm brushed her bosom. He moved in concert with her so expertly the brush would be thought accidental. She continued to inspect the selection, unaware he stood so near the material on the front of his trousers touched against her skirt when she bent.

Basil edged closer to the large window. The butcher eased away from his customer and turned. His searching gaze met head-on with Basil's and he shrank back a step.

"A coward and a cur, I've killed better men than you."

The glass partition kept Basil from being heard, still the butcher retreated farther.

Basil moved up the sidewalk. When he caught up, Elinor and Guy had wandered into a bookstore. They were talking by a display showing the author of a sex therapy book. He lingered in the background as she tried to explain the difference between the conscious and subconscious mind. Guy listened as Elinor expounded on how the insecurities bred in the subconscious could affect conscious behavior. Sometimes, she told Guy, those issues resulted in sexual performance difficulties and required the aid of a therapist.

Basil slid up beside her. "This should be good," he whispered.

"What a lot of twaddle." Guy sneered at the author's photo. "He's just a modern-day gypsy." He challenged the theory of paying a stranger to chit-chat about one's tupping troubles. "Tis a fool of a man who gives away hard-earned coin and only gets blather in return. In my time, if a lad had difficulties, we sent him to Hilda. She'd sort him out properly, and not with a load of gibberish." He jabbed the air with his index finger for emphasis.

"The point of a therapy is to get help without the services of a Hilda," Elinor said.

Guy snorted and stalked away.

Basil joined Elinor as she walked around the other displays. They stopped at a table of new releases. One caught his eye. Opening it, he grimaced as he flipped the pages.

"The Supernatural Sleuth by Margaret Mellon." Elinor read the title out loud.

Absorbed in the book, Basil didn't respond. He turned to a particular page and moved his hand so she could see the picture. "Oh, my God, I can't believe your castle is here." Elinor ran her finger down the page to the paragraph discussing Ashenwyck. She picked the book up and read aloud. "Castle Ashenwyck, long rumored to be haunted by ghostly apparitions, was a major disappointment. Although our cameras were there for several days, we saw nothing but the cold, nasty mists of the Fens. In my opinion, Ashenwyck isn't worthy of being on any serious ghost hunter's itinerary."

"Old bat," Basil grumbled.

"So, you refused to deign Mellon with your presence." Elinor laughed softly as she closed the book and put it down.

"She's a mad old cow," Basil said, "who irritated the hell out of Guy and me. We stayed long enough to hear her and her fellow invaders speak about us. They called us *entities*, things that should be speculated upon and examined. Ashenwyck is my home, and we are not things to be analyzed."

Remembering the experience made him furious all over again. He signaled to Guy and walked away, out of the store.

#

They were back at the car within the hour. The plants and jardinières loaded in the trunk. Coming around to the driver's side, Elinor remembered she wanted to pick up a couple of steaks. "I'll be back in five minutes. I have to run a quick errand up the street. Wait here." She darted off as the knights stayed with the vehicle.

The overhead bell on the door jingled.

"Hello, can I help you?"

Elinor immediately wished she'd worn more make-up. The butcher wasn't like any butcher her mother went to. Dark blonde hair well trimmed, bright blue eyes, handsome. He directed a totally disarming smile at her. Only men on billboards could smile like that, or so she thought until now. Elinor gave him her order, and tried to act cool.

He wrapped the meat and walked to another counter, his hand brushing against her as he passed.

"Would you be interested in a roast for you and your husband? They're on sale this week."

"I'm not married, so a roast would go to waste."

He flashed that smile again, revealing a tiny dimple. "Have you just moved to the village?"

"Yes, into the manor down the road, near the old castle." She took as long as possible digging for money in her purse.

He took her money. "I'm Jeremy Barnes, by the way," he said, wiping his hands on his apron before he made change.

Elinor self-consciously touched a fingertip to the mole by her upper lip. "Thank you, I'm Elinor Hawthorne." She managed to smile in what she hoped was a flirty way. "My friends call me Nora."

"Nice meeting you, Nora."

Elinor approached the car lost in thought, wondering if Jeremy would ask her out. Wouldn't it be too perfect if a hunk_from the village turned out to be Mr. Right?

"You were gone a long time, longer than you said you'd be." The accusatory tone shook her out of her musings. The look he trained on her could freeze a lava flow. For a split second she felt a twinge of guilt as though she'd cheated on him. The reaction was too ridiculous to give any credence, so she didn't.

"Sorry for the wait. The butcher and I were chatting."

Basil stared at the packages she hugged to her chest. "The butcher? Is there nowhere else you can purchase meat?"

"Probably, but why should I? I like this little shop." Elinor canted her head and studied Basil. He looked fierce and grim, and rather scary. "What's wrong?"

"Nothing, everything's fine."

He was lying. However, happy to let the topic go, she casually agreed, "If you say so," and got into the car.

Chapter Ten

Elinor trailered Guardian over the day after workmen finished the split rail fence. He'd been stabled at a nice farm, but the facilities were shared with other boarders. Here, the pasture was lush, green, and all his. It took two weeks for delivery but finally, today, installation of the modular barn began.

The entire operation proceeded under the scrutiny of the knights, the framework established amidst much clucking and critical comments. Out of the crew's view, they strutted from corner to corner, their whispers followed by an occasional hand or arm gesture. Fed up with their antics Elinor went back into the house.

She sat at the kitchen table paying bills while keeping track of the progress. The toes of black boots appeared by the table and into her line of sight as she moved an invoice aside. Elinor took a moment to prepare before looking up. Call it woman's intuition, but she had a feeling he wasn't there to compliment the carpenters. Basil stepped closer, hands going to his hips. His normally well shaped mouth tightened into a harsh thin line. No intuition needed. He was in a snit, undoubtedly about the barn.

"Is something wrong?" she asked, sweet as pie.

"Elinor, think you those puny pieces of wood and paltry bits of metal are fit to hold a powerful beast?" he asked, casting a menacing glance at the workmen. "For surely, they are not. I understand there'll be no stone, but where is the oak? Where is the proper framework?"

She shifted in her chair to face him straight on. "Basil, I've seen many stables of similar material. This company puts these structures up all the time. They're more solid than they look, trust me."

He dropped to one knee, in front of her. His head tipped down just enough so his eyelashes looked like dark caterpillars against his cheek. His inky, blue-black hair fell forward, framing his face. Tempted, her fingers poised, wishing to touch its silkiness. Kneeling, with his head bowed, she imagined this was the position he'd take if he were about to propose. For one moment she lived the fantasy. *Rise, Sir Knight, I accept your suit and would be most pleased to marry you.*

Basil's expression softened as he raised his eyes to hers. "What do you think?"

The question brought her back to the present and the rude intrusion of reality. The fantasy of pretending Basil was proposing was marvelous fun while it lasted. It was also daft.

He stared at her quizzically. Had Basil guessed? Horrified he might've read her thoughts, she tried to sound unruffled. "What do I think about what?"

He moved his hands up as though to enclose hers, were it possible, and a slight tingle passed over her skin as he did.

"Elinor, it's our belief these men or their superior have played you false. We'd be most willing to advise them we're fully aware of their perfidy and put the situation to rights."

The sweetness of the gesture overwhelmed her. She'd love to throw her arms around him and hug him. Here was this splendid, charming man offering to defend and protect her interests. It was so chivalrous and gallant.

"Basil, trust me when I tell you those lengths of metal and board will do just fine. I don't need oak." She tilted her head coquettishly, a smile meant only for him on her lips. "Truly, Guardian will be okay. Please remember, this building doesn't have to withstand a siege."

He stiffened, his proud features taut, but he made no rebuttal. Elinor was afraid he mistook her explanation as a rebuff of his advice, of his experience.

"Please don't do anything yet. Let's see how it turns out. If it's lacking, you've my blessing to do whatever you think necessary," she said in an effort to mollify him.

Basil agreed with one curt jerk of his chin and started over to Guy as visions of what sort of justice they'd mete out flashed in her mind. He was the liege lord once. The position gave him carte blanche over local lawbreakers to order flogging, branding, even death.

"Ah--Basil, you do know you can't run them through, don't you?"

He stopped, and she waited for him to argue. The moment of debate passed, with a simple "Aye," he moved on.

Guy leaned against the doorjamb, arms folded over his chest. Basil said something she couldn't hear. From the way Guy's mouth quirked, he didn't approve of her answer either. They felt she was out of her element. These fourteenth century men were happy to mete out justice to someone they suspected of playing her false. Sadly, no one among the twentieth century men she knew would've given the problem a second thought, if at all.

By mid-afternoon the crew had finished and left. Basil came into the stable as Elinor put the tack away. She continued storing equipment as he scrutinized the interior. His displeasure evident, she was ready for the negative comment she knew he'd make.

"Would you care to go riding with me, Elinor? I'd be most pleased if you say yes. It is a lovely day."

The invitation, sounded so formal in his old world accent. It resonated on the ear, rich and warm, the way hot fudge on ice cream tastes.

Surprised by the invitation, Elinor blinked, mentally switching gears from the prepared response for the criticism she expected. "Yes," she agreed in a cheery voice not used since her teens. "I'd love to."

She hurried to tack up Guardian, grateful for her diligence keeping his bridle and saddle clean. The immaculate Basil would notice slovenliness. He waited outside by Saladin. Elinor's grip on Guardian's reins tightened as they neared the door. He might freak encountering a ghost horse. She held her breath anticipating the worst from the unpredictable Thoroughbred.

Guardian's ears pricked forward then swiveled to the side several times as he listened. His neck arched and went rigid before he relaxed, dropping his head with a whinny. If he perceived the presence of Saladin he didn't feel threatened by it. Relieved, Elinor relaxed too and mounted.

"Where to milady?"

Elinor gave the woods brief consideration. "How about the castle? I haven't been since I was a child."

Basil wore a linen surcoat with a leopard *rampant* embroidered on the front over a short hauberk. Golden spurs etched with an elaborate design were strapped to high boots. His polished cuffed gauntlets held Saladin's reins with innate surety. The picture of courage and grace, he was a history book's illustration of the chivalrous knight. The impeccable image the modern aristocracy wants to portray, but falls short.

Someday when she was too old to recall her name, she'd still remember this. She'd remember living every little girl's dream. *Once, a knight in shining armor took me to his castle.*

Elinor sat straighter in the saddle and tried to rise to his level of elegance.

Chapter Eleven

They rode across a long, grassy field beyond her property. The once visible path was now overgrown with wildflowers. Basil grinned, watching her. "Such delight you take in the flowers."

"They're lovely. What an amazing shade of purple on that one with the round, plump blossom. I especially like those tiny blue and yellow ones." Elinor pointed.

"Over the centuries I've ridden here countless times. I never paid them much attention."

"I'm sure your mother or her ladies mentioned them."

"I don't recall." Try as he might, Basil couldn't remember if they had. He dug deep into his memory to no avail.

"Tell me about your family. What happened after you were killed?" Elinor asked.

He hadn't talked about Grevill in a long time. Until Guy compared him to Theresa's son, he hadn't thought about his brother in recent memory.

Basil rode relaxed with one hand resting on the pommel and one on his thigh, as he had so often in life when on his land.

"After Poitiers, my brother Grevill inherited everything. He was an excellent liege lord, very perceptive. Neither our heritage nor our villeins suffered as a result of my loss. My brother was always mindful of the needs of the people who served us. It would be hard to find a more caring or generous man."

"How old was he when you died?"

"A score and one."

"As the oldest male, you inherited everything. If you had lived, he would have been a landless knight. Had he already made a name for himself in tournaments and such? He sounds rather mature for twenty-one? Was he at Poitiers, too?"

"No, he didn't go with the army to France. Grevill was born with a deformed and useless arm. Even so, he trained as hard as any other knight. Being fit in the lists is vastly different than warfare. His gift lay in areas less brutal. He oversaw my interests while I campaigned. It was a relief to me."

"Did he marry?"

"Yes."

"There's an Earldom attached to Ashenwyck, yet your family name is not well known to me, from a historical standpoint."

"The last of his descendents died fighting for the king during the Civil War."

"Cromwell again."

Basil nodded. "Dreadful man."

They made their way down into the ditch that was the moat. Elinor reined Guardian in at the top of the slope.

Basil halted next to her and sat quiet for a long time, taking in the ruin. He lifted his hand indicating two places on each side in front of them.

"This was the barbican. The gates were just beyond. These stones were part of the first curtain wall." He pointed to a long row of rubble. "A second curtain wall manned by our archers protected the inner bailey. Attackers were forced to fight in a confined space while pinned by bowmen."

They trotted on into what was the bailey. Elinor walked Guardian around the courtyard's perimeter. "I'm trying to picture how it was, how it must've bustled with activity."

He showed her where the stable had stood, marking off the dimensions of the impressive structure.

They returned to the entrance of the old Keep and dismounted. Basil walked Saladin over to a mound bordered by brush and wild trees and tied the reins over a sapling branch.

"Why did you do that? Tie up a ghost horse?" Elinor tied Guardian to an oak a few feet away.

He patted Saladin's flank as he walked past. "Old habits die hard I guess. Come let's go up to the parapet." He held out a hand and she laid hers on his, not truly touching as they climbed the rampart's loose stones.

Where the stairs narrowed, he let her take the lead, watching as she mounted the old steps. Her hair was done up in what she called a ponytail, secured with a pretty pink ribbon. The tail portion swung in rhythm to the movement of her hips. At one point, midway, she smiled at him over her shoulder. The sunlight gave her cheeks and nose a girlish shine. He smiled back, and for a fleeting moment felt like a lighthearted young man again.

What weakness of mind took possession of him, Basil couldn't say. He reached out to tug her ponytail then caught himself and dropped his hand to his side.

On the way, he pointed out the sites of various buildings and general layout of his home. She strained his memory a couple of times with her questions. At the top of the rampart he walked her over to the corner with the best view.

"You can see forever from here. My house seems so insignificant."

Basil caught a whiff of the mild scent from her shampoo when Elinor glanced up. It reminded him of the air after a fresh rain and he moved a fraction closer.

"You needn't point out my pitiful stable, Milord Manneville." She winked at him and with a sweeping arm gesture mimicked a haughty, upper class accent. "Sir Basil, lord of all you survey."

Another time, another place he'd have taken the wink a step further and kissed her into the next day. "Do you see that outbuilding?" He gestured to a spot a half mile away.

"Yes."

"That's where the woods used to start. They were much denser then. Over the years, many of the ancient oaks were chopped down for building and other needs. My family lands stretched well beyond the forest."

"The river was also much wider and deeper. It was the source for our well and supplied water for the moat. In the spring, at its peak, the flow took the runoff of the moat's stagnant water downstream."

Basil rested both arms on the wall as he reminisced, another old habit. In life, he often walked the parapet when he wanted to be alone to think.

"I didn't know many people considered the problem of stagnant water in those days. We've all heard about the disgusting matter thrown into the Tower's moat." Elinor wrinkled her nose. "It's pretty remarkable your family was concerned with the moat's upkeep. How do you drain a moat, anyway?"

He loved technical questions of that sort. Management of the castle was something he'd trained for all his life.

"Originally, a dungeon had been built in the lower level of the Keep. My family stopped using it for that purpose in my father's youth. They constructed a tunnel that accessed the moat with a lower exit channel on the other side. The walls of the tunnel and channel were reinforced with stone to prevent seepage. From a platform, the gate raised to allow in fresh water. The stagnant water was forced out. Once the gate lowered, the moat filled. Villeins dug the channel to the river out then replaced the dirt after the water was exchanged."

"Ugh! Poor villeins!"

He grunted but kept his gaze on the scenery. "I knew Lords who tried to maintain the moat water, and I knew others who didn't." The corner of his mouth curled in disgust, "Trust me. If you ever smelled a moat at the end of summer, you'd lend a hand with a shovel yourself."

"You're probably right."

Elinor leaned back against the blonde stone merlon and turned toward Basil.

He felt her eyes move from his hair to his lips and knew the second they lowered to his chest.

“Of course, the river was a serious problem at times. So much of this area is wetland and susceptible to flooding.”

Green eyes roamed every inch of him.

He’d known many women in his life and recognized what the nuances in a lady’s perusal conveyed. There'd been summer jousts where he thought he’d burn up in his armor. Elinor’s desire scorched him more than the hot metal. *Her flesh and blood desire.*

He stared straight ahead, because if he looked at her, he'd be lost, his strength of will would falter. There'd be nothing to keep him from trying to do what he couldn't. A painful reminder of the man he no longer was.

Basil propped a foot on the crenel, his thoughts in disarray as he attempted to describe the land. The temptation to touch her, hold her, was too strong. Fighting the urge, he closed his eyes. He envisioned how she'd recoil if she sensed the emptiness of his existence. She is joy and laughter, she is life...*she is life,* he told himself. He opened his eyes and then foolishly turned.

She smiled when he looked over, her lips glistening with a pink cast in the sun. His resistance crumbled.

I am lost.

Basil closed the gap between them. Gauntlet gloves gone, he lifted a hand to the side of her face. It didn't matter he couldn't physically touch her. He started at the skin behind her ear, continued downward as his thumb stroked a path over her cheek and along the pale arch of her throat.

"Basil," she said softly and tilted her chin.

Whether it was a faint tingle or tickle he didn't know, didn't care. She felt him. Slowly, he dragged a finger along the underside of her jaw. A shiver passed over her, but she didn't recoil.

"Basil," she whispered again and closed her eyes.

He concentrated all his energy. His cold lips pressed against her warm ones and Basil escaped in her kiss.

Her eyes flew open. Like a watermark on paper, his image was dim and faded as she reached to pull him closer. He rejoiced and despaired when she responded. It had cost him to feel her lips move under his, to sense her intake of breath. Longing he'd thought forgotten returned with a force that rocked him to the core. Masculine hunger had been aroused, and for one, sweet moment, he'd forgotten what he was.

The flash of bliss plummeted into abject shame. He stepped away, giving her space, giving him space. Anger surged. He looked to the tranquil blue sky and questioned what manner of God would allow this. He wondered for the thousandth time what he'd done to offend God so.

She watched him with such heartbreaking confusion in her searching eyes. He ached to be somewhere, anywhere, else.

"Basil." She stepped closer and lifted her hand to his face.

"Don't." He moved farther away and she lowered her hand. "Heaven plays a jest on me and I am a fool to have given in to it."

Filled with bitter self-loathing, he tried to concentrate on the panoramic view, purposefully avoiding eye contact. But, he only saw the vision of her reaching for him, responding to him.

"You're not a fool."

The Fates hadn't been totally cruel. They'd let him see the desire she carried for him. He'd make the thrill of that lost pleasure satisfy him.

"We should continue our visit around the castle."

"Basil—,"

Without waiting, he walked towards the steps of rubble, his boots silent on the gritty stones.

He headed for the Keep as she rushed to catch up. Several minutes went by as he silently surveyed the remains of his home. When he spoke, his voice was heavy with remembrance.

"This was the great hall. Two stories high, the hammered oak beams arched to a peak in the center. Rather like a giant sea beast. A staircase at the far end led to private chambers."

He held his hand out and motioned for her to stand beside him. "A massive fireplace stood along this wall with large Gothic windows on either side. Stone fretwork with triangles of stained glass inserted topped each while the lower portion consisted of clear leaded glass."

"Tapestries of saints hung on either side of the windows," he said, pointing. "Larger ones draped much of the opposite wall since no fireplace interfered."

The hall came alive again for Basil. His words painted a picture of the room. "The first tapestry my distant relatives brought back from the Crusades. It showed a Frankish knight battling a Saracen." Every detail took shape as he elaborated. "Woven with threads of silver and gold, you could almost feel the metal of the Saracen's helm. The second was of a white hart. It was my mother's favorite. The next tapestry was of two leopards bringing down a horse. The leopard is the badge of my family, as you are aware. An immense tapestry hung behind the dais of a sole leopard with our motto embroidered across the top, *Virtute et Armis*, 'courage and arms.'"

He studied her as she wandered around the bailey. What was it about this woman he found irresistible, and why now? "You have no idea how good you look dancing with such abandon to your rock and roll," he whispered low. The vision brought a smile.

Perhaps, he reasoned, the attraction went beyond his realm of experience. Elinor was unique in many ways from the women he'd known. For one thing, she was intelligent, a rarity for a woman to be sure. Nor did she pretend timidity. She spoke boldly and never hesitated to argue a point if she felt her cause just. Sometimes he thought her logic correct. However, he saw no reason to admit it.

In his mortal life, there'd been no shortage of women who wanted him. They'd wanted him for his wealth, his influence, and some just wanted him in their beds.

Here and now, he had no worldly things to offer Elinor yet she acted as if his company alone was enough...strong stimulation for a man's pride, even a dead man's.

"I guess we should start back." Elinor came towards him.

With each step, his heart silently said what he lacked the courage to say aloud.

In another time, I'd have brought you to my castle, kept you, loved you, and made you mine. What would you do milady, if you knew my thoughts?

He kicked at a rock that didn't budge as he walked to Saladin.

Chapter Twelve

The first month of her summer vacation was gone already. Elinor hardly noticed since it had also been the first month in the manor. She'd worked nearly everyday decorating the house. From now until the start of school she wouldn't have the luxury of dedicating so much time to the manor. Her superiors at Stoneleigh demanded early preparation for the upcoming semester. Which translated, meant hideously dull meetings in advance.

That morning, the school staff meeting ran late as usual. It was the same every year. The unchanged curriculum was discussed ad nauseam. Lesson plans were submitted and approved and for the most part mirrored those presented the year before. Elinor did win her battle to spend more class time on the Hundred Years War. She couldn't wait to dig into the middle ages, considering what fantastic resources she had.

Ravenous and tired, Elinor debated whether to throw something together at home, or stop at the village grocery and hope to find a ready made anything. The food didn't have to be tasty, only convenient. She opted for the market.

After three trips down the store aisles, nothing seemed in the least appealing. The food that sounded good needed time to cook. The easy to prepare dishes were less than inspiring. Even the pictures on the boxes couldn't make some of the meals look appetizing. She gave up and tossed two cans of tuna in the hand basket and headed for the cash register. Someone called her. She turned and spotted Jeremy.

"Hi, I wasn't sure at first it was you. I didn't recognize you immediately with your hair up and you're wearing a suit." He smiled just enough to reveal the dimple at the corner of his mouth. "I hope I'm not being too forward. I assumed you'd remember me. We met a few weeks ago when you came into my butcher shop."

"Of course, I remember you. I just came from work and haven't had a chance to change. So how have you been? Busy at the shop?" she asked, noticing how the little dimple deepened as he talked. He wore jeans and a rugby shirt. The shirt showed off the broad shoulders his butcher's coat hid.

"Yes, business is good, thank you for asking. It helps when you're the only butcher in town." He reached over and took the hand basket from her and put it on an empty counter. "How about I put these in my basket?"

"All two cans," Elinor said, dropping them into his basket.

"So, where exactly do you work? You look very official."

"I teach history at Stoneleigh."

Jeremy's brows lifted a tad. "The posh girl's school, I'm impressed." Between them they blocked most of the small aisle. "Perhaps we should walk before someone mows us down." He grasped her elbow, his fingers brushing her ribs as he led her towards the front.

"Why don't we have dinner at the Falcon's Nest?" The pleasant smell of soap wafted over her as he bent close. Such a refreshing change from the heavy scent of most aftershaves many men drown themselves in.

"I'd like that very much," she said, pleased for once the school meeting ran late.

#

She'd hesitated and almost changed her mind about dinner as they stood in the pub's doorway. It was well past the time she usually came home. Basil might worry. She resisted the sudden urge to leave and reminded herself not to let her feelings for him to get out of control. Especially when she had an attractive man in arms reach. *A living, breathing one.*

A hazy cloud of stale smoke that irritated her allergies and eyes hung like fog inside the pub. Elinor waved her hand in front of her face while they worked their way through the crowd and found a small table.

Jeremy didn't wait for the serving girl and placed their order with the bartender. He returned with the drinks and set Elinor's on the table. He sucked down a swallow from his filled to the top pint of beer and managed not to spill any as he squeezed onto the tight corner stool.

He licked away a thin layer of foam from his upper lip and smiled across the table at her. Such a sexy smile, Elinor thought as her cynical mind questioned her luck. Why would a man who looks this good and has his own business, not have a girlfriend? She sipped her whiskey and soda, while she contemplated the possible reasons.

"Penny for your thoughts," Jeremy asked, as she sorted through the mental list.

"I was wondering why you don't have a girlfriend."

He didn't flinch at the question, which she thought was a good sign. "Well, the shop is the main reason. It belongs to my father and he'd like to retire soon. Taking over the business hasn't left me with a lot of time to dedicate to my social life, let alone a girlfriend."

Elinor was instantly suspicious. Experience had taught her the next statement would involve some sad tale of being too busy to go anywhere. She could almost hear the "Why don't you make us a little dinner and we can watch television at your place," suggestion. Translation--*you can make me dinner and we can have sex, then I'll go home.*

"It's taken a few months to get all the details worked out, and my schedule manageable. But, even with more time available to me, I haven't found anyone who really interests me, until now." Jeremy placed both elbows on the table and leaned forward. "That question goes both ways you know? Why don't you have a boyfriend?"

"I haven't found anyone who interests me either, until now."

For a long moment neither said anything letting the innuendos hang between them.

Jeremy was the first to break the silence, "I like your hair better down."

The barmaid walked by with a plate of roast beef and potatoes, the aroma of onions and mushrooms trailed behind her. Elinor's stomach growled loudly. "Sorry, I'm a bit hungry."

"I'm starved too." Jeremy signaled the waitress.

The next two hours flew by. "It's almost 10:00, I should go. I open early on Saturdays," Jeremy said.

Elinor nodded and tried to hide her disappointment. He hadn't indicated any desire to see her again.

All the way to the car he didn't say a word. Elinor retrieved her keys and started to thank him when he put his arm around her. "Would you like to go to dinner tomorrow night?"

"Yes, I'd love to, what time?"

Jeremy pulled her close. "I'll pick you up at 7:30."

Her mumbled "Okay" was lost in a sloppy wet kiss. His soft, fleshy mouth covered hers as the kiss reached beyond the outside of her lips. She broke it off and subtly moved her purse between them. "Let me give you my number. Call before you leave so I can give you directions to my house."

He took the paper with her number and opened the car door. "I'll see you tomorrow. Don't forget to lock your doors."

Distracted, Elinor smiled wanly back, thinking more about the kiss, than his concern for her safety. She hoped he was a better date than a kisser. "I'll be okay."

Once out of sight, Elinor wiped her mouth with her fingers. The memory of Basil's expert and delicious kiss came back. It occurred to her that Basil would rather fall on his sword than kiss like a fish. *A big mouthed fish.*

Chapter Thirteen

Elinor heard the music to *Born to be Wild* from the end of her driveway. When she parked and got out, a voice not belonging to Steppenwolf sang along in a clear, fine baritone, *Guy*.

Inside, record album covers were strewn over the drawing room floor. Guy, in the center of the mess, stood putting on a one man show.

"I see you like rock and roll," she said and closed the door.

He stopped singing and turned the volume down to a civilized level. He gave her a quizzical look. "Rock and Roll? If you mean the music with the loud drums and people screaming, then the answer is yes, it's brilliant!"

"Brilliant? I've never heard you use the term before."

"Heard it on the BBC, David Frost called *Star Wars* brilliant."

Elinor cringed. “Admitting to me, a teacher, you’re updating your vocabulary from the telly is like a knife in my heart.” She laid her hand over her chest and feigned a wound. Guy grinned and pulled a couple more albums out.

She carefully stepped around the records on the floor to put her purse and keys down. A quick scan of the titles showed a remarkably eclectic side to Guy. Elinor put several back into their jackets and tried to establish some order to the chaotic mess as Guy came over. He beamed in an odd self-satisfied way.

"Have you been up to something?" She quickly scanned the room.

"No, why do you ask?"

"You have a mischievous air about you."

Guy picked up an album by the Moody Blues. "I have discovered they wrote a song about us." He inclined his head toward the chair where Basil sat, legs draped over the arm, reading Horse and Hound magazine.

"The Moody Blues wrote a song about you and Basil," Elinor repeated. "You...and Basil?"

"Not us exactly but about medieval warriors." Then, with all the aplomb of the chivalrous knight he once was, Guy announced, *"Knights in White Satin."*

She started to tell him it was *Nights in White Satin*, but stopped. He was so thrilled she couldn't bring herself to tell him he misunderstood. "Of course, it's a pretty song isn't it?"

"Yes, it's quite nice indeed." Guy put a record on the turntable and moved the arm over to a specific song. He bowed slightly from the waist and held his hand out to her. "Lady Elinor, would you do me the honor of dancing with me?"

"I'd love to."

He held himself farther away than most dance partners and kept looking down, watching her feet. The steps were new to him, so Elinor found a way to gently suggest a lesson.

"We're usually closer together when we dance to a slow song. It's considered very romantic. I can show you if you like. Why don't you play another slow song?"

Guy agreed and rapidly went through the stack of records. The beginnings of *Unchained Melody* by the Righteous Brothers started. She showed him where to put his hands along with a basic box step. A natural, he caught on fast and played the song again, softly singing along.

"You know, nowadays, if you danced with a woman and sang to her, she'd melt like butter," Elinor teased, batting her lashes at him. "You'd absolutely be invited into her bed."

"They melted in my time too. Some things have not changed." He raised his chin in self-mocking haughtiness. "My charm transcends the ages."

Elinor rolled her eyes, "You are a conceited devil and the most incorrigible man I've ever met."

"Tis true. Those are but a few of the qualities I wear well, milady." A light tingle teased the small of her back through her clothes where his hand hovered. "I think you find me charming."

"No, I don't." Elinor refused to look at him, certain the lie would send her into a fit of giggles.

"Yes, you do. You are a woman. This charm is a boon and a curse."

"Oh do hush up and dance."

Guy's image faded slightly as he employed the same energy force he had when she hung the pictures. Although she couldn't actually lean on him, he lessened the weight on her arms. They continued dancing as the next song played. The Lou Rawls's hit from a few years earlier, *You'll Never Find Another Love Like Mine* began as Guy moved closer. Her one hand covered by his, the other at the back of his neck. The intimacy of the dance brought a beguiling smile from Guy, who was obviously in his element.

Her gaze locked onto Basil's, watching them with fierce intensity. Elinor smiled and waved her fingers, but he just sat fixed, staring. When Guy spun her a second time, Basil stood and headed for the back door.

At the end of the song she offered to teach Guy *The Hustle.* They were rooting through the stack of albums when a fearsome cry sounded from off in the distance.

"What was that?"

Elinor rushed for the kitchen door, but Guy intercepted her. He held his arm out, as though to bar her path.

"What are you doing? Someone might need help."

"It's Basil's war cry," Guy said in a somber voice. "Come, your presence won't help. There is no help for what troubles him."

She hesitated, and then walked back to the stack of albums, Guy beside her.

"You're not going to tell me what's wrong, are you?"

"If he chooses, he will tell you."

Chapter Fourteen

The knights left early that morning to go riding. Elinor planned to use the time alone to clean house. She brought her motivational tape downstairs to listen to while she worked when the doorbell rang.

"Yes," she said, puzzled seeing the van in her driveway when she opened the door. She wasn't expecting any deliveries.

"Are you Miss Hawthorne?" A teenage boy with grimy blue jeans, a yellowing tee shirt and an equally dirty jacket stood on her step. A flower box from the village florist and clipboard with pen attached were jammed under his arm. The disgusting jacket provided a buffer between the box and his armpit, for which she was grateful.

"Yes, I'm Elinor Hawthorne."

He pushed the clipboard at her. "Sign here."

She'd barely finished when the boy snatched the board and shoved the box in her hands.

"Wait, who are these from?" If he answered she didn't hear him. The lad leaped into a van and pulled away, the wheels throwing stones up in all directions. "Rude Bugger."

Elinor opened the box in the kitchen. A dozen roses of the softest peach color lay inside with a card, her name printed in the block letters. "The roses made me think of you." She recognized Jeremy's handwriting, the same bold lettering he used when he labeled her meat wrapper.

She removed the flowers one by one, laying them in a quasi arrangement on the kitchen counter.

"What's this thing?" Basil asked, returned from his ride.

"It's a Walkman," she said and took a vase out of the cupboard and set it on the counter. "You clip it to your waist, put the headset on and it plays a taped recording."

Elinor popped the cassette out for him to see and then put it back. She turned the volume up and held out the earpiece so he could hear.

Learn to Stop Smoking. Basil scrunched his face up. "What kind of music is that?"

"It isn't music. It's a motivational tape."

"How does this motivate you?" Basil asked, with more than a little skepticism, fingering the Walkman.

"You listen to it while you sleep, at least I do, and the message plants the idea of not smoking into your subconscious."

"Is this the same subconscious you told Guy about in the bookstore, the one that suffers tupping troubles? If so, I don't think I'd care to possess one."

"We all have one that's unique to us as individuals. Even you have a subconscious, although I doubt you've tapped into it very often." Elinor waited for Basil to fire off a snide retort.

He pointedly glanced at the pack of cigarettes on her table and back at the tape. "Tell me again how this works?"

"Okay, I don't listen to it as often as I should," Elinor said with an exasperated sigh. "When we're awake our conscious mind comes up with all sorts of road blocks to hinder us from doing what we'd really like to do. For example, deep down I want to quit smoking. My conscious mind, however, will find a reason to light a cigarette, like 'you've had a terrible day at work, Elinor. A cigarette will help you to relax.' So, I light a cigarette. The tape, if-I-played-it-enough, would eventually enable my subconscious to override the interference of my conscious mind."

Basil snorted. "Perhaps you should just stop purchasing cigarettes."

"That's such an irritating and simplistic answer." Annoyed by his straight forward logic, she turned back to the box of roses.

"What are you doing with those?" Basil peered over her shoulder.

She removed the remaining flowers with care, giving each a gentle shake to loosen the stems from the greenery. "They're a gift. Aren't they pretty? Pale pink and peach are my favorite colors for roses."

The open card sat on the counter. Basil picked it up and his curious expression changed into a scowl. "Who's Jeremy?"

"The fellow I have a date with this evening. Why?"

"Who is this man? What do you mean when you say you have a date with him?" He tossed the card down and leaned against the counter, his arms folded across his chest.

She was well acquainted with Basil's moods. The angrier he got, the smoother his facial features became, except for his mouth. Right now, his lips had tightened into two slashes. On occasion, when he was being especially belligerent, he'd stand, feet braced wide apart, like an executioner on the scaffold.

Elinor tried to figure the best way to explain what a date entailed. "A date is kind of the prelude to a courtship. People go out together to see how well they get along. Usually, they go to a restaurant, get to know one another. Sometimes they go to a movie or dancing," she said and returned to her flowers.

"I've never heard you mention this Jeremy. Have you known him long?"

"I met him the day we went into the village. He's the butcher."

"What!"

Startled, she jumped and stared at him.

"He's a...a tradesman. A tradesman you don't know well. For all you know he could be the worst sort of blackguard."

"How dare you look down your nose at his profession?" she asked, shocked by his class-conscious attitude. "There's nothing wrong with being a butcher. Nor, do I care for your tone. Pray tell, were you never attracted to the daughter of a tradesman?" she challenged.

Basil glared down at her, his expression rigid with suppressed fury. He was a hair's breath away from assuming his executioner's pose.

"Do not try and muddy the waters, Elinor. We are not talking about me. We're talking about you. But, since you seem keen to pursue my past, I'll tell you. If I'd been attracted to a tradesman's daughter, and if I'd pursued that attraction, it would only have been a minor dalliance. Under no, and I repeat no, circumstances would I have considered it a 'prelude' to courtship. It wouldn't, and couldn't, be more than a dalliance. As Earl of Ashenwyck, my future was preordained. That future did not include courting milk maids or blacksmith's daughters." He stepped closer, trying to intimidate her.

Elinor had no intention of budging.

Basil took a small step back, "Let me ask you a question." An odd calmness laced his voice.

Apprehensive, she agreed. "Okay."

"You're a well educated woman, as are your parents, I assume." She nodded and he continued. "As such, I imagine they have certain expectations for you, comparable to the standard you've set for yourself. Is that not so?"

"Yes."

"Suppose the cleaning person, the man who empties the dustbins and sweeps up at your school, a pleasant sort of fellow, asked you on a date, as you call it. Would you go?" He held his hand up, "Think before you answer. Be honest with yourself. Would you accept, or would you politely refuse and offer some kind of lie as to why not?"

Elinor stayed silent. They both knew the answer.

Basil's attitude softened and his manner became more conciliatory. "Will you admit to yourself he's not in the same social class? Can you admit you would turn him down for that reason?"

His observation was painfully accurate. "I'd find an excuse not to go." Ashamed, she refused to meet his gaze.

Her chin tickled as Basil held his hand under it until she lifted her eyes. He pressed his advantage, "Would you agree it doesn't matter how pleasant or attractive someone is? It's futile to pursue a courtship if there's little common ground?"

"Yes."

"Elinor, I believe your sympathies in this matter are well intended, but naïve. Since time began, every society has had its own class structure. There will always be slaves and chieftains, serfs and kings."

He cupped his hand along her tingling cheek. "Take heed, milady, that you don't paint yourself into a corner with the same brush you'd paint me."

She couldn't let him finish it this way, because times had changed and so had the class structure. "I understand your point of view, Basil. Truly I do. However, please understand our society has become more egalitarian. There's no taint now in being a tradesman."

His expression remained skeptical.

Curious, Elinor didn't want to let the topic go. "What about love? Some people who fall in love have learned to overcome their differences. Or don't you believe in love?"

"I believe love is something that helps bards and poets put coin in their pockets."

"That's the most cynical thing I've ever heard."

"What do you mean?"

"I mean, your opinion of love is horrible. I'm stunned you believe such a thing." Elinor leaned back against the counter and like him, she folded her arms. His attitude shocked her. "Haven't you ever wanted to be in love or be loved?"

"I never gave it much thought, but since you require an answer, no."

"What an intriguing revelation," she said. "Did your father and mother love each other?"

"I don't know," he said, pausing briefly, as though remembering and clearly having to think about the answer. "Perhaps, when I was young, they might've been in love. As a small boy I often heard talk and laughter coming from her chamber. One night while Grevill was still an infant, I heard my father shouting at my mother about him, about his deformity. She was weeping. I'd never heard him speak harshly to her before. After that, he stopped visiting my mother's solar."

"Your father blamed her for Grevill's handicapped arm, didn't he? How awful for your poor mother." As a history teacher she realized the cultural differences between those days and now. Still, she couldn't stomach his father's behavior. She suppressed the urge to rage at Basil for it. With trepidation she asked, "How did your father treat Grevill?"

"Grevill received almost the same education as I. I told you how hard he trained. No one abused or ignored him. Of course, as the future Earl, my training had to be more extensive. My father made certain I understood my duty and what was required of me. My brother was not mistreated."

From his tone, she'd insulted him. "I apologize; I don't mean to cast aspersions against your family. But, I despise your father's attitude. It was cruel and wrong to blame your mother."

The apology worked, and some of the tension left his face. "My father was a man of his time."

Guy passed through the door and into the kitchen. "Lovely flowers. Are they from the neighbor's garden?" He brought a rose from the arrangement to his nose.

"They're from Jeremy, the village butcher," Basil said with a sneer before she could answer.

Guy laid the rose down with a quizzical look at Elinor, "Why would a tradesman give you flowers?"

Elinor put it with the rest of the bouquet and picked the vase up. "I'm not discussing the matter any further with you or anyone else." She aimed a piercing stare at Basil as she left.

They followed her into the drawing room.

"You're not leaving those there are you?" Basil demanded when she centered the vase on the coffee table.

"Yes. Is there some reason why I shouldn't? Other than they weren't sent by a prince or a duke or some other toffee-nosed fellow?"

"They'd look better somewhere else. Maybe the library."

Guy frowned at Basil like he'd lost his mind.

"Don't be an idiot. The flowers are beautiful. They should be seen and appreciated," Elinor told him.

Basil spun and stormed out of the room.

Chapter Fifteen

After Elinor left that evening, the knights rode to the castle ruins. Neither spoke until they reached the parapet.

Guy propped himself against the wall and stretched his long legs out in front of him. The night breeze blew leaves over the stones and across where he lay.

Basil stood, elbows on a crenel and where he had a view of Elinor's house bathed in the moonlight.

Guy tilted his head back and closed his eyes. "Do you want to talk about that scene you made over the butcher's flowers?"

"I have no idea what you're talking about."

"Don't be evasive. It ill suits you. You're jealous, although, I cannot fathom why you'd be so upset over a silly gift from some tradesman."

"That is ridiculous. I have never been jealous in my life."

"If you were cut right now you'd bleed green. It certainly wasn't your aesthetic sense that was offended by her display of roses. Admit it, you're smitten with her." Guy cracked one eye open and peered at Basil.

“You’re trying to irritate me.”

True, he was fond of Elinor, too fond. He enjoyed being with her more than he cared to say, even to Guy. However, jealousy was too preposterous to entertain seriously.

"I will grant I like her very much, but so do you, do you not?" Basil said.

Guy shifted so they faced each other. "Yes, I like her, enough to wish I'd met her a long, long time ago." The unexpected confession got Basil's attention. "Elinor has none of the brittleness I've known in many women. She's a warm, witty, comely lady. She's also flesh and blood."

Uncomfortable under his friend's scrutiny, Basil turned away and focused on the house again. "Is there a point to this discussion?"

"She's a flesh and blood woman with visions for her future." Guy rose and joined Basil. "You are but a vision of a past flesh and blood man." He laid his hand on Basil's shoulder, "Make sure it's enough for her my friend." Guy walked away, leaving Basil alone with his thoughts.

Chapter Sixteen

Elinor said goodnight to Jeremy and came into the house. The vase of flowers was gone. What had Basil done with them? About to ask, the primary suspect's sour expression made her hesitate.

"What's wrong? You look like you found something distasteful on your boot."

"I find it distasteful you spend your days influencing young girls and your evenings playing the part of a tavern wench." His eyes bore fiercely into her as he made the snide observation.

"What are you talking about?" She was more than a little taken aback by the harsh accusation.

"That disgusting display on the doorstep."

Elinor set her purse on the coffee table and sat at the other end of the sofa from Basil. "Are you talking about the good night kiss I gave Jeremy? It was just a kiss."

"Well, it wasn't just a kiss now was it," he said with exaggerated innuendo.

"Yes-it-was-just a kiss," she stressed.

"His hands were all over your bodice, fondling your breasts and if I may be so bold, fondling them rather badly. In my time, I wouldn't have let a buffoon like that work in my stable. I wouldn't allow him to touch my horses, let alone a woman. He should be flogged for considering himself talented enough to touch a lady. He squeezed your breast like he was judging fruit at a fair. And you, milady, should be beaten for behaving in such a disgraceful manner."

Elinor fumed. How dare he put her on the defensive? She hadn't done anything wrong.

“First,” she snapped, ticking off her points finger by finger, “why were you spying on us? Second, it wasn't as though I let him put his hand under my blouse and actually fondle me. I agree, he lacks finesse, but I don't see how it's your concern. Third, how dare you refer to me as a tavern wench? As I recall, ‘in your time’ there was quite a bit of sneaking off to not so private corners for quickies against the castle wall. A tad more disgraceful than fondling I'd say."

Basil shifted so they were face to face. "I admit, in my time, I did partake of certain stolen moments in the shadows of a castle or two. Unlike the butcher--"

"Stolen moments! Talk about a euphemism, how can you say that with a straight face, why--"

"May I finish?"

Elinor swallowed her next statement and nodded.

"Unlike the butcher, I was a charming and skilled lover. I flattered and delighted the ladies before taking my ease. I did not flounder about."

"Bully for you,” she said with more heat as her anger increased. He was acting like a toad and she had no intention of letting him get away with it. “You make it sound as though you did them a huge favor by taking your ease in whatever spot you found vacant."

"In truth, women found me quite desirable, and they frequently sought me out." Basil ignored her muttered “Oh, brother,” but she knew he heard.

"I never wanted for female companionship. My touch was invited. Was the butcher's touch invited?" he asked and canted his head, so arrogant and accusatory.

The urge to choke Basil, or at least throw something heavy at him, grew with each pointed question.

She hadn't invited Jeremy's touch. She didn't stop it either.

She stammered, trying to avoid a direct answer. "No. Yes. Not really, but it's none of your business anyway. I don't have to answer to you. I'm a grown woman in case you hadn't noticed. And, don't change the subject. I believe you were rattling on about what a stud you were. So, let me ask you, didn't that inflated opinion you have of yourself get in the way of consummating the act?"

"Yes, I've noticed you're a grown woman. I am dead, not blind. As to the rest, I will regard this abuse as female petulance because I expressed the wantonness of your behavior." He pointed a finger at her. "Rest assured, letting that oaf touch you with such familiarity guarantees he feels he will have his way with you sooner or later."

"How did you come to that conclusion? Please enlighten me. Did you feel you had the right every time you touched a woman's bodice?"

"Since you ask, I never had to bumble about with bodices like some beardless youth. The outcome was never in any doubt." Basil smiled in a most annoyingly superior way.

He was the most maddening man she'd ever met. "How perceptive of you. So you're saying no woman ever told you no? They all just hung around with their knees up waiting for you to ravish them?"

"In their own way, yes."

"Really?" Elinor drawled.

"You think I'm lying?"

"No, I think you are a pompous ass."

Basil shrugged. "Perhaps." He scrutinized her with the hauteur of a noble dealing with a troublesome villein.

"What has your back up, Elinor? It's not because I said you behaved like a wanton. If that had been the reason you'd have told me I was all wet and gone about your business, you often do."

"Fine, you're all wet." She got up and poured a glass of wine. She grabbed a book from the mantle and sat in another chair, pretending to read.

Basil pressed on. "There's a strange pattern to your ire, and I think it's related to my past. The more I tell you, the more piqued you become. Why is that, I wonder?"

Her refusal to spare him even a cursory glance while she pretended to read failed. He was so damn full of himself she couldn't let the conversation go.

"You say Jeremy warrants a flogging for fondling me, then it's logical I do too since I didn't stop him. Tell me, do you think it's all right to beat a woman?"

"I've met some who would benefit from a thrashing. But no, I don't feel it's right for a man to strike a woman, even if she deserves it." He looked away briefly, "I didn't beat my betrothed, even after I discovered she'd given herself to another man while I attended to matters at court."

Anger and hurt washed over Elinor. Basil had been engaged. For some inexplicable reason she felt betrayed. He was a ghost, yes, but he was *her ghost.* It was easy to talk about his life and see him as a noble knight he'd been. Even envisioning him surrounded by beautiful women wasn't difficult to accept. But picturing him with a specific woman, the woman who'd have his children, who'd grow old with him, was another thing entirely.

"You were betrothed? You were going to be married?" Questions tumbled out. Her voice notched higher and she lost the battle to discuss his fiancé with any logic. "You said you didn't believe in love. Did you love her?"

"There was never any love between us," he said in a flat tone. "She was a well bred lady and I had no quarrel with the negotiations between our families. I required a wife who'd be able to run my large household and provide an heir. She seemed capable. If our coupling proved less than adequate, I could satisfy my needs elsewhere."

"What did she look like?" Elinor already knew the answer. A man like Basil wouldn't be engaged to anyone less than a raving beauty. The thought nagged at her.

"I find it odd to speak of her. It has been such a very long time and I rarely thought of her when I lived." He closed his eyes, a deep furrow formed between his brows. "Fair of face, she had blue eyes or green, light anyway, and blonde curls to her waist. I recall her skin appeared...I believe the word you'd use today is translucent. Perfect really."

"What was her name?"

"Gwendolyn," Basil said, opening his eyes.

"Gwendolyn," Elinor repeated the name in a sugary voice.

The fact that Gwendolyn was peaches and cream fair to Elinor's more Mediterranean appearance fueled her feelings of betrayal. Her hurt was childish and silly, but she didn't care. "Why do men always want blondes? What is it about them that sets men all atwitter? Stick big breasts on them and you're hopeless!"

Basil fixed a look on her so hard Elinor turned away and tried to focus on the book in her lap. When she braved a glance up, he sat smirking.

"Elinor, are you jealous?"

"Don't be ridiculous. Why would I be jealous of some woman who's been dead for over six hundred years?" Elinor wasn't sure what she felt, but it certainly wasn't jealousy. "Why would it matter to me if you married? I'm surprised, that's all. You don't seem the marrying kind."

"Why does Gwendolyn's prettiness offend you?"

Elinor squirmed under Basil's analytical scrutiny.

"Do you not believe yourself comely?"

She stared at her book, her eyes not moving, fingers not turning the pages.

Basil leaned into her line of sight and kept leaning until she grumbled and closed the book. "Your lovely russet hair catches the golden light of the sun. You have a full mouth that invites a man's kiss, even when you stick your lower lip out, as you are now. Although rather French, the beauty dot by your lovely lips is most pleasing. Surely, you must know how extraordinary your eyes are. Like a changelings, they go from deep green to near gold, depending on your mood. Your breasts are lovely, creamy and firm; they sit nice and high."

Elinor sat quiet for a moment thinking about what he'd said. "When did you see my breasts? Have you watched me dress?"

"Only once. By accident." Basil didn't elaborate.

"That's voyeuristic." Part of her was flattered, but she certainly wasn't going to tell him. No, she should be angry with him and was-or so she told herself. Her inner voice whispered she was really angry because of Gwendolyn. A fact she didn't feel the need to address in front of Basil.

"What about you?" She twisted to face Guy and with her best school teacher, disciplinarian mien, "Have you also watched?"

Guy jumped at her sudden query. Looking guilty, but acting unashamed, he confessed, "I am no monk."

"What does that mean?"

"It means I might have seen you. I don't walk around with my eyes closed. It's possible I have passed by when you left the shower."

From the corner of her eye she saw Basil make some frantic hand signals.

Guy went blithely on, "I find your body most appealing, although your bottom is not as round as I would prefer, a bit on the flat side. You do have fine legs, and I like your other little beauty mark, the one on your breast, quite intriguing." He smiled first at her, then at Basil.

Basil attempted to salvage the situation with what he must've considered the best of all possible compliments. "You have good hips for child birth. You are hale," he looked over at Guy who encouraged him with a firm nod, "and hearty. A man knows he could make strong sons with you."

"Hearty? You find me hearty? Unbelievable! Both of you, stay out of my bathroom and my bedroom." She glared at Basil. "And for the record, I'm not in the least hearty, you big toad." Elinor threw the book down and stomped upstairs, slamming the bedroom door.

Baffled, Basil shook his head. "She seems upset. Why? Did I not compliment her eyes, her hair, her breasts?"

He got up and walked to where Guy sat. "What are you doing?"

"Playing backgammon with myself. I rather like it, I'm winning." At the sound of Elinor's heavy footsteps, Guy tilted his head toward the ceiling.

Basil pulled a high back chair over to the table. "Reset the board, I'll play a round while her temper cools." He sat rubbing his chin as Guy set up the game. "Perhaps we missed something she wanted us to flatter her about, though I cannot think of anything we forgot."

"There are times you flatter a lady, yet she takes offense for no apparent reason. Since there's never any logic involved, a man can make no sensible argument or defense," Guy said and rolled a four-three. "She becomes like a dog with a bone." He brought two checkers down to midpoint, positioning for a quick blockade.

Risky and bold, this early in the game, Basil thought as he planned his strategy.

"If you try to show her the error in her thinking, you will find yourself like that bone my friend--shredded," Guy said, as Basil rolled his dice.

Chapter Seventeen

Elinor awoke the next morning still peeved. Basil's reference to her as hearty trumped her unacknowledged jealousy over his engagement. "Hale and hearty," the words were burned in her brain. How could the thick-headed dope think that was a compliment?

After a fast shower, she dried off at warp speed. Wrapped in the towel, she took a quick spin around her bedroom and the hall. If she felt the tiniest tingle or tickle on her skin, there was going to be big trouble for two ghosts. Satisfied she had privacy, she returned to the bedroom. She dropped the towel and stared at her naked reflection in the full length mirror. She turned to the right. "Not bad, tummy's flat, titties firm and high," she said, jiggling them. Then, facing front, "my hips look okay, no big bulges." She lifted one arm to the side and wiggled it, "no bat wings, nothing wobbly," she repeated the action with the other arm. She turned her backside to the mirror and groaned. "All right, not my best angle. It's not a perky bum, flattish, but far from hearty." With a sigh, she decided it served no purpose to dwell on the matter. The sun was out. The weather was beautiful. The woods seemed like a good place to relax. She dressed and headed that way.

#

Elinor sat cross-legged on a dry patch she found on the forest floor with a handful of walnuts. A grey squirrel watched her from a nearby alder tree. For several minutes, she held the nut out and made what she believed were excellent squirrel chirps. The grey hesitated at the base of the tree before scurrying over to sniff the offering. Deeming it suitable, he delicately removed it from her fingers and dashed off.

Out of the corner of her eye Elinor saw Basil appear. He sat down just as the grey hopped over to take another nut.

"Trusting little fellow."

"Yes, he came down rather fast considering they don't come in contact with many people." Elinor remained still so the squirrel wouldn't be scared off.

As though sensing Basil's ghostly presence, the squirrel laid his half-eaten walnut down and scampered over. He sniffed furiously, sat on his haunches and chittered at Basil. The noisy chirping continued for about a minute before he stopped and appeared to wait. Apparently concluding he wasn't going to get anything worthwhile, he showed his backside, gave his tail several hard shakes and scurried back to the walnut.

Elinor leaned close to Basil. "I believe there was a rude comment about you in that tail action."

"Probably still bears a grudge over the squirrel-trimmed cloak I gave my mother one year." He peered over Elinor's shoulder and noticed her little walnut pile.

Basil shifted so he knelt on one knee and pointed to the nuts in her hand. "Do you want to know an old custom of ours?"

"I'd love to."

He placed his hand over hers so she'd close her fingers. "We used acorns, but walnuts will do. You throw a handful into the air and make as many wishes as you can before the first one lands."

Elinor stood and threw upward as high as she could. The squirrel's ears perked as the nuts landed softly in the leaves. "I got three wishes in. I've never heard of that custom."

"I'd be surprised if you had. I just made it up. I needed to lure you away from your woodland friends so you'd go for a walk with me." Basil extended his hand, and they strolled along the bank of the stream.

The mist hung thicker and heavier in the places where the stream widened. The trees formed a canopy, thinning only where the spring sunlight filtered through. The alder leaves had a silver hue in the light, intermingling for a pretty mix with the greens of the oaks and ash. Surrounded by the forest's neutral tones Elinor felt part of an artist's watercolor.

They walked without speaking. Basil kept his hands clasped behind his back and the pace slow.

When he first sat down, she hadn't paid attention to his clothes. Now, as he got a few steps ahead, she noticed his white linen shirt and black breeches resembled the attire he'd tried to wear to the village. Were those breeches as formfitting and thigh hugging as the ones today? She'd been too nervous that day to take in all the details. Her gaze slid down his thighs where soft black boots came up to his knees. Elinor surreptitiously scanned his backside. *Oh yeah, you definitely benefited from all that time in the saddle.*

His hair was pulled back into a queue again only today he sported a small gold earring. In a million years she'd never have pictured Basil wearing an earring. Guy yes, Basil no. It suited him. He looked like a pirate, a very sexy movie pirate. She reluctantly broke off the lusty perusal before she got caught and embarrassed herself.

Good thing too, because Basil turned to her a moment later.

"Last night you asked me whether I loved Gwendolyn. And by the way, I forgive you for your outrageous outburst. You seemed quite curious about her."

Elinor stopped several feet back, hands jammed into her jeans pockets. She gave him her best, stone-faced stare, feigning umbrage. Basil's "forgiveness" didn't offend her, not really. However, she didn't want the haughty devil to think the audacity of his comment went unnoticed. Her pretended indignation failed.

Basil impatiently motioned for her to catch up. "Don't get your feathers ruffled and come here while I'm talking to you."

"Devil," Elinor huffed and joined him.

"I wondered if you've ever been in love."

Although they stood side-by-side, Basil's face was shielded from her view when he posed the question. A shrub with small, spiky pink flowers appeared to hold his interest. The delicate petals lifted when he reached to touch them.

"No." Elinor shifted position so she could see his face. Why was he interested? She studied him, trying to guess his purpose. Did he feel as muddled about her as she did about him?

Basil glanced up. "Is something amiss?" She shook her head and he returned his attention to the bush. "Out of curiosity, if you were to fall in love, how do you picture your ideal man?"

Maybe she read his expression wrong, but Elinor thought he seemed relieved when she'd said she hadn't been in love. She wasn't sure what to make of his response and her mind wandered as Basil rolled the pink buds between his fingers in a slow caress. Elinor gave herself a mental shake and asked for clarification. "Are you asking how I picture him physically or what character traits are important to me?"

Basil waved his hand in the air as though it didn't matter "Start with the physical. How do you envision him?"

Two different answers came to mind and she paused to consider the choices. Keep the description generic or tell him the truth? The truth won out.

At first, she thought it better to gaze into the distance, be less obvious, more contemplative. But then, with a rare burst of bravado, she thought, hell, if I'm going to tell the truth, I may as well look straight into my vision's eyes.

"He should be tall. I like tall men. I'd like him well built, broad shouldered and strong. His face should be nice and this is important--" Elinor leaned toward Basil, thinking, hoping he'd be able to read between the lines. "He should look very masculine. Maybe, he'd even bear a less than perfect aquiline nose. Men who have soft features make me uncomfortable. I always suspect they'd be more attractive in a dress than me. I like dark hair, especially when it's long." She tapped her lips with a forefinger. Smiling, she said, "Oh, a nice bum would be a bonus."

Basil's soft laugh sounded almost shy and more than a little self-conscious as he touched a finger to his nose. He started to reply and hesitated, then said, "Ah...should we start to wend our way back?"

They turned away from the stream, leaving the wood to walk on the grassy field. Basil clasped his hands behind his back again but didn't say a word.

"What were you going to say?"

"Nothing."

"Not fair! I answered your question. Did my description upset you?" She hated having to ask.

"No, not at all. I'm a bit confused." Basil didn't elaborate and continued walking. When they were within sight of the house he stopped and faced her. "Does Sean Connery look like this man you described?"

"What--what?" The strange question came out of nowhere. "Yes. How do you know about Sean Connery?"

"I heard some women speak of him." Arching a brow, he narrowed his eyes at Elinor, "Some of the things they said were quite shameless."

"Why are you looking at me like that?"

"Well, you said your description fits this Connery fellow."

If only she could shake him until his teeth rattled. Then, when she had his attention, she'd tell him. Idiot, it fits your_description too. Since that wasn't an option, she went with a noncommittal response. "It describes a lot of people."

"This Connery is a Scotsman. Do you prefer your ideal man a Scot?" he asked, eyes fixed on her.

Elinor caught on to the purpose of his question. "No. An Englishman would be more than fine with me."

Neither moved. More than anything she wanted to touch him, touch his hair, his face, his mouth. Her gaze fell upon the scar over his neck. Dull white at the edge, the rest had acquired a slight pinkish sheen as some scars are wont to do.

She traced the length of it with her finger. It started at the base of his ear, curved down and ended at the hollow of his throat. How forceful the killing blow must have been to cut through his mail. Above, another scar perhaps three inches long ran straight across his throat. Did the same French blade make both or was there another? Did it matter?

Basil stepped within inches of her and ran his fingers down her cheek near her ear, tickling the baby fine hairs. His hand continued slow and light as he moved his thumb over her lower lip. Elinor edged closer wanting more. His large hands cupped the air near her face as he bent and whispered, "Elinor."

She closed her eyes in anticipation.

"Nora!" Someone in the distance called. Elinor jerked, and opened her eyes, turning towards the house. Lucy stood at the end of the pasture fence waving.

"I forgot Lucy was stopping by on her way to Nottingham this afternoon," Elinor mumbled with a long sigh of disappointment. When she twisted around Basil had gone. "Basil?" No one answered. She plastered a smile on her face and headed for the house.

"Sorry, Luce, I didn't realize the time."

Lucy tilted her head and stared hard at the area Elinor came from, before she turned around. “Who were you talking to out there?”

"No one," she said, without missing a beat.

"I could have sworn I saw you talking to a man dressed like a highwayman."

"It must've been a shadow. Trust me, if I'd been talking to some gorgeous, tall, dark-haired fox, you'd know about it."

Lucy blocked Elinor's path. "Hold on just a second," she said and wagged a finger. "It's funny you should say he was tall with dark hair, because I don't recall saying that. You're supposed to tell me, your best friend, when someone tall, dark and looks great in boots crosses your path."

"You're right. You didn't say tall. Knowing you as I do, I simply filled in the blanks." Elinor stepped past Lucy and forced a laugh. "Don't worry. If someone fitting your description drops from the sky into my drawing room, you'll be the first to know. Now, let's go inside before you start seeing ghosts again."

Inside, Lucy went straight to the refrigerator. "How did the date with Jeremy go? More importantly, is he going to ask you out again?" She took a soda and sat across from Elinor at the table.

"The date went okay." The evening with Jeremy was the furthest thing from Elinor's mind. "He called me early this morning." One shoulder lifted in a lazy half shrug as she told Lucy about the short conversation. "He sounded strange. He talked really fast and was so muffled, I had a hard time understanding him. If I didn't know better, I'd say he had his hand around the receiver. The call couldn't have been more than a minute long."

"What did he say?"

It wasn't one of those male-female conversations a woman commits to memory. "He asked me out to dinner Thursday."

"You don't seem very excited. Are you going?"

"I guess so, but I told him it would have to be an early night. I have school in the morning." Deep down, she was relieved the date would be short. "He has to get up early too, but Thursday was the only night he had available. On Saturday, he leaves with his mother for Yorkshire."

The corners of Lucy's mouth curved down, "He's not a momma's boy is he?"

"No, it's not what you think. She asked him to drive her around while she shops for retirement property."

"All right, that's acceptable." Lucy put her bottle down. "You're oddly unenthusiastic about a handsome and charming man. Let's get to the interesting stuff. Is he a good kisser and did you sleep with him?"

"You know I don't sleep with men on the first date, and he's not a good kisser." Elinor got up and busied herself with kitchen chores. Even if he was a good kisser, Jeremy's couldn't compare to Basil's. No amount of busy work could put that thought from her mind.

Lucy walked over and took Elinor by the arm. "You know you're being silly. Nobody. I mean nobody waits anymore. It's stupid. Men don't put up with women who play hard to get. They don't have to. The sooner you realize it, the better off you'll be. No one will think you're a slut, believe me. You need to get with the times. Besides, it's not like you're a virgin."

Elinor rolled her eyes and went back to wiping down a counter. "News flash, there's a good chance I'll never sleep with him."

"How bad was this kiss?"

"Like kissing a plunger, is that bad enough for you?"

Lucy wrinkled her nose at the comparison. "Kissing badly doesn't mean he's bad in all areas."

Elinor patted Lucy's hand and walked away. "I agreed to go out with him again, a date, that's all. I am what I am. I'm not turning myself inside out for anyone, and I won't be badgered into having sex. Okay?"

"Whatever you say, my Victorian friend. Just out of curiosity, your reticence doesn't have anything to do with that dark Zorro look-alike I hallucinated does it?" Lucy cackled and grabbed her purse, "No need to give me your Medusa stare, I'm on my way out, t.t.f.n."

"Oh, ta-ta for now yourself," Elinor grumbled at Lucy's departing back, "and I'm not in the least Victorian."

Chapter Eighteen

Elinor heard the car drive away as she stood at the archway to the drawing room. Guy, ever fascinated by the record player hovered around the machine for hours on end, today being no different. He'd recently taken to listening to his favorite songs, over and over. She debated her options. Should she risk sitting in the drawing room with a good book? Could she bear hearing *Born to Be Wild*, for an hour straight? Or should she try to find Basil? Common sense dictated when he wanted to return he would.

She ventured into the drawing room. As expected, she found Guy picking through rock albums.

"Have you listened to some of the classical records I have? I think you might like Mozart or Beethoven," Elinor suggested, curling up at the end of the sofa.

"I have heard them. Their music is just that, only music. I like the songs with words. I like to listen to the story." Guy turned to her. "Can I play one or two for you?"

"Certainly."

"Pay attention to the lyrics. You'll see what I mean."

"Yes, sir, I will, sir." Elinor snapped a hand to her brow in mock salute. Guy's eyes narrowed and the tiniest of frowns came and went before he fixed his attention on the stereo.

The rich bass voice of Bill Medley came on with the first lines of *You've Lost That Lovin' Feeling.* Elinor stretched a leg out and rested her head on her arm. The song was one of her favorites.

Guy sat on the floor next to the sofa. "Listen, can you not feel the heartbreak in his voice?"

"Every woman I know loves this song. It's great to dance to, even though it's about a breakup."

Guy tipped his head and looked up at her. "One day we will have to dance to this." It ended and he got up to put another record on, "Now this one is most perfect for a man to woo a lady by."

Her eyes widened with curiosity. A statement like that, coming from Guy, would have a saint holding her breath in lusty curiosity. Exile's *Kiss You All Over*, came on, and Elinor couldn't resist laughing. If ever a song suited a man, this one fit Guy to a "T."

He lay down on the floor with his arms folded behind his head. A slow smile crept across his face as he closed his eyes and tapped his foot to the music. A low, primal growl preceded one stanza, "I love this part about being her fantasy," he said, with another soft growl.

In spite of his teasing manner, his love of music and lyrics made Elinor suspect he was a die hard romantic. "Guy, were you ever in love?"

He opened his eyes and stared at the ceiling, no longer tapping his foot.

"I believe I might've been. It's hard to say I was very young at the time."

"Tell me about her. If you remember a girl from your youth, you must've been in love."

A few seconds passed before he added, "I guess you could say I was."

Elinor fussed with the sofa pillows trying to situate herself to see him better and get more comfortable.

"Being in love is like being pregnant, either you are or you aren't."

Guy sat up on one elbow and glared at her, "Who tells this story Madame, me or you?"

"Jeez, don't get your knickers in a knot. Go on, I promise I'll be quiet."

"As I was saying." He cast a stern glance in Elinor's direction. "I was quite young, only twenty summers. She was but ten and five years and besotted with me. She seemed happy just being near me. I enjoyed her company too. We did simple things. We'd take long walks and talk, sometimes she'd sing. Her name was Lorraine. She was kind and gentle with the voice of a lark.

"Her father approached mine about marriage negotiations. My father asked me. I told him I'd no interest in marrying anyone. My plans, you see, did not include being saddled with a bride."

"If you loved her, couldn't you have agreed to be married at a later date?"

Guy laughed; a quiet, almost bitter laugh. "As I said, I was young. I had battles to fight, dragons to slay, a full court of women to conquer." He twisted his hand in the air, mimicking the movements of a sword. "I wanted no burden of any kind to slow me down."

"What happened?"

"After a few years, I tired of court intrigues, the gossip and the boring sameness of it all. By then, Lorraine had married someone else."

He got up; pulled an album from the stack and stared at the disc for a long moment before putting it on. This time when he sat on the floor he kept his back to Elinor and rested his hand against a propped up knee.

The song was *Dust in the Wind*, by Kansas. Guy's head hung a little as the song began and he softly sang along. When it ended he stayed silent and still as the next song started to play. She'd never seen him so solemn and tipped her head to peer at his face. When he glanced at her, his sparkling eyes had dulled.

Quickly looking away, he said, "Interesting lyric, wouldn't you say? All we are, all we do, crumbles and blows away, like dust in the wind. Before we left for what turned out to be our final campaign, I'd decided I'd return to my holding once the war was over. It was time to be the future baron."

A couple of heartbeats later, Guy made eye contact with her, the light back in his brown eyes. "Death milady is a plague to the best of our plans."

The sudden silence when Guy turned off the stereo blanketed the room in the sadness of the poignant memory. He put on *Born to be Wild*, and resumed his original position, stretched out on the floor, keeping time to the music with his foot.

Elinor laid her head down on her arm and thought about what Guy had said. How short sighted she'd been regarding he and Basil. Caught up in the novelty of their ghostly presence, she hadn't really thought about their lives as men. They'd been in their prime, with hopes for a future that ended one bloody morning on an overcast September day.

What would have happened if they'd lived and had children? Would history have played out the same? What difference might their lives have made? What was changed by their deaths? The unfairness of their loss troubled her for the rest of the afternoon.

Chapter Nineteen

That night Elinor put her headset on and went to bed early with her motivational tape.

Basil lay next to her for a long time watching as she slept. Sprawled out, her hair was in wild disarray on the pillow, the headpiece had slipped, but the earplugs still remained in place.

He ran the back of his knuckles along her face in a long caress. His fingertips drew a path along the smooth flesh under her jaw. He buried his face in her hair, inhaling the mingled scent of her shampoo and exotic bouquet of her perfume. He slid a fingertip across her collarbone, lingering at the hollow then up a blue vein, wanting to feel her heartbeat. Basil bent close and brushed her warm lips with his.

He lay back with his forearm across his eyes, "For six hundred years I've wished only for true death. I never imagined there'd be something I'd want more. Now I find there is, and it's more elusive than death. I wish with all my soul, such as it is, you could know me as the man I once was."

Elinor moaned softly. He turned, afraid she might've awakened and heard the tormented whisper. Her eyes remained closed and she sighed again. He wondered what she dreamed. Basil rolled onto his side and was quiet for several minutes, thinking thoughts he knew better than to have. Then very gently he removed the headset. His lips almost touching her ear, he began to speak.

Elinor dreamed.

She stood at the base of a stone archway that housed a dark metal portcullis. Bracketed torches lit the stone interior.

No sound came from the bailey beyond. Unafraid, Elinor walked into the courtyard and stopped in front of Ashenwyck's high Keep.

The thick oak doors of the imposing structure were three times her height and dotted with large iron studs. They opened,_bathing the area in light from the great hall. Fresh rushes cushioned her bare feet and she stepped inside.

So much more than she imagined, the room was warm and inviting, rich in detail and textures. Rough stone complimented carved stone, aged oak swept upward into the ceiling's skeleton of cross beams. Prisms of light from the torch flames bounced off the window glass. The circle from the blower's pipe in the pane's center reflected a rippled pattern on the floor.

She walked to the tapestries Basil described. All appeared new, but for the one dating to the Crusades. The hanging of two leopards bringing down a horse was both horrific and beautiful in its depiction. The golden leopards were majestic with their black and bronze spots. Their claws of shiny black silk were a sharp contrast to the varied pale hued threads used on the white horse. Scarlet bloodlines of silk marked the claw's trail over the horse's flanks.

The largest tapestry hung over the dais. A sole leopard stood proudly; lush jungle vegetation in various shades of green and brown surrounded him. Above him in deep gold, the words Virtute et Armis.

Basil came towards her. Dressed in the dark breeches and soft shirt he'd worn in the wood, his untied hair inky against the white of the shirt.

"Elinor," he murmured and kissed her.

She wrapped her arms around his neck, and her fingers wound through his hair.

Unhurried, feathery kisses skimmed the corners of her mouth. Basil lifted her and pressed her close. She rose up on her toes and grasped his shoulders for support, moaning in protest as the kiss ended.

He eased her down and moved away. His image began to fade. She was losing him.

In her sleep, she called his name.

Basil rolled onto his back and stared at the ceiling. Release her from the dream, he told himself, before it goes too far. An honorable man would take the moment he'd been given, hold it as a cherished memory and go no further.

Elinor's eyelashes fluttered as she called his name again.

His moral battle was lost. Tonight he'd be the man he used to be, the man he wanted her to see. He lowered his lips to her ear.

Basil's image grew stronger as he closed the gap between them and embraced her again. She felt his warmth as his arms wrapped around her waist. She ran her hands over the hard contours of his biceps and down the well defined forearms. She slid her palms down to his waist, over the silk shirt, and the planes of his chest.

There was no tickling, no tingling sensation, only firm flesh. She raised tentative eyes to his, afraid the answer would disappoint, "Is this a dream, Basil? Am I dreaming you?

"Yes, and no." He paused, as if telling her too much might wake her or change how she felt. "You see what you desire to see. I can paint a picture with words. You give it life and breath. It's what you called your subconscious allowing you to dream what is in your heart. The dream is both of ours to make."

"Yes, it is. Ours alone."

Her journey continued. She sought fulfillment to the erotic promise of his words. She curved her hand along his jaw and traced the outline of his lips now pink with life.

He kissed her temple, teasing her skin with his breath. "You memorize me with your touch."

"If you're only a vision, Basil, then I'll commit this to memory and hold onto it after the vision fades." Desperate, she flung her arms around his neck. "I'm afraid to let go."

"Don't be..." the rest of his words were lost, buried inside a hard kiss, seductive and heated, filled with a thirst long denied.

As his strong thigh wedged between her legs, her foot rubbed against the supple leather of his boot. She clutched his hair as he slid a hand under her dress and with light sweeps_caressed her hipbone with his fingers. Arching at the_sensations, her head tilted back, he nipped the tender skin beneath her ear and down her throat.

She lost herself to him completely. All her fantasies and yearning merged with the urgency fear begets, fear this reality would disappear too soon. As tight as Basil held her, she clung to him harder. Some part of her wanted to believe if she held him close enough, he wouldn't go anywhere, couldn't go anywhere.

"Come," he held out his arm and led them towards a wide, stone staircase. Centuries of foot traffic had left depressions in the middle of each.

They entered a large, high-ceilinged room. The sweet scent of beeswax from the candles filled the air. A helm and sword she recognized as his lay on a wide, plain chest. A long wooden table stood under the window with two ornately carved pewter goblets and a flagon on top. She circled the room touching things, his things, fingering the copper basin where he washed.

A massive bed with a goose-down mattress dominated the remaining space. Four tall posts supported a railing that ran around all sides of the bed. Heavy velvet curtains in dark indigo blue were attached to each post and tied back with silken bronze cords and tassels. Pillows of chrysanthemum colored_Tripoli silk with embroidered dragons rested against a fat bolster.

Basil stepped close and pushed the hair away from her neck to place a kiss there in its stead. He bit her lightly at the nape.

"Dance for me," he commanded in a hushed voice, as his warm hands trailed down her arms.

She didn't hear the strange exotic melody at first. Then, from somewhere, came a male chorus singing a repetitive pagan chant. Strong primitive drums drove the beat of the chant, the power of the song building. He lay on the bed as she found the music's rhythm and began to move.

His gaze never left her as she danced. His fascination excited her and she danced closer. The dress floated in waves around her ankles while the light from the fire silhouetted her form through the gown's gossamer material.

The music was freeing, the hypnotic melody her guide. A light sheen of sweat covered her body. Elinor lifted the hem of her dress. Caressing her slick thighs in sensual strokes she edged toward the bed. With a glistening wet palm, she beckoned to him.

Basil swung his legs to the floor. She straddled one, buried her hands in his hair and lowered herself down. She ground along the length of the captured thigh, the erotic contact making her bold. He cupped her bare buttocks, licking the tiny rivulet of sweat that rolled between her breasts.

He brought her with him as he stood, deft fingers undid the laces of the dress. Strong arms laid her back on the bed.

She cradled his face in her palms, and kissed his lips, his chin, his neck, his cheeks. He smelled of soap and chamomile.

Surrounded by the soft down of the bed she watched him undress. The nobleman and warrior slowly stripped away, now becoming her fantasy lover.

She opened her thighs, reaching out as he lowered himself onto the bed. He held her wrists and kissed her hard, relentlessly, and then he abandoned her mouth. Gentle kisses made a path down to the sensitive hollow above her collarbone. Goose bumps rose where he skimmed his lips over her skin.

"Look at me Elinor," he said, raising his head. Glassy, black marble eyes locked on her. "Tell me what you want."

"You, all of you, as much as I can get."

"Be sure."

"I am."

He slipped his hands under her buttocks, raised her hips and buried himself inside her. Basil pulled out and thrust into her again. She drifted to a place somewhere between intense pleasure and the need for release as he moved inside her.

The palms of her hands moved in wide strokes across his hard back, traveling down his spine. She felt a shiver ripple through him at her touch. She began to climb. He took her to the_top of a cliff, where she teetered so close, so very close. He withdrew and stayed her fall, only to rock his hips over hers till she cried out. "Please." He drove back into her. Her *nails marked his skin in tiny half moons where she gripped his shoulders. She closed her eyes and fell.*

Her breath evened and they rolled over. With tender fingers he smoothed away the strands of hair that clung to her face. His hand made a slow arc over her thigh from the back of the knee up as he lowered his head and grazed her lips with a gentle kiss.

He laid her on her back. "I'll never willingly release you. Never. Even in your dreams." Poised above her, the flames from the candles made squares of light in his fathomless eyes. In their depths she saw his uncertainty. He doubted her acceptance of his passion.

She kissed his chin, his lips, the tip of his nose; she dotted his jaw with a dozen kisses and murmured, "Then don't."

He rolled over and pulled her close. Elinor used a length of her hair to tickle and tease his chest and navel.

"Cease your torment woman." The faint lines around his eyes crinkled as he laughed. "You shall make me forget the time and the dawn comes soon. We'll have another night, I promise you."

"You said you'd never willingly release me. Is that a promise?

He was silent for a long minute, then in a barely audible voice said, "Yes, and may God have mercy on my soul."

Elinor's eyes flew open; she bolted upright and scanned the room. The sky had just begun to grow light although the moon and stars shined low on the horizon. She picked the headset off the pillow and placed it on the nightstand, admonishing herself for not being able to keep it in her ears.

She shifted into a sitting position, fluffing her pillows behind her back and drew her knees up. Never had she dreamt such a realistic or erotic dream.

When the sun peeked over the horizon she went downstairs and started a pot of coffee. Guy appeared and sat at the table, with the London Times. Everyday he rummaged through the paper searching out lingerie ads. A few minutes later Basil came in. Heat instantly shot through her.

"You look especially lovely this morning," he said, with an innocent smile and brought his hand to her face. "Your cheeks have a very pretty blush to them. Did you sleep well?"

"Yes, remarkably well, thank you." In a moment of panic she touched her lips, checking for swelling.

Chapter Twenty

The five days since her dream had whizzed by. It was Thursday and she had a date with Jeremy. She told herself to keep an open mind. It wasn't fair to judge him so hastily. Elinor stood at the dining room table silently repeating those words as she went through the day's mail while Basil railed at her.

"You can't mean to see that bounder again. I've told you he's not your sort."

She'd hoped, apparently in vain, he had softened his opinion since their last discussion. "Basil, please don't start that talk again about him being base born, or a peasant, or whatever label you choose." She tipped her head back and blew out a frustrated puff of air. They'd been arguing all afternoon, since Basil found out Jeremy invited her to dinner. "I'm not breaking the date, period."

"Base born is not the issue. I believe that's something diligence and hard work can overcome, on the rare occasion-"

"I knew there'd be a caveat thrown in." She tossed the mail down and she squared off with Basil.

"As I was saying, not everything can be so easily changed." Basil pointed a finger at her, "He's--"

"He's what?" Elinor snapped, "Not an Earl. Not the darling of the court? What?"

"There's nothing I can say to convince you he is bad for you, is there?"

"Come up with something credible and I'll be convinced."

"You're not his." Basil's eyes had glittered with anger then flattened.

Did she read accusation and hurt in the charge, or did that interpretation stem from her own guilt and ambiguity? Elinor couldn't say. The name Delilah resonated in a corner of her brain. A sense of disloyalty to Basil ate at her all week, illogical and troubling as it was to admit.

"No, I'm not his." I'm not anybody's, she thought. I've no one to read the paper with on Sunday mornings, no one to share a New Year's kiss with, no one to give me a valentine. For those reasons, Jeremy deserved another chance.

"Basil, it's only dinner. We're not intimate."

"It's none of my affair. Enjoy your evening." He said crisply, and then disappeared through the back door.

Elinor hurried up the stairs to shower and get ready. Jeremy was due in less than an hour and she wanted to be at the door when he pulled up.

Basil's vocal and adamant disapproval made his feelings clear. The argument had played and replayed a dozen times in her head, as she dressed. She didn't want this sore point between them, especially now. Ever since the night of the dream, Basil brought her roses, always the pale colored ones she favored. Every morning she awoke to find two or three beautiful blooms on the kitchen counter. The charming little gesture made her want to kiss him senseless. However, she also suspected he acquired them from the neighbor's garden.

When asked outright if he nicked them, the question was met with a dramatic wounded look and complete denial. Basil reiterated he was a knight, not a thief. She subsequently cast an inquiring eye toward Guy, who stared back with a wide-eyed face of innocence. Elinor dropped the subject. Some things a woman is better off not knowing.

Finished dressing, she stood in front of the mirror, her thoughts a jumbled mess. Her undefined emotions about Jeremy didn't help. Maybe tonight's date would ease her mind. Maybe she'd discover she really liked Jeremy and stop thinking about the dream. *Maybe pigs would fly*!

Jeremy drove up as she scurried out the door, locking it as he stepped from his car and walked over. He wore a black dress shirt and black jeans. The dark color complemented his light hair and made his smile even whiter and brighter. He greeted her with a long, deep, and wet, wet kiss.

"I'm sorry this has to be an early night. You've no idea how I missed you." He squeezed her shoulder hard ignoring Elinor's flinch as his fingers bruised the tender area under her collarbone.

"I've missed you too."

Liar. Elinor hadn't thought of him, not in the way he expected. She tried to list his attributes in her mind. He's attractive. He's pleasant to talk to, intelligent and articulate. He's--brutish. The adjective popped into her head as she absently rubbed the spot he'd hurt. The painful greeting didn't endear him to her. She told herself to not condemn him by this incident. He's used to handling heavy cuts of meat and might not realize his strength.

Perhaps he had a delightful sense of humor and she only needed to talk to him at length. "Could we have dinner someplace in the village? It's close. Afterward we can go somewhere and chat for awhile." She wanted to bite her tongue afraid he'd interpret "go somewhere" meant his flat. She definitely wasn't ready to sleep with him.

"Actually, we're going to a little place outside of town." He kissed the palm of her hand, turned on the radio and started down the road opposite the village.

As they exited her driveway Elinor glanced back, half afraid she'd see Basil standing there and sighed aloud when he wasn't.

They arrived at the tiny, dark restaurant in about fifteen minutes. Jeremy held onto her waist or she'd have tripped several times. He chose the farthest booth with the least amount of light in the establishment. Their second date and both times he picked a remote table in a dim place. Their dinner was fine, the conversation constant. Jeremy liked to talk. The humor and charm Elinor hoped for didn't emerge, in spite of his loquaciousness.

There'd been a minute when she questioned her excellent memory. She'd asked him where in the Yorkshire Dales he planned to go with his mother.

"Yorkshire Dales?" His expression was blank.

"You said you were going there with her this weekend."

"Sorry, you're right. I guess I put the trip out of my mind. I'm not looking forward to it. Bound to be bored senseless. It'll be two days of following her around, while my mother finds fault with every house she sees." He rolled his eyes, his lips curving into a tiny smile as he checked his watch. "Let's leave."

His speed taking her home bordered on reckless. The country road was pitch black and filled with tight bends and turns. More than a little frightened, she shut her eyes twice when the rear end of his car fishtailed on a curve. Her fear grew the closer they got to her house and Basil. She tried to occupy her mind by making small talk. He kept his answers brief while his hands were anything but quiet.

Jeremy steered with one hand and stroked her thigh with the other. She wasn't enjoying the attention. He was getting closer and closer to the juncture between her legs with each stroke. She didn't care for his assumption, although she shouldn't be surprised according to Lucy. She moved his hand away and laid it on his thigh.

Jeremy chuckled and swiftly wrapped his fingers around her wrist. He dragged her hand over and pressed her palm against his crotch. Caught in his firm grip he forced her to rub him through his jeans, until the zipper strained under his erection.

"Stop it!" Elinor tried to pull her hand away.

Moments earlier, she'd been afraid of Jeremy's driving. Now her fear ratcheted up another notch and had nothing to do with his driving.

Elinor turned as much as possible in the seat and tried again to tug her hand free of his grasp, to no avail.

"Let go!" The words were no sooner off her lips when the car stopped in front of her house and she jerked her hand free.

Thank God.

She unbuckled the seatbelt and grabbed her purse, one foot on the ground before she opened the door all the way. She pushed off the seat using it to give herself added impetus, and bounded out of the car toward the house. He caught her at the waist and spun her around just as she reached the steps. His chest firm against hers, Elinor stumbled backwards until her back hit the exterior wall. Jeremy raised his free hand and laid it flat on the wall, blocking any escape. The masonry was cold and rough through her thin blouse as he pressed closer.

He kissed her cheek and neck, "You can't leave me like this." His breath hot on her flesh, she heard him unzip his jeans. Nausea filled her. "You can see how much I want you. I know you're not a virgin. No woman your age nowadays is. So what's the problem?"

He found the hand she'd held tight at her side. She was no match for his strength. Unable to wrench herself free, he wrapped her hand over his erection.

She tried to reason with him. "Jeremy please don't. I'm not ready." In the past, she always thought of herself as too proud to beg. "Please, please don't do this." She was wrong.

"You think it's fun to lead a man on?"

"I didn't."

"You happily joined me the night we met at the grocery store. You acted as happy to go to dinner with me again the next night and again this evening. If you didn't want to fuck me, you shouldn't have gone out with me."

Maybe, he was right. If she'd told him no when he called the other day, she wouldn't be in this position now. She hated him but hated herself more.

His breathing changed as he began to move back and forth, crushing her fingers tighter around him. "You've got me so turned on. If you won't screw me, at least do this." His rapid pants sounded like a train in her ear, and he moved faster and faster in her palm, finally ejaculating. Elinor closed her eyes in revulsion as the warm, sticky fluid oozed between her fingers, dripping over her hand.

He dropped the arm that blocked her path and stepped back to zip himself up. Opening her eyes she stood frozen, wanting to slap him with the same hand he'd cum in. She started for the door when he placed a folded handkerchief into her palm.

He walked with her as she rummaged through her purse with the unsoiled hand. She shook with rage as she tried to get the key in the lock and fumbled.

"In spite of our little struggle I had a good time tonight. It didn't have to be one-sided you know. I'd rather we had a head banging fuck. I'll call you soon."

He casually turned and headed for his car as she managed to unlock the door and dash inside.

Hard black eyes followed the vehicle down the road. "We'll meet another day, butcher."

Chapter Twenty-One

Guy was stretched out on the sofa listening to music when Elinor came in and rushed upstairs.

A moment later Basil appeared, his image faded as he drew a fireplace poker from the stand. There was a flash of battle-hardened malice in the set of his jaw, dangerous determination in his eyes Guy hadn't seen since Poitiers.

Basil sliced the air with a powerful downward stroke of the poker. His image disappeared completely with the blow. The jardinière shattered scattering potting soil and the dwarf palm Elinor had ordered from Scotland. With the same unseen fury he drove the iron rod into a log in the grate.

"What is amiss? I haven't seen you like this since France, when you caught that man-at-arms raping a child."

Basil related what had transpired. Guy sat up and shook his head. "I've never understood forcing a woman to do anything against her will. The world is filled with obliging women. Why compel one who is not?"

"The cur has no remorse. He thinks to call on her again. I won't allow it." His stronger image returned. Basil's large hands flexed over the arms of the chair, his eyes alive with renewed rage at the mention of Jeremy's intention.

Both knights looked up to the ceiling at the sound of Elinor's shower. "He mocked her when she refused, then bullied her, trying to instill doubt in her for saying no. Distressed as she is, I fear she'll question her convictions."

"Why would she doubt herself? No, the butcher is the dishonorable one. He's a base and common man without a shred of chivalry, nothing to do with her."

Basil rose and lingered near the stairs. "I heard Lucy say it didn't matter if a woman was a wanton. In this day and age, no one judges her badly. She said Elinor's attitude was silly." Basil started to pace. "I should talk to her."

"No, you should not. I will." Guy didn't give Basil the chance to argue. "It would shame her to know you witnessed what happened. I've perceived of late, the relationship between the two of you has...changed."

Arms crossed over his chest, Basil refused to make eye contact focusing on the staircase instead.

"I see I'm correct. I'll be most interested to hear how this was accomplished. Surely, it has to be better than any bard's tale ever told."

“Do you intend to speak to Elinor or tarry here, plaguing me with questions until the next millennium?”

Guy ignored the withering look he got. "I'll go and speak with her now. But don't think to escape the telling of this recent closeness with the lady."

Basil nodded curtly, and Guy headed for Elinor's room.

#

Elinor sat on the edge of the bed in her robe with the towel in her lap.

“Elinor,” Guy called softly from the hall. “May I enter?”

She didn’t feel like seeing anyone.

“I’d like for us to talk,” he added.

With a heavy sigh, she said, “Come in.”

Guy walked through the door and joined her on the bed.

"What do you want to talk about?" She had a sinking feeling he knew what happened.

"You remember a week ago you asked me if I'd ever been in love and I told you about Lorraine."

"Yes."

"I told you when the campaign ended, I wanted to settle down."

"Ah, huh."

"We never got a chance to really finish that conversation."

"Later perhaps. If it's all right with you, I'd rather-"

Guy interrupted her. "Actually, I think tonight is a perfect night to talk."

She couldn't argue without going into details she'd prefer to keep to herself, so she relented. "Fine."

He laid his hand over hers and it tingled from the fingertips to her wrist. "As you know, I had numerous liaisons with women. I can tell you without exception, I was happy to bed them, but reluctant to wed them. Once, I decided to search for a wife in earnest, I knew my choice would be a lady, like yourself. I'd give my name proudly to this woman who'd be a good example for our children."

"By good example, you mean a virgin. Guy, I know what you are trying to say. Hundreds of years ago virgins were rampant and cherished. The times have changed. Besides, I'm not..."

He laughed. "Elinor, look at me." He waited until she did. "Trust me. Virgins weren't as plentiful as you believe. Would I have married a woman if I bedded her first? Yes, if I cared deeply for her. Like all men, I'd want to be her first. But if there had been another I'd understand. However, I couldn't if she had been intimate with many."

"Would you have married a woman if she carried another man's child?"

Guy shook his head. "No. That I could not do. I had a title, lands, my heir needed to be mine and mine alone."

"Of course." Elinor was silent for a moment. "I'm not a virgin," she confessed in a quiet voice. "When I was younger, I slept with two men because I thought they'd like me more. I never saw either again. Afterward I swore I'd never sleep with anyone for that reason again. There's been one other since."

"You're not a wanton."

"It's difficult to know the right path."

"Don't change because others around you are or taunt you because your ethics are higher."

"You know what happened, don't you? If you know, Basil knows." Mortified, she wanted to bury her head under a pillow and be alone in her embarrassment. She'd fought the tears, trying not to break down in front of him. Losing the battle, they streamed down her cheeks.

"So, you have known the occasional man." He shrugged. "Let me tell you what Basil and I and all men know. No man wants to sit in a *crowded* room and wonder how many other men know what only he should about his lady."

"I understand. I don't mean to cry."

"Shh, you're being silly. It's just the two of us. Cry if you need to."

"I can't help it. I keep thinking about that Beatles song, *Eleanor Rigby*. The words keep repeating in my head...lyrics about a woman who no one loves and who dies alone. Only the priest comes to her funeral. I'm afraid I'm going to wind up like that."

Guy put his finger under her chin until she tipped her head up. He dabbed at her eyes with the towel. "I don't know the song, but its dark with mean words. I have no idea why the..." he waved his hand in the air. "The bug group would sing such a hurtful tune. I do know that terrible fate would never happen to you. I'm six hundred years old and know a thing or two. You are not this tragic Eleanor Rigby. You are the delightful and lovely Elinor Hawthorne."

His sweet reassurance made her smile. "Thank you for making me feel better."

"Are you okay to sleep?"

She nodded.

"I'll go then." He rose and went to the door. "Stay as you are." Guy disappeared.

Chapter Twenty-Two

The next morning Elinor called in sick when she wasn't. Something she'd never done before. Guy's talk had brought her spirits up, but she awoke upset, still feeling soiled. Was he right? Was her lack of wantonness, as he charmingly put it, something to be treasured by a man? Or, were Lucy and Jeremy right? Was she a walking anachronism destined to be alone? Would Elinor Hawthorne become Eleanor Rigby?

Lyrics from the song tortured her as she dressed and went into the kitchen. Elinor wished she hadn't remembered it. She wished the Beatles hadn't written it. *Stupid song, stupid Beatles.*

After downing a couple of cups of coffee, she decided to take Guardian out for a pleasant ride. The distraction might help banish the specter of the song from her mind.

She'd yet to ride him across the nearby road. Only one narrow lane ran in each direction, but the country byway was heavily traveled as it connected to the main carriageway into King's Lynn. Guardian hadn't been ridden near traffic. The possibility he might spook worried her.

There was one house between hers and the roundabout. Elinor didn't know the family who lived there. Since moving in, she'd often seen the lady tending her flower beds. A variety of rosebushes, tea, floribunda, heirlooms and others she couldn't name lined the fence surrounding the woman's garden. Their tops spilled over the picket points. Elinor glanced over as she rode by and hoped the shrubs in her favorite colors hadn't been mysteriously stripped bare.

She stopped short of the road and waited for the opportunity to cross. So far, Guardian seemed unperturbed by the cars and the noise. She'd just eased him forward when a large truck came down the rise to her right. The noise from the heavy vehicle's diesel engine was twice as loud as that of regular traffic. The skittish thoroughbred tossed his head back, crow-hopped, and spun. Startled, Elinor tightened hard on the reins, harder than necessary, until he halted. Once she was sure he'd sufficiently calmed, she trotted without trouble across the road.

She rode for a couple of hours in the peaceful woods when dark clouds filled the sky and thunder rumbled in the distance. Elinor didn't want another incident with the excitable gelding. She turned Guardian towards the house, taking a different path, one farther away from the blind rise in the road.

Elinor entered the grassy field behind her house as the thunder of the fast-moving storm grew nearer. She spurred Guardian into a canter, trying to beat the rain. Behind her, a gunshot loud backfire from a truck sounded. Guardian bolted, breaking into a full gallop. His neck stretched further forward with each stride as the reins slid through her gloves. Elinor clamped down onto his barrel with her legs. She tried to maintain a balanced seat against his powerful gallop over the uneven terrain. She grasped his mane with one hand and held on hard until she managed to gain control of the reins. Elinor yanked with all her might. Guardian refused to slow and flung his head around rebelling at the taut bit.

Elinor desperately fought the sweeping panic at the sight of her pasture fence coming closer and closer.

Guardian was never trained as a jumper. She worried he'd either run into it, injuring both of them, or try to jump the rail. If he leaped the fence, she'd never stay astride. Her riding skills weren't that good.

"Pull steady but firmly on the right rein, bring it all the way back to your hip." Basil rode next to her on Saladin, keeping pace with Guardian. Elinor acknowledged Basil's instruction with a stiff nod, afraid to turn her head. She screamed as her foot bounced out of one stirrup. The girth slipped and the saddle canted at an unnatural angle with the shift in weight. Only the strength of her legs kept her from being thrown, while the loose stirrup banged hard against her boot.

"Straighten and pull harder on the right rein. Force him to turn. Do it now!"

Basil's command shook her from her panic. Elinor struggled and righted herself, and drew back as instructed. With a steady and strong hold, she kept her hand on her hip. Guardian's head came around, and he slowed. She maintained the steady pressure until his front feet finally stilled, and his rear flank circled around.

She sucked in new air with great gasps as Guardian snorted, his sides heaving. When they both caught their breath, Elinor headed for the house. Her grip relaxed and his head dropped and bobbed as he walked.

Basil guided Saladin closer. The great warhorse held his head high, flicked his ears and pranced like the jaunt had been enormous fun. "Always remember, if you use a steady pull on one rein, he has to turn. He'll do it to relieve the pressure of the bit. He has to slow down to accomplish the maneuver."

Elinor nodded and stared straight ahead.

"Elinor, look at me. Are you okay?"

She shook her head. "I'm so ashamed. I screamed like an idiot. My old riding instructor would disavow any knowledge of me."

"So, you screamed. We've all been scared at one time or another. You just have to learn not to let fear get the better of you." Basil leaned over. "Once in France, Guy woke up, saw his bedmate in the morning light and yelped like a pup."

Elinor laughed. "Thank you." She smiled at Basil. "I don't know what would've happened if you hadn't come along."

"But I did. I always will."

"Will you?"

Chapter Twenty-Three

They rode along at a relaxed pace now. In spite of the impending storm, Basil suggested they ride a little longer.

"Guardian should not associate bad behavior with the reward of going home." He told her. Elinor remained shaken but agreed because Basil was near.

A question had nagged at her since the first night, a sixth sense that Basil hid some deep, troubling issue about Poitiers.

"Will you tell me about Poitiers?"

He continued to face straight ahead without answering.

"It's not my intention to pry. If the topic upsets you, we can talk about something else." She wished now she'd kept her mouth shut.

"Don't regret your curiosity. It's natural."

Basil was silent for a long moment as if remembering the painful details.

"We formed up and watched as the French numbers grew, aware of how desperately out-manned we were. The situation left little choice but to wait for them to attack. A tremendous stillness settled upon us as we made ready, an eerie quiet, no one really wanted to talk.

"First there is always the time of fear and anticipation. Then, there's the reconciliation as each man makes his peace with God. That is when the quiet sets in and the waiting begins, which is the worst part. It's the tension only a man in war knows."

He spoke in a curiously even tone like a radio story teller reading Shakespeare.

"The prince rode to the front of our lines to speak encouragement to the men. He addressed them not as a prince but as an Englishman who'd share the field with them. He told them to let their voices ring out for England. No man felt left out. Even the chests of the Welsh bowmen puffed up with pride."

His regard and loyalty to the prince spoke volumes to Elinor. She made mental note to pay more attention to Edward in her class lectures.

Basil's chin notched up with a defiant air. "Aye, the French couldn't miss our voices that day. You've heard of a warrior's battle cry? Some say it's to scare the enemy, which is true. But I think it's also the release a man's soul needs in order to fight.

"Most of the French knights could be seen dismounting and moving their horses to the rear. The best of their cavalry remained mounted and intended to charge our line of longbowmen. A great cry rang from their side and the attack came swiftly.

Our archers showered them with a constant hail of arrows. Their horses reared in terror, stampeding back through their lines in confusion. The noise was beyond imagination."

His voice was no longer so restrained. Elinor listened and watched him with intense interest. His gaze grew distant. It wasn't the Norfolk horizon he fixed on, but France, as the tableau played out again for him as raw and vivid as the day it occurred.

"How many hundreds of years must pass for the spectacle to dim an iota? Will I ever not remember the air smelling thick with blood and fear, the putrid stench of eviscerated horses and men? The stink of death."

The question wasn't meant for her. It wasn't even meant to be answered. She sensed he'd forgotten her presence. "Basil?"

Without acknowledging, he went on, "We charged. The struggle had turned into a blood bath. With their sheer numbers they managed to overrun our lines. The French knights on foot slashed at our horses as we came over the hedge. Saladin went down. I couldn't dismount in time and was caught underneath him. My thigh bone snapped." Basil paused. "My cause was lost," he said, the flat narrator voice again. "I knew it. I could see Guy fighting to reach me. I tried to wave him off, to leave me, to go. He couldn't see in the bloody chaos."

Basil stopped with his back to her and for a second, his shoulders sagged. The pain of what he felt had shown through the image he manifested. An accidental reveal she doubted he intended.

He quickly straightened. "Guy was surrounded, overwhelmed. They dragged him off Thor while a half dozen blades rained down on him. It was almost the last thing I saw."

Elinor remembered seeing how extensive the vicious scars on Guy's arms were when he wore the tee shirt. Her heart broke for him, broke for both of them.

Basil halted Saladin, the corner of his mouth tipped up in a sardonic mock smile as he turned to her. "So, I guess you're wondering how we ended up like this, yes?"

A flood of emotions ran through her, regret, sympathy, and shame she asked him to tell her about that day. Still, she was curious.

"Don't fret so. I'm fine. It seems it wasn't Guy's destiny to die that day. In his effort to save me, he died before his time. As a result, his fate became entwined with mine."

"You can't blame yourself. If the situation had been reversed, you'd have tried to save Guy."

A small twitch in his cheek was the only evidence of the guilt he held close. "But it wasn't the reverse, was it?

No words of consolation would ease his tormented soul and Elinor agonized for him. "What about you? Why...?" She struggled for a suitable description. "Why aren't you at peace?"

"I don't know."

He gestured with his hands either in supplication or resignation. Perhaps both. In the unguarded moment, the veil fell away from his rugged face, revealing a half-millennium of blame and sorrow. The weary face of a man who battles a war he cannot win.

"How can you not know? What about Guy? You know about his fate. Who told you that, God, or St. Peter or some archangel?"

"No one so lofty or grand." He laughed a little at the notion. "I have no idea what his title was or is, guide, messenger, squire to an angel. It seemed the mission was to inform me about Guy only."

"That doesn't make sense," she insisted and stared in disbelief at the incredible statement. "Surely a day doesn't go by that you don't wonder or ask why?"

"I stopped asking why four hundred years ago," he said wryly. "Oh, I demanded answers for awhile. Was I not brave enough, honorable enough, generous enough? What failure of mine caused my banishment?" He pressed his lips together at the bitter recollection and repeated the answer. "It's something I must learn for myself, I was told."

Words tuck in her throat. She was helpless as to what to do or say.

"I'm all right, Elinor, truly I am." His straight face made the lie appear convincing.

After they rode in silence for a few minutes, Basil nudged Saladin closer. "So, what other questions do you have for me?"

The casual remark ended the tension. Relieved, she racked her brain for a light-hearted question. "I was thinking, you've seen enormous changes in the world. Is there anything you dislike about the twentieth century?"

He pursed his lips as he considered an answer. "Yes, the noise. Your world is terribly noisy."

Who'd have dreamed he'd find something as mundane as noise objectionable. She'd expected a more global response.

"Basil, we live in the country. It's very quiet here."

His brows lifted a fraction in challenge to her statement. "On the contrary, it's still noisy, even out here. In my time, if a man sought solitude, he merely rode a small distance from the castle. The only noise was the occasional sound from the wood. Now, no matter where you go, there's noise. Noise from the sky, noise from the road, radios, televisions, it's constant. You're so used to it, you don't notice."

Elinor nodded. "Perhaps. On the flip side, what do you like the most about these times?"

He answered without hesitation, grinning wickedly. "Short skirts."

Chapter Twenty-Four

It had been an emotional day for Basil, between Elinor's frightening ride, his retelling of Poitiers and the ghostly circumstance he and Guy found themselves. Now everything was calm and quiet. This was Basil's favorite time of night. He liked to walk Saladin around Ashenwyck in the moonlight and pretend his home looked as it did in his lifetime.

Tonight a bracing wind blew through the ruins, but it paled compared to the tempest that swirled within him and the moral dilemma Elinor presented. Never in his mortal life had he faced such a difficult problem. How easy it had all been then. Certain of what course to take, his decisions were swift. Emotions hadn't colored his actions. But, he'd never been in love when he was alive. He debated if everyone found love so disconcerting or just him.

How different might his life have turned out if Elinor had been around then and they'd married? Would he have had a son, an heir, a hearty little boy with his dark hair and her green eyes?

A car on the road honked, bringing his attention back to the issue. Was his coming to her at night unethical? Perhaps. Was it immoral? No, he told himself, because he loved her. Was it dishonorable? Basil acknowledged it wasn't sterling behavior for a knight, but not comparable to the butcher who was truly dishonorable. The memory of Elinor trapped against the wall flared again. "I've not forgotten about you and what you did to my Elinor."

In the distance, the upstairs light came on, and her shadow passed by the window. Basil rode toward the house.

Every night since the dream, Elinor listened to the tape. Tonight was no different.

Basil lay next to her and removed the headset. She didn't wake, only rolled over onto her side toward him. He contemplated what to do. The idea she returned his love, even if it was limited to her dreams enchanted him. All the emotions he shunned in life and thought impossible in death converged to shred his self control. He bent his lips to her ear, his whispered seduction brought life to secret wishes.

Elinor dreamed.

Flames licked and lapped the inside of the huge fireplace and cast a honeyed glow over the banqueting hall.

Basil stood motionless, elegant in a cobalt blue velvet tunic. A scroll design was embroidered in bronze silk along the hem and repeated on his tunic's high collar.

Three long strides brought them together. Powerful arms surrounded her. Crushed to him, the heat from his body and the hearth enveloped her. Wisps of his hair tickled her nose and upper lip as he lowered his head to kiss her.

She returned his kiss with a fervent one of her own, aware of nothing but him. Only when she ran out of air did she pull away. Elinor smoothed his hair from his cheeks and temples while she caught her breath. The glimmer of the torchlight softened his features and gave him a provocative and playful air. She stroked his forehead in faint little caresses with her thumbs down his temples then leaned forward so they were nose to nose.

"Good evening milord."

"Good evening to you, milady. Does the gown please you? I would have you in my colors."

Her dress of bronze samite silk matched the embroidery on his collar. The garment fit snug under the bodice and accentuated her bust. A gentle flare in the front cutaway revealed an underskirt of cobalt blue silk covered in a fine woven mesh of gold that sparkled in the light. Tight sleeves edged in the same gold netting ended in a vee just past the base of her wrists.

"It's beautiful. I feel like Cinderella." She swayed back and forth, captivated by the shimmering mesh.

His hands stilled her as they inched upward to rest along the sides of her breasts. "I don't know Cinderella. I'm sure she pales in comparison though. It pleases me you like my choice."

Elinor tipped her chin, hinting for a kiss.

"It would also please me if you'd dance with me like you've danced with Guy." Basil's lips grazed hers, the barest of touches, the words a caress on her mouth.

"Now I really do feel like Cinderella at the ball."

They weaved an easy pattern in the firelight to Roberta *Flack's, "The First Time Ever I Saw Your Fact."*

"You look far away," Basil said.

"I was listening to the lyrics."

"Do you like the song?"

"It's lovely. The lyrics are wonderfully romantic."

"I'm glad." He pressed his hand tighter to the small of her back. "I asked Guy to help me choose some pretty music. I'm afraid I'm not a musical person. Guy has often accused me of being a Philistine."

She kissed the corners of his mouth and teased the outline of his lips with her finger. Basil's smile widened just enough to snag it in his teeth. He drew the digit in further, rhythmically sucking as the tip of his tongue skimmed the pad.

He brushed her hand away and kissed her again. Each kiss lasted longer and longer. Savored by the lovers, each was as thrilling as a first kiss and desperate as a last.

The silk of her gown was an erotic whisper on her skin. He slipped his warm hand under the skirt and made a wide arc up the outside and down the inside of her bare thigh. The back of his knuckles teased her excited flesh as his hand progressed.

Her nerve endings became tiny needle pricks. One finger became two as he made come hither motions inside her. The strokes grew faster and penetrated further. She clamped hard onto the firm muscles of his shoulders. The husky cry of "no" turned to unintelligible moans as his grip anchored her while the climax ran its course.

He slid his hand out slow and hugged Elinor close. She nestled against him. "I believe we should go to your chamber milord." She glanced down, then up, and wiggled her brows, "Unless you want me to take you here on this stone floor."

"You are a bold woman to think to take a warrior in his own hall."

"I'm brazen enough to take you anywhere I can," she said, delighting in the vibration of his laugh through the cloth.

"Shall we?" He motioned toward the staircase.

They walked with arms wrapped around each other's waist. She tilted into him, the cushiony velvet of his tunic soft and luxurious on her cheek.

Fresh candles burned in the stanchions and a hearty fire warmed the chamber. "What is your pleasure tonight?" Basil's words muffled as his lips grazed her forehead.

She placed her palms on his chest and held him at bay. "No, tonight you will tell me what you want. This night, satisfying your wants is my pleasure."

"As you wish, it would be unchivalrous to deny a lady her desire."

He turned her around and untied the laces of her dress. His fingers lingered at each sliver of exposed skin the open laces left. The gown fell away from her shoulders and rough palms eased the sleeves down, freeing her arms. He inched the dress over her hips, unwrapping her like a gift, the silk pillowing at her feet like a bronze cloud.

He came around and kneeled in front of her. He lifted each leg to push the skirt aside, then rocked back on his heels and slid his hands up her calves. Soft pressure behind her knees pulled her to him. She sucked in air as he kissed a path up her thigh.

She grabbed a handful of raven black hair and forced him to look up. Taking as much of his tunic in her fists as she could, she tugged until he stood.

"You are my prisoner." She struggled to hold his wide wrists with one hand while undoing the tunic's toggle fasteners. He crossed his wrists offering a more manageable hold for her smaller hands. It gave her the advantage she needed.

"Hah, victory," she declared and removed the tunic, then continued to undo his breeches. "A lesser woman would've given up. Now, I will know what you desire, milord."

Basil brought his lips to her ear. "I want to make love to you with each of my senses. I want to smell you, inhale your scent," he told her and nuzzled her neck.

She forgot her hold and tilted her head to give him full access to her throat.

"The perfume you wear, it is L'interdit, yes?"

"Yes."

"L'interdit." The word sounded almost holy when he spoke it. "I want to know where on your body the perfume lingers strong and where it grows faint. Here on your neck it is exotic and bold." He buried his face in her breasts, "Here it is tantalizing but distant." He knelt again. "I want to feel the intake of your breath when I touch you."

As he intended, she gasped softly and her stomach drew in as he dragged his tongue along her abdomen, blowing warm air in its wake.

She wove her fingers through his hair, deaf to everything but his voice as he chronicled her every response. His palms cupped her buttocks and pinned her as he progressed downward.

Behind him, the candles burned bright then soft. The flicker from their flame danced on his skin. Riveted, she watched the play of light and shadows move across the muscles of his arms and shoulders.

"I want to taste your need for me and hear your cry of ecstasy. I want to feel your body contract around my tongue then contract even harder when I am inside you." Her skin tickled as he whispered the words against her thigh.

He rose and crushed her to him. A punishing kiss claimed her mouth. A kiss that affirmed ownership that she was his to take. "I want to see your eyes grow cloudy and darken with your hunger, only for me. Tell me. Say the words. You hunger. Only for me."

Her whole body throbbed, coherent thought shattering before reaching realization. The glow from the fire and candles dimmed and flared, and dimmed again. Basil appeared like an avenging angel in the eerie light, his strong grip imploring her to answer.

"Yes. Only for you."

He led her to the bed, setting her in front of him so she sat cradled within the contours of his body. He surrounded her with pillows like one of the houris from a sultan's palace.

"I thought I was to pleasure you." She tried to turn her head but he held her in place.

"Shh, lean back. This is what I want and it will please me." His arms encircled her, cupping her breasts, teasing and toying with her nipples.

One hand stayed high giving equal attention to each breast. The fingers of his other hand splayed across her taut stomach, their padded tips circling and dipping into her navel. His whispered intentions grew more graphic and erotic as he delved lower on her body.

"Spread your legs and open for me, Elinor." She pushed back hard into his chest as he pressed his palm on top of her pubic bone. His fingers tormented her until she exploded into a violent climax.

Her breathing still labored, he rolled them both over. She rolled one more turn so she was on top. Straddling him, she wrapped her hand around his cock. With the pad of her thumb she slickened his velvety tip with the semen that teared from it.

She inched down and peered up. "Now, I would taste you and hear you cry my name." She wanted to go on and repeat his passionate words back at him.

Elinor jerked awake, panting like an excited puppy. She turned a lamp on and saw her headphones on the pillow. The night breeze teased the edge of the sheet she'd kicked off. She swung her legs to the floor and sat on the edge of the bed. The explicit dream vivid in her mind, she padded into the bathroom and drank two full glasses of cold water. How would she ever face Basil again, straight-faced, without thinking of what they'd done, if only in a dream?

Chapter Twenty-Five

Elinor and Basil spent every day and night together during the remaining weeks of the school's summer break. They rode or had picnics in the woods and at the castle ruins. Sometimes Guy joined them on their rides and often when they played board games. She taught them to play Monopoly and Castle Risk. They caught on to Castle Risk with remarkable speed and trounced her on a regular basis. Neither were gracious winners.

"Am I not a brilliant warrior?" Basil said, gloating. "Once again, victory is mine."

Guy was equally obnoxious when he stormed her imaginary territories. The last time the three played she lost her temper.

"Lucy once said all men are little emperors, you two are empirical proof of the statement's veracity." Elinor dumped the game pieces in the box, folded the board and went off in a huff.

Basil, in turn, tried to teach her to play chess, and eventually gave up. Her inability to plan several moves ahead stretched his patience to the limit.

"'Tis a game of strategy," Basil barked, capturing her rook with his bishop. "I have demonstrated more than once how to anticipate and plan your tactics accordingly."

"What can I say? This whole war scenario escapes me."

Secretly, he suspected she pretended to be simple minded.

"I refuse to play with you anymore if you won't use your wits."

"I understand and don't blame you."

Basil looked suspicious, check-mated her in two moves, and left with a scowl on his face.

Guy popped a tape into the stereo. "You dislike the game and wanted to quit I think," he said to Elinor who was storing the chessboard in a cabinet.

"My God, the game is dull as dry toast. I have no idea why people find it so bloody entertaining."

Guy pulled a record from a stack of albums and put it on the turntable. He adjusted the volume and began recording. He'd discovered how to make custom cassette tapes of his favorite songs from albums. According to him, this was nothing short of miraculous.

"Tell the old warhorse when he returns that I went shopping," Elinor said.

Preoccupied, Guy nodded without looking up.

She was still out when Basil came back from a ride. He found Guy laying on the sofa and talking back to the actors in a movie on the television.

"Sit down, the movie hasn't been on long."

Basil joined him.

"Bloody awful!" Guy said two hours later and snapped the television off. He grabbed the program listing. "It says right here, '*Casablanca*, a World War Two classic that pits Humphrey Bogart against a Nazi Captain.' The perfidy of the BBC luring innocent folk to watch such rubbish."

"War movie indeed," Basil said. "There wasn't one battle scene. But then there wouldn't be with that passel of cowards. All they did was try to outwit one another for the papers to sneak away on."

"Sam the piano player was good," Guy conceded.

"At least he could sing," Basil agreed.

As they wandered out still voicing their disgruntlement with various plot points the phone rang.

Elinor's answer machine came on, followed by Jeremy's voice. He left a number to call.

Elinor walked in the door an hour later, played the message and rushed to call Lucy to tell her Jeremy had phoned. "Guess who rang me up? I'll give you a hint. He's the biggest jerk in the universe." She paced behind her desk in the library while Lucy tried to figure it out. "Yes, Jeremy."

Basil stopped in the doorway when he heard his enemy's name. Unseen, he eavesdropped.

"He said he wanted to see me again, soon." Elinor said, a bit breathless.

Basil heard enough, something had to be done to thwart the butcher. He spun and headed for the village. A few minutes later, Elinor reiterated to Lucy she had no intention of going out with Jeremy ever again.

Chapter Twenty-Six

A teacher's meeting kept Elinor late. Basil used the opportunity to convince the school secretary to pass the message along. A number of times in the past he'd whispered suggestions to mortals. They always credited a “little bird” being responsible for the suggestions. The logic of this phenomena escaped Basil. To his knowledge, England did not possess an abundance of talking birds.

Sarah, ran over as Elinor walked to her car. The secretary apologized for not giving the message to her earlier. "A little bird told me I was forgetting to do something."

Elinor sat in her car and stared at the note. Her brain screamed to tear the aggravating request up and go home. But, one tiny part of her felt guilty about ignoring a plea that claimed to be an emergency.

“Why won’t he leave me alone? Fine. I'll see what is so urgent, and then never, ever see him again.” Elinor balled the note up and drove into the village.

Jeremy’s eyes widened and then sparked with anger when he opened the door. He stepped into the hall with the speed of a man who’s just seen a cobra, slamming the door shut behind him.

“What the hell are you doing here?”

Elinor’s shoe caught on the carpet, nearly tripping her as she tried to get out of his way. Bewildered by the malice in his tone, she didn’t answer at first.

"I asked what are you doing here?" He took a menacing step closer. His skin was flushed all the way down his neck and dark red blotches colored his cheeks.

Elinor refused to retreat, desperate not to let him see how he intimidated her. "I'm here because of your stupid message. Why else? You ass."

The door opened again and a pretty brunette in a short kimono started to enter the hallway. "Who's she?"

"A customer. Go back inside Caroline." He shot a warning glance at Elinor. "Do what I said," he ordered. "I'm taking care of this."

The brunette didn't move, inspecting Elinor instead. "What does she want? Did she follow you home?"

He shoved the woman inside and closed the door. His voice was low when he confronted Elinor again. "I don't know what you think you're playing at coming here. That's my fiancé, and I swear if you say one word to her about us, I'll make you regret it."

Stunned, Elinor fixed on the spot the brunette had vacated. When Jeremy issued his threat, she finally turned back to him. "Were you engaged when we went out?"

"Yes, and don't think to act the wounded puppy. It's not like you were hurt. I needed a diversion, a little side action and you seemed promising." His lip curled into an ugly sneer. "Christ, what a mistake. I had to fight you for a lousy hand job. I only called last week because Caroline was out of town and I was horny."

Jeremy gave Elinor a bruising push with the heel of his hand to her shoulder. "Get out of here!"

Elinor flinched and slapped his hand away, the sound echoing down the empty hall, "Go to hell!"

Basil and Guy watched Elinor race out of the building before following Jeremy inside. The knights lingered in the shadows and waited. They listened as the brunette told the butcher to be less friendly with his customers. "Really Jeremy, some of these sad, lonely types like that woman will think you're flirting."

The brunette left the room and a moment later the shower started. Jeremy came out of the kitchen with two glasses of red wine. He didn't notice the ottoman had been moved and blocked his path.

His elbow slammed hard into the wall as he fell. The glasses went airborne and shattered, spilling wine over the wood floor. Jeremy cradled his elbow as he tried to sit up. The eyes that sparked with anger aimed at Elinor, reflected terror now, seeing the blade of a sword hovering above his throat. The semi-transparent figure of the knight who held it grew stronger.

"Who the hell are you," Jeremy asked in a strangled voice.

He used his hip and good elbow to crawl back a few inches. Glass fragments crunched under his weight as Guy flanked him.

Basil watched the butcher's nostrils flare and his eyes dart nervously, between him and Guy. The symptoms of fear were something Basil had seen a hundred times in men he fought. The butcher's struggle not to panic pleased him.

"Who we are doesn't matter. Hear me well, butcher, never speak to, or touch Elinor again, ever. And if you think to threaten her," one side of Basil's mouth lifted in a sinister mockery of a grin. "...Pray God for his mercy, for it's the only mercy you'll know."

Jeremy snorted with false defiance, "I'm not in the habit of taking orders from psychopaths. I'm calling the police and having all three of you arrested."

There was only a flash of steel and Guy's blade stopped an inch short of Jeremy's neck. He jerked back, banged his head hard into the wall and lost control of his bladder. The wet stain darkened the front of his jeans and the acrid odor of ammonia filled the air.

Light bounced off Guy's sword as he held it under Jeremy's ear. "I do not know what a psychopath is, but I mislike the word."

Jeremy recoiled as Guy tilted the blade's edge closer.

Basil sheathed his sword and kneeled down, the hair on Jeremy's arm raised as the knight neared. "Heed my words butcher, or you may find yourself in a place where all you hear is silence."

The knights disappeared.

Jeremy stared vacantly and started to cry.

Chapter Twenty-Seven

Elinor sat up in the corner of the sofa with a stiff whiskey. The circumstances of the incident nagged at her. If Jeremy hadn't sent the message, then who did? Only five people knew she'd dated him, excluding the two of them, it left Lucy, Basil and Guy.

Lucy had no reason to get involved, that left only Basil and Guy. Her heart sank at the thought either of them would do such a thing. But, there was no one else. Hurt and angry, she tossed the whiskey back, drinking it in one swallow. She never drank hard liquor straight. The burn fed her anger.

She'd brought the bottle with her and poured another two fingers in her glass when Basil and Guy returned.

Without looking up, she took a sip and asked, "Why did you do it?" She slammed the glass down onto the coffee table and lifted her eyes to Basil. "Why?"

Guy began to explain, but Basil raised his hand and cut him off. "This is my doing and mine to answer for." Guy inclined his head with a nearly imperceptible nod and disappeared.

"You deliberately tricked me."

"I understand you are distressed. But, you must understand I was trying to help."

There was such anguish in his plea, she wanted to console him. In an effort to hold onto her anger, Elinor crossed to the other side of the room to separate herself from him.

"Do you have any idea what you did? I was humiliated. He mocked me. He threatened me...threatened me for God's sake!" She rocked back and forth and stared at the floor, away from the misery in his eyes.

"Elinor, I swear to you I never meant to cause you pain. You're the one person I'd never want to hurt." Basil moved to where she stood and reached for her. "You must believe me, I swear to you on my honor as..."

Her head snapped up at his words. The gesture implored her for mercy she couldn't give. "Don't. Don't swear to me on your honor as a knight. It would be a very bad tactic on your part right now. Or is there some part of the Chivalric Code I missed, some part that says lies and betrayal are acceptable? Or is that just part of your particular code?"

Basil looked disconsolate. She meant to hurt him, meant the vicious indictment to wound.

"I am so sorry. I learned he had a betrothed. I thought if you saw what a blackguard he was you'd have no desire to see him again."

Basil's torment evident, Elinor felt a pang of regret over her harsh charge. She pushed the emotion aside, unwilling to forgive and forget.

"After what he did on our date, I know what a jerk he is. I had no desire to see him again. Why would you even think that?"

"I heard you talking to Lucy on the phone. You said Jeremy called and wanted to see you. I believed you intended to do so." Basil hung his head as awareness he'd misunderstood seemed to settle over him.

"For the record, I also told her I had no intention of seeing him. If you had bothered to ask me I'd have told you the same thing." Weary, her nerves raw from the confrontation with Jeremy and now Basil, she sank into the chair opposite him.

"You know what you don't get, Basil? You don't get it was my mistake to make. If I wanted to see him, it was my choice. Mine. You don't own me. "You had no right to interfere, no right. Stay out of my business. Stay out of my life."

He flinched at the stinging words she couldn't stop herself from wounding him with.

She turned from him as conflicting emotions tore at her.

Basil knelt in front of the chair and held his hand under her chin as she lifted her face to his.

"I've meddled where I shouldn't have and I'm ashamed to say for selfish reasons in part." Her cheek tingled at the nearness of his palm. "I used to be an honorable man."

An uneasy silence stretched between them. When Basil spoke again, he appeared to choose his words with the same hesitation a man in a mine field chooses his steps.

"I apologize for any harm I've caused. If you believe nothing else about me, believe I love you Elinor. I will always love you." A sad smile touched at his lips. Then, he stood and walked away.

Elinor watched him disappear and fought the urge to call out to him. The sting of remorse over the things she'd said made her feel worse than what he'd done.

She stared at the empty space. "Damn it, I won't be a pawn, not even for you, Basil."

The heat of her anger spent, it ebbed away as she finished her drink. She listened for Basil's return. After awhile, when he didn't come she went to the kitchen door. She opened it, and standing in the doorway, called out, "Basil, I'm sorry. I didn't mean what I said. Please come back."

She waited and then called out again. She continued waiting and watching for a sign of him. When it finally dawned on her, he'd gone off with Guy for the remainder of the night, she closed the door. She closed it slowly, still looking for him as she did.

"Tomorrow, I'll tell him I'm sorry for the hurtful things I said. Tomorrow, we'll put this behind us."

Sleep eluded her that night, even after two more stiff drinks and two aspirin. The pain in Basil's eyes before he left haunted her. She'd gotten up several times during the night and stared out at the castle. What did she expect to see? A glitter of armor, the silhouette of Saladin and his rider crossing the bailey, *anything,* she told herself.

At first light Elinor ran downstairs, made coffee and waited for the morning paper. The paper always brought Guy. If Guy was around, so was Basil.

Midday--the paper had arrived hours earlier, she'd drunk the entire pot of coffee and still the knights hadn't come. She saddled Guardian and headed for the castle.

Elinor rode every inch of Ashenwyck, calling out every few minutes. No one answered. The longer she called the more her stomach knotted and twisted in alarm. A shadow of dread she didn't want to acknowledge grew inside her. *He can't be gone.*

Desperate, she dismounted, tied Guardian up and climbed the broken steps to the parapet where Basil first kissed her. Over and over, Elinor cried his name with no response. Exhausted, she sat down in the rubble and slumped against the same wall where Basil had stood and told her about the castle, his life, his world. The vivid memory flooded her thoughts, the image of how he looked, talked, gestured. The reality of him as a man and not the handsome spirit who haunted her took hold that day.

She closed her eyes. "Where are you?"

She stayed until sunset, believing if he saw her he wouldn't have the heart to turn away.

The moment she stepped inside, Elinor knew the house was empty. A ray of hope seized her, maybe they'd come while she was gone, hurrying to the stereo she checked Guy's tapes. He did something with the tapes every day, play them, or record more, something. Nothing had been moved. Hope flickered out.

"When we feel happiness ebbing away and we don't know what to do, we do silly things," so her grandmother used to say. Elinor grabbed a flashlight and started back towards the castle in the dark.

Wet field grass clung to the riding boots she hadn't bothered to remove. Several times, she tripped on small animal holes and gouges made by Guardian's hooves. At the edge of the old moat she stopped.

"Basil," she called again, determined to see him. Her voice echoed off the stone.

No one came.

The early fall days were growing shorter, but the nights remained warm. A good sweat covered her by the time she gave up and trudged home. Again, she tossed and turned and found no respite in sleep.

The next morning, Elinor wandered from room to room in what had become a ritual of loneliness. How could a house so familiar seem so desolate and alien to her now? Would she ever again love it like she used to?

With no particular destination in mind, her wanderings took her to the library. It had taken a lot of time and patience to furnish the room the way she wanted, but the effort paid off. The room reeked of old world style and grace, leather and suede chairs on richly colored carpets were perfect companions to the antique desk.

A huge stone fireplace dominated one wall. The artistry of the stonemason was reflected in the detailed work of the surround and mantel. Carved dragons in high relief graced the sides of the surround. Their tails started at the hearth stones, their scaly bodies ran upward, as the heads spewed flames across the mantel. Basil loved the fireplace. Elinor gravitated to it.

A porcelain swan, a favorite piece of her grandmother's, sat on the mantel. Picking it up, she held it to her chest.

"Please Grandma, I need your help. Please, please, please help me find him. Please help me to talk to him."

Basil leaned on the doorframe, a safe distance away so Elinor wouldn't sense his presence, and listened as she implored her grandmother's aid.

Chapter Twenty-Eight

The next night a full moon bathed everything in silver and grey light as Elinor walked to the castle. Again, she called and called.

"Elinor."

She froze, staring at Basil. Afraid he was a creation of her imagination. And looking at him, she knew. In a matter of seconds, her mind saw the truth. A terrible decision had been made. The finality of it written on her lover's face, the determination and resolve in his sad eyes.

"No, please no," Elinor whispered, blinking back tears and hysteria, her mind set off on a race it couldn't win. *I'll tell him how sorry I am, that I didn't mean what I said. I'll convince him everything is all right.* It's *just a hideous misunderstanding.*

Her words tumbled out in a mad scramble of apologies and explanations and love. She spoke fast not even sure if she was coherent. Afraid to move, afraid to stop and take a breath, her fear spilled out.

"Shh, Elinor...no more, please." Basil cupped her face in his hands. "Do not do this. I would hear no words of regret tonight."

Only his nearness made her stop speaking.

"Come walk with me."

Trance-like, she moved forward. How she managed to get one foot in front of the other she couldn't say. *I have lost him.* With that painful admittance, a strange numbness took over where the hurt left off.

"Elinor, interfering with your mortal life was the worst thing I could have done. It was unfair to you and wrong of me." Basil held a finger to her lips as she started to protest. "Please, let me speak." Reluctantly, she remained silent.

They walked together in a slow, measured pace, Basil guiding her away from spots where she might stumble.

"I lived my whole life doing what was expected of me. I was brave and I hope honorable. I gave of my time to my family. I gave of my knowledge to the villeins who depended on me, and ultimately I gave my life for my king. But, I never gave my heart. I never loved, not until you, Elinor." He stopped and turned to her. The light from the night sky cast his face into shadow, his expression hidden.

"I believe now that to live a life never having loved is not to live at all. I don't know why I'm the way I am. Maybe this is what I needed to find out for myself. The lesson I needed to learn." Basil wrapped his arms around her, as close as possible.

Elinor felt the power of his embrace. Whether through wishful thinking or some other unknown source, she didn't care.

"I believe I also needed to learn that to truly love someone you must put what's best for them ahead of your own desires."

She lifted her face to meet his sad gaze. He closed his eyes for a moment before looking away. Her breaking heart knew he was gathering strength for what he had to say next.

"You have your whole life ahead of you. I can offer you nothing. You deserve to be loved by someone who can give you joy and children and happy memories for your old age. I'd give everything I owned in this world to be that man." Basil's hand moved to stroke her hair.

"I've never been a victim of jealousy. Now, for the first time, I envy someone."

"There's no guarantee I'll have all that if you leave me."

"No, there are no guarantees in life. I should know. But, there are possibilities and I know you, my love. You will never look for or see the possibilities around you if I stay."

"You said you'd never willingly release me, you promised." She lost the battle. Tears fell.

Sorrow etched his handsome face. "I don't willingly do this, Elinor. It's what is best for you." A long moment passed before he spoke again. "Your tears stab my heart. They make no armor to protect against such wounds."

Basil took a small step back. "Let us talk of something else. Tell me milady of something you always wanted to do."

Elinor stopped crying. She wiped her cheeks with a shaky hand and tried to focus on his question. The struggle to concentrate and think of an answer took a minute.

"Istanbul, I've always wanted to go to Istanbul."

"I don't know where Istanbul is."

"You know it as Constantinople."

"Ah, I always wanted to go there too. I think you should go, for the both of us," he said, his smile sadly encouraging.

"I will. I'll go at Christmas break...for the both of us." Elinor's voice broke. She swallowed hard. She refused to cry. She wouldn't ruin these last moments.

Basil extended his hand, "I must leave soon. Will you give me the pleasure of one last dance?"

Elinor hadn't paid attention to how he was dressed until now. He wore the black breeches and white silk shirt he'd worn the first time he came to her in the vision as she slept.

“How dashing you are.”

His smile changed to a shy grin.

She moved into his arms, his presence tickling her bare arms and throat. *As Time Goes By* began. Elinor didn't question how he managed for the music to play. The how of it didn't really matter.

"Guy picked this song for me. He said it’s a pretty one a lady would like."

In spite of the circumstances, Elinor had to laugh a little. Basil, by his own admittance, was unmusical. Lyric obsessed Guy his sole guide and mentor in all things related to the subject.

"Basil, how did Guy find this song? I don't believe I have a recording of it."

"Hmmm, to be honest, we heard it in a foolish movie we watched." A small furrow formed between his eyes, "We were misled by the BBC into watching a war movie which wasn’t a war movie at all. No battles, but it had this song."

As the song ended Basil continued to hold her close for a few minutes before touching his lips to hers. Elinor thought she might be willing to sell her soul to feel their warmth again.

"I will always love you, Elinor. Always. Never doubt that." He cleared his throat unnecessarily. "You must go now. I'll watch from here and see you safe to your door."

With those words he moved away to stand at the entrance of the bailey. The breeches and soft shirt were gone, he wore his mail and surcoat again, the medieval knight once more.

"Goodbye my love. My only love," Basil whispered as she passed where the outer gates to his home had stood.

Elinor crossed the field. She forced herself not to look back, not to fall to her knees on the soft ground and weep. It wasn't until she reached her door that she gave in and turned to face the ruin. Passing clouds threw the castle into shadow. She couldn't see any sign of Basil. A bleak feeling that he hadn’t watched filled her. The clouds continued on, then, in the moonlight, she saw the glint from his armor.

Chapter Twenty-Nine

December

"Why can't you wait and go to Istanbul, when I can go too?"

Lucy sat on the bed while Elinor extracted different outfits from the closet. Various pieces she eliminated right away. The rest, she separated into either the "take for certain" stack or the "maybe" pile.

"I told you. This is something I have to do now, not later. And, please don't be offended, but it's something I need to do by myself."

Elinor's shoulders sagged and she raised her eyes heavenward at Lucy's crestfallen expression. For the last five years they'd vacationed together and a hurt Lucy didn't understand the sudden change. Because Elinor couldn't explain, her dear friend would have to stay hurt for awhile.

"I'm sorry. Look, I promise we'll go wherever you want in the summer." Elinor returned to sorting the clothes.

"Nora, does this have anything to do with what happened a few months ago?"

The directness of the question sent Elinor into a mental tailspin. On occasion, over the last couple of months, Lucy asked if everything was all right. She never solicited more than Elinor's sketchy information supplied.

Elinor mustered as much passivity as possible before she answered. She wanted to extinguish Lucy's interest. The emotional topic wasn't open for discussion, not yet, maybe not ever. "I don't know what you're talking about. Istanbul has a special meaning for me. That's the only reason."

"You really are a god-awful liar. I know something happened last fall. It changed you. There's a terrible sadness in you now that wasn't there before. I didn't want to press you. I stayed quiet and hoped you'd volunteer. But you haven't and I don't understand. Why won't you tell me?" Lucy lingered at the door of the closet. "The dark-haired man is involved, isn't he?"

Elinor puttered, adjusting hangers that weren't out of order.

Lucy stepped closer. "The man I saw in the field that day, with you."

The two friends locked eyes, one stare a challenge for the truth, the other recalling a happy memory. Elinor debated what to tell Lucy.

"You saw a ghost." Pithy and all she intended to say. "Now, if you don't mind, I'd like to get out of the closet."

"You don't trust me," Lucy said, sounding offended and wounded as she followed Elinor through the bedroom and down the stairs. "Why? Why not?"

"Please Luce, no more questions."

"Will you tell me about him someday?"

"Maybe one day, but not now."

A couple of seconds ticked by, Elinor watched Lucy's expression change from disappointment to acceptance. She didn't protest or argue only grabbed her purse from the end table.

"What are you doing tomorrow? Do we have time for lunch?" Lucy asked, digging in the handbag for her car keys.

"Absolutely. I'm going to take Guardian out for a ride in the morning. Meet me here at noon, and we can eat in the village. I'll pack in the afternoon." Elinor's mood lightened as she discussed the trip and walked Lucy to the door.

#

Typical for Norfolk, the winter day was cold and blustery. A biting wind blew in strong gusts from the channel. The damp chill invaded places normally protected by Elinor's wool jacket. Ominous, black clouds loomed in the distance over the coast. She decided to make it a short ride and headed for the woods on the far side of the road. The wood near her house and the castle were too full of memories, the loss of Basil too fresh.

Elinor rode for an hour surrounded by trees grey and bare, like her broken heart. A loud thunder-clap sounded close. She circled Guardian around and started home, mindful of the slick cushion of wet leaves that blanketed the forest floor. In spite of her caution, Guardian slipped and went down hard on one knee. After several firm tugs on the reins, Elinor managed to raise his head, but he slipped again before he worked his way up. The fall and struggle had him agitated and stressed. Elinor sat quiet and let him snort and blow while he calmed down.

Lightning struck, searing a nearby tree. Elinor jerked, but kept a loose hold on the reins. A frightened Guardian bolted, yanking the reins out of her hands with that first leap. She tried not to let terror override her senses and grasped his mane with one hand. She stretched, leaning far down the side of his neck, struggling to reach one rein and regain control. She'd do what Basil told her and force Guardian to turn. The turbulent movement from his long strides kept the rein just beyond her fingertips.

Elinor braved a glance up. He'd crossed out of the woods, into the flat area, seconds from the road. Panic replaced coherent thought. Desperate, she pushed against the stirrups and lifted completely and precariously out of the saddle to stretch further forward. Only the pressure of her knees and calves kept her astride while she maneuvered.

As it came over the rise and onto the straight patch of empty road, the Range Rover picked up speed. The driver divided his attention between the road and the car radio.

At the edge of the pavement, Guardian came to a sudden halt. The abrupt stop sent Elinor airborne, over his head.

The driver glanced up from the radio. There was no time to slam on the brakes. The impact sent the bags filled with Christmas gifts flying across the cargo area of the Rover.

Chapter Thirty

Lucy couldn't remember a traffic jam this bad on a country road. At least a mile long, it moved at a snail's pace.

The cars inched along for fifteen minutes before she saw the police car ahead. Another five minutes passed before she saw the animal control officer holding a horse by the bridle. In seconds, she recognized Guardian and pulled over onto the embankment. A Range Rover sat fifty yards ahead, the hood dented, the windshield a web of cracked glass. A man Lucy guessed to be the driver rested in the grass being treated by paramedics, talking to an officer.

A second policeman approached and told her to drive on when she got out of the car. "Just tell me, was the rider of that horse involved in the accident?"

Stoic and composed, the officer's professional demeanor betrayed nothing. "Do you know the owner of this horse?"

Lucy nodded.

"Would you come with me please?" She trailed after him firing off questions, which went unanswered.

With the aid of animal control, Lucy got Guardian back to Elinor's and untacked. The police told her not to call Elinor's parents. They'd send someone to notify them. The officer said she could meet the Hawthornes at the hospital.

Lucy wandered around Badger Manor and tried to think what to bring to the hospital beside the usual robe and toiletries. The policeman's refusal to discuss Elinor's condition was ominous. How bad was she?

At the door, she spied dozens of cassette tapes. None of the holders listed the songs or artists names. The lack of detail struck her as odd and out of character for Elinor.

She hurried to the hospital and found Mr. and Mrs. Hawthorne already there. They hugged her and thanked her for helping, then informed her Elinor was still in surgery. Other than that, no one would offer any opinions. Except for the initial small talk, they all waited in quiet, alone with their thoughts. Every time a nurse walked by, Elinor's mother straightened, her anxious gaze following the staffer only to slump down when they walked on.

"Why do you think hospital waiting rooms are painted green?" Mrs. Hawthorne circled the room as she commented on the décor. "Not just any green, but a green with no name. It's never ivy or sage or even lime green, but some shade they must save just for hospitals." She stopped and stared up at the florescent ceiling lights. “And then there’s the lighting. Have you ever noticed it somehow makes those of us waiting look like we should be admitted?” She circled again, same path, opposite direction.

Neither Lucy, nor Mr. Hawthorne, had an answer for her, assuming she really wanted one. Mrs. Hawthorne sat down.

At last, the surgeon came out and spoke to them. His assessment was brief. He'd done everything possible. However, the internal damage had been tremendous. Elinor's parents tried to question him more. The doctor met each inquiry with an evasive response. He cut them off before they were finished. He ended the conversation by saying she'd be moved to a private room. The staff would be advised her family could stay as long as they liked.

The room was Spartan, even by country hospital standards. Elinor lay motionless. Her skin was paler than the white hospital gown, the back of her hand bruised where they'd inserted IV needles. Lucy stared at the heart monitor, the green blips coming sporadic and slow, logging the inevitable.

She walked down the hall to the water fountain near the exit. The glass doors were shut tight against the black night and the storm's cloud cover that still loomed. As she bent to drink, cool, crisp air filled the corridor. Lucy turned to see if the doors had blown open. Her eyes widened as her throat worked to swallow the mouthful of water.

Basil stood silent.

"I know you," Lucy blurted, her eyes alight with sudden recognition. "I saw you in the field with her. Nora told me I saw a ghost. I thought she was being sarcastic. I never believed in ghosts."

Basil smiled. "Neither did I."

"You..." The words trailed off while she adjusted to his presence and sorted out the meaning in her mind. "...You've come for her."

He gave a small nod.

"She always loved knights," she whispered with a quiver in her voice.

"I know."

Lucy's tears echoed softly off the walls of the empty corridor.

Basil approached. With an upturned palm, he raised a hand towards her cheek in an open gesture she knew was meant to reassure.

"You were her dearest friend. She loved you very much."

She tipped her head, eyes to the ceiling, Lucy blinked hard several times. More composed, she lowered her head and returned his gaze. “Sorry, give me a moment.”

He waited.

When she was certain she could maintain her emotions, she said, “I'm fine.”

He dropped his hand. "It is time."

She studied Basil. He was all she hoped a knight would be. "This will sound strange, but, I kind of envy Nora." Lucy took a deep breath and managed a weak smile. "Don't tell her."

"I won't." Basil gave her a courtly bow, "I take that as a great compliment, Lady Lucille."

#

Basil's kiss warmed Elinor's lips. Her eyelashes fluttered open and he lifted her into tight embrace. "You came."

The color high in his cheeks emphasized the flash of white teeth as he smiled. "You're the keeper of my heart, how could I not?"

Dressed the same as the last time she'd seen him, the polished pommel of his sword and shiny mail reflected the light. Understanding without regret filled her. Elinor's fingers slid over the fine material of the bronze silk dress she wore in her dream. *Now, the dream comes true.*

Basil rose and waited at the door, resplendent in his medieval armor. Elinor whispered good bye to her parents. “Don't be sad. I'm not alone, and I'm happy.”

Mrs. Hawthorne sat on the edge of the bed and took Elinor's hand and kissed her forehead as the monitor flat lined. "My baby's gone."

Her father went to the window. His back to the others, the former Royal Marine's shoulders shook with the stout man's quiet tears.

Lucy watched as the magnificent knight led her friend away. The bruises gone, Elinor glowed. Her complexion was flushed with a healthy pink color. Her eyes bright with new life, she never looked more beautiful. The fine gold netting on the dress sparkled as she turned and waved, the dark knight holding her close. Lucy smiled and waved back as they faded from view.

Chapter Thirty-One

Outside, Elinor ran to greet Guy who had waited with Thor and Saladin. He opened his arms wide and pulled her up in a strong embrace. The beloved charmer of Edward's court bent her backwards, "Milady." Mischief and light danced in his eyes as his lips came within an inch of hers.

"That will be quite enough." Basil expertly extricated Elinor from Guy's grasp. "What do you think you're doing?"

"What? I'm merely showing our lovely Elinor how happy I am to see her," Guy's brows rose in mock innocence, "how much I have missed her." He gave Elinor a flirtatious wink and a rakish grin.

Basil snorted as he lifted her onto Saladin's back and mounted. "Shall we go?"

Elinor shifted in the saddle and turning her head, stretched so her lips touched his. She savored their firm fullness and the heat of his kiss. A lock of his hair fell forward tickling her nose. She wrapped the inky strand over her finger and sniffed it, "Your hair does smell like chamomile, so clean. I dreamt it did."

"Did you?" He covered her neck with small kisses that teased her skin when he spoke. "I never favored soaps of a strong scent, I'm glad you like my choice."

Thor sidled close enough for Guy to lean over and lay a warm hand on Elinor's. "Do you see a white hart keeps us company?" He said, nodding towards the right.

"So, it does." The gentle animal gingerly kept pace with them, then ran ahead a short distance and stopped until they caught up. It reminded her of the hart in Basil's tapestry.

"A coincidence," Basil said.

Elinor twisted around, "How did you know what I was thinking? Can you read my mind here?"

"Men can rarely read a woman's mind, even here. Women's thoughts are usually so fleeting, 'tis difficult for a man to get a fix on them." Basil clasped her hand in his before the swipe she took at him connected.

"What a toffee-nosed chauvinist you are."

"Tsk, tsk, name calling, and here of all places." He rested his chin on Elinor's head and held the other hand down too. "What's a chauvinist?"

"A chauvinist is someone, *usually a man,* who believes in the superiority of his own gender. The word derives from the name of a French soldier." Basil and Guy remained strangely quiet. She'd at least expected some argument. "What, no denial?"

"Well, my lovely lady, my beautiful, sweet Elinor--"

A set-up. Elinor tried to wriggle her hands out from Basil's grasp. Whatever came next would deserve some retribution, but his grip held firm.

"I'm in a bit of a quandary. It's difficult to argue with the belief that men feel themselves superior to women. After all, they are. However, you credit a Frenchman for creating a philosophy which is actually common knowledge. That's the arguable part. The French aren't usually that astute."

Basil frowned and pursed his lips in a failed attempt to appear serious. "What do you think Guy?"

A better actor, Guy managed to contain his amusement. "I must be the devil's advocate." He brought a hand to his chest in a mock gesture of sincerity. "I've always tried to be a fair man. If a woman chooses to take a superior position I feel it's only right to extend her the opportunity."

He played the part well and allowed for a dramatic pause. "I rather like it when the woman is on top. It leaves my hands free to play with her other bits."

Both Basil and Elinor rolled their eyes.

The hart pranced faster through the fields, disturbing nothing.

Basil nudged Saladin and they changed directions and rode towards a long patchwork of green meadows. Off in the distance, at the bottom of an escarpment, a herd of wild horses grazed. "What do you think will happen to Guardian?" Elinor's mother and father were animal lovers. They wouldn't order Guardian put down because of the accident. She worried they might sell him. What would the new owners be like?

"Your parents will give him to your friend with the thoroughbred farm in Warwickshire. He'll have a contented existence."

"How do you know? I mean, if it hasn't occurred yet, how can you know?"

Basil put a finger under her chin and turned her face to his, "Elinor, trust that some things I know." He gave her his best *I have secret information* look.

She relaxed against his chest. "Good, I wouldn't want him to suffer because of my poor riding skills."

"Your skill as a rider had naught to do with the end result."

Elinor took a moment to mull over the implication of his statement. She wondered if he'd foreseen her death.

Basil and Guy stopped at the edge of a glade more beautiful than any they'd passed. Granite stones enclosed a brilliant blue lagoon. Outcroppings of rock formed little waterfalls.

The knights dismounted and Basil helped her down. Neither accompanied Elinor as she walked about.

The pool was covered by an arched stone bridge with three steps and two pillars on either end. Another pair of pillars stood in the middle, one on each side of the walkway. Atop, lanterns burned, so no part of the bridge fell into shadow.

“Incredible. Have you been here often before?”

"I heard of it, but never--" Basil faltered a moment, "had the opportunity to visit." Something flickered in his eyes and then was gone as fast as it appeared. *Regret?*

In the sky above the hill, an immense blue-white disc illuminated everything around her. An aura clung to it like a gossamer veil that thinned as it trailed outward. Leaves on trees and shrubs where its beam shone brightest had a translucent quality.

The knights allowed her to enjoy the wonder of the place. At last, she came back to them, thrilled by the experience and elated they'd brought her. "Do we stay here or go on?"

Basil clasped his powerful arms around her and hugged her tight. They kissed. A kiss not of passion but poignancy. Elinor noticed. She brushed off the difference, choosing to believe it had been her imagination. One hand slid to her lower back, and with great tenderness, Basil explored her face with the other. A kiss followed each touch and then he drew away.

"You must cross the bridge now."

Guy laid a hand on Basil's shoulder. Basil nodded and stepped back.

Mail clad arms encircled Elinor as Guy sweetly kissed her forehead. "Fair warning Milady, when next we meet, I shall give you a proper kiss." He wiggled his eyebrows and smiled a faint, lopsided, smile, letting her go, he remounted Thor.

Secure in Basil's presence and captivated by the beauty around them Elinor thought the comment odd. But considering where they were she didn't over think it.

"Shall we?" She turned and started up the steps, then glanced over her shoulder to find the knights hadn't followed. A brief jolt of apprehension shot through her. "Aren't you coming?"

Basil shook his head, "Not right now. You must cross this bridge by yourself. All will be well. Trust me." He made a little shooing gesture with his fingers urging her forward. Guy said nothing and fixed his attention elsewhere.

Elinor rushed over the bridge and ran straight to the bank of the stream. Basil stood by Saladin, "Basil?"

He didn't move, didn't speak. Alarmed and confused, she waded in. The long dress slowed her, the wet material dragging her back the direction she came from. "Basil?"

He ran into the stream and met her halfway as she threw herself at him. "I can go no farther Elinor, neither can you."

She shook her head in disbelief, refusing to give his words any credence. "You're wrong. You must be wrong. This isn't the way it's supposed to be." Elinor sought some sign, some indication Basil could be mistaken. His stoic expression was the worst possible answer. "I can't bear to lose you again. I can't." Basil caught her as her knees buckled.

They stood in the crystalline water as tears of grief racked her body. Basil rocked her, murmuring words of comfort, and patiently waited for her sobbing to subside. "Shh...You mustn't cry. There's supposed to be no tears here. It's not as bad as you imagine. Will you listen to what I have to tell you?"

She nodded yes, seeing no other choice.

"You gave me your unconditional love when I had nothing to give you. I spent my life thinking romantic love was an emotion of no value. With you, I saw what love could be. In your eyes, I was a different man, a better man."

He gently nudged her chin up. Resigned and heartbroken, his image blurred behind her watery eyes. "I've been given another chance at life. Love it seems is quite unique, while binding our hearts, it releases our soul."

"I don't understand. If you love me, why are you leaving?"

"This isn't our time. But, we will have our life together. One that's complete in every way. We'll meet again."

Defeated, Elinor sagged against his chest. No soothing words could ease her pain.

"Truer words I cannot speak. I will come back to you." He cradled her face. "This is a promise I make to you. I broke the last one. I won't this one. This is a promise yet to be fulfilled, but I swear by all that's holy it will be kept. You trusted in me as a ghost. Trust in me as a man. We'll be together sooner than you think. Believe and it will be so."

Basil's words offered cold comfort. Bereft of all except the smallest of hopes, Elinor clung to them. Her fragile hold on hope was all she had, and hold it she would. "What about Guy? Is he going too?"

"Yes, he's also been given another chance at life. Long ago his fate mistakenly became entwined with mine. Now we're both free." Basil pressed his forehead to hers.

"It's my turn to extract a promise from you-" His quiet request spoken with lips close and warm to her ear, she hesitated then acquiesced.

"You must promise to look for me. In another time and place, we'll meet. I may look different. But in your heart, you'll know me. Trust your instinct."

"Do you think I wouldn't know you anywhere Basil?" Elinor challenged in a hoarse voice that cracked as she spoke. She cleared her throat and held tighter onto the front of his surcoat, the soft material bunching in her hands.

Basil laughed, and a small laugh even bubbled out of her. "Forgive an old warrior his caution. Plan well and expect the unexpected."

He hugged her close. Both took one last feel of each other. Basil buried his lips in her hair. Elinor ran her hands down his arms, over his back, his face. They would carry the memory of this last embrace until they met again.

Basil kissed her tenderly then pulled back. Water swirled around his boots as he returned to the far bank. "Watch for me." In an instant, he mounted Saladin and the two knights vanished.

End of part one

Part Two

Chapter Thirty-Two

London-Present day

Miranda Coltrane hurried to finish preparing the last two tapestries. Hugh Glencoe, a popular host on the channel she worked for wanted them for the set when he interviewed Ian Cherlein. A noted historian, Cherlein had produced and narrated a highly acclaimed television series on medieval life. Unlike many of his predecessors he infused the show with humor and colorful anecdotes. The program made him an in-demand advisor to movie and television studios on various historical productions.

Hugh was a nervous wreck over the interview. “Everything has to be spot on,” he told her.

Her reassurance that morning was ignored. He'd been up Miranda's nose all afternoon, rechecking and repeating every fact and detail she'd supplied him. Fantasies of choking Hugh and kicking Cherlein in the shins for all the aggravation he caused crossed her mind.

The company she’d worked at for three years owned several channels, all specialized in different areas of interest. Her channel produced historical programs. Since half of the shows involved English or European history the company kept a small studio and staff in London. For the most part, the Yank executives left them alone.

Dust motes filled the air as she shook out the first tapestry. Miranda quickly covered her mouth as a trio of violent sneezes exploded out of her. The initial attack over, she pinched her nose to stifle further blasts.

"Ugh!" She checked her new blouse for errant sneeze spray. "Thank goodness," she said, seeing none. Thanks to a recent trip to Barcelona she had a great tan and her deep red hair shimmered with copper highlights from the sun. The sheen of the gold satin blouse against her darkened skin gave her a rather sultry look...in her opinion. She didn't need the effect ruined with spittle dots.

Miranda laid the tapestries out on the floor. On her hands and knees, she began running a bar through the loops of the first. She was still on her hands and knees straightening the loops when Kiki dashed through the door. Her co-worker barely missed toppling over her.

Miranda snatched the tapestry and stumbled to a stand. "Dammit Kiki, you almost trampled on my prop and me. What's wrong with you?"

"Ian Cherlein is due anytime," Kiki panted.

"So."

"Aren't you excited?"

"Not especially. He's just another guest."

"Not true and you know it. You're being arbitrary for the sake of being arbitrary."

Ian entered the studio through a rear door and signed in with the security officer. The uniformed guard directed him to Hugh Glencoe's office. As a polite gesture, Ian wanted to stop in before the interview to say hello.

Ian thanked the guard and headed towards Glencoe's office. The corridor was lined with cubby-hole workrooms. He paid no attention to the occupants. They were mostly behind the scenes staff he rarely had occasion to meet. Ahead, a buxom attractive blonde skittered into a room, her short curls bouncing. She looked a promising option for late dinner and drinks at the flat.

Ian lingered in the doorway, as the blonde mentioned him by name to a long-legged redhead whose back was to him. Tall, she wore high heels which made her nearly 5'10. He liked it when tall women were confident enough to flaunt their height and not try to hide it behind flat shoes. The redhead swayed invitingly to a U2 song playing in the background. Her black leather skirt pulled taut then relaxed with the side to side shift of her hips. An erotic vision of her naked, her hair loose and blowing, riding a chestnut Thoroughbred rose in his mind. He wished she'd turn around. If she didn't have a face like a horse, she might work out better than the blonde.

The women continued talking. He waited for a break in their conversation rather than interrupt them. Curious, he leaned against the doorframe, listening unnoticed by either lady.

The redhead fussed with the tapestries and tried to stifle a sneeze as the dust floated around her.

"I'm fully aware he's a special guest-" She pinched her nose and turned her head to the side. Her head bobbed once with the loud chirp of a half-formed sneeze. "I'm doing these tapestries because of him. Hugh wants the set to have an old world feel for Cherlein's appearance. So why are you so excited about him?"

"I talked with Zandra. She says Hugh, a station rep., and Cherlein met a couple of weeks ago. Apparently, the Americans want him to host a weekly program on medieval life...and they're going to do the shoot over here."

"Makes sense. As I understand my history the Americans didn't have much of a medieval life."

The blonde lowered her voice conspiratorially. "That's not all. Zandra said he's suck the breath out of your lungs handsome."

"Gaw, talk about hyperbole. His promo picture's plastered all over the lobby. I grant you, he's easy on the eyes. If...the photos are accurate and if any icky flaws haven't been airbrushed away."

"He doesn't have any icky flaws."

"You don't know that. He might have dangling nose hairs..."

The redhead wiggled her fingers under her nose in an unpleasant charade of said offensive hairs. Ian nearly spoke up, if only to put an end to the silly suggestion.

"Or warts," she continued. "He might be covered in them for all you know."

"Don't be ridiculous," the blonde argued. "You saw Cherlein on his special from a couple of years ago."

"I was out of the country when it was broadcast."

"You don't get it. Zandra said he's way better in person. In fact, she's begged Hugh to let her be the production assistant on the show. She hopes to do more than just work with him." The blonde stretched the "just work" part.

"Kiki, I'd take Zandra's description with a grain of salt. I've been to office parties she's attended. She fell in lust with a different man at each one. They ran the gamut from relatively all right, to looking like the dog's breakfast. So, when she says he's woo-woo handsome, it could mean he has two eyes, two lips and a nose, where they should be.

"First of all, he's probably married." The redhead unfolded another tapestry and laid it out on the floor. "If he isn't married, he's very likely gay. They usually are. I've noticed there's direct correlation between the degree of hunkiness and those possibilities. As one increases so does the other."

Ian refrained from snorting out loud.

"Wrong on both counts. He's not married. Zandra checked. And he's definitely not gay. My cousin's friend was production assistant on a movie he worked on in Florida and slept with him."

Ian smiled, remembering the charming Cuban P.A., Ava, who taught him several Spanish swear words.

"How do you know she slept with him?" the redhead asked. "Not that I care a whit about Ian Cherlein's boudoir romps."

"Don't be stupid. Long weekend, mansion with a private beach, bathing suits optional, they weren't playing bridge.

"According to my cousin, they spent most of the time in the sun and in bed. When they did venture out it was only to do the most romantic things. One night they went to a Latin nightclub, and they tangoed for hours."

"They did the tango? Really? I thought only middle-aged women vacationing in Rio did that," the redhead scoffed.

Middle-aged women indeed. I bet I could tango you right out of your panties, young lady. Now, more than ever, Ian was more determined to see the redhead's face.

"My cousin's friend said the weekend was brilliant."

"What was brilliant, the tango, the mansion or the man?"

"All of it, but especially the man. It seems his reputation is well deserved. He's...ummm, inventive, shall we say and has great stamina." Kiki twirled in a circle on her toes as if enjoying the event if only vicariously.

Ian ducked out of sight and scarcely avoided being discovered as the blonde spun his way.

"You done?" the redhead asked as Kiki completed her little dance. "Is he all invention and art, or has nature been kind to him also?"

Kiki demonstrated with her hands.

"Really?"

The redhead sounded impressed...*finally*.

Ian was both flattered and embarrassed, and not much embarrassed him. Various ladies had complimented him on how well nature blessed him. The compliment whispered or moaned, usually followed some head-banging, balls-to-the-wall sex, but never before came in the form of mime, at least not to his face. He actually felt the heat of a blush.

The redhead smoothed the tapestries and started to run the bar across the top of the second one. He stepped back for a different perspective as she tilted her head from side to side. She knelt to straighten the material, tucking her hair behind her ear.

Ian stood at a different angle so he could see her face better without being in the women's line of sight.

She wore only a soft pink gloss on her lips. She had high cheekbones, a straight Patrician nose and large eyes. She didn't wear much makeup judging from the faint shine on her cheeks and nose. He liked that.

The natural quality attracted him after living in Los Angeles for the past few months. He looked forward to dating women with soft breasts that moved in the same direction as the rest of their body.

The redhead placed a library ladder against the wall. She tried to set the bar the tapestry hung from onto two large wall hooks. But the pole teetered as the hanging slid to one end. She straightened both and instead of resting the bar in the hooks, she held the prop up to the wall, arms raised.

Ian watched her skirt come up, offering him a lovely view of thigh high stockings. What man isn't a sucker for silk hose_and high heels? The temptation to run his hands up those legs was tough to ignore and was felt all the way to his loins.

Chapter Thirty-Three

The unwieldy and heavy hanging was killing Miranda's arms as she held it up. Plus, the weight shifted when the material slid to one end of the pole. She balanced herself against the wall but her arms were stretched too far. The awkward position gave her no leverage to either adjust or move down a step on the ladder. She tried, but after several attempts couldn't manage to lift the tapestry off the wall. Fed up, she saw another option and pushed back hard. It was a tactical error. She wavered precariously before a pair of strong hands grasped her waist and helped her to the floor.

Saved, she laid the tapestry across the top of the ladder and turned around to say thanks. She found herself eye level with a man's jaw.

She glanced up into eyes the color of India ink that sparkled in a most beguiling and puzzlingly familiar way. On closer look they weren't black but deep brown. The Romanesque nose, although prominent, lent an appealing masculine quality. It softened his angular cheekbones. Miranda recognized him instantly.

Ian Cherlein wasn't the Adonis Zandra made him out to be, but he was better looking in person than in pictures. His dark hair was longer than in his promo photos and hung to his shoulders. He reminded her of...of...she struggled, trying to come up with the best comparison. King Arthur.

A powerful vision of him wearing a sword and high black boots flashed in her mind. A tidal wave of intimacy hit her fast and she choked on a gulp of air. Then it vanished.

She wasn't an intuitive person by nature. The common concept of *gut instinct* was alien to her. In fact, she found the notion foolish. She quickly corrected friends who attributed a good choice to gut instinct by explaining the fallacy in their logic. "The law of probability states a right choice is bound to be made on occasion. 'Even a blind squirrel finds an acorn once in awhile,' as the saying goes."

Although, she'd at times experienced the impression of déjà vu, the encounters left her feeling unsettled. Ian Cherlein was a stranger to her. This inexplicable powerful sensation of familiarity for him bothered her more than other déjà vu situations.

Shaken by the extraordinary reaction, Miranda locked eyes with him. Ian winked and broke into a broad, sexy smile. In addition to her brief loss of sanity envisioning him as King Arthur, she was mortified for gaping at him.

Miranda composed herself and tried to move away. He embraced her, pulling her close instead. Then, his expression changed. He cupped her chin in one hand and slowly turned her face to the left and then right. His eyes searched hers. It was intense and a bit unnerving. What was he looking for? Cherlein touched a finger to the beauty mark by her upper lip. He stopped and remained perfectly still as though under a spell. He bent and sniffed her cheek near her ear. It wasn't bad. Rather sensual, actually. However, it was far too bold.

"Elinor?"

He'd spoken so soft, she wasn't certain if he called her by someone else's name. "Pardon?"

"Hmmm?" Cherlein murmured as his scrutiny of her continued.

Miranda couldn't guess what had him so fixated. "You said something, I'm afraid I didn't hear it."

"It wasn't important. Your perfume, it's L'interdit, right?"

She nodded. "I'm surprised you know the scent. It's not a trendy perfume."

"It's my favorite."

"That's nice. You should let go now." Miranda pressed her palms to his chest. Ian didn't seem inclined to release his hold. Although, being his prisoner was far from unpleasant, if Hugh came by, he'd wonder what the devil was going on. "This is quite inappropriate." She pushed harder against his chest. "For a minute you appeared to recognize me," she said, making idle conversation while continuing her effort to free herself.

"You remind me of someone I knew long ago," he said and released her. "I thought I might've looked familiar to you also." The smile returned, a little tighter. "Do I?"

"No, I'd have remembered if we had met." Miranda thought it best not to mention her strange moment of recognition.

He kept hold of one of her hands and drew her back as she started to move away. "I'm Ian Cherlein."

"I know. Your photo's in the lobby, Mr. Cherlein."

"Call me Ian."

Miranda watched, transfixed, as he brought her hand to his lips and grazed her fingers with a light kiss. The man had her completely muddled. She finally gathered enough of her wits to comment on how fortunate she was he happened by.

The corner of Ian's mouth curved up ever so slightly. "I wasn't walking by."

A rush of panic shot through her. How long had he been there? Had he heard them talking?

"You haven't told me your name."

"Miranda Coltrane. Out of curiosity, how long were you standing in the hall?"

"Long enough."

Kiki uttered something unintelligible.

Miranda gathered the first tapestry. "Again, I appreciate the rescue Mr. Cherlein...Ian, but I have to go now. I need to get these props to the set designer for Hugh's show."

"I'll take them for you."

What would Hugh say if he saw his guest moving scenery for her? Concerned, she declined the offer.

"No, please, I can manage. Thank you anyway."

Kiki found her voice and introduced herself, stepping on the hem of Miranda's tapestry in the process. "Hi, I'm Katherine Kingston but everyone calls me Kiki." She stood frozen as a statue and owl-eyed as Ian kissed her hand too.

Pressed for time, Miranda had to physically shove Kiki off the prop to get her to budge.

Ian took the tapestry from her in spite of her protest and then bent to grab the other one.

Miranda reached for the smaller second tapestry. "I'll get this. It's only painted canvas and not heavy." She held the tapestry up and out. "Beautiful isn't it? It's called-"

"*La Belle Dame sans Merci,* by Frank Dicksee."

"Yes, that's right. How did you know?" The minute the question left her lips, Miranda could've kicked herself. She'd just asked Ian Cherlein, medieval expert how he knew a famous painting of the period. "Sorry, of course you'd know this picture and artist. We'd better go." She started down the corridor before she blurted out some new idiocy.

Julian, the set designer dashed over as they entered the studio, miffed, judging from the tight white line of his mouth. The short, balding man squinted at her, "It's about time. We have less than an hour until the show, stupid girl."

"Yes, I know when the show is," Miranda said with a grimace, embarrassed.

He started to make another snippy remark when Ian stepped forward and fixed him with a stony stare. "I'm Ian Cherlein, Hugh's guest, and I delayed her. If there's a problem perhaps you'd like to discuss it with me."

The designer shook his head, mumbled everything was okay and then wandered off with the property. Ian watched the man's retreat, "Wanker."

Miranda laughed, "Oh, absolutely. You didn't have to do that you know. He always has his knickers in a knot. I ignore him." She extended her hand. "Thank you for your help. Hugh's office is past the next corridor and the makeup room is at the end of this hall, on the right. It's been nice meeting you."

Ian stopped her as she turned to leave, "Do you work for Hugh?" He'd wrapped his hand around her arm and idly rubbed his thumb across the area just above the elbow.

The tiny caress made her heart pound so hard Miranda suspected Ian could see it through her clothes. "No, I'm a researcher for the channel." With a self-conscious sigh, she added, "The resident bookworm."

Most men rolled their eyes or even yawned in her face when she mentioned her job. Ian didn't.

"Those pieces you found are quite good."

"Thank you; I've always had a penchant for knights."

Something sparked in Ian's eyes, his gaze intensified and Miranda wondered if all women found it as hypnotic. Did they all stand like rooted trees, unable to walk away until he blinked or something and released his hold? Probably.

"Will you be watching the interview?"

"Most of the time I don't." The soft rubbing on her arm felt strangely erotic. No one ever said the elbow was an erogenous zone. Distracted to the nth degree, speaking with a modicum of normalcy demanded all of her concentration.

Goose bumps rose from her wrist to the nape of her neck as he slid his hand down her arm. Her pulse fluttered like hummingbird's wings. Once his fingers found her wrist he'd feel it too.

"Would you stay this afternoon? I'm interested in your opinion on the topic." He smiled seductively when his fingers reached her wrist.

"Um, sure, if you like, I'll just go up to the sound booth. I can see the stage from there."

"Can't you watch from here, off stage?" He gestured to an area behind the curtain with his hand clasped around hers, their two arms side by side as he pointed. It was a silly thing, the way she mirrored his movement. One look at his grin and she knew he intended to tease her into relaxing and it worked.

"What beautiful green eyes you have." With his other hand he brushed aside the hair that had fallen in her eyes .

"Isn't that what the wolf said to Little Red Riding Hood?"

Ian leaned close so his lips brushed her ear and whispered, "Yes. Just before he mentioned he wanted to eat her."

Miranda groaned but couldn't help smiling.

"I'd best head up to the booth."

Ian held onto her wrist. His gaze shifted to the sound booth, then back to the stage area. He glanced over to where the set designer directed the grips. "What's the wanker's name?"

"Julian."

Her hand was still in Ian's firm grip as he pulled her close and called out, "Julian, do me a favor."

The designer pranced over. In the most nauseatingly ingratiating voice she'd ever heard him use, he said, "Whatever you want Mr. Cherlein."

Ian ignored the moony look Julian gave him. "I'd appreciate it if you'd find a comfortable chair so Miss Coltrane can watch the show from backstage."

His lips compressed at the request and irritation registered on his face. "She can watch from up there." He indicated the sound booth with a dismissive wave of his hand.

"No, I don't want her that far away. She can sit off stage, over there," Ian said in a gracious but firm tone, pointing to a spot beyond camera range. "I'd really appreciate the favor."

Julian sniffed and raised a disapproving brow. His nostril might have been attached to his eyebrow so well timed were both actions. "Fine, we'll find her a chair." He spun around like some old movie queen, and ordered a grip to bring a chair.

Ian's thumbs ran along the edges of Miranda's ribcage as his hands circled her waist. "I'll pop in and say hi to Hugh, then run to makeup. Come to dinner with me after the show."

His dark eyes were luring her to some secret destination. Wolf eyes? Maybe. Maybe not. Without hesitation, she said, "Yes." She stepped back and turned to go the other way.

He didn't move.

"Go. I'll see you later," Miranda made a shooing motion then headed down the corridor. She summoned all her self control and kept walking, refusing the temptation to sneak another peek at him over her shoulder.

Once out of his sight, she sprinted to her office. After a quick check of her handbag and desk for the cosmetics she wanted, she hurried out the door. A rush of air blew over anyone in the hall caught in her wake as she made a beeline for the ladies room.

Kiki emerged from her office. Miranda was besieged by a barrage of questions.

"Well, you certainly have Ian Cherlein's attention. Did he ask you out? I told you he was hot." Kiki both asked and answered everything for herself. The rapid fire questions continued the entire way to the powder room.

“He invited me to dinner.” Miranda almost didn’t recognize her own breathless voice.

“Ahhh, you are so lucky. Where is he taking you? Tell me everything he said, start at the beginning."

They passed several staff members in the corridor who stared, their curiosity aroused by an animated Kiki, half skipping next to Miranda.

In the privacy of the bathroom, Miranda tried to answer the questions in the order asked. A tough task since Kiki still rattled on about Ian.

"Stop!" Miranda held up a hand in a desperate attempt to stop the mini inquisition. "We're going to dinner after the show and I've no idea where he's taking me."

Kiki sat with one hip on the edge of the sink. Her expression was somewhere between a soothsayer and a Mother Superior. "Are you going to sleep with him? This is Friday. If he likes you, he'll probably stay the whole weekend." She crossed her arms with a smug smile like she'd just imparted the secret of the universe.

It was a good thing Miranda's mouth was filled with toothpaste. She couldn't respond with the immediate acerbic retort on the tip of her tongue. The few seconds it took to spit and rinse gave her time to answer.

"I realize its Friday and the beginning of the weekend, thank you Mrs. Stephen Hawking. For your information, I've no intention of sleeping with him tonight. I may never sleep with him. As far as I know this may not go any further than dinner. Satisfied?" She meant every word.

Kiki stared at her as if she'd grown horns and a tail. "You're joking, right?" Kiki poked Miranda's arm with a finger, "Swear you aren't going to play hard to get. Men like that don't just happen along everyday."

"This may come as a shock to you, but I won't sleep with a man on the first date, even if the man is Ian Cherlein. If he's truly interested in me, then he'll ask me out again."

Miranda didn't owe anyone an explanation for her standards. And, damned if she'd allow herself to be put on the defensive. With a mix of anger and righteous indignation she said, "I'm not defined as a person by the men in my life."

Kiki pinned her with disbelieving eyes. "You're a fool."

She started to counter when Hugh's imperious assistant Zandra stormed into the bathroom and forced Kiki aside. She sidled up to Miranda. The poor lighting made Zandra's mouse brown hair look even duller. Worn in a precision cut bob she never had a strand out of place. Miranda suspected it was a wig. Petite and thin, with a pointed chin and pinched features, in Miranda's opinion, she appeared every bit the evil headmistress seen in bad movies.

"Well, it seems Mr. Cherlein has taken a liking to you," Zandra said in her snippy tone. The hollow sound of the rapid tattoo she tapped on the tile floor bounced off the walls.

"What do you want Zandra?" Miranda brushed her hair keeping a close watch on the stupid cow from the corner of her eye.

"You don't fool me for an instant. I know what an ambitious witch you are. If you think you're going to get the job of Mr. Cherlein's assistant by sleeping with him, think again. Hugh's already agreed to suggest me for the job." She inched closer. "You'll do well to remember I'm on friendly terms with all the station executives. You could find yourself doing research for the culture channel...in Wales."

Nice and slow, Miranda put everything away and then wheeled around to confront Zandra. They'd have been nose to nose if Miranda didn't dwarf her.

"Now, I'm going to tell you something, you little piss-ant. I'm very tired of you. We're all tired of you." She loomed in and forced Zandra to take a defensive step backward. "What goes on between Ian Cherlein and me is nobody's business. I don't plan to pursue the position of his assistant. If he requests me, it won't be Hugh's decision or Ian's whether I accept or not. It will be mine and mine alone."

Miranda leaned closer, enjoying the confrontation. "Never speak to me like that again, and never threaten me. Now, move."

Zandra's thin lips disappeared from view with the warning. Air whooshed into the room as Miranda whipped the door open and regally left.

She walked to her office with Kiki hot on her heels. Miranda nonchalantly sorted through the paperwork on her desk.

"I can't believe you did that. Are you crazy?" Kiki grabbed her arm and gave it a hard shake.

Miranda jerked her elbow free and continued to clear her desk surprised at how good she felt. The clash had been a long time coming. Everyone despised Zandra, but they all walked on eggshells around her, afraid of her influence.

"The surly bitch should have had a set down ages ago. She's a shrew. Quite frankly, I don't care what she tells Hugh."

Kiki looked worried and unconvinced.

Miranda hugged her and tried to ease her mind. "I'll be fine, don't worry. I won't be threatened by someone like Zandra. I hate bullies, and that's what she is. If you let a bully get away with dictating to you once, they'll do it forever." Miranda gave her another quick hug. "I have to go. Have a good weekend." She was half-way down the hall before she heard Kiki yell that she wanted a full report.

Chapter Thirty-Four

Ian stood on the stage as Hugh discussed some of the questions for the interview with him. Cindy, the makeup girl tucked protective white towels into their collars and began powdering them off. Ian expected to be shown to the makeup room, but Hugh requested they get together on the set instead. Several times as the two of them talked his host checked the monitors.

Cindy remained close. As soon as the conversation ended, she led Ian back to a chair at the side of the stage. The minor touchups took longer than usual. Cindy's chest brushed against him a remarkable number of times, more than necessary. Every time Ian said something she touched his arm. He maintained a pleasant and polite manner as she flirted and kept his hands on the arms of the chair.

A loud disagreement drew everyone's attention. Hugh didn't yell, but the heated conversation carried across the small studio. Twice, he'd tripped over electrical cables taped to the floor. He argued with the cameramen, the director, and the lighting crew about flattering angles and shadows cast on his "good" side. A special filter was brought in and attached to the primary camera for Hugh, which appeased everyone. His host's vanity amused Ian. Working in Los Angeles, Ian learned that in the early days of television, they commonly smeared Vaseline on the camera lens. It was de rigueur with the shows starring "middle-aged" actresses making the switch to the small screen. The more "seasoned" actors were mollified with a vodka rocks.

At last, Cindy finished and left. Ian immediately looked over to Miranda. His eyes lingered on her crossed legs as she sat relaxed. He'd been sneaking peeks towards the off stage area the entire time. She'd arrived between glimpses.

He was about to make a mad dash off stage and attempt to steal a kiss, when a reed thin, petite woman walked onto the set. The woman leaned over and whispered something to Hugh. Ian found himself eyelevel with a flat derriere in a too short skirt. Two scrawny legs and knobby knees had him wishing he'd sat in another part of the room.

The woman straightened and smoothed her skirt. She scanned Ian, hard. Her pink tongue emerged and she slowly licked her lower lip, her gaze fixed on his mouth.

Empathy for Christmas hams shot through Ian.

She gave him a coy look, strolled over to him and introduced herself. "I don't know if you remember me. I'm Zandra, Hugh's assistant." An involuntary shudder passed over Ian as her hand skimmed his thigh. "If there's anything you need or want I'll be happy to get it for you. I'll be right up there." She tipped her chin towards the sound booth, her hand still on his thigh.

Christmas hams be damned, Ian thought. The woman could put a wolf off his food. She reminded him of a bird of prey with her angular haircut and beady eyes. The talon-like squeeze on his thigh jerked him out of his silent observation. He flinched.

Enough was enough; Ian removed her hand from his leg. "I'm quite sure there isn't anything I'll want from you. It's very kind of you to offer though. Thank you."

Ian slanted a furtive glance in Miranda's direction wondering if she'd seen the woman stroke his thigh. She not only had witnessed everything but found his discomfort funny. The minx bit her lip to keep from laughing, shoulders shaking with the effort. Ian caught her eye and faked a disapproving scowl. Miranda crossed her eyes and stuck her tongue out taunting him more.

He yanked the towel from his collar and affected one of his better warrior faces and went to her. A soft "oh" escaped her lips as he pulled Miranda into his arms.

"What a cheeky sausage you are Ms. Coltrane, and one with a very cruel streak, I see. Couldn't you feel me willing you to come and rescue me?"

"What?" she exclaimed, in feigned wide-eyed innocence. "You didn't find Zandra enticing? Didn't her touch send a warm, fuzzy surge down your spine?" she asked in a sugary sweet voice, straight-faced.

"The woman's a raptor," he said. "She's worse than an ice cream headache." His hands slipped to a spot below the small of Miranda's back, above the cleft of her buttocks so her hips nestled against him. "I like a woman with some sauce, although, I'll have to do something about this cruel streak of yours. One day soon you'll want my mercy and I shall be very slow in giving it. Very slow," he warned with a devilish grin and bent to kiss her.

It was shockingly bold of him considering the set was filled with the crew. A usually private person, she wasn't given to such brash behavior in front of her co-workers. When his hand slid down her spine, she knew she wouldn't resist. She couldn't explain. That was a lie. Truth was, she liked it too much. The other employees were going to gossip anyway. So what the bloody hell, she might as well give them something to really talk about.

The kiss was tender and unhurried and filled with promise. When she closed her eyes, Miranda saw him, not as he was, but standing someplace else. His hair was tied back in a queue. He wore dark breeches and black riding boots and a white shirt open at the collar. The illusion grew more detailed. A woman pressed into him as they stood in a field. He leaned over and kissed her blocking the woman's face from view.

Different from a dream or fantasy image, this vision had dimension, with a compelling reality attached to it. Miranda swayed at its force. Her eyes flew open as Ian broke off the kiss. He was staring at her with a strange expression. She almost believed he had the same vision. The intensity in his face puzzled her. Was he looking for confirmation of a shared hallucination?

The experience stirred up strange and contradictory emotions, all potent. The sights stimulated a voyeuristic curiosity about Ian and the woman. They intrigued her yet frightened her at the same time. Where had the fear come from? It was too weird to dwell on. Today, she only wanted to be the woman who'd caught Ian's eye.

"What a penetrating stare. Are you plotting your revenge because I laughed at you?" Miranda joked, pushing the effect of the vision from her mind.

"No. I already know what your punishment will be." Ian teased in a provocative tone, half expensive scotch, half smoke.

"I'm not worried," Miranda said. "In general, men have rather poor memories for anything except sports."

"You couldn't be more wrong," he said, giving the flippant remark more weight than it deserved. "I won't argue the point right now." He smoothed her hair back over her shoulder and stepped away toward the stage.

Miranda watched the interview certain Ian had to be the most charming man in the universe. His kiss was like being caught in a tornado. *Cheeky and saucy, that's me.* She caught herself giggling and glanced around to see if anyone else noticed. Kiki was the giggler, not her.

Her attention span shrunk to that of a puppy's as she tried to focus on the discussion between Hugh and Ian. The problem increased as the program progressed. Every time the stage director moved she excitedly sat up in her chair, hoping he was about to hold up fingers indicating minutes left.

A blonde she had never seen before stood behind the painted backdrop, engrossed in the show. More to the point--engrossed in Ian. Where had she come from? Visitors to the studio were always provided an escort and never allowed backstage when taping was in progress. Alarmed by the possible security breach, Miranda approached the woman.

"Excuse me, who are you, and how did you get past the guards?"

In profile, the woman appeared attractive. When she faced Miranda, the lights from the set illuminated her. Miranda reevaluated. Not attractive, but breathtaking. The blonde had ivory skin, a full pouty mouth, and bright blue eyes. She resembled a young Michelle Pfeiffer, dressed like an ad from Vogue or a model from a couturier's runway.

Not a single wrinkle marred the cream-colored silk Armani suit. This fact alone irked Miranda who had a love/hate relationship with silk. She loved silk and it hated her. Never did it remain pristine on her. An hour on her body and the silk was rumpled to the point it looked slept in. She fervently hoped the beauty was an intruder who needed to be ousted.

"Oh, security did stop me. I explained I'm Ian's girlfriend and that he expected me, so they let me through. I'm Jennifer, by the way." A limp handshake followed the honey sweet introduction.

A bottomless crevice opened and sucked Miranda down into a hole of misery and humiliation. Jennifer's words echoed in Miranda's ears as her nauseating descent continued. *I'm Ian's girlfriend.*

Only bits and pieces of the woman's conversation got through Miranda's numbed sensibilities. Something about Ian's return from Los Angeles, a comment about how long the wait had been, how his schedule kept them apart.

"You say he's expecting you?" The question came from a disembodied voice Miranda vaguely recognized as hers.

"Of course, he knew I'd meet him." The beauty's eyes narrowed into suspicious slits. "Why do you ask?"

"No reason. No reason at all," Miranda mumbled and turned to leave.

Jennifer laid a restraining hand on her arm. "Do me a favor. The program's almost over and I have to go to the loo. Will you be an angel and let Ian know I'm here?" She didn't wait for an answer and headed down the hall.

Nonplussed, Miranda sat down.

The show ended. Ian shook hands with Hugh and started toward her. His fine woolen trousers outlined lean muscular thighs with each stride. Miranda hated herself for noticing. He had made her the butt of a cruel joke. Under no circumstances would she let him see how much it hurt her. With his every step, her resolve hardened. With every step, her anger deepened.

She grabbed her purse and rose from the chair as Ian slid his arm around her waist and drew her close.

"Give me a few minutes to get this makeup off and we'll go."

Miranda knocked his arm away.

Ian looked stunned and confused.

"We? We are going nowhere. I'm going home, and you, Mr. Cherlein, can go to Hell."

Ian's puzzlement and distress appeared genuine. She mastered the most dignified face she could under the circumstances.

"Bastard!"

Chapter Thirty-Five

Ian stood still, his arms out in the position of the broken embrace, trying to understand. Fury sparked in Miranda's angry eyes, gold flecks floated in a sea of green, like the eyes of a great African cat. The glare of a lioness toward her captors as the net closes around her. But, why?

Surprise rendered Ian temporarily speechless and allowed Miranda to put several yards of distance between them. He dashed after her. It never ceased to astonish him how fast women walked in high heels.

"Miranda! Miranda! Would you please stop and tell me what's wrong?" Ian reached for her and missed. "Talk to me, what's this about?"

Two arms tried to encircle his neck. He winced as a familiar and unwelcome "Ian" vibrated in his ear. He snatched Jennifer's wrists, broke free and stepped back, still holding her wrists to keep her at bay.

Miranda continued. The commotion hadn't slowed her a bit. Ian glanced up in time to see the exit door swing shut. The scent of her L'interdit perfume lingered in the corridor. Bitter frustration swept over him. Furious, he confronted the ex-lover.

"What are you doing here?"

Jennifer tilted her chin up and acted offended. "What do you mean, what am I doing here? I'm here to see you, of course."

She changed tactics and eased closer to Ian until she tried to trap one of his thighs between her legs. He shifted so she couldn't.

"I was patient and waited for you to return and now you're back. Things can finally be normal again, like before. I have the entire evening planned, all the ways I'm going to welcome you home."

Ian recoiled as she rubbed her hand over his crotch and he pushed her away harder than he intended. "Jennifer, I thought we sorted this out months ago. There was nothing special between us. We had a good time for a couple of weeks, that's all."

Her chin began to tremble and her lip quivered. Any minute big, fat, crocodile tears would fall. Of the ten things he hated most, fake tears were in the top three. Women who cried on cue only did it once with him. That was a relationship breaker. Jennifer strained his tolerance, but he needed to know what she'd said to Miranda. If he could find out what crazy nonsense the obsessive blonde told her he'd have an idea how much damage control was necessary.

The tears flowed. "How can you say that? I love you. I know you could love me back, in time. Why are you being so mean?"

Ian held Jennifer in a loose, generic hug. Stiff and robotic, he patted her back. She buried her head in his shoulder. "I'm not being mean, just honest. I'm never going to feel for you the way you feel for me." Jennifer struggled against him. Prepared for the move, he tightened his hold. "Now, tell me exactly what you said to Miranda."

The reply was muffled by Jennifer's sobs and difficult to understand, which only aggravated him more. "Who's Miranda? Is she the redhead that walked out?"

"Yes." Ian lessened his grip.

Jennifer's tone verged on shrill. "Why? Why are you so interested in what I said?" She cocked her head to the side, "You fancy her, don't you?"

"Just answer me. What did you say?"

Jennifer pushed hard on Ian's chest. The tears had stopped as easy as they started. She glared at him, her wet eyes glassy with neurotic jealousy and contempt. "No, I don't think I'll tell you. You'll just have to chase after her and find out for yourself." She drew back to slap him.

Faster, he grabbed her wrist and brought her arm to her side.

"Let me go. I hate you. And now, she'll hate you too."

The histrionics were wasted. Ian ignored the dramatic whimpers. Nor did he care enough about her for the words to provoke him. "I'm tired of playing this game with you Jennifer. Tell me what you said."

"Let me go, you're frightening me."

She wasn't afraid in the least and he knew it. "Answer me."

"I told her I was your girlfriend."

"And?" Jennifer refused to look him in the eye. Ian squeezed her wrist harder. "And?"

An evil smile twisted her pretty mouth into an ugly sneer. "I told her you expected me. You know what she thinks? She thinks you invited her out as a back-up date in case I didn't show. Poor Ian, you'll never convince her she was anything more than second choice."

He stared at her for a moment as the impact of what she said sunk in. For once, the little twit was probably right. It's exactly how Miranda would view the situation. Ian dropped Jennifer's wrist and stalked out, contemplating what to do next.

Chapter Thirty-Six

Miranda didn't look back. Her palms slammed against the bar on the security door that led outside and she hurried up the street.

The office buildings cast long shadows onto the sidewalk in the setting sun. She yearned to hide in those shadows and avoid the world. Usually, she took the underground to Victoria Station then caught the train home to Norfolk. The tube's obnoxious rush hour crowd was too much for her to deal with in her current mood. At the moment, she wished her country manor house was a London flat instead. She decided to black cab it to the train station. If it had been financially feasible, she'd have taken the cab all the way home. She wanted to be alone in her misery. She'd acted like an idiot over a man and in front of everybody at work to boot.

The cab made slow progress in the evening traffic. Miranda muttered to herself and every so often a deep, tragic sigh escaped. Three times the driver slid the plastic window open to ask if she was speaking to him. After the third inquiry he stopped.

In the greater scheme of things, she had only herself to blame. She'd broken her own rule. It had always been her practice never to accept a date with someone she didn't get to know first.

Miranda's spirit sank further as she remembered her previous affairs. Some were short and disastrous. Some lasted longer and ended on a good note. None were special.

Deep down, she agreed with Kiki, though she'd never admit it to her. Men like Ian were rare, if what was said about him was even half true. And, she was powerfully attracted to him. She believed he had that special something and she wanted to experience it. Was that so much to ask?"

The cabbie turned onto Park Lane. A twinge of sympathy flitted across her mind as they passed the pack of cars in the Marble Arch round-about. The lead cars in each lane crept forward desperate for a break in traffic, a chance to merge.

A short time ago, she thought she was getting a break. If only she hadn't been so drawn to him. If only he wasn't so handsome and charming. If only he hadn't acted so interested in her.

A red, double-decker passed. An advert for Derbyshire Dairy with the picture of a grass-eating black and white cow was pasted to the side.

"If—if—if. If only indeed. If only cows had balls they'd be bulls!" she said, under her breath.

Chapter Thirty-Seven

Morning sunlight streamed into the bedroom. The light caught the shimmery threads of the moiré wallpaper. A cheerful brightness warmed the room. Miranda groaned and swung her legs over the side of the bed. She sat for a few seconds, rubbed the grit from her eyes, then got up and yanked the drapes closed.

She went into the bathroom and splashed water on her face. After brushing her teeth and hair and pulling it into a ponytail, she took a long look in the mirror. Rat eyes, bloodshot and red-rimmed, looked back. Depression had finally given way to sleep three hours earlier at four in the morning.

She slogged into the kitchen and tried to forget the previous day's nightmare. The best way out of her doldrums was to focus on work. She'd stay occupied and put the events of the previous day behind her. The ruin of Ashenwyck Castle loomed in the distance, "looks as good a place as any to start."

The phone rang as she poured her first cup of coffee.

"Christ Almighty's sake, who'd call anyone at this hour?" She moaned, "Kiki," sure her friend wanted to find out how the *dream* date went. *Oh, he went all right. Out the door on another woman's arm.*

"Kiki, you'll have to wait to hear the sordid details. I'm not in the mood to talk about it, not with you or anyone else right now." She said to the mug, ignoring the phone.

The message machine clicked on after the fourth ring.

"Miranda, it's Ian. Please pick up. I need to talk to you and explain about yesterday." He stayed on the line, waiting. She could hear him breathing. "There's been a terrible misunderstanding. Please give me a chance to explain."

She glared in silent challenge at the cordless still in its cradle. If the inanimate object wanted to avoid being ripped from the wall it should end the tape and disconnect.

Fortunately, it did. Miranda still raged at the machine.

"Bastard! Bastard! Bastard!"

She fumed over a cup of coffee and then fumed some more over another cup before deciding to tack up her thoroughbred, Zulu.

Fifteen minutes later, she yanked the stirrups down and prepared to mount when a young man called out to her from the side gate. He held two boxes and shifted his feet to a beat and tune only he could hear.

"Are you Ms. Coltrane?"

"Yes." Now what?

"I was told to deliver these to you personally, so here." He shoved two long white florist boxes at her like they were burning logs.

"Wait, tell me who sent you?"

The delivery boy turned but continued to walk backwards as he answered. "The man didn't say his name." Again, he spun around and scurried towards his van.

"What did this man look like?"

"I don't really look at blokes, lady." He stared at the ground as though he expected to find the answer lying there. "He was dark, you know, dark hair, tan, tall." The boy perked up and grinned at her, "His car was the dog's bollocks, noticed it straight away, a Lotus Esprit. They don't get any sweeter." With that the boy sprinted off, his car keys jingling in his hand.

Ian! Miranda considered running after the young man and flinging the boxes back at him or under the van's tires. The option was lost by the speed of the boy's departure.

Peevish, she took the boxes into the kitchen and laid them on the table, talking to herself the entire way. "I'm not opening these up. I'm not looking at these flowers. I'm throwing them away. If you were here Mr. Cherlein, I'd be sorely tempted to beat you over the head with them till you were bloody and they turned to potpourri."

But, she didn't throw them away. It served no useful purpose to throw the flowers out. Of course, she could donate them to a local hospital, *or not.* Miranda stood, hands on hips, and stared at the boxes, at war with herself. She opened one box. There lay one dozen, perfect long stemmed roses, the most beautiful shade of pale peach. A soft, steady hiss escaped as she inhaled. Somewhere in the back of her mind a voice commanded her not to react, not be swayed, not weaken. Remember the wicked sender of the prettiest flowers she'd ever received. Insubordinate, treasonous fingers started pulling the roses from the box. She fussed and cooed and stroked individual velvety petals with her fingertip before she brought the blooms to her nose. Ever so gently, she laid them down and opened the second box. These, for sure, were going to the hospital, no doubt in her mind. She'd just give them a quick look first.

"Oh, they're magnificent," Miranda said, unaware she'd spoken out loud. The second dozen were a soft, pale pink. She brought these out with the same reverence as the first dozen.

That inner voice came on strong again, the words “fool” and “pathetic female,” bounced around her head. Another voice, tiny but suggestive whispered, maybe he deserves a chance to explain.

Miranda considered it for a moment, then tapped into her reserve of anger and groaned, "I don’t think so. Burn you, Ian Cherlein, burn you to the bowels of whatever place you come from. How dare you send me flowers? And how dare you send them in my favorite colors? Why couldn't you send stupid red roses like everyone else, or yellow, or any other color, but these?"

Swearing harsh epitaphs, Miranda divided the flowers up. The vast majority went downstairs in a huge blue and white oriental vase. She put one into a small vase in the bathroom and several from each bunch she placed by her bed, not to remind her of Ian, of course. No, that wasn't it. They added a pretty touch to the décor, no other reason.

"I'll keep your flowers, but I'm still not taking your calls. Let the devil take you. Buy every flower in the whole of England, I don't care," she said as she strode back to the stable.

Zulu's ears twitched and pricked up at the sound of her raised voice. He began his standard dance of anticipation when she neared. The big bay loved to stretch it out. His canter invariably turned to a gallop over the grassy field behind the house. Miranda grabbed his reins and led him through the pasture gate. Like a woman who had been riding all her life, she mounted and spurred him. The well trained thoroughbred leaped into a canter from a standstill.

Her next project dealt with castles. The channel planned a series on various ones all over England, Scotland and Wales. They wanted the Norman fortresses that suffered the bloodiest battles, to those reputed to be haunted. They'd finish with castles renown for their design or beauty. The research required lots of field work to numerous locations. She relished the opportunity to see each, to be surrounded by their history, their individual stories. For her, nothing replaced the tactile experience of being there rather than reading about them.

She hadn't ventured inside the Ashenwyck's grounds since moving into Badger Manor. She'd ridden around the exterior, of course. Whenever she did, mixed emotions she couldn't explain tugged at her. Part of her was desperate to walk the grounds, touch the ruins that remained, feel the stones under her feet, close her eyes and let her imagination take her to another time. Part of her wanted desperately to run away. In the past, the latter won and she rode away.

But not today.

A rush of sensations filled her as she crossed the ditch and rode toward the old curtain wall. She reined Zulu in and stopped at the edge. Melancholy washed over her only to be overwhelmed by an undefined desire, for...what? Where had the powerful feeling come from?

Mystified, Miranda shook her head and pushed the odd sensation from her mind. She nudged Zulu past the wall into the outer bailey. A gnarled oak grew off to the side of an outbuilding's crumbled foundation. The stable. She knew it with unshakeable certainty but couldn't say why. She dismounted and tied Zulu to the tree, then walked over to the old corner stones wondering where the strong impression about their purpose came from.

Drawn towards the remains of the parapets, she climbed up the damaged stairs. She picked her way through the broken stones over to the wall. Resting her elbows on one of the crenellations, she began to relax and took in the panoramic view.

What a fortress this must have been. For five centuries, untold numbers of garrison soldiers kept watch here. She tried to create a mental picture what life was like for those who lived within the castle grounds. What did they see when they looked out? What did they talk about night after night? What did they dream? What did they hope? All her life, she'd been fascinated with the medieval world, sensitive to her affinity for the people and events.

Did the people like their liege lord? Were there many handsome knights, skilled in the joust and the bedroom? Were any dashing epitomes of chivalry in their armor riding on destriers? Or were they yellow-toothed, tubs of lard who abused the female servants? Both, she figured.

She lingered there awhile, absorbing the spirit of the place. Finally, she decided to move on and explore the rest of the ruin. She brushed crenel grit from her sleeves as she went down the steps, mentally forming a description of the castle.

In what was once the bailey, her immediate thoughts were to walk around and get a feel for the place. Then, for some unknown reason she found herself in front of the Keep instead, captivated. Faint laughter and voices came from the great hall, or so she imagined. Miranda closed her eyes and cocked her head. She strained to hear more, but the sounds were gone. The wind playing tricks on her ears, no doubt.

"The hall was originally two stories high with arched Gothic beams and massive windows."

Ian!

She whirled around to confront him, taken aback by how near he stood. How very lord of the manor he looked, in his fawn colored riding breeches, tall black boots and dark blue hunt coat. He'd drawn his hair back into a ponytail. The breeze caught the tendrils where they came loose. She gave him the once over, his proud stance, so aristocratic, so confident and concluded the otherwise good attributes were wasted on the biggest jackass that walked the earth.

Resolute, Miranda squared her shoulders and folded her arms across her chest. Hostility or indifference, she did a fast analysis on which of the two options she'd use to make her point. She went with the handiest, hostility.

"What are you doing here?" she demanded. "How did you know where to find me? Where did you get the clothes and horse?" Miranda gave him another cursory and disgusted perusal, and then waved a dismissive hand in his general direction. "Don't bother to answer, I really don't care. Just leave, you're not wanted here." With a light slap to her forehead, she added, "How silly, why limit ourselves? I think it's safe to say you're not wanted on the entire continent. Go back to America. It's a much bigger place. Gobs and gobs of people, I'm certain a good percentage are smarmy arses like yourself. You should blend in with relative ease there."

Ian presented himself as neither contrite, nor smug, but committed. He advanced a step.

She retreated a step and he stopped.

"Hugh told me where you live. I stayed in the village last night planning to straighten things out today. Since you won't take my calls, you left me no choice but to track you down. The delivery boy said you were saddling your horse when he came by. I followed you to the castle on a hunch. The horse and clothes belong to a friend who owns Avalon Farm down the road. The boots are mine. I've had them in my car for awhile." He gave her a small smile and took a deep breath. "I believe that's the sequence of your questions."

"What a convenient place the world is for you, Mr. Cherlein." Maybe if she was unpleasant enough he'd get the message and leave. "Thanks for the information. I'll pass it on to someone who cares."

“Let me explain, please.”

She wouldn’t be dazzled a second time. He wouldn’t humiliate her again.

"There's nothing to explain. Don't bother yourself anymore with the matter. If you'll excuse me, I need get on with my business, so please go. Good day."

Ian didn’t move.

“Perhaps you misunderstand, byeee, adios, au revoir, arrivederci baby.” Four wiggling fingers accompanied the last. Ian slid his hands into his pockets and just watched her. Miranda didn't budge. She refused to be the first to give ground. She dismissed him. He should go. “Go!”

"I can't do that. I can't leave. I have to talk to you and you have to listen." Ian moved closer, until they were less than arm’s length apart.

The tactic took her choice away. She had to leave. To stay meant the risk of capitulation. She hated herself for being so drawn to him. Compelled to look one last time, she turned to him, angry with her own weakness.

Something was wrong. It wasn't Ian she saw in the courtyard, not the Ian who had spoken with her a moment ago. She gasped. No, she thought. This isn't real.

Ian wore a knight's armor and sword. She shook her head in disbelief. I'm hallucinating, Miranda told herself without conviction. A shiver went down her spine when the phantom remained. With trepidation, she reached out and expected the apparition to disappear.

Her arm dropped and she backed away as the vision came to life. Moonlight shined down into the courtyard and reflected off his armor. He was speaking to a woman. Their mutual caresses indicated a shared intimacy. Then, they kissed. The face of the woman stayed hidden yet there was a familiarity about her. Mesmerized, Miranda watched Ian and the woman. She knew this moment in some vague way. Déjà vu? They loved each other, she could sense it, touch it, the feeling palpable.

"Ian?"

She blinked. Ian the knight and the woman were gone. Waves of desolation and loss flooded Miranda. With a plaintive moan, she buried her face in her hands.

In the space of a heartbeat, Ian wrapped his arms around her. His lips grazed her cheek and temple, and he held her until the distress passed. Calmer, she stared up at him. A myriad of emotions, love, heartache, loneliness, and joy all rippled through her. More feelings she didn't understand.

Rattled and confused, now she had the added embarrassment of looking like a crazy person. A problem made worse by the fear she just might truly be crazy. Why the eerie visions? And, why only with Ian?

Miranda let go of her tight hold on Ian and moved, giving herself space. "I apologize. I don't know what came over me." She spun and tripped, then walked on. "Goodbye."

She heard him following. Miranda quickened her pace to where Zulu stood and hurried to free the reins from the branch. Ian caught up. She quickly mounted, forcing Ian to leap out of the way as she spurred Zulu into a gallop before getting fully seated.

Chapter Thirty-Eight

Miranda sank into the saddle and touched her spurs to Zulu's barrel once more. The light cue was all he needed. Like most thoroughbreds, he loved the faster gait. With each stride, his heavy rear haunches reached further under himself. Rear hooves landed in the imprint the front ones left. Under different circumstances Miranda might've relished the thrill of the gallop too.

Fairly confident she'd outmaneuvered Ian, Miranda relaxed. The respite was short lived as the sound of hoof beats rapidly approaching from behind reached her.

"Unbloody believable," she ground out through gritted teeth. She pulled up hard at the pasture gate and slid out of the saddle, tugging Zulu inside. A loose stirrup banged into her arm and would leave a nasty bruise. She didn't care.

Ian approached the far end of the pasture. Miranda rushed to bolt the gate, confident Ian wouldn't attempt to jump her fence. Satisfied, she started for the barn with Zulu when a thud sounded. She knew the sound of a heavy horse landing a jump. Ian, the persistent, bloody, devil had leapt her fence.

Miranda kept walking. "You might think twice about dismounting. As soon as my horse is stabled, I'm calling the police."

Ian dismounted and tied his horse to a rail at the side of the barn. He tucked his riding gloves into the waistband of his breeches and followed her inside the barn. He stayed quiet with his shoulder propped against the exterior door while she untacked Zulu and led him to his stall.

She didn't spare Ian a second look as she walked to the house aware he trailed her. She grabbed the kitchen phone and made a great show of calling the police. She hit the on button and held the receiver up so he heard the dial tone and then pressed it to her ear.

"You're acting childish." Ian snatched the cordless from her hand and replaced it in the stand. "There's a very reasonable explanation for what happened last night, and you're going to listen." He clamped his hand around her elbow so she couldn't leave.

Miranda twisted away, but Ian blocked her escape. No matter which way she picked she'd have to circle around him. "It appears I have no choice." She crossed her legs at the ankles and leaned on the sink counter with her hands pressed hard against the tile. If she appeared hard and unreceptive...good. Perverse as it was, a glimmer of hope deep inside her still flickered but damned if she'd let him see how he affected her.

"Mind if I sit?" Ian made himself comfortable. He glanced at the remains of her morning coffee. "You could offer me a cup of coffee." He ignored her dramatic sigh and waited.

Miranda made no attempt to do what he asked. A staring contest resulted. She finally caved. At times obstinacy is rewarded. Ian didn't gloat. He wasn't a fool. His eyes followed her every move as she got a mug from the cabinet. She banged the cupboard door and kept her back to him while micro-waving the coffee.

"You're an excellent rider. I'm impressed."

"Thank you." She appeared to relax for a split second, then stiffened again. "Not that I care if you're impressed or not."

The momentary softening in her demeanor encouraged him.

"Did you grow up with horses?"

"No, as a matter of fact I had a morbid fear of them most of my life." Miranda popped the microwave open on the first beep. "I decided I wasn't going to let fear get the better of me. So, five years ago I started taking lessons."

His exact words to Elinor, hearing them repeated, Ian flashed back to the day her horse bolted. She'd been so ashamed because she was scared and screamed out. She needed reassurance. He told her she just had to learn not to let her fear get the better of her. His gaze shifted to Miranda. This could've been a perfect opportunity to talk about their history if her mood wasn't so hostile. He had so much he wanted to say and so much he wanted to ask, like how she came to live at Badger Manor.

"Black or white?"

"Black."

Miranda gingerly set the hot cup down and took up her original position.

"Why Ian? Why explain anything about yesterday? What do you care? It was only dinner."

"Miranda--"

"How about I explain it to you in two words? Two words and we'll let it go at that and you leave?" She didn't give him a chance to speak, "You say it was a misunderstanding. I say it's a case of Mea Culpa."

They weren't the two words he'd expected. Intrigued, Ian folded his arms and sat back. Stretching his legs, he crossed them at the ankle, mimicking her stance. "Mea Culpa?"

"It's Latin for my fault."

"I'm familiar with the term...*and the language*." He stressed the last in a subtle retort, after all not many people could claim his knowledge of Latin. “Go on.”

"My fault for being stupid. You stroll into my workroom, the sexy, smart, sophisticated scholar and pretend you're interested in me."

"Good alliteration," he interrupted. Her eyes narrowed, and he waited for the fallout from his flip remark.

She surprised him and acknowledged the compliment with a cursory nod. "Idiot that I am, I believed you were sincere. Too gullible to see this is a game you play. You used me to amuse yourself while you awaited the arrival of your girlfriend."

As Miranda waffled on about Jennifer's arrival, his mind wandered for a minute. Did Elinor jabber this much? He tried to remember. Miranda seemed able to ramble on and on without taking a breath, an amazing ability he conceded. Ian concentrated on her mouth as she berated him. How long could she kiss without taking a breath?

Miranda abruptly stopped.

Ian sipped the coffee and waited to see if she was finished or just refilling her lungs. Her tight-lipped silence continued. A clue. He assumed his chance for rebuttal had come.

"Are you done with your rant?"

"I wasn't ranting."

"Actually, you were darling."

"Don't call me that. I'm not your darling."

"Miranda, Jennifer isn't my girlfriend and we didn't have a previous commitment last night."

Miranda stared straight ahead. The lack of eye contact made it impossible to judge her reaction.

"I briefly dated Jennifer before I left for Los Angeles. It wasn't serious and definitely not an exclusive relationship, as least not for me. I told her it was over. I guess she thought there was more to it or didn't believe me, who knows?"

Ian took Miranda's hand and pulled her to the chair next to him. He sat her down so they faced each other, knees touching and kept her hands in his while he talked. A brief tug of war ensued as she tried to free them and failed.

"I don't lie Miranda."

"Not true. Everybody lies. Everybody."

"You're right. I stand corrected. But, I'm not lying about this and I'm not lying to you. By everything that's holy, I swear to you I had no idea she was going to show up yesterday."

Ian leaned closer, their foreheads nearly touching. When she didn't move, he brushed her cheek with the back of his fingers. "I wouldn't do that to you. I wouldn't do that to anyone."

She looked wary. He tried to think of alternative ways to win her trust if she didn't accept his honest explanation.

"If you dumped Jennifer, why did she come to the studio and tell our security you expected her? If she had any doubts about the finality of your previous relationship wouldn't she have gone to your flat?"

"Everyone knows Hugh's show is broadcast live. With all the promos on my appearance, it doesn't take a Rhodes Scholar to know where I'd be yesterday. Maybe she thought if she just showed up, I'd take up with her again." Ian shrugged. "Who knows? Jennifer is clearly a bit of a head case."

Miranda still didn't look convinced. Frustrated by the situation, he added, "I live on Cumberland Terrance near the Regent's Park barracks in a brick Edwardian. You know the ones, solid outer doors, brass deadbolt locks and high wrought iron fences. I oversaw the installation of the security myself. I'm away on location a lot and security is important to me. She knew she couldn't get into my place."

"She made it into the station without any problem."

"What do you want me say? My security is better than your security."

Miranda didn't comment and neither did he. He thought it best to give her several minutes to think over what he said. Most of the storm and fury had left her eyes. He could almost see the wheels of her mind spinning, analyzing the veracity of his explanation. Sunlight from the window only lit part of her face. The part in shadow heightened the dark circles that colored the area underneath her lower lashes. He guessed she hadn't gotten much sleep and hoped the weariness would work to his advantage.

"I don't know Ian," she sighed. "I want to believe you. I just..." Her voice trailed off.

"Then do believe me. I don't make a habit of galloping across the countryside to plead my case before angry damsels." *Not anymore.*

'I've never been called an angry damsel." She looked away at the roses he sent. Finally, she turned to him. "I believe you."

Ian placed a gentle test kiss on her lips, not a hundred percent sure of the depth of her belief. He didn't want to give her too much time to think and change her mind. He kissed the corners of her mouth, her nose, the baby soft skin in the base of her ear. Hesitant at first, then with more conviction, she returned those kisses. The tension between them faded.

She pulled away. Quiet, she studied him for a moment, her thoughts unreadable.

Ian scanned the room. "I like your kitchen. It reminds me of an old French bistro with better appliances."

"Thank you."

Ian looked around more, taking note of what else had changed over time. He had a clear view of the drawing room through the archway and locked on the Leighton pictures. Elinor's paintings.

He went into the drawing room and stood in front of the paintings. Memories of the night Elinor hung them flooded back. Her struggle with their weight and how pleased she was with herself when she thought she'd managed the job alone. Her shocked disbelief at first seeing he and Guy.

"Ian?"

"Hmmm?" He turned his attention to Miranda standing in the archway.

"You had one of those thousand meter stares."

"I like your paintings," he said and joined her. "I'm curious. How did you find this place? It's a marvelous location." An incredible understatement, he thought. "Come on, you can tell me while we walk in the woods."

Miranda owned Elinor's house. The coincidence was too unusual to be an accident, in his mind anyway.

Chapter Thirty-Nine

They set a leisurely pace and Ian let her talk.

"I discovered this house by chance, in the back of an estate agent's distinguished properties book. I wanted a place closer to London. I work at home or in the field a lot. But, on the days I have to go into the studio, I didn't want a long commute. The affordable price swayed me to inquire." She paused and shot a glance his way, "Aren't you going to ask why it was so reasonable?"

"This is your story. Tell it the way you want."

"The agent tried to put me off when I asked to see the house." Miranda lowered her voice an octave. "Bad history to the place. It's totally unsuitable for a woman alone."

She laughed lightly at the retelling of the warning. Miranda put a hand on his arm as she shared the details. She probably wasn't aware of the casual touch or how much he cherished the small intimacy it held.

"I asked him to show me the property anyway. After that mysterious comment, who wouldn't be keen to see the house?"

"I can't wait to hear these tales." Ian's curiosity soared. He suspected he knew what the "bad history" consisted of but wanted to hear her version. Maybe the combination of his presence and her talking about the manor would trigger some memories.

Say it. Say how, once you saw the manor you were inexplicably drawn to the house. Tell me the moment you entered you felt the warmth of love, some nostalgia.

"Ages ago, the young woman who owned it died in some kind of accident." Miranda fluttered her hand, as though the fact had little bearing on her story. “Her family put the place up for sale. But whenever someone came to look at the house, weird things happened and potential buyers were scared off. Soon, rumors spread about the manor being haunted."

Miranda's cavalier description of Elinor disconcerted Ian. There'd been no indication she felt any connection with her past life. He worried whether her lack of attachment included him.

"A family finally bought the house but within months they too complained of spooky happenings and sold the place. The manor changed owners a few more times. It always went back on the market shortly after the new people moved in.”

Miranda’s enthusiasm spilled out. She stopped every few feet to emphasize different parts of the story. “A few of the previous owners left all kinds of things behind in their rush to leave. To my benefit, I might add. I found those reproductions of the Leighton paintings in the attic."

Ian found her enjoyment contagious. Her voice rose and fell as she described what she liked and didn't like about the place. The words clipped and rapid fire as she discussed her ideas for change. As they strolled hand in hand, his thoughts dwelled on Elinor, but not in a way he'd have guessed. Instead of sweet remembrance, he caught himself watching Miranda and tried to recall if Elinor had ever been so animated. He didn't think so. To his surprise, he liked Miranda's gregarious nature more.

"You’re staring. I’m boring you aren’t I?"

"Not at all." From the skeptical look on her face she didn't believe him. He had lost track of the conversation but was too charmed to feel guilty. "Do you have any idea how pretty you are when you're excited?

Your cheeks turn the loveliest shade of pink all the way to your chin."

"Thank you," she said, a note of skepticism in her voice. "You really don't want to hear about my house, do you?"

"Yes, I do. Multitasking, I can listen and appreciate your beauty."

"Anyway, the manor remained unsold for ages. The only people interested were a few ghost hunting groups. They didn't want to buy, only lease. You know the type, the ones who want to set up cameras and equipment to record sightings."

At the mention of ghost-hunters, Ian tightened his grip on her hand.

"Do you know about these groups?" she asked.

Preoccupied, he didn't notice the sudden strain in her voice. "I've seen several at work. Ghost-hunters, what a misnomer that is, more like interlopers. Fools playing silly games in a world they can't understand."

"Ow, Ian you're hurting me."

Ian stopped. He saw how red her fingers had turned and relaxed his hold, his anger receding. "Sorry darling."

"As I said, no one had shown genuine interest in buying the place until I came along two years ago."

"Weren't you afraid of encountering these alleged ghosts?"

He held her face in his hands and stared with a strange intensity, she didn't understand.

"No. Intrigued by the possibility, yes, but not afraid. To be honest, the house was in such bad shape after all the years of neglect, ghosts were the least of my problems. Plumbing and wood rot were my primary concerns, not to mention the wiring, which hadn't been updated since 1980."

His eyes seemed to look deep into her soul as if he sought another answer, something more.

Miranda explained, "I've never felt threatened by the superstitions involving my house. If the manor is haunted, why would the ghosts hurt me? I'm only trying to make the place pretty again. If ghosts exist, I imagine they're people like you and I, whose spirits, for one reason or another aren't at rest. What do you think?"

"I think that's a very reasonable explanation."

They continued on, stopping again next to a flowering bush. He ran his index finger down the fullest pink petals of the blooms in a gentle caress and bent to inhale their scent.

A hazy recollection unfolded as she watched him. Recognition of the scene played in her mind, like a distant echo, something about the sight she should know. A piece to a puzzle she couldn't put together.

The sensation hammered at her memory. She couldn’t recall where or when she’d been a part of a similar, if not exact, scene like this. The feeling she was forgetting something important nagged at her. What was so important? She needed to--to what? Remember? Solve? Like a song whose words you recall but not the title. The answer hung there, just out of her reach, then slipped away. She couldn’t fix on how Ian played into these feelings.

"Should we start back?" he asked, oblivious to her perplexity.

They made their way towards the house, arms wrapped around each other's waist. Miranda stayed quiet, her mind awhirl as she tried to sort out what the odd sensations meant.

"Come with me while I return my friend's horse to the farm then we'll go to lunch. I don't know about you but I'm ravenous. Besides, I have to discuss a matter with you."

Ian’s curious statement broke her train of thought.

Chapter Forty

As usual, parking on the High Street was at a premium. In a rare occurrence, a space opened as Ian drove up. Like most urban drivers, he pounced. He slid his sports car into the spot in one maneuver. Miranda was impressed. It would've taken her multiple attempts.

Ian kept a firm hand on the small of her back as they stepped up to the sidewalk. The sudden loss of warmth when it was removed made her turn. He'd walked away and stood in front of the shop near where they parked. She followed his gaze fixed on the J. Barnes, Butcher, sign over the door. His attention shifted to the glass window and the activity inside. A glacial coldness came into his eyes as he watched. It bordered on hatred she'd only seen in movies. Spy movies and the like, where the villain drags the hero out, ties him to a chair and wheels a table of torture instruments over. Instead of fear, the defiant hero faces his torturer with pure hatred in his eyes.

"Is something wrong?"

His demeanor changed from ramrod stiff to casual, as he dismissed the question with a simple, "No, nothing." He slipped his arm around her and hugged her close all the way to the pub.

Something disturbed him, no matter how offhand he might try to act. She couldn't imagine why the butcher shop would elicit such a negative reaction. For a few moments, she'd swear he was somewhere else. Wherever it was the butcher shop took him, she didn't want to go.

They took a few seconds to let their eyes adjust to the dark interior of the Birdcage Pub. The Elizabethan tavern was well known in the shire for its unusual façade. The narrow building had pink cob walls with a half-timbered upper level. The structure had settled unevenly over the centuries with a slight but unmistakable cant to the top floor gable.

Miranda wolfed down everything put in front of her and cast covetous eyes on Ian's uneaten chips. He slid his dish over to her side of the table.

"What did you want to discuss with me?" she asked and greedily dove into his plate.

"I talked to the American representative for the station last night and requested you as the researcher for my show. You'll work for me exclusively starting Monday." From his broad smile, he was quite pleased with the arrangement.

She stared at him, an uneaten chip in her fingers and her stomach somersaulted. She wanted to be special to Ian, like a girlfriend, not a personal researcher. Miranda did a mental recount of all her notable sins, which she was getting paid back for now, in spades.

Ian said something. She picked up on the key words, but the rest sounded like white noise. Disappointment and uncomfortable questions made it difficult to concentrate. Was all his talk and kisses a disingenuous flirtation to butter her up, get her to agree to work for him? She thought he was interested in her as a woman. How could she have been so wrong?

"You haven't answered. I'd hoped you'd like the idea." Ian's smile disappeared. He reached across the table and moved the plate of chips out of the way. "I have the feeling I've offended you."

"It's--it's a fine idea." She hesitated, debating whether or not to ask him outright about his intentions.

She weighed the pros and cons and decided to bite the bullet. Better to know.

"I was under the impression you wanted to see me socially, or have I misinterpreted everything from the start?"

"What an odd question." The tips of his eyebrows drew together into a quizzical frown. "I assumed I made my desire to see you quite clear. Why would you doubt it? The fact you're my researcher too shouldn't make any difference."

"I'm afraid it makes all the difference. I can't date you if you're my boss. I've seen enough office romances to know they never work out. They're death on a relationship, especially when one party is the boss and the other is a subordinate." Miranda slumped against the padded booth back.

"We'll be the exception."

"No, we won't be the exception. I can't and won't go out with you while you're my boss."

There was no romance to office affairs. They always seemed tawdry to her. The next statement practically choked her to say, but she saw no other choice.

"When the show is finished, I'd love for us to see each other, if you're still interested."

"Are you crazy? That's six months away! I can't believe you're imposing this Draconian ideology on us."

"I'm sorry Ian, but I've had friends who had office romances and it never went well for them. I'm sticking to my guns, it's--"

"Don't talk about guns. I called the big guns at the channel to have you switched. After you stormed out last night, I rang the station manager who waffled, so I went over his head. Living in the U.S. for the past year, I learned a thing or two about the Yanks. They don't shilly-shally, not when it involves revenue. They've already sold the commercial spots for my show. At this point, they'd give me the Dalai Lama if I asked." He sighed. "Serves me right for thinking I'm so clever. I outwitted myself."

"What do you mean?"

"My plan was faultless. If you refused my apology and explanation, I'd win you over while we worked together. A simple enough plan."

The sticky situation made her heartsick. It was a big risk. All she could do was hope he'd still be interested in six months. Then there was the issue of his sex life. Obviously, she couldn't expect him to remain celibate which opened the door for another woman to worm her way into his affections. On the other hand, he hadn't intimated theirs would be an exclusive relationship anyway. If she didn't take the job, Zandra might. And if Zandra got it, she'd say hateful things about Miranda every chance she could. Miranda racked her brain for a compromise.

"Ian, what if you ask for someone else and I'll assist them if there's a problem?"

He shook his head. "I can't ask to change now. I was adamant in my demand. No, you'll be my researcher." Ian reached over and covered her hand with his, "We'll work this out one way or the other." His forced smile didn't hide his agitation over the situation. "There's something else I'd like to ask you, something that has no bearing on work."

"What?" she asked, leery of getting more bad news.

"Do you ever go to the butcher a couple of doors down?"

How casual he made the question sound, but his grasp on her hand tightened imperceptibly.

"No. I went there once when I first moved here. But Barnes gave me the creeps. I get everything at Sainsbury's. Why do you ask?"

He relaxed, pleased with her dismissal of Barnes. "Just curious. What do you mean he gives you the creeps?"

"I can't explain it. He didn't do anything necessarily bad. He came out from behind the counter when he didn't need to and stood too close. He kept brushing against me. It gave me the willies. I'd have turned and left, but I was the only customer in there and it would've been awkward. I bought one item and got out of there fast. I know I sound paranoid."

"No, some people affect us in strange ways," Ian offered. If the time were right, he'd have told her, it's the part of her that's still Elinor reacting to Barnes.

Ian studied the subtle changes in body language. They offered him a delightful view. She'd loosened the high collar and unbuttoned the first few buttons on her riding blouse. When she moved a certain way, the change in position pulled the bodice snug. The lace of the low cut bra was well defined through the thin cotton.

Barnes couldn't be faulted for wanting to touch Miranda, his actually doing so incensed Ian. The modern world has its conveniences, but the old world had its own advantages. Impaling the head of your enemy on a pike to warn other scoundrels was an advantage he missed.

"He's icky," she said with a wrinkled nose and bent forward to stress the point gifting Ian with a better view of her cleavage. Grudgingly, he focused his attention back to her eyes.

"Icky, huh? I like that description." He laughed and brought her hand to his lips. Her fingers smelled of potato and malt vinegar. She smiled, watching him with a mix of humor and mischief in her eyes, the way Elinor often did.

The pub was about to close for the afternoon and they had to leave. "Do you mind if I run a quick errand. I need something from the chemist," Miranda said. "I'll only be a minute."

"No problem. I'll catch up with you at the car." He glanced down the street to Barnes's old wooden sign. "I've got something I want to do too." He gave her a light kiss on the cheek and they both walked away in opposite directions. Ian waited till he saw Miranda go into the drug store before he stepped into the butcher shop.

The overhead bell jingled. The sound surprised him, it was so old fashioned.

A young man, thin with a shaved head, came from the back. "Can I help you?"

Ian hesitated with second thoughts, wondering if the bastard would even recognize him.

He decided, he wanted to stir Barnes's long buried fears. He wanted the satisfaction of seeing the look on his face. "Is Mr. Barnes around?"

"My father doesn't deal with customers anymore. Is there something I can assist you with?"

"I knew your father years ago. I thought I'd stop and say hello."

Ian wouldn't have guessed the young butcher was related to Barnes, let alone a son. He had his father's height, but that was all. The father at least had a strong build. The son's butcher coat hung loose and droopy, the way a heavy coat does on a wire hanger. His lean face bordered on gaunt and made his cheek bones more prominent and his chin more pointed.

"If you'll give me your name, I'll let him know you're here."

"I'd rather surprise him."

The younger man shrugged and left. A few minutes passed. The son was taking longer than he expected. Ian went to the front window and stretched as far as he could and looked up the street. He worried Miranda would finish and see him in the shop. He couldn't do what he planned if she came inside. Relieved she wasn't in sight, he turned his attention to the rear of the shop, where the son had disappeared.

The swing door had a glass window that ran from midway to a couple of inches from the top. Ian positioned himself to get a better view of the work area. Then he saw him, Barnes senior. All Ian's anger, all his desire for revenge, faded.

The former butcher moved with what Ian could only guess from his limited line of sight, slow, shuffling steps. Barnes used a stainless steel cane in his left hand while the son held the right elbow and assisted. The elder man's stroke ravaged face sagged on the right, his lower lip hung at an odd slant, and the eyelid lay half closed.

Ian felt no sympathy for the low grade predator. He wouldn't forgive the abuse Barnes perpetrated against Elinor. But, Ian didn't feel the hate anymore either. He eased out from the two big cases he'd been standing between and left before father and son got to the backroom door.

Miranda waved as she walked towards him. He hurried down the sidewalk to meet her, slipping his arm around her waist.

"Is your business finished?" she asked.

“Yes, the loose end is taken care of,” Ian said, conscious of the shop’s display windows as they got into the car.

He merged into the High Street traffic and put Barnes from his mind. He concentrated on Miranda. He drove her home the long way. The less traveled country road with its bends and curves lulled him into a pleasant daydream.

In the perfect world of his fantasy, the memories would rush back to her, and she'd be in his arms. He'd make short work of the tiny shirt buttons. She'd tip her head back and grant him free access to the sensitive skin of her throat and collarbone. He'd taste, and touch, and savor until his senses reeled and she cried out for more. The daydream's rich details took on a life of their own as Ian wended the car through the lush green landscape of Norfolk.

Miranda tapped him on the shoulder as his erotic journey had progressed to her panties. "You missed the turn for my house."

"Sorry, just daydreaming." Ian fidgeted. His groin strained uncomfortably in the tight breeches.

"About what?"

"Pardon?"

"What were you daydreaming about?"

He doubted Miranda was ready to hear his sex fantasy. Thinking quickly, he said, “Umm, well I thought we might go over the program's subject matter,” he said, looking for a spot to make a U-turn. “Put our heads together and kick around some ideas, come up with different ways to entertain while we educate the audience." Ian gave himself a mental pat on the back for his fast recovery.

"I'm really flattered you want me to contribute. I'd love that. I'd love to be more than the research lady." Miranda planted a kiss on his cheek.

Ian held her hand as he drove along, encouraged by the kiss. His pleasure marred only by the looming problem of convincing her they could date and work together.

Chapter Forty-One

Miranda lay in bed that night and tried to hold her thoughts to only the best parts of the day...Ian's kiss, their walk in the woods, the lovely drive back to her house. Try as she might she couldn't keep the unexplainable visions and roller coaster emotions that accompanied them at bay. She forced her brain to stop working overtime. She fixed Ian's face in her mind, closed her eyes and dreamed.

She stood at the gate of Castle Ashenwyck, a ruin no more. The flames from torchlights flickered behind the leaded windows of the keep. A tall man appeared in the moonlit bailey and walked towards her. He stepped through the portcullis and extended his hand.

"Ian." She whispered.

"I've been waiting for you." He took both her hands in his and pulled her to him. He slid the hood of her cloak down, then cupped her face in his hands. He kissed her like a ravenous man, making a banquet of her lips, tasting every deep place of her mouth with his tongue. The massive oak doors of the Keep opened. Ian wrapped his arm around her waist and swept her along with him, the doors shutting as they stepped through.

Logs blazed in a fireplace big enough for her to stand inside. Ian led her over to a thick sheepskin rug that lay before it. She held still as he undid the frog clasp of her cape, letting the garment fall and pool at her feet.

A dress made of a gossamer material lighter than silk and softer than velvet clung to her body. The rosy circles of her areolas and dark nest of pubic hair were revealed. She felt no embarrassment, no self-consciousness.

Ian ran his hands down her arms and up her ribcage to her breasts, his palms warming her nipples. He wove his fingers into her hair and kissed a path down her throat and over her collarbone. Everywhere his lips touched and left a damp spot, he blew a warm breath.

"More," she whispered

Lifting his head, his fingers moved to the top of her gown. He bunched the material in his hands and ripped. That garment too, puddled at her feet and she was naked. Ian bent and suckled a nipple, softly at first, then harder and harder. He shifted, paying homage to the other until it too pebbled.

Then, he dropped to his knees. She spread her legs in anticipation. He planted his strong hands on the backs of her thighs and held her in place. He kissed the inside of her thighs and she thread her hands in his hair. She pulled him against her until his mouth was at her entry. He ran his tongue along her crevice then dipped it into her, sucking for a moment before pulling out. She moaned in protest and he tasted her again. He entered and withdrew mimicking the sexual ritual. He did it_again and again. When she thought she'd explode with pleasure, he did things she only heard about. She cried his name as she came.

Before her heart could slow, Ian drew her down onto her knees facing him. He was naked too. He kissed her and she tasted herself in his mouth. He lay her down onto the woolly rug and she locked her legs around him. He drove into her. Braced on his elbows, he moved his hips in a circle on top of her, first right then left, dancing inside her. He withdrew until only the tip of him remained in her, then he thrust deep within, far, and hard. She came again.

Miranda sat up in bed and switched on the lamp. The sex was so graphic she looked at the pillow next to her. Ian wasn't there. She knew he wouldn't, couldn't be there, they'd said goodbye hours earlier. But she looked anyway. Her bed was a mess. The covers hung half on, half off the mattress. The duvet lay bunched on the floor. You'd think I really had a round of bang-up sex, she thought.

She plumped her pillows against the headboard and leaned back thinking about the dream. The very realistic dream. The very explicit dream. Once, after seeing the play, she dreamt the Phantom of the Opera kissed her while she was in the shower. She was wet and naked. He was dry and dressed in his usual mask, cloak and tux. This was way more than a musical theatre actor canoodling with you. The details of this dream were worthy of sharing. She wondered which of her friends she could tell. Not Kiki. Kiki would blab. Keeping secrets wasn't her strong suit. Actually, this was strictly best friend material. She'd tell Shakira. Miranda glanced at the clock to see what time it was and how long before she could phone Shakira.

Chapter Forty-Two

"This is ridiculous!" Miranda complained. "In the brief time I've worked for Ian, I must have taken a thousand calls from different women."

"A thousand? Do you think you might be exaggerating because they're all from females?" Kiki asked with an annoying smirk.

"No. A little, maybe. All right, yes. But I bet it's at least a hundred."

Kiki looked unconvinced. "I'm going back to my office. I'll see you later when you're not so cranky."

Miranda swore as the phone rang again. "No, he's still not in. Yes, I'll take *another* message Carla. Yes, I know how it's Carla with a C." Miranda rolled her eyes and fumed. "Bye," she said and banged the receiver down. Unsatisfied, she picked the receiver back up and banged it down three more times.

#

Ian returned from the afternoon meeting in a good mood. He stopped by the studio's security desk to tell the guards a bawdy joke. They offered to email him a couple good ones they'd received before he continued on his way. This was the start of the second week working with Miranda. He believed he was making progress with her. Ian smiled as he passed Miranda's office, which was open as usual. He only caught a portion of her phone conversation, enough to stop him in his tracks. Ian blanched and took two steps backward. He stood in the doorway and patiently waited for her to finish.

She took her time writing out the message, not bothering to acknowledge his presence. Miranda still didn't look up after the call ended. He cleared his throat. She ignored him and added the slip to the other messages. Then with slow and excruciating precision, she tapped the stack together with each rotation.

Ian waited, observing with every turn her lips alternately tightened or pursed. She was pissed about something. From the cold shoulder he got, Ian guessed the root of her anger involved him.

Finally, she looked his way. "*My liege*, is there something I can do for you?" Her honey-coated drawl oozed sarcasm, and made "my liege" sound like a sleazy invective.

"Your liege? Interesting. So, tell me, my little serf, did I hear correctly? Did you answer the last call as the 'Hussy Hotline?'"

"As a matter of fact I did," she challenged with a *what are you going to do about it* look written all over her face?

Only the slight flare of Ian's nostrils hinted at the smile he suppressed battling to keep up an imperious façade. Her little rebellion had his mind wandering. Mental pictures of kissing that impertinent expression off her face diverted him from the subject.

Ian knew the role of imposing liege lord well. He moved out of the doorway, over to the front of her desk.

"Your unique salutation could be an embarrassment. I do get business calls. I'm sure you have a reason for it." He leaned closer and gripped the edge of the desk, upping the intimidation level a notch. "Would you like to tell me what's got your feathers so ruffled? I'm sure I can guess, but I'd rather hear it from your own sweet lips."

Puffs of Ian's breath fanned the top of her hair. Her eyes widened a fraction, but she didn't budge. A mutinous Miranda stuck her chin up in a blatant refusal to be cowed.

"I'm not a fool. I know Zandra is responsible for all your paramour's calls being routed to me. I've worked out a system with the switchboard operators. When it's a familiar female voice they put the call on line two, all the others are sent to line one. I only answer Hussy Hotline on the secondary number.

"None of your women seem insulted by my greeting. As a matter-of-fact, *Carl--la* has called back twice in the last half hour alone."

She'd worked herself into a waspish snit. He waited for the second volley.

"You saunter in and stand around like some dark archangel, a hand on each side of the doorframe, your unbuttoned jacket winging out." She pointed her index finger like a lethal weapon. "Well, that avenging angel attitude doesn't work on me. I'm not intimidated, so you can stop looming over my desk."

"It was worth a shot," he said, unable to keep the humor from his voice.

"I am supposed to be your research assistant, not your personal secretary. I came in a half hour early this morning to get a jump start on those weapons you wanted catalogued. And all I've done is take messages from your lovesick mistresses."

Miranda slammed the slips down in front of him. Her angry eyes sparkled even in the unflattering office light. Ian tucked the stack into his coat pocket and sat on the corner of her desk.

"You're right. You shouldn't have to take my personal calls. I'll get them to end."

"Start with that Jennifer person. She's a loon. The whingeing and whining when she can't get you on the phone is working my nerves."

"Who'd have guessed?"

"I had the impression she'd been dealt with."

"Me too. I'll take extra care to make certain she understands completely."

"Please do. The sooner, the better."

Ian touched his palm to her cheek. "Green is a very becoming color on you. It goes with your complexion."

The comment earned Ian a look worthy of Medusa. "What is that supposed to mean," the mumbled words vibrated against his palm.

"Your dress, it's a lovely shade of green."

Ian rubbed his thumb across her cheek. His fingers brushed the length of her jaw line as he withdrew his hand. He stood and walked to the door.

He raised a flat palm over his heart and bowed his head. "I'll sort out the telephone issue." After a brief pause, he added, "Oh, you do know that as your liege lord you have to do anything I ask, and I do mean anything."

The thrown pen missed as he quickly ducked out the door.

Chapter Forty-Three

Alex Lancaster walked along the corridor to Ian's office. Ian sounded tense on the phone and suggested he stop by. Their lifelong friendship extended far beyond the definition normally applied to the term. A whole new meaning is added when you've fought and died together, let alone haunted the earth. Granted a second chance at life, they'd each fared well. After all that had happened to them, there wasn't much either found stressful. Naturally, Ian's call stirred his interest.

Alex smiled to himself as he walked, his thoughts dwelling on their accomplishments. He had his work as a music producer and was considered a powerhouse in the industry with a knack for predicting trends. Ian had found success in his history outings. Lovely, open-minded women were in abundance. Life was good.

More out of habit than curiosity, he took a fast glimpse into the rooms as he passed. He stopped at the door of one.

A woman sat bent, reading. Stacks of open books surrounded her. Straight hair the color of polished red mahogany hid her face. It didn't matter. He had a knack when it came to women too. And, he had a feeling this one was delicious under that curtain of hair. The faint scent of familiar perfume reached him as he lingered in the doorway. The fragrance invoked memories. Curiosity piqued, he entered.

She stuck a post-it note on the page she'd been studying and looked up. "Do you need assistance?" she asked with a polite smile.

Alex didn't answer. Instead he scrutinized the woman. The hair was darker, thicker. She had the remains of a nice tan. Her complexion seemed on the olive side without the additional color. She had a clever little beauty mark by her upper lip. But, it was her eyes that made him pause. Could it be?

"Is there something I can do for you?" Caution had crept into her tone.

"Sweetling, you may do anything you like to me, or with me, or if you're so inclined, for me. As to assistance, well I've never needed any in the past. I believe I'll be able to rise to the occasion whatever you choose to do."

She cocked one brow. "Sweetling, sounds like a medieval endearment. Something rakish knights used to avoid committing a damsel's name to memory."

Alex threw his head back and dramatically covered his heart with one hand, "*La Belle Dame sans Merci*, you wound me." His teasing manner faded as he spoke from memory.

"And there we slumber'd on the moss,
And there I dream'd, ah woe betide,
The latest dream I ever dream'd
On the cold hillside.
I saw pale kings, and princes too,
Pale warriors, death-pale were they all,
Who cry'd-La Belle Dame sans Merci
Hath thee in thrall!"

"That's my favorite Keats poem. I thank you for the 'beautiful lady' part, but surely I'm not without mercy?"

He started to answer and the words stuck. He cleared his throat. "Fair lady, were I a dying medieval knight I can think of no face I'd rather look upon in my last moments than yours. Your lips suggest a passionate soul. Where there is passion, there is mercy."

"Do you always say the right thing?"

"It depends on the woman."

She laughed softly. "Seriously, is there something I can help you with?"

"I'm Alex Lancaster, an old friend of Ian's. Can you direct me to his office?"

He reached over and took Miranda's hand, kissed the back of her fingers, then smelled the inside of her wrist. "Ah L'interdit, that would make you Ian's Miranda." *And his Elinor.*

"Yes, I'm Miranda, Ian's research assistant. He's spoken of you often, Mr. Lancaster. I'll show you to his office."

She stood and started across the room when Ian walked in. "Alex, I knew I heard your voice. I see you two have met."

As he and Ian talked, Miranda passed very close on the way to her desk. She stopped. "Excuse me Mr. Lancaster, but you seem very familiar to me. I feel like we've met before."

Alex glanced over and caught the fleeting, pained look on Ian's face. "Some people say if you feel like you've done something or met someone before, you have," he said, turning to Miranda.

She nodded. "Well, I guess it will have to remain a mystery for now."

"We'll be in my office," Ian said and left with Alex.

Ian poured two straight scotches, handing one to Alex as he sat. "I need your advice. It seems all the minions from hell are conspiring to thwart my progress with Miranda." He tossed the stack of pink message slips across the desk towards Alex.

Alex spread them out in front of him. "So you get messages. What's the problem?"

"If you'll notice they are all from women, Jennifer, Suzy, Carla. Miranda took them."

"Beautiful women are calling you, pretty standard stuff, nothing new there. Miranda’s your assistant. Isn't taking messages part of her job?" Alex gave him a quizzical look. "Enlighten me, I don't see the problem."

"The problem is I don’t want Miranda to think I'm a playboy and only want a tumble. I'm not seeing these women anymore and don't intend to ever again. How can I convince her of that if they keep calling?"

Alex leaned back and stretched his legs out. "Why don't you just go to the switchboard operators and tell them to take the messages. Instruct them not to forward anymore to Miranda."

Ian sipped his drink and dismissed the suggestion with a shake of his head. "I've done that. They were told by Zandra, one of the executive assistants, to send the calls to Miranda. And believe me, they're a lot more afraid of Zandra than they are of me. The woman's a harridan. She's doing it to spite Miranda. The two hate each other."

"I think I passed her in the hall, the face of a peregrine falcon, right?"

"That would be her, although comparing the two is cruelty to falcons everywhere."

"You're known to have considerable charm. Perhaps you should apply some of your legendary wiles to Zandra one evening." Alex wiggled his brows.

Ian's lips curled in disgust. "I wouldn't touch her with a Frenchman's dick. But, since you've made the suggestion, why don't you beguile her, take her to new heights?" This time Ian wiggled his brows.

"She's not my problem."

“Very droll.”

“I'm willing to take one or two of these ladies off your hands though," Alex offered as he sorted through the stack. "What about Jennifer, what's she like?"

"A borderline stalker, I thought I was rid of. I'll have to handle that one myself. Again."

Alex put all the slips from Jennifer aside. "And Suzy?"

“What’s the best way to describe Suzy?” Ian sighed and tried to be at least kind, if not nebulous. "A dancer, nice body, appeared in every chorus line, in every West End musical for the last decade. High maintenance."

Grunting, Alex put Suzy's messages in the same pile as Jennifer's. The last two words made his decision, as Ian knew it would.

"How about Carla?"

Ian smiled. "I think you’d like Carla. She’s smart, claims to have gypsy blood and she likes games."

"I'm pretty good at them myself. I play a sharp game of poker, and as you know, a mean game of backgammon. Maybe a little strip backgammon to entertain her."

"Not those kind of games." Ian exchanged a meaningful glance with Alex.

"I'll take her." Alex pocketed the slip with Carla's number and pushed the stack of rejected slips across the desk. "Introduce us tomorrow over drinks."

Zandra flounced into the office without knocking. "Hello Ian. The station manager would like a word." Her head snapped around to where Alex sat.

"Tell him I'll be there in a minute." Her rude habit of barging into his office irritated the hell out of him. He ground out his reply with the idea that Zandra might realize her obnoxious behavior wasn't acceptable. She didn't react, oblivious to all but Alex.

"I know you. You're Alex Lancaster, the music producer," Zandra said. "I'm Zandra Rhodes, executive assistant to Hugh Glencoe. We'd love to have you as a guest on his show."

"I'll keep it in mind."

Ian stood, aimed a malevolent glare at Hugh's assistant and slipped on his jacket. Her attention stayed fixed on Alex, as she moved closer to him. From the corner of his eye, Ian thought he saw Alex cringe.

Alex grabbed his drink and darted past them and into the hall. Ian ushered Zandra out by the elbow and again instructed her to tell the station manager he was on the way. If it had been Miranda, he'd have given her a pat on the bum before sending her off. Zandra, he was reluctant to touch in any but the most perfunctory way. Instead, he reverted back and engaged the old medieval, Earl of Ashenwyck brook no argument attitude. Ian waited until she got the point and left.

"Where are you going?" he asked Alex.

"Into Miranda's room, I'm not staying alone in your office where that thing can swoop down on me like a sitting duck. Did you see the way she looked at me?" He made a face and shuddered.

Ian would've laughed at Alex's grimace and alarmed tone if it wasn't Miranda's room where he sought refuge.

Chapter Forty-Four

Miranda looked up from the screen, surprised when Alex set his drink on the desk and pulled a chair up to hers. Ian dogged his steps.

"Miranda," Ian said.

"Yes?" she said, turning from Ian, distracted by Alex. Thumbnail pictures of medieval swords were displayed on her computer. He clicked on several, blowing up the images on the screen.

Ian barked. "Miranda!"

She turned to Ian. "What?" she asked with a small, impatient open-handed gesture.

Alex sat unperturbed as Ian pointed a finger at him. "Don't let my friend here charm you out the door with tales of déjà vu possibilities. He'd love nothing more than to beetle off with you to some cozy spot. If anyone is going to beetle off with you it will be me. I don't care if he says the studios on fire, unless a fireman personally tells you to leave, you're to remain here. Do you understand?"

She nodded and he left. "Wow, too weird."

"Just ignore him. He's always been a fusspot. Tell me what you're working on, sweetling."

"Ian's first show is on the Hundred Years War. The initial segment ends with the capture of King John. Much of the beginning portion is the battles of Crecy and Poitiers. I'm trying to find the exact type of sword the Black Prince used."

Miranda found the swords under consideration and enlarged her preferences. "Of the two I've found, one has a rather ornate pommel with a lion's head carved in the wheel. It's from his effigy in Canterbury Cathedral. I like this one though," she pointed to a second picture. "I think the simpler design is the better choice."

After a cursory glance at the more elaborate sword Alex said, "You're right, take this one. The prince could be very flamboyant at court. But in battle, he was a serious warrior. He used a sword with a simple unadorned pommel, the cross-guards straight and plain."

Alex leaned back in the chair and appeared to choose his words carefully as he described the Black Prince. "Edward had one of the finest military minds England has ever known."

"Without a doubt. Please, go on."

"There's a time when a leader must follow his own counsel, or follow his advisors. He was wise enough to know the difference. On the battlefield he was a brave, and in general, an honorable man. Although, I'm sure exceptions could be found to his chivalrous nature."

"Like Limoges," she added.

"Like Limoges. War brings out the best and worst in men, sometimes the same man. In my opinion, a knight couldn't serve under a finer leader. The speech he made to his soldiers on the field of Poitiers was better than any playwright's fiction."

Miranda listened, engrossed, struck by the intensity of Alex's description and how personal his knowledge sounded. Only one other person made the images and personalities of the time so colorful and three dimensional, Ian. When he discussed Crecy, and specifically Poitiers, the battles came to life. She heard the thud of a morning star landing against a shield or the whoosh of a sword as it cut the air. With a little imagination, she could picture the field of dying horses and men, the ground blood soaked and reddish black.

How unique for two modern men to have such a strong attachment to a long ago time.

"You speak as though you really knew him." Miranda wondered at the cause of the enigmatic, almost sad emotion that briefly entered his eyes.

"This period in history is of particular interest to me. Perhaps I identify with some of the personages too much and it affects my opinions. Did you want to continue with swords or shall we go on to other weapons?" He didn't wait for her response and advanced the page.

They spent their time leafing through page after page of arms and armor. Alex impressed her more and more as they went through each section. He grew especially enthusiastic when they came to the examples of warhorses and their decorative bridles.

A clear picture of Alex on a strong stallion came to Miranda. Distinct enough for her to remark, "I can visualize you on a great destrier, a huge grey Percheron maybe."

"Can you? How uncanny. I happen to have a grey Percheron and several black ones too."

Ian had quietly entered the room. Only when Alex acknowledged him with the barest of nods did she become aware of Ian's presence.

Excited with the results of their search, Miranda gave Ian a dazzling smile. "Hi."

"You two appear to be getting along rather well. Can I hope the research also went well in my absence?"

"Ian, you won't believe how much we've gotten done. Alex has been an enormous help. He's a fountain of information."

She expected him to be pleased. Instead, he looked disappointed, although she couldn't swear to it, but he seemed a little hurt. Neither made sense to her.

"Great," he said, with a weak smile.

The sentiment sounded stiff and added to her confusion.

"I have a couple of things I need to talk to him about. Afterward we can go over what you've found."

"Belle dame, it has been my pleasure." Alex stood, kissed her hand, and they both left.

Miranda rested her chin in her palm curious as to what was bothering Ian when Kiki came flying into the office. "Okay, out with it. What's your secret, perfume, witchcraft? Confess!"

"What are you talking about?"

"Don't play dumb. I'm talking about the fact you have the attention of two of the hottest men in London, and we want to know your secret."

"If you're referring to the man who just left, that's Alex Lancaster and he's a friend of Ian's. He passed the time with me while he waited for Ian. Don't make it into something it's not. And, who is 'we' exactly?"

"Every female in the building, that's who. Or didn't you notice the parade of women who strolled by your office?" Kiki fluttered her hand and prattled on, "I take back the question. If I had that hunk sitting next to me I wouldn't notice anything either. Since we're on the subject of "his gorgeousness," how's it going with Ian?"

"It's going fine. We're not dating if that's what you want to know. I told you I wouldn't go out with him while we worked together." Miranda swiveled back to her computer. Maybe Kiki would get the hint and leave.

She and Ian were already fodder for the office gossips. This was exactly what Miranda deplored but she had no one to blame but herself. She'd let him kiss her in front of everyone that first day. At the time, she hadn't dreamt she'd wind up working for him. Let the rumor mills grind away. Her relationship with Ian wasn't open for discussion.

Kiki didn't take the hint and refused to be put off. "Why are you so opposed to dating him while you're his assistant? Seriously, do you expect a man like Ian to wait around?"

Miranda had to answer Kiki or she'd never leave the subject alone. "No, I don't expect him to hang around, I hope he will, but I don't expect it. It's just--well, I like him. I like him so much I can't see straight sometimes. But if we were to date and he wound up dumping me, I'd still have to work with him. I'd be shattered. I couldn't do it, Kiki. I couldn't have my heart broken, then work with him every day and pretend I was all right. Don't you see?"

"No, I don't. I don't understand why you assume he's going to dump you." Kiki's flighty manner evaporated and she turned serious. "It's you who doesn't see. You're so afraid, you're blind to the truth. He's crazy about you. I can see it. We all can see it, everyone but you. The way he looks at you. God, I'd give up chocolate for a year to have a man like him look at me that way."

"I know he likes me. Sometimes I think he likes me as much as you think. The thought of that frightens me as much as it excites me." She checked herself. She hadn't meant to reveal so much to Kiki, to anybody.

"Hmmm, sounds as though you more than like him," Kiki bent close. "Take a chance Miranda, Columbus did."

"Yeah right, easy for you to say."

"I'm available for a double date with you and Ian, if you'd care to let Alex know." Kiki winked and left.

Miranda sat mulling over her friend's suggestion, then dismissed it. How could she get Kiki to understand what she didn't understand herself?

How could she explain about her visions? Visions that came unbidden, flashes and images of Ian as a knight, or in a castle courtyard with a mysterious woman. After his visit to her house, she could add graphically erotic dreams to the list. Over the past week working closely together, the images had come with increased frequency, grown more vivid, more intense. There was a woman in many. A woman whose face she never saw. Some of those imaginings were so sensual she could almost feel the heat where their skin touched, hear the carnal words, the woman's words, his words. A premonition of him leaving sometimes accompanied a vision. The pain of the loss so tangible it invariably tempered her fantasies.

No, she couldn't tell Kiki or anyone. They'd think her mad, and rightfully so. Hell, even she was beginning to doubt her sanity. Ian's to blame for this disturbing problem, she thought in a huff. After all, she'd never experienced fantasies like this before he came into her life. Therefore, he should shoulder some of the responsibility for her deteriorating mental state.

Chapter Forty-Five

Ian removed his jacket and slumped into his chair, while Alex freshened his drink. Tension mingled with impatience and colored his tone as he brooded over Miranda's warm reaction to Alex.

"I strain and fight everyday to see some sign of recognition in her eyes. Every morning I endeavor to find the key to unlock her memory. Can you tell me how it is she remembers you? How she has this feeling of having met you and not have it with me?"

"No. I've no idea." Alex candidly replied. "I could venture a guess, but that's all it is, just a guess."

"I'm open to any and all theories, go ahead."

Alex hesitated and took a deep breath, "Perhaps it's because I never hurt her."

"What do you mean?" Taken aback, Ian fought the impulse to become defensive.

After taking a long, slow sip of his scotch Alex explained, "Well, I think it's like the lyric from *The Way We Were*, what's too painful to remember, we choose to forget."

The lyric meant nothing to him. Ian wasn't certain he'd ever heard the song.

"I should have known," Alex mumbled to himself. "You know the song *The Way We Were*?"

Ian shook his head.

"Barbra Streisand's big hit," Alex added as a hint. Several seconds passed as he waited in vain for Ian to confirm he knew the song or at least nod in affirmation. Nothing.

"Do you ever listen to music, other than when you're riding in an elevator?"

"Yes, I listen to music. I'll have you know I've a very fine collection of CD's."

"By fine collection do you mean the odd six or seven left at your flat by various females?"

Indignant, Ian said, "Yes."

"So tell me Mr. MTV. What are the names of the CD's, or perhaps you can name the artists?"

Ian absently rolled a Pelikan fountain pen over his knuckles back and forth. His favorite pen, the one he found closest to writing with a quill. He kept a watchful eye on the instrument, never lending it.

"You know I'm not musical."

"Not musical? Compared to you, Attila the Hun was a song and dance man."

Alex brought the glass to his lips and put it back down without touching the tawny liquid. "Ian, I've no idea how to help you with your predicament. I wish I did. I don't understand why you feel this urgent need to have her remember to begin with. Why can't you forget it and just court her? Take her to dinner, buy her flowers, go dancing, win her heart that way."

Ian sat pensive and considered his answer. He'd asked himself that exact question several times. It always came back to the same thing. "Elinor loved me when all I had was my word and my honor. A man can be penniless and still be wealthy, if he is true to his word, and can keep his honor in a world of deceivers. I broke my word. I failed her. If Miranda recalls you, then there must be a way for her to remember Basil and our love. Perhaps some deep-seated part of her will know I kept my final promise."

Alex's crooked mocking smile said it all, half, *you're having me on* and half *you crazy bugger.* Either way, Ian got the drift Alex didn't buy the explanation. "Out with it. I've seen that look before. What's on your mind?"

"I know honor is and always has been important to you. You've always been a man of your word. But, I think in this situation you're like a dog chasing his tail. Frankly, I suspect this has more to do with ego than you care to admit. You've done a bang up job putting a rosy spin on it, but to what end? Pride goeth before the fall, be careful my friend."

Alex finished his drink. "I'm going to get on my way. I have a date. I'll see you ..." he slid the message slip from his pocket and peeked at the name, "and Carla tomorrow for drinks."

"Do try and remember her name tomorrow, will you."

"Not a problem, I'll just call her sweetling," Alex said, checking his tie as he stood. "The ladies love it. They say it sounds romantic and old world."

"You love this modern time, don't you?"

"Victoria's Secret, birth control, liberated women, it's brilliant."

They shared a laugh, lightening the mood.

Alex turned serious. "Ian, God knows you've been around a long time. You'll think of some way to reach her. Give it time. If she never remembers, so what, maybe it's not such a bad thing."

Ian gave a low grunt and watched as his friend headed for the door. "Alex...thanks."

Ian stared at the closed door and contemplated what they'd discussed. Alex was wrong. How could Miranda not want to know they're destined to be together? He evaluated several different ways to go about convincing her before a simple but shrewd plan came to him. He needed to be a stronger presence in her daily life. It would take a couple of weeks. If she subconsciously sensed the prior hurt like Alex suggested, then she had to have the good memories buried there. He just needed to unlock them. Tonight was the perfect time to start.

He walked into Miranda's office, a man on a mission.

Chapter Forty-Six

Miranda was standing at her desk, pictures of weapons spread in front of her. She looked up as Ian came in. "Hi, I saw Alex leave. I was about to go to your office. I've printed out the pictures and descriptions of the weapons we might use." She started to gather the examples. "When you approve the choices I'll send copies to the production assistant to forward on to the re-enactment group."

Ian came around to Miranda's side of the desk, never slowing his stride, a strange glint in his eye. She watched him with a mixture of wariness and excitement. With one hand he took her by the wrist as he pulled a chair over with the other.

"Sit."

Ian tugged her down into a chair and arranged the two of them so they were face to face. Instead of knee to knee, he placed himself so both her legs were between his. Hunched forward, his forearms rested on his thighs.

"Show me the pictures. By the way, I don't want a re-enactment group. Make sure the production staff is made aware. Tell them to get stunt men. I want the battle scenes to look and sound as realistic as possible. Those weekend warrior clubs won't do."

The examples were laid out in sub-categories so Ian compared swords to swords, daggers to daggers, armor to armor. He kept his head down, reviewing, but slowly with each stack he edged further forward until his hands were over Miranda's lap. A faint whiff of Dunhill, his after shave, drifted up. The subtle scent never overpowered her.

She gazed down at the back of his bent head and wondered what his pillow smelled like. She bet there was the underlying odor of linen, crisp and clean, with an overlay of him, and a touch, but just a touch of Dunhill.

What a distraction the man was. Subtly, she studied him as he sorted through the printouts, noting the way his broad shoulder muscles curved, stretching the cotton shirt when he shifted.

She fantasized him making love to her. For the hundredth time this week, she envisioned where his arms bulged as he supported his weight and covered her body. She saw her hands slide under his biceps and up and over his wide back. Her palms would register every flex of his muscles as he moved across her body kissing, teasing, arousing. His thick hair would tickle her breasts and stomach as she ran her hand down the indentation of his spine.

Ian sat up. Startled, she tried not to look flustered.

"I've marked the weapons I want to use."

He'd said something. His lips had moved and there'd been vague sound coming out. She was caught like a rat in a trap, wallowing in an X-rated daydream.

"Sorry?"

He stared at her hard as though he'd read her mind. "I've marked the ones we're using, take them to production and then meet me in my office and we'll go to dinner," he said after a few seconds.

A ripple of relief ran through Miranda when he stood. Grateful her inattention hadn't been questioned; the invitation went over her head. The thought of declining never formed.

She stopped in the ladies room on the way back from production for a quick critical appraisal. The make-up and hair needed only a minor touch up but the dress--.

The ivy green flattered her. Long sleeved with a mandarin collar the dress hugged her figure well and ended an inch above the knee. A modest slit over one thigh added a little sex appeal. Unfortunately, it was silk. Unlike the pristine silk Armani worn by "Jennifer Perfect," as Miranda labeled her, this dress had serious wrinkles.

"Why am I doing this?" She mumbled, digging through the toiletry bag she kept in her desk. He swore he wasn't seeing other women. How can that be true when they keep calling? If she had the sense God gave a goose she'd decline the invitation and leave.

She knew the answer. Deep down she wanted to believe he could be as attracted to her as she was to him. Miranda straightened her dress as best she could, brushed her hair and glossed her lips.

"Let Jennifer Perfect and the rest eat cake."

It occurred to her quoting a woman who'd had her head chopped off wasn't the wisest choice.

Chapter Forty-Seven

Ian sat in his office using the time to marshal his wayward thoughts. He'd had one devil of a time concentrating on the pictures. When they sat so close with their thighs touching, he thought he'd never make it through the stacks of examples. Then, when he leaned over her lap and his hand came into contact with that sexy slit in her dress, *bloody hell!* The slit stopped just short of the top of her stocking. If he'd moved his fingers one inch he'd have been touching the soft skin of inner thigh.

Miranda had driven him crazy all day in that dress. He loved the way it clung to her as she moved and the quiet rustle as it slid against her skin. When she reached for a book on one of his shelves the material drew taut outlining the shape of her bottom. For a few seconds, he considered closing the door and ravishing her. Fulfillment of that temptation would have to wait. Miranda wasn't likely to appreciate the spontaneity, *yet.*

Dinner was the first step in his plan. They belonged together. He'd no intention of waiting months for her to come around, but he needed to walk a fine line. Too suave and he'd come across as a shallow playboy. He had to be charming enough to win her trust and confidence.

There was a soft knock and Miranda peered around the door.

"Ready?"

"Absolutely," he replied. More than you know, he said to himself.

His splayed fingers covered her lower back as he led them out, passing a group of co-workers. Ian paid no mind to their curious looks. He didn't care in the least about the whispers that started before they were out the exit door.

"Where would you like to go?"

"Well, if you're up for curry, the Rangoon Club is only a few blocks from here, near Grosvenor Square," Miranda suggested. "We can walk."

*

As they waited to cross Oxford St. a tenor sax started to play behind them. The melody caught Ian's attention. He turned.

The musician stood at the entry of the Marble Arch underground. He played without sheet music, black case open on the sidewalk. Without letting go of Miranda's hand, Ian went over to the busker.

"He's often here during the week," Miranda said and smiled up at Ian.

"What's the song?"

"*Space Oddity*, the old David Bowie tune."

Ian listened and let the music take him back to a day when he and Guy had been unmerciful to Elinor during a game of Castle Risk. They'd trounced her in record time. This was a favorite song of hers. She'd put the album on the stereo towards the end of the game. This song had just started when she stomped off.

Ian threw a pound coin in the sax player's instrument case .

"Play it again, will you?"

The busker nodded and replayed the haunting melody. When he finished, Ian thanked him and they walked back to the corner.

"Do you like that song?"

Miranda shrugged. "It's all right. Sad. I don't listen to Bowie much."

That wasn't the answer Ian hoped to hear.

At dinner he wanted to know about her life, her childhood, every detail of her twenty-five years. Miranda spoke about her family and how she came to be fascinated with history. Ian danced around direct questions regarding his family and background. He kept his answers vague while still satisfying her questions. If she thought his responses superficial she didn't indicate it. They lingered over drinks until she mentioned catching the last train to Norfolk.

The evening had been so much more than Miranda expected. That was a lie. She expected it to be wonderful, and it was beyond wonderful. She loved the way Ian touched her often with small intimate gestures. A thumb that circled the inside of her wrist, or the way his fingers slid the length of hers, up and down and in between. She concluded Ian's touch on any part of her anatomy would feel erotic.

She was reconsidering her office romance policy. What sort of impression would abandoning her ethical stance after one evening out give him of her? Did it show a complete lack of conviction to her personal standards? That's the type of woman he's probably used to dating. He had to see she was different. But, she really did want to make an exception to her rule. Coward that she was, she thought it best to let him make the overture. On the rethink, since she'd been so adamant about her policy, he might not make a move. Maybe he wanted a sign from her first. It was a conundrum of her own making.

They took their time walking to his car and reached it all too soon for Miranda, who still mentally vacillated.

"I had a lovely time. I wish..." her words trailed off. "Never mind, it's not important. If you don't mind could you drop me at King's Cross Station?"

She cursed her loss of nerve. Then, in a defensive internal about face, she justified chickening out. She told herself the original plan was for the best.

Could she get more schizophrenic?

"I'll drive you home."

Ian wrapped his arms around her, the protest she was about to make silenced with a kiss. The kiss stole Miranda's breath and thought away. She almost forgot what she intended to say. He lifted his lips from hers; still keeping the embrace tight.

"It's too far, you--" he stopped the rest of her words with another kiss, deeper than the one before. Ian changed positions, each new slant brought a tantalizing difference to the kiss. Every new probe offered the invitation to be returned and Miranda wouldn't decline.

Just one more, then she'd stop him. Just one more.

He locked her body to his. She held hard to his neck and shoulders, wanting more intimacy than the embrace allowed.

Ian's hand slid lower. Strong fingers urged Miranda's hips forward. Iron thighs pressed against her softer ones. The thin barrier of clothing between them a poor shield as his erection pushed against her. Her hips ground in unison with his.

Never breaking contact, Ian walked Miranda backward. The cold cement wall of the garage chilled her shoulders as Ian's hot hand skimmed up her thigh. His calloused palm caught on her stocking as his thumb circled an erotic pattern on her flesh.

She slipped her shoe off to hook a stockinged foot over the back of his leg. When he broke their kiss off, a breathy Miranda didn't let the opportunity pass. She kissed his neck, his chin, his throat.

His hand moved further up and a small shudder traveled through her as he glided over the sensitive hip bone. Ian cupped a buttock, while another firm hand held her in the position of his choice.

The shrill sound of a car alarm invaded their privacy and jarred them out of the moment. Ian froze. His hands stilled and he glanced in the direction of the offensive noise. He turned back, a look of disgust on his face.

She'd acted like all the other women, crawling all over him in a public garage. Slutty. Everything lovely about the evening was lost, sullied.

Ian withdrew his hand from under her skirt, straightening it as he pulled away. Cool air blanketed the area left empty of his body heat.

Sudden and strong, a weird premonition filled her thoughts, a sense of devastating loss and emptiness. Was the apprehension related to her visions and Ian, or a result of mortification? She didn't know. The experience troubled her as much as the sad feelings brought on by it. Until now, she'd pigeon-holed the existence of premonitions as nonsense along with gut instinct and intuition. But, she couldn't deny the power of the visceral warning.

She remained motionless, trying to sort out what to do, what it all meant. Of course, now Ian probably figured she was a tramp, so why should she be concerned about the rest? At least the car alarm shut off.

"Come, I'll drive you home." He slipped an arm around her waist, drawing her from the wall while she put the shoe back on.

Finished, she tried to step out of his encircling arm. She wanted distance, a safe zone to regroup and gather the scraps of her pride. Embarrassed by her conduct and how cheap he obviously thought of her behavior, Miranda struggled with him to no avail.

"Please, let go of me. Just take me to the train. I can make my own way." She snapped and glanced away before he could see her distress.

He tugged harder. She inched closer. He touched his lips to her hair, even as she refused to make eye contact.

A long silence passed with Miranda not moving a muscle.

"My car is parked at the Downham Market Station," she said at last. "You can't take me home. I've no way of getting to the train tomorrow."

"I'll pick you up in the morning. Don't bother to argue. It's not open for discussion." His firm hand on her back urged her forward.

"We're not at the office, Ian. Don't order me around. I'm not one of your whip crème headed mistresses who you tell the earth is flat and they nod in agreement."

"Fine. Then, don't treat me like a bounder who'd dump you off at the train with no thought for your safety."

She noticed him wince when her hand brushed his groin as she climbed in the sports car.

Ian slid into the driver's side and started the engine. He shifted into gear and gunned it, chirping the tires as he exited the garage.

"What's wrong, you act like you're in pain?"

"Nothing, except my testicles feel like they're attached to an anvil."

Miranda couldn't resist an unladylike snort. "I hope you're not looking for sympathy from me."

"No, darling. I've been around enough women to know that would be foolish."

Chapter Forty-Eight

Miranda was determined not to repeat her mistake. All week Ian continued to ask her to dinner. She politely refused, which wasn't easy. She'd like nothing better than to see him outside the office atmosphere. He never pushed the issue, but he didn't hide his disappointment either. Her determination weakened with every refusal and the desire to throw caution to the wind grew.

She discussed the pros and cons with her childhood friend, Shakira. The approach worked well with her. Shakira was a successful attorney. The pros and cons of a sticky situation was her strong suit.

Shakira said, "Personally, I refrain from dating anyone here at the firm. But, it's an easy choice for me. None of these peacocks in pinstripes appeal to me."

Her final warning to Miranda helped, *maybe.*

"At the end of the day, don't wind-up with regrets because you didn't go after him out of fear."

She thought about that. If she agreed to date Ian, the circumstances had to be right. No parking garage scenes.

She was rethinking her negative philosophy regarding office romances when Kiki walked past. She and several other female staff members were on their way to lunch and invited Miranda.

Miranda declined, although she wanted to get out of the office for a little while. She'd worked through lunch for the last three days and deserved a break. Not to mention the Marks and Spencer sale started today and by tomorrow all the best things would be gone. She had to go. She double checked her wallet for both cash and credit cards and dashed out.

#

"Hello, belle dame."

Miranda's head snapped in the direction of the familiar voice. "Alex. Hi. What are you doing here?"

"That's a broad question. By here, do you mean, the lingerie department, Marks and Sparks's store, or London?" He asked and took the white brassiere she'd been considering from her hand. Alex held it up for inspection. His gaze slid from the garment to Miranda's chest and back.

She felt herself flush under his perusal. To her greater embarrassment, Alex checked the size of the bra, before setting it on the display table.

"London, I can figure out. I meant this specific department in this specific store. I figured you more for a Victoria's Secret kind of man," Miranda explained. She imagined he knew of stores she couldn't name that sold a variety of underwear she probably wouldn't know how to put on.

Alex flashed a sexy, *I know more than any one man should*, kind of smile and continued to check the size labels on different bras.

"Here," he handed her a frilly, bronze one, cut so it pushed the wearer's breasts high and together. "This is a much better color for you. It compliments your complexion and hair. As to your analysis, I generally don't shop for women's undergarments. I trust they'll know what appeals to me. But, I saw you pop in here and followed.

"What size panties do you wear?"

"Pardon?" Miranda's brows shot up. She wasn't sure what surprised her more, the bold question or Alex's nonchalant expression. He acted like they were discussing the weather.

"I asked what size panties you wear. While you go and try on the bra, I'll find the matching undies for you."

He studied her hips then spun Miranda around and scrutinized her butt.

She squirmed and wrenched herself out of Alex's hold on her waist to face him. "If you think I'm going to stand still while you gauge how big my bum is, you are mad as a hatter."

Unfazed, he casually suggested, "I'm guessing a medium thong or should I grab a small too?"

"I hate thongs. I'd rather go commando. For the record, there are only four women on the planet who can wear a thong well enough to use their real names. As for anyone else who's contemplating wearing one, I advise...don't, not until you see your backside in a 360 degree mirror first." Miranda pointed an index finger at his nose. "And, I'm not trying the bra on either."

Alex's eyes dropped to her chest, "Pity." He took Miranda by the hand and led her to another table. "We still have to find you some matching panties."

"We?"

"You needn't be embarrassed." He bent close. "I've seen my fair share of lady's *smalls*. When we're done, we'll go for coffee."

There was no arguing with him. He stood over her as she sorted through a half dozen different styles of panty in the same shade of bronze. Every so often, he'd hold up a pair and she'd tip her head from side to side and give him an indecisive shrug. Most of what she held up, he'd vehemently shake his head no to and made a sour face. At last, they both agreed on a pair with delicate lace on the front and high French cut legs.

"Do you have some place special in mind?" Miranda asked as they left the store.

"Yes. A coffee house called The Octavo. It's not far."

"What a strange name."

"I'm sure that's not the original name." Alex said and hurried them across the street mid-block. "It's decorated with wallpaper that simulates a library. The door to both loos are covered and you have to figure out which book to push to get in. I like watching people as they get more and more frustrated trying to find the toilet."

"That's mean."

"No, that's someone easily amused." He turned down a well hidden mews. The cafe sat at the end of the alley. "Here we are." Alex held the door for her.

She didn't know quite what to make of Alex's invitation. Unsure of his motives at first, she couldn't articulate what she'd expected. He never struck her as someone who'd betray a friend, especially a close friend like Ian. But, he did have a serious womanizer reputation and they had spent a bit of time handling intimate garments. Shopping for lingerie with a man was a first for her. Shopping with a man like Alex contributed to her discombobulation.

When they first sat down, Miranda kept her guard up. Then, as the hour progressed, she lowered it. At no time did Alex say or do anything she'd deem licentious, or unsavory, or in questionable taste. He'd been a perfect gentleman and a marvelous conversationalist. He had a curious way of seeing the world, droll, a bit caustic, definitely astute, but judgmental in a medieval way in some matters. Occasionally, he'd make a comment that sounded rather old world.

She wanted to understand him better and her mind would wander as her brain picked apart something he said. As a result, she'd lose the gist of the conversation and he'd have to repeat himself. The third time, she asked him to repeat what he said, Alex studied her and took a long pause before he complied. She figured he suspected her of being ditzy. After that, she paid closer attention.

Her second cappuccino arrived. Alex sipped a double espresso. She felt at ease and as she relaxed the same strong feeling of connection to him she felt the first day returned. It was the sense of deja-vu again that made her blurt, "*Dust in the_Wind.*" The conversation had turned to their shared appreciation of music and the old Kansas song popped into her head. For reasons she'd never be able to explain, she saw Alex singing to it. Most of the fleeting picture was a blur. A hazy vision made more bizarre by the fact the room in the brief glimpse looked similar to her drawing room.

"What did you say?" Alex asked, staring hard at her.

Miranda fidgeted in her seat under his scrutiny. "This is going to sound a little crazy, but I had this weird flash of the song *Dust in the Wind*, and pictured you singing it."

"I don't find that at all crazy. I find it...how shall I say...more than interesting."

She could almost see the wheels of his mind turn as he ran a finger along the rim of the cup, his eyes never leaving her.

"Tell me how you pictured me."

"There's not much to say. Like I said, it happened so fast." The illusion of Alex didn't generate the tumultuous emotions the visions of Ian did. She had no idea why.

"Really, it was like a camera flash. For that instant, you looked old fashioned." Miranda's hand stirred the air as she searched for the words, "Oh, you know, boots, breeches, and a tunic thing. You appeared sort of sad."

Alex passed the espresso under his nose and then took a sip. "Have you ever seen these flash pictures of Ian?"

A guttural, piggy sound emanated from her as air and liquid went down the wrong way, choking her. Thank God, it had been a small swallow or she'd have sprayed Alex.

He rushed over and alternately patted and rubbed her back.

"Are you all right?"

Miranda mumbled she was fine and Alex returned to his seat.

"Why do I think you're uncomfortable with this subject?"

Miranda shrugged.

"Perhaps, if I rephrase the question," Alex said and watched her with analytical eyes. "If you had to see Ian in some other, let's use the term persona, for lack of a better word. How would you see him?"

Miranda wanted to answer with a complete recapping of every strange vision she'd had of Ian. She wanted to unburden herself and share what she'd experienced. She wanted someone else to tell her she wasn't crazy. Self-doubt and fear the response might go the other way made her rein in her temptation. Not completely though.

"I see him as an intellectual Clive Owen."

Alex's gaze flickered over her and she sensed the wheels of his mind turning again.

"*Gosford Park*, Clive," or, Alex quirked a brow, "*Closer*, Clive, or *King Arthur*, Clive?"

"*King Arthur*, Clive."

"Hmmm."

Chapter Forty-Nine

Alex kissed Miranda on the cheek and said goodbye then returned to Marks and Spencer. He searched the display tables in the lingerie department. He couldn't find a bra and panties exactly like the ones Miranda bought. After spending several minutes trying to hunt down a sales girl, one happened by. He hooked her elbow.

"You had a very feminine, bronze colored bra on the sale table this morning?" The clerk stared vacantly at him. "Satin ribbons, loads of lace." Her gaze didn't alter. "It was the fanciest one on display. There were matching panties in the same color, also with frilly lace," he told her with growing impatience.

Her head bobbed up and down then stopped. Silence.

Alex waved his hand in front of her face. "Hello."

"What?"

"Think you can handle a trip to the stockroom to check on another set?" She nodded but didn't move. "Now."

"Oh, right. I'll look for a nice black set too in case I can't find the others."

"No. They have to be the same style, the same color." Alex said. "Bring out whatever size you find."

The sales girl disappeared behind the "employee's only" door. After several minutes, she returned with the matching pair. The wait had almost made him late for an appointment.

Finished with the business meeting, Alex rang Ian. "I'm over here on the west end, not far from your studio. Meet me at the Thistle Club. I've a complimentary invite. They want me to join. We'll have dinner and drinks. I have some intriguing information for you."

"I can't believe you're considering joining a club." Ian said.

"I'm not. You know me. All these clubs filled with walrusy old men, flaunting their old school ties. Too bloody dreary for my tastes. However, the dinner is free and they are supposed to have a fine chef."

Ian laughed. "I'll be there in twenty minutes."

#

Over the rim of his glass, Alex saw the maitre'd lead Ian to the tap room. The tuxedoed host snapped his fingers and an ancient waiter appeared. Ian ordered a double Johnnie Walker Blue Label on the rocks.

The waiter returned with the drink and a humidor the size of a laptop computer, only deeper.

Alex rummaged through and selected a long, thin Cuban. He twirled the cigar between his fingers and passed it under his nose. "Do you think these are really rolled on the thighs of Cuban women?"

Ian clipped the end of one he'd already removed and handed the cutter to Alex along with his lighter.

"One can hope." Ian inhaled deeply and leaned back into the chair. He blew out a cloud of smoke and said, "I'm looking forward to trying the steaks here. I understand they're better than the Maze Grill."

"I love the Maze, brilliant filets. You can cut them with a spoon," Alex added between puffs. He eyed a waiter carrying a tray of hot hors d'oeuvres. "Isn't it amazing the different and delicious foods available to people now? Meat that isn't dried, or tainted or maggoty."

"—or at one time, whinnied or brayed prior to hitting your plate," Ian chimed in.

A bluish-white cloud hung around their heads. Whenever it began to dissipate, the fog of smoke was replenished by the exhalation of one or the other.

"Those last few weeks in France when our supplies were almost exhausted we foraged along with the horses, I'd have called you a liar if you told me one day we have shops with aisle after aisle of every food imaginable. To use a modern cliché, that morning at Poitiers, I was so hungry, my stomach thought my throat was cut."

The irony in Ian's comment brought a small chuckle.

Both men sat silent, smoking, each lost in memory.

Alex swallowed the rest of his drink. "I had an interesting conversation with *your* Miranda."

"When?"

"Today."

"Today? Where did you see her?"

"I ran into her at Marks and Sparks."

"Isn't it unusual for you to be over this way before late afternoon?"

"I had business in the area. Running into Miranda was a lucky coincidence."

After a few minutes, Ian said, "What did the two of you talk about that you found so interesting?"

"You, as King Arthur."

"Oh? Go on."

"She had a vision of me, a brief one according to Miranda. I think she was remembering a day when Elinor and I were talking about music. I can't recall where you had gone off to."

"What do you mean she had a vision of you?"

Alex leaned far back in the chair and blew out a long stream of smoke. "The name of a song I sang while Elinor lay on the sofa and listened. It's a sad song and the words struck me as reflective of our circumstance. She remembered me singing. She remembered most of what I wore." He smiled. "I can't believe she recalled such a small thing."

Ian didn't say a word.

"Look, don't take what I said wrong." Alex sat up straight. "I didn't mean anything by it. I was flattered, simple as that."

"A busker the other day played one of Elinor's favorite songs. Miranda was with me so I had him play it twice. It meant nothing to her."

"Ian—,"

"Let's talk about something else. How does Miranda see me as King Arthur?"

"She actually sees you as kind of Clive Owen type—Clive doing King Arthur to be specific."

Ian blew on the end of his cigar. The burning tip flared red then receded back to a dull orange. "I can see that. Did you tell her I'm taller than Clive?"

"No. I've never met the man. I've no idea how tall he is."

"Well, I have. He's tall." Ian tapped the ashes of his cigar and added with a smug grin, "But I'm taller."

"You tell her. I figure I've chatted you up enough. If I talk about you too much, she'll think I'm a poof."

Ian's grin broadened.

#

Carla opened the door. "Alex, what a lovely surprise?"

"Hello, sweetling. Are you up for a late night date?" he asked and came inside, the Marks & Spencer box in his hand.

Carla stepped close and kissed him hard and slow. "I'm always available for a late anything with you."

She slid her fingers into his waistband, low enough for the tips to drag along the heavy line of hair that trailed to his groin. "Make yourself a drink. I'll just go and change."

Alex handed her the small box with a bow around the outside. "I'd like you to wear these tonight."

"Ooh, a present. I love presents," Carla cooed and unwrapped the gift. "I've never had a man buy me lingerie before. Well, not...hmmm...conventional lingerie."

"Yes, they're definitely different than your usual style."

She ran her hand over the lace that bordered the high, French cut legs of the panties. "I like your taste though. Pretty color, bronze."

Chapter Fifty

The phone hadn't rung in the last hour. All the little brush fire crises of the morning were extinguished. Miranda and Ian sat talking, enjoying the rare peace. Then Charles, the production assistant, and Evelyn the wardrobe mistress, dashed into Ian's trailer. A flushed and agitated Charles started babbling before Ian could put his coffee down.

"Terry and some of his men are refusing to wear the equipment you designated."

Behind him, Evelyn nodded in agreement.

The Poitou-Charentes regional authorities refused the production company permits to film at the actual location of the battle. What was the English side of the battlefield now had a tract of up-scale homes. "The presence of a film company is an unacceptable disturbance to the residents," the authorities said.

The production company chose the area near Rutland Water, an English location with similar countryside. They'd rehearsed with props for the last three days. Today, they were supposed to rehearse in full costume with both types of props Ian requested. In two days, they'd shoot the Battle of Poitiers scene. He was very specific about the sequence and involved himself in every aspect of its filming. Tempers flared more than once between him and Terry Gatcombe, the stunt coordinator.

"I've had it with Gatcombe." Ian's patience snapped as he spotted the source of his anger through the small window. "I'm putting an end to his bullshit," he said, throwing open the trailer door. Ian ignored the little stairs and jumped onto the grass and strode towards his nemesis.

Terry and his assistant, Duncan, a bear of a Scotsman were stretched out playing cards on the grass. Neither man bothered to stop their play at Ian's approach.

"I understand you have an objection to the equipment." Ian snatched the cards from their hands and tossed them aside.

Miranda might've picked them up before they blew away, but she didn't want to miss a word. Besides, she rationalized those two didn't deserve to have their stuff rescued. As far as she was concerned, Terry and Duncan were crude buggers at the best of times and bottom dwellers most of the time.

In one smooth and quick motion, Terry rolled to his feet. A large man, he stood tall as Ian, but about a stone heavier.

"Yeah, I do. There's no reason for my men to suffer wearing the armor you ordered. The lighter weight replica stuff will look like the real thing on camera."

The two men stood face to face each assessing the other.

"First, not all of the men have to wear the custom made, more authentic gear. Just the men in the foreground where the heaviest action is depicted and the camera will concentrate need wear that armor. Secondly, it appears the same on film, but the effect is not the same." Ian's level tone was civil but firm.

Only Miranda knew him well enough to know the extent of his anger. She'd seen him get pretty pissed the last few weeks, never had he raised his voice. On the contrary, the more intense his outrage, the more stoic he became. This wasn't an area he'd tolerate disobedience.

Ian lifted several items of replica armor one by one from the table. He tested the weight, moving each from hand to hand.

"The better pieces here are carbon steel. This new steel is very different than the steel used in the fourteenth century. Some of the rest of this junk is aluminum. The men in the close-ups wearing the light steel bits will look like Robin and his Merry Men. The ones in the beer can material will come off like ballerinas."

Terry had no opportunity to respond.

"Fatigue was always a factor then. A knight accustomed to the weight was neither slow nor ponderous in his movements, but more deliberate. He had to focus his attack. He had to try and wear his opponent down, while conserving his own energy. Prancing around like Sherwood Forest Nancy Boys would've gotten a knight killed." Ian tossed the armor down on the table with the same disregard he's shown the cards.

"I'm sure to a his-to-r-i-an like yourself it might seem to make a difference." Terry dragged the word out accentuating each syllable.

Miranda sucked in air through her teeth and remained close to Ian, morbidly fascinated by Terry's stupidity.

"Your set and this set are both steel. At the end of the day, the difference will be negligible on film."

"You think so?" Ian replied with a note of provocation in his tone. "A short, mail hauberk was about twenty pounds. Add another seven or so for the helm, three to three-and-a-half for the arming sword, add in the individual plate sections, and it's roughly fifty pounds." He stacked the pieces of the replica armor Terry swore by and lifted the pile. "I'm guessing yours to be twenty to twenty-five pounds, maybe."

Terry's contemptuous attitude grew more evident with the information. "There you have it. You expect my lads to carry the extra weight, easy enough request when you aren't doing it yourself, *historian*."

One corner of Ian's mouth curved up in an unpleasant smile.

"Is that a challenge?"

"I'm in as long as you're willing to make it interesting. Shall we say one hundred pounds if I win and my lads wear the replica equipment of our choosing?" Terry nodded with a self-satisfied smirk to his supporters who had gathered around.

Ian appeared neither impressed nor intimidated. "All right. But if I win, I'll take your money. You'll wear my armor selection, and I'll not hear one whimper from you the rest of the shoot."

"Agreed."

Both men went off to don the armor.

Stuntmen and crew had formed a circle, eager for combat. Heavy wagering began between the two groups, most of the money on Terry. All the stunt people were well aware of his reputation as an excellent swordsman and bet accordingly.

The production staff backed Ian, but bets were small. Miranda hoped they backed him out of faith in his ability, or at least out of loyalty. Her blood boiled hearing several cover their bets on Ian with larger ones on Terry. She felt like slapping their traitorous faces raw.

In a booming Highland brogue Duncan announced, "One hundred pounds to any here willing to take my wager and back the historian against my man."

Miranda stepped forward, glaring at the turncoats from the staff who bet against Ian. "I'll take your bet Scotsman."

Duncan nodded in acceptance, then turned and made a big show of laughing at her foolishness with the other stuntmen. She watched him "high five" several and flick his head in her direction.

"You'd bet against me, sweet lips? I should be hurt." Terry eyeballed her with a gaze as bold as it was lusty. "Since you're in a mood to lose, want to wager with me?"

Miranda disliked him from the start and figured him for a conceited lager lout. She wondered more than once what sort of woman would be attracted to his cheesy charm.

"Sure, what do you want to bet? Your lackey was willing to go a hundred," she said sarcastically and jerked her head in Duncan's direction.

"I'm too chivalrous to take a lady's money. How about you meet me for a drink when I win and..." leering at her mouth, he added, "a kiss."

She countered his prurient stare with a disdainful one of her own. "I doubt you can spell chivalrous, but I'll accept your wager and when you lose I'll take two hundred quid."

Terry laughed. "I won't lose sweet lips."

Miranda spun on her heels and raced back to Ian. "Did you hear that last bet?"

Ian grunted and continued to work on a fastener.

She took it as a yes. "I'd rather suck a bulb of garlic soaked in vinegar than kiss that cretin."

His gauntleted hand wrapped around hers, dwarfing it. "I guess I'll just have to win." He smiled and ran a leather covered finger down her nose. The glove's riveted, overlapping plates that protected the back of his hand clinked as he did. "May I carry a favor of yours into the contest?"

Ian's warm breath tickled her skin as he bent close. Miranda searched for something, anything. She settled on a ribbon from her ponytail and tied it around his arm.

"I guess this makes you my knight in shining armor, literally."

"Yes, I am, *literally."*

The time for their fight approached. A nervous Miranda fussed over Ian checking and rechecking fasteners. "Promise me you'll be careful. Promise you won't do something to get yourself hurt because of that fool."

"You have my solemn word." Ian kissed the area where her brows drew together in worry. "What about us? Shall we have a wager, milady?"

He was trying to put her at ease. She knew it and adored him all the more for the gesture. "Name your terms, Sir Knight." Miranda batted her lashes and made a deliberate pouty mouth hoping she didn't look like a guppy.

His helm cradled in one arm, Ian stood absorbed, watching Miranda as she stroked his plated arm and chest. To anyone who bothered to notice, a dozen naked sex symbols couldn't drag his attention away from the woman in front of him.

Worry etched her face. She leaned into him and pressed her cheek against his. Ian kissed her brow ever so lightly in return and the lines of concern on her forehead smoothed.

"When I win you can make dinner for me tomorrow night."

"And if you lose?"

"I like beef stroganoff," he said, winking.

Miranda was scared witless as the combatants took the field. It's just a mock battle she tried to tell herself. The fact they were using real swords had her stomach in high speed turmoil. On various programs, Ian had demonstrated the use of different medieval weapons, including swords, but he was still basically a historian. Terry's bread and butter were dangerous stunts. He'd worked with dozens of weapons on dozens of movies, taking risks was no big deal to him.

The adversaries faced off. Terry came on strong, his blows rapid, each from a different angle. Ian reacted with equal speed, simply angled away with minimum movement, countered with defensive steps only when necessary. Miranda watched the clock. They'd been at it for five minutes. It felt like five hours to her. Ian had yet to take offensive action. She kept her distance from the other spectators while changing spots constantly to get a better view. Their cheers for the sleazy stuntman grated on her nerves and fed her fear.

More minutes passed. Terry's blows were slowing down but no less forceful. A hard strike caught Ian on the forearm, and dented his vambrace. Ian reeled momentarily. The effort and impact even staggered Terry and it took him several seconds to regain his balance. Miranda flinched, but stifled a cry of alarm, afraid she'd distract Ian. She sent up a silent prayer. *Please, don't let him get hurt. Just keep Ian unharmed and if you could help him win this quick that would be okay too.*

After that vicious blow it became clear Ian had deliberately waited till Terry tired to retaliate. Miranda wondered if Terry had listened at all to Ian. Ian told him straight off wearing an enemy's energy down was a common tactic. If the jerk was too arrogant to believe Ian, oh well, and damned good for her side.

Ian raised his sword. With incredible and surprising speed, he struck and struck at the stuntman, always forcing him to take a step backwards. The technique effectively limited Terry's ability to counterattack.

Ian pushed Terry all over the field as the stuntman's breathing became more and more labored and his reactions slower. Several times Terry was unable to keep his sword at the ready.

Transfixed, Miranda followed each step Ian took. It seemed choreographed, part of a dance he'd done a thousand times. She stayed riveted on him. Brilliant to watch, all power and grace, his movements had an economy to them, nothing flamboyant, nothing wasted, none of the artifice seen in movies or staged sword fights. Miranda hugged herself and rocked back on her heels in sudden realization. She wasn't simply projecting Ian's face on the imaginary knight. *He and the knight of my visions are truly one and the same.*

Ian knocked Terry's sword from his hand into the air.

The stuntman bent and rested his hands on his knees, panting, sweat leaked out from under his helm. "I surrender. You've made your point."

Terry took the hand Ian offered. Some of the stuntmen and other supporters grumbled but begrudgingly congratulated Ian. The more sullen ones drifted to the rear of the group.

Terry managed a smile and a half laugh as he turned to the other losers, "Sorry about your losses, I shall make amends at the pub. The first round is on me." He gave Ian a curt nod, "Of course, that includes you, historian." This time no derogatory intonation accompanied the word.

An elated Miranda ran through the crowd and launched herself at Ian. He beamed at her like she was heaven sent and captured her with one arm. She kissed him full on the mouth in front of the company. Miranda told herself she only intended to hug him. His reaction made her dare to kiss him in spite of the crowd. Right. And cake eaten a spoonful at a time had less calories than eating it slice by slice.

Ian deepened the kiss as the crew egged him on and finally broke the kiss off when they both came up for air.

Terry scanned Miranda like a hungry wolf.

Ian aimed a piercing stare at his former opponent. "Thanks for the offer, but *we* have other plans."

"Sorry, I didn't know." The stuntman lifted his hands in a mock surrender and turned to mix with the group of onlookers.

Ian hugged Miranda tight so only she could hear, "I've changed my mind. Tomorrow is too long to wait for my winning dinner. Tonight sounds much better."

Their kiss had exposed the relationship the office rumor mongers alleged. She didn't care what people said anymore. She was thrilled with his victory. What better time to cast her fate to the wind and do what she wanted. And, this would be a lovely dinner, just the two of them, at her home, with no parking garage scenes.

The crowd dissipated and they were left alone. Miranda had an incredible urge to tell Ian about the visions. What would he think if she told him he was the knight?

"We'll stop at my hotel so I can have a quick shower and change," Ian said, stripping off the rest of his gear.

Miranda abandoned the idea of telling him about her knight. Things were going too well at the moment to complicate matters with talk of wild imaginings.

Chapter Fifty-One

Miranda sat on the bed. The large hotel room had a sitting area to one side and a king bed and desk on the other side. The tasteful décor was a traditional style in muted tones of chocolate brown, tan and steel blue. Too neutral for Miranda's taste, she'd add a splash of color with bright jewel tone throw pillows or oriental vases.

Ian began to undress. "I won't take more than twenty minutes, unless, of course, you want to join me."

A giggle bubbled up at the playful invitation. Another giggle. They were coming with more frequency. Good Lord, she was turning into Kiki.

The light laughter didn't stem from humor as much as a self-conscious effort to cover the temptation of the invite. The man was the wave of warm water that laps at your knees, your legs, your chest, higher and higher until you're over your head. How long can a woman be expected to tread water? The question danced in her thoughts as she turned her head while he disrobed.

After the bathroom door shut, she wandered around the room. Extremely neat, he left nothing lying around. His paperwork was tidy and organized on the desk like at work. She continued while listening for the shower. Miranda peeked into the closet, not really sure what she expected to find other than clothes. Everything was lined up neatly, shoes with shoe trees, suits, shirts, and slacks were separated by purpose and color.

The fastidiousness of a man who's endured chaos.

She stood with one hand still on the doorknob and one on her hip puzzled as to where the assumption came from. She let the question go and shut the door. It was one of the mysteries about Ian she just seemed to know.

The shower stopped. She sat on the bed again and picked up a book from the nightstand. A picture of the American General, Norman Schwartzkoff stared back at her. She wondered if Ian had ever considered pursuing a military career.

He came out bare-chested and in jeans with the top button undone. His skin was the color of polished cedar in the afternoon light. He stood in front of her towel drying his hair.

Clothes didn't do justice to his powerful build. His lack of fatigue during the exercise with Terry made sense now. Miranda let her gaze trail down past the indentation under his pectorals. His waist was trimmer than it looked in business attire. Black, silky hair added another sexy layer to his tanned chest.

In the erotic dream she had of him, he didn't have a hairy chest. She'd burn this sight into subconscious. If she had another erotic dream, she wanted this fun feature included. It was so unsubtle, but her eyes dropped to the darkened line under the open waistband. He should just paint a "down here" arrow on his stomach.

She looked up. He grinned and smoothed his hair back with his palms. What a great smile he had. There was nothing contrived about it. If he didn't like someone or something he never faked a pleasant response.

She loved his smile.

She loved him and probably had from the start. Love at first sight? Something else she never believed in before Ian. He made her laugh even when he was being awful. He always had an acerbic, but accurate comment about the administrators and their hare-brained suggestions, which occurred regularly. Of course, he whispered undeniable remarks when the subjects were in her line of sight and she had to suffocate her laughter. Conversely, his courteous deference to other employees, a reflection of the quality of his character, always struck her. Even tactless Zandra received her share of pleases and thank yous from him.

Miranda never considered herself vain, but how Ian could make her ego soar with just a look. Sometime's his dark eyes were all sensuality and sometimes deviltry and appreciation. He made her blood churn in her veins. She was lost from the moment he grinned like the wolf in *Little Red Riding Hood* and suggested eating her.

Ian winked obviously approving of her intimate perusal. She clutched the book harder. Caught ogling him, she fumbled for something neutral to say.

"Nice tan."

"Thank you, the result of a year in a sunny climate."

Miranda cursed herself as her eyes darted downward when he unzipped to tuck in his shirt. She brought them back up with all speed and hoped he hadn't noticed the transgression.

"You've a lovely tan yourself," Ian said and took what in Miranda's opinion was an excruciating amount of time to zip and button up.

"It's nice, but not as rich or deep as yours, and I vacationed in the hot Mediterranean sun. Yours is..." Miranda scanned him suspiciously as he fixed his belt, "Very un-English."

She was grateful for the silly conversation. A moment ago, she'd been too close to blurting out, "I love you." There are some things a man should say first, I love you, being the primary one.

"Are you saying you don't think I'm English?" His brows furrowed and he tipped his head to the side. He appeared confounded by her remark.

"I didn't say that, but you are swarthy for an Englishman. You should recheck your family tree. I think there might be some pirate skeletons in your closet."

"Perhaps I've just spent more time in the sun topless than you have." His attention fixed on her breasts. "Not unfixable." Ian sat next to her on the bed and began to put his shoes and socks on, "If it weren't for this shoot, I'd be sorely tempted to take you away for a long weekend. Somewhere hot, so I could show you what happens to 'mad dogs and Englishmen' in the sun."

"Be careful, I might hold you to that." Miranda felt coquettish and charming, two things she'd never strived at being good at. She never thought the qualities important enough.

"Shall we go? Although I'm loath to suggest it now that I have you here on my bed...after all, there is room service." He slipped one hand around the nape of her neck and softly kissed the corners of her mouth. "Have I told you how impressed I am with your multi-tasking skills?"

"What multi-tasking skills?"

"Your ability to gawk at my body, while maintaining a strangle hold on General Schwartzkoff."

“What ego. I didn’t gawk.”

“I’m not complaining.”

Ian pushed her onto the mattress and held her there with one hand and extricated the book from her death grip with the other. He ignored her squeal and buried his face in her neck, his shoulders shaking with laughter.

"I was not gawking at your body." Miranda grabbed a handful of his hair and gave it a little shake to emphasize her point.

"Ow, those hairs are attached you know. Are you miffed because I dressed too fast?" He laughed out loud now, in spite of the pain she continued to inflict. "Ow, ow, ow, sorry, I'll try to go slower next time."

"Get off me you big, conceited oaf!" She let go of his hair to shove him hard with both hands. He didn't budge.

He threw a leg over and covered half her body with his as she tried to wriggle out from under him. "I've been called many things, never an oaf."

"Well you are, now get off." Miranda renewed her struggle.

"I don't think so. I like having you under me. It brings out my pirate blood. You look ripe for plundering. You feel it too, with your hips writhing against me like that." He braced himself on his forearms and rocked his hips.

Stilling, she said, "Pillager of innocent women, that sounds about right." Miranda bit her lower lip and turned her face away to keep from laughing.

"I only want to pillage and plunder you so I'm not sure I qualify as a true pirate. Besides, I suffer terrible mal de mer, which limits my buccaneering drastically."

"You get seasick?" she asked, surprised. "I'd never picture you with your head hanging over the ship rail."

"Some trips, I didn't always make it to the rail. Not a pretty picture, believe me." Ian wrinkled his nose at the memory.

It was a sweet, boyish gesture. Miranda couldn't resist nuzzling his exposed neck. "That was plural. How many sea voyages have you made?"

"Several, all across the Channel."

"Why would you cross by boat more than once knowing you get seasick? Rather lame. Why not take the Chunnel or fly?" It's more than lame, she thought, it's damned odd.

Ian dropped his head and laid a passionate kiss on her, his stomach rumbling the entire time.

"Well?" She mumbled against his lips as he was about to take a second plunge.

He sighed. "Ah well, it was a very long time ago, and I was traveling with a large group. We were required to stay together. Plus, we had quite a bit of equipment and going by ship was the...um, most economical. Shall we go before my hungry belly embarrasses me further? Unless, my little booty," he stretched her hands far above her head. "You'd prefer to continue with my despoiling of you."

"We can stop at this nice market I know on the way to my house," Miranda said.

She smiled to herself as Ian rolled off her, muttering about the pitiful end of his buccaneering career. She'd made up her mind to seduce him. Forget her rule about dating while he was her boss. She saw the whole scenario in her head. He'd never expect it of her. She'd never expect it of herself.

Ian grabbed his car keys and wallet. Miranda waited in the open doorway of the hotel room. Another thirty seconds and they'd have been on the elevator, but the phone rang.

"Damn. I have to answer in case it's a problem with the production."

He slammed his keys on the desk as he listened, arguing for a few minutes with the caller. He hung up, looking apologetic at her. "I'm sorry, darling. The prop department sent the wrong pieces for the prince's tent. I have to drive to London and oversee the rush delivery of the proper set pieces."

"Why do you need to be there? Can't the London staff handle the problem?"

"If it was for any other episode, I'd let them. But, the Battle of Poitiers is too important. Can you forgive me? I'd love a rain check for tomorrow night."

"You don't need to apologize. I understand," she said, hiding her disappointment. "Tomorrow's fine. How's 7:00?"

"Can I come over earlier?"

"Absolutely."

"I'll drop you off on my way to the city," he said, and kissed her.

Chapter Fifty-Two

The mist surrounded her. Disoriented her. The cool damp chilled her legs and swirled about her knees as she walked. Nothing in the vaporous world looked familiar. Her feet made no noise in the soft soil. A horse snorted. She stopped. Uncertain she really heard a horse, she cocked her head and listened. The silence engulfed her again. Her hands trembled. She hated being lost.

Breathing...something was breathing nearby. A large dark shadow came toward her. All she could make out was a black shape. The mists circled around it too. Then, she saw him. Ian, in armor, on a black warhorse.

"Miranda."

He pulled her up and placed her in the saddle in front of him. How he managed she didn't know. She couldn't remember what she wore a moment ago when she was alone and afraid. Now, she wore a beautiful gown of silk. Gold netting trimmed the lower half and glittered even in the fog.

"Where are we going?"

"Home, to Ashenwyck."

A moment later his armor disappeared and he was in front of her, shirtless and barefoot and in jeans. She still wore the gown but the sleeves had slipped down on her arms. They stood in a great hall as he unbuttoned the front of her dress. He cupped her breasts and ran his thumbs over the lace of the bronze colored bra.

He kissed upwards from her cleavage to her chin. He cradled her face in his hands and ran his tongue along the seam of her lips. He made a slow invasion of her mouth. Delving deeper and deeper, he controlled the kiss, channeled her passion.

The room spun around them. They were dancers without music. His urgent fingers tugged at the slippery material until the top of her dress hung about her waist. The bra fell away under his warm palms. He swung her up in his arms, carrying her to a high backed Gothic chair. She straddled him as he sat. He pushed her skirt up high and stroked her bare thighs. He spoke to her in a language she didn't understand that sounded archaic and erotic.

She slid down the length of him, off his lap and onto her knees before him. Now, she would control.

She held his wrists and brushed her lips across his chest, the soft hair tickled her nose. She made her way in slow sweeps to his stomach and released his wrists. She ran her tongue in and around his navel. The muscles of his abdomen flexed beneath her lips as the tips of her fingers slipped under his waistband.

As she unbuttoned the jeans, he *tried to pull her up, urging her with his strong hands. She resisted. "Stand," she said and he obeyed.*

She peeled his jeans down and circled the tip of him with her tongue. She relished his groan as she bent taking as much of him as she could in her mouth.

Miranda hit the floor with an unceremonious thud. "Christ Almighty!" She rose up on her elbows. "I don't believe this. I haven't fallen out of bed since I was four." At least, she fell off the bed while only having a sex dream about Ian. Thank God, it didn't happen while actually having sex with Ian.

She gathered the blankets and pillow she dragged with her to the floor and she checked the time. Midnight. The bewitching hour. She debated whether to wake Shakira and tell her what happened. To Miranda's knowledge, her friend had never fallen out of bed. But, Shakira never met Ian.

Rolling over on a buttock that would be bruised in the morning she sat up, turned on the light and dialed.

Chapter Fifty-Three

By midday, Ian finished supervising the loading of props onto several lorries. He considered driving straight to Miranda's house from London. Instead, he drove to the hotel, showered and used the time rethink other scenarios that might help her remember. He still arrived early.

Ian juggled the two bottles of wine with the big bouquet and knocked. She answered right away.

"I brought a Pouilly Fuisse and a Bordeaux. I wasn't sure what you prefer." He handed her the flowers and put the wine down on her dining table.

"I like both." Miranda smelled the flowers. "Lovely roses, thank you," she said and kissed him. "There's a drinks cart in the drawing room. Please make yourself at home."

Without asking he brought her a drink too. "I didn't see much of your house last time, mind if I walk around?"

"Not at all."

Ian noticed the two Leighton paintings the first time he came. There'd been no opportunity to discuss the artwork that day. Later of course, Miranda told him she found the pictures in the attic. Interestingly, she'd hung them in the exact same place as Elinor.

He remembered how adorable Elinor looked that night swaying as she sang to those disco songs. Nostalgia swept over him. He closed his eyes. *Elinor.* How long had it been since he tried to picture Elinor's face. Ian opened his eyes, studying the similar but different looking Miranda as she arranged the flowers. Could it really have been a couple of weeks?

A ripple of remorse ran through him, yet watching Miranda filled him with mixed emotions. She was his today, his tomorrow. If only she'd remember even a smattering of their yesterday, how much richer their new lives would be.

He turned his attention to the room again. Nothing else in the drawing room was reminiscent of Elinor. Miranda surrounded the area in textured fabrics. A contemporary taupe suede sofa with throw pillows in an Asian leaf pattern of deep green and gold silk complemented the khaki green moiré draperies. Miranda was eclectic but warm in her tastes and definitely a change from Elinor's adherence to William Morris's traditional designs. He stroked the soft nap of the coffee-colored velvet chair.

Curious, Ian ventured up to the bedroom. If a room can be a contradiction, Miranda's fit the term, romantic and exotic, enticing and bold. So like her, he thought, standing in the doorway. A satin blanket with a half-dozen appliquéd pillows of *in-your*-face rich jewel tones covered the bed. A delicate embroidered throw with seed pearls lay across the foot. Draperies in bright, dark blue hung in fat folds behind tasseled tie-backs. Miranda's display of Oriental porcelains, intricate and unique contrasted to the ultra feminine atomizers Elinor collected.

An inexpensive carved wooden screen of East Indian design, common to any London flea market served as a headboard. The allure of this room was the sensual beauty of material. The last time he was in this room, Elinor's antique Jacobean bed of heavy dark oak dominated the space. Ian sat on the edge of Miranda's bed and made a silent comparison. Elinor was like that collectible old bed, everything about her lay on the surface. She was what she appeared to be and would be loved for herself. *Except for ghosts. We were her secret.*

Ian gave the room another visual once over. Miranda is like a glassy-surfaced lagoon, but break through the smooth veneer and underneath's riptides, and surprises. With her you've got to risk all and dive in. How could she be so different? He went back downstairs not sure whether to be dismayed or unconcerned.

He sought solace from his confusion in the library. How much could it have changed, he thought? Once his favorite room, the simple furnishings, comfortable club chairs, large desk and potted plants all similar to what Elinor had picked, eased his anxiety.

The books Miranda used as reference material for the battle armor lay open on her desk. Ian thumbed through them reading the comments on her post-it notes.

She walked in and took his hand. "It's our day off. No talking about the production, understand?" Miranda closed the book he'd been reading. "Come to dinner, the stroganoff is ready."

"The last time I had good stroganoff was in a hole-in-the-wall Russian restaurant in a shabby Hollywood neighborhood," Ian said and let her lead him.

"You haven't tasted my stroganoff yet. That Russian restaurant may still be your last good stroganoff."

During the candlelit dinner, Ian seized the opportunity to discover any useful clue to Miranda's buried memories. Answers to his subtle questions didn't give him much information.

"Do you ever wonder about Ashenwyck?" He poured the last of the bordeaux as she cleared the dishes.

"All the time. I try to picture it filled with castle folk, bustling with activity. In my imagination, I even furnish it. You have to understand, I do that everywhere I go. I imagine how it used to be."

"Really? Tell me how you see the great room." Ian clasped her hands and tried to get her to sit while she talked. Miranda laughed and pulled away to gather the rest of the dishes.

"You told me a little the day you found me there but in my head, I've filled in more details. Give me a minute, and I'll join you."

Ian nodded and returned to the library.

After walking around the house earlier, he realized he had to rethink his plan. Badger Manor hadn't triggered Miranda's memory, neither had working with him. The Leighton paintings were the key. Elinor loved them. Miranda loved them. In her dreams, Elinor loved the Ashenwyck he whispered of. He'd remind Miranda of that dream castle.

He sat on the edge of the desk and mentally organized what needed to be done for the plan. He stared at the two tall bookcases in front of him, filled to the brim. One held mostly fiction paperbacks. In the other case, books on medieval history clearly outnumbered other reference material.

Curious about the abundance of information in that one area he pulled books from the shelves. Several were about knights and the Age of Chivalry, along with numerous biographies of the Black Prince and Edward the Third. Others were different accounts of the Hundred Years War; each contained bookmarks. Ian assumed it was research for the show.

In some, she'd inserted handwritten notes with dates. Ian didn't pay attention to them as he went on to the next book. Then, one note, written in red ink caught his eye, dated prior to the show...way prior. His was the first television series in four years that detailed the war against France and the English campaign. What was Miranda doing with all this documentation? He backtracked to where the memos started and checked them individually. All were before she came to the station. In each she marked the same place, and the same people, like she'd been searching for someone. Searching for him?

Ian closed the last book, sank into a nearby chair and propped his feet up on the desk. Perfect. I'm the knight you_seek. Once I give you Ashenwyck and you learn our history, you'll know it too. What started as a slow, humorous chuckle, rumbled up until he found himself laughing.

That's how Miranda found him, sitting behind a stack of books, wearing a silly grin. "What's so funny?"

"You're funny. Life is funny." Ian stood and held his hand out. "Come here."

She looked suspicious but came around the desk. Ian stepped behind her so she had a clear view of the shelves. "What do you see?"

Miranda blew out a long, impatient sigh.

"Okay Ian, I'm going for the obvious here, books. I see books."

He wrapped his arms around her and draped her hair over to one side and kissed her nape. "What kind of books?"

She tilted forward giving him better access to the spot he knew was highly sensitive.

Ian traced a path of kisses from the base of her ear down the side of her neck.

"Ian."

His name was lost to a moan as he found an especially vulnerable place. He'd remember this weak spot for when he needed it down the road, whenever she was mad at him.

"Hmmm...Yes, darling."

"I don't want to talk about books. I...I want-"

He lifted his head so his lips brushed her ear. "What? What do you want?"

"No, don't stop." The plea spilled out. "I want more kisses, here and here." Miranda touched a finger to the hollow above her collar bone and then back to the susceptible area on her neck.

Ian followed her finger with his lips. "What kind of books?" he asked, gliding his hands up Miranda's ribcage to stroke the sensitive inner flesh of her arm. His thumbs continued the erotic motion over the sides of her breasts as he trapped her nipples between his fingers. "Tell me about them."

"Uh, history, they're my history material." She closed her eyes and dropped her head back against his chest. "Ian, why are we talking about books? Why are we talking at all?" Her voice had gone from a soft whimper to a low seductive invitation.

A part of him wondered the same thing, mostly the lower part. "Miranda, you're not paying attention. What kind of history books?" He ignored the pressing need of his own body to pursue an answer. The answer he wished to hear.

"Umm, I don't know. Medieval."

Ian stilled his hands.

"Why did you stop?"

"Ah, I take it you like this." He caught a nipple and made small circles over the nub. "And this."

Kisses on her neck turned to little nips. She murmured something unintelligible that he took as a good sign. "I have an unlimited supply of these which I'm most willing to share, but you have to answer my questions."

"That's blackmail."

"Yes, it is."

"The devil take you, Ian Cherlein. They're history and other various reference books. I'm a researcher, remember?"

"The devil didn't want me. And I'm aware of your profession. I want to know why you have so many medieval ones. Why is the fourteenth century bookmarked in all of them?"

"I don't know. I guess I've always had a fascination for that time. Kiss my neck again." Miranda tapped a finger impatiently on the exact place she preferred.

This wasn't going as planned. Ian wanted to soften her up so she'd be more relaxed, more open-minded to his suggestions. Instead his strategy made her like silly putty, not to mention an erection he could cut diamonds with. Frustrated, he decided on a different approach.

"Do you believe in reincarnation?"

Miranda shifted and tried to face him, but he held her tight. "You know I don't go for that woo-woo business. But, I do get these déjà vu moments. So, I'd say where reincarnation is concerned, yes. Do you?"

"Yes."

"Interesting, I thought mostly women believed in reincarnation."

"You're probably right. Most men are keener on instant gratification than future gratification, I'm an exception. But we've digressed, try and stay with me." He gave her bum a light tap. "What do you think I might have been in a past life?" He asked with strained casualness. It was difficult to hide his anxiety as he waited for her to say knight.

"Definitely, a Roman general. I see you riding roughshod over some poor Celtic village." Miranda nodded as though the panorama played out in her head. "There you'd be in your shiny breastplate and fancy cavalry helm, on a giant warhorse oppressing the locals."

Behind her back Ian rolled his eyes. "I was almost flattered for a moment there. Oppressing the locals indeed." He leaned in and whispered, "Can you see me as a knight?"

Miranda made a huffing sound and gave him a sidelong look. "Of course, I already have." She lowered her gaze and took a deep breath. Ian felt her ribcage expand with the effort. "Ian, I--I've seen you. Today, I-"

"Forget the sword fight," Ian interrupted. He didn't want her to rehash what she saw that afternoon. That wasn't the picture he wanted to recreate for her.

"Tell me this, are you at least in the scenario with me as the Roman general?" He turned her so she faced him, his fingers spread along her spine.

"Yes." Miranda slipped her arms around his neck. "I'd be one of the downtrodden Celts you took as a slave," she said, covering his jaw in kisses.

"I'm starting to see the merit of being the oppressor. You'd be my sex slave."

"What if I want to be a kitchen slave?"

"I'm the general. I get to pick what kind of slave you are."

"How do you know I wouldn't murder you in your sleep?" She arched and looked up at him with arrowed brows.

"You wouldn't." He ground the words out with some effort. With her back arched the way it was, her hips pushed against his groin slightly every time she spoke. Agony never felt so good.

"How do you know?"

"I'd keep you too tired to lift a weapon."

Ian trailed his hands along Miranda's tailbone and over her buttocks. He struggled for control. For a tortuous moment he held her hips pressed against his arousal. She nestled herself in a perfect fit between his legs. He groaned as he brought his hands up, fisting them in her hair, oblivious to her small whimper. Desperate to bury some part of himself, he kissed her roughly, a choking kiss that penetrated deep. She angled so he could take more and in a violent frenzy of her own, Miranda thrust back.

Ian lifted his head so his lips hovered a mere inch from hers. One week. In one week, he could bring everything he needed together. He was bursting to tell her everything now but giving her the dream back, the memory, was worth the short wait.

Miranda slid her hands down his chest, her nails dragging over places that made him shiver in response. He had to make her stop. As her fingers dipped under the waistband of his pants, Ian grabbed her hands.

"I can't do this." It took his last vestige of will power. "We have to stop...for now."

Pain and confusion flickered across her face.

"Why? I don't understand." The pain disappeared. She stiffened and asked, "Why is it when I say I don't want an office romance you argue, then when I give in you stop?"

A fatalistic dread crept into his thoughts. What if her confusion morphed into rejection?

"You must trust me. I have my reasons. Believe me, there's nothing I'd rather do than make love to you. The time isn't right, but it will be soon. God help me, it better be."

"Now, the time isn't right. Interesting turnabout."

Miranda tried to jerk away, but he held her close and hoped she'd understand when he explained.

"Don't be angry. Please trust me, just a little. Give me one week, okay?"

His hold eased a bit. She sprang from his arms. "Sure." A myriad of emotions danced in those green eyes. No longer dilated with passion they were jade ice floes, cold, wary, condemning, but not sad. He'd turn those feelings around.

"You're upset and you shouldn't be. There's a lot you don't understand. This will all make sense in a few more days." Ian smiled as he offered his reassurance.

Her expression didn't change.

It would be so easy to play to the present, forget the past, win her over and sort the details out later. He refused to take the coward's way. She deserved to know what they were to each other. This was the fulfillment of the dream they couldn't live then. Once he recreated the scene, she'd remember. What she didn't remember he'd explain. Their past will merge with the present and the moment will be that much sweeter.

She broke away and went into the kitchen. He watched her work at the sink, her movements compact and robotic. The sight tore at his resolve and his heart.

The last thing in the world he wanted was to hurt her, even temporarily.

"I think it's best if I leave," he said, joining her in the kitchen.

She didn't argue. For a moment, she didn't respond. Then, she only nodded.

"Thank you for dinner. It was delicious. But, mostly thank you for the company." He stood close. So close, he felt the warmth of her body heat.

She dried her hands and briefly turned to look at him. "I'm glad you enjoyed the meal."

"And the company."

"Me too," she said, stepping from him. "I'll walk you to the door."

Worried, Ian didn't move. "You're angry."

"I promise I'm not angry."

He didn't know what to do. At a loss, he went to the door.

"Good night, Ian."

Her lips remained closed when he kissed her.

"You may not be angry, but you're clearly upset. I--"

"Ian, stop. I'm not angry or upset. You asked for time. Take it. Take as much as you need to do whatever," she said with a smile as warm as the one she greeted him with when he arrived.

He relaxed. On the front step, he paused to kiss her again.

The door shut before he had the chance.

Chapter Fifty-Four

Saturday night's debacle with Ian continued to weigh heavy on Miranda's heart. She'd immersed herself in various duties around the house to keep her mind occupied. Badger Manor never looked so immaculate. Zulu's tack shined. Zulu shined. He'd always been brushed and groomed after each ride. But this past weekend, his mane and tail were trimmed and combed, hooves polished, and his coat warm water shampooed. Too bad, none of it helped Miranda wash Ian from her mind.

He called Sunday. She broached the subject of the production's shooting schedule for the upcoming week. Three, twelve hour days were blocked out for the filming. It was a tough sell, but Miranda convinced him she should return to London. No production, whether for the small screen or big, ever goes smoothly.

"I'll handle any unforeseen administrative problems," she said. "You're needed to oversee the location shoot."

Ian balked at first and then finally agreed. He wanted to come over and spend the rest of Sunday with her. Miranda begged off with a lie.

"Lovely as that sounds, Ian, I have a nasty migraine. It's better if you stay at the hotel."

Filming was completed early and Ian returned on Wednesday by noon. She avoided him most of the day while he attended production meetings. When he came back to his office, Miranda kept her door closed. The few times he came in to speak with her, she laughed at his jokes, offered opinions when he solicited one and did everything he asked. Unless, she had a business question, she didn't seek him out or go to his office.

Thursday didn't go as well. Ian managed to be a constant presence in her office. Or, so it seemed.

After he tracked her down hiding in another part of the station, she escaped to the British Museum's library. A favorite haunt, she'd visited often. A peaceful place, the high ceilings, the recessed wood paneling that lined the walls, the old brass lamps with their pleated shades eased her troubled mind. The emotional razor blade she balanced on at work seemed a bit less sharp here, her frayed nerves a little less ragged. She loved the smells of the venerable building, an odd mix of musty linen, leather, and the pipe tobacco that clung to scholarly men of indefinite age. She wandered among the new volumes and ancient texts. Nothing here could hurt her.

Miranda caught the Oxford Street bus westbound to Bond Street heading back to work. On board, she climbed the dimpled metal stairs to the upper deck. She loved the views of the city the second level offered.

As she transferred buses, a quick glance at her watch showed the noon hour sneaking up. No reason not to blend the library and lunch into one journey. Not that she was hungry. One positive thing about relationships gone awry, they were good for losing weight. Too bad, they were so brutal on the system in every other way.

Miranda rode this route on a regular basis. The next stop was in front of Sound City, the biggest music store in London. Every woman knows, shopping is an excellent alternative to food.

When the bus stopped, she hopped off and went inside. An old-fashioned place, the store had multiple sound booths. A customer could listen to demo

CD's in their entirety rather than the thirty-second sound bites online.

She gave the rock section a cursory check then moved toward movie soundtracks. As she rounded the end of the aisle, she almost bumped into the broad back of a tall, long haired man, one she knew.

She tapped him on the shoulder. "Hi. I can't believe I'm seeing you here. I thought all you had to do was pick up the phone and CD's were laid at your feet."

"Hi yourself. Don't you look pretty." Alex held her fingers between his warm palms and kissed Miranda on the cheek. "Actually, I do have tons of CD's and digital files laid at my doorstep. But I also like to visit the shops. I like to hear what people are saying about different groups. It helps me to predict trends. Other times, I'm looking to add to my personal collection. Walk with me while I check out some new remixes."

Alex went to the solo artists section and pulled out a Frank Sinatra and a Shirley Bassey.

The selections surprised Miranda. "I never saw you as a Sinatra or Bassey type. They're ancient. I always think of you as a rock and roll kind of guy."

Alex frowned. He appeared somewhat offended by her comment. "I try to keep an open mind when it comes to art and music is art. I enjoy all kinds of music with two exceptions--weird Japanese instrumentals that sound like someone plunking on something hollow in a cave. I don't get it. There's no melody, just plink, plink, plink. And, I am not a fan of Hawaiian music or songs involving coconuts and ukuleles," he commented with a distasteful shrug.

Alex added the two CD's to the stack already in his hand. "Come, let's listen in one of the booths."

The store manager knew him. Instead of opening one of the small, more commonly used booths, he unlocked the biggest one in the front. Alex put on the Sinatra CD. *Night and Day* was the first cut. He took Miranda's purse, set it on a stool at the side and extended his hand. "Shall we, milady?"

Miranda and Alex simply swayed for the first few bars while Frank Sinatra spoke the opening lyrics. Then as the melody started and the speaking turned to singing, they moved in perfect time with each other and to the song. Within the confines of the booth, they somehow managed to dance in more than shuffle steps.

Sinatra's *Where or When* followed, the dynamic of the lyrics rocked Miranda. She'd done this. She didn't know where or when, but she'd danced with Alex before. She saw the two of them. It was a brief image and as real to her as dancing with him now was. The random flashes of Alex didn't distress her like the ones of Ian. Why they didn't puzzled her. But part of the inexplicable pieces and roller coaster emotions since meeting Ian came together for her. Just as she knew she'd danced with Alex in a place she couldn't name, she knew all the visions of Ian were based on a truth she couldn't remember. What role she played in those vignettes remained a mystery.

Sinatra went into another Cole Porter song. As she and Alex continued to dance to the romantic music, Ian's behavior the night of their dinner drifted into her thoughts. She'd practically offered herself to him on a silver platter and he'd turned her down. Why?

"I'd like to ask you something. Please, be honest. This is important." Miranda hated the tone in her voice. Whining or sounding needy and weak wasn't her style. The slippery slope to utter wimp loomed yet she couldn't stop herself. "I know I'm attractive. But, would I ever be attractive enough for a man...well, like you?"

Alex's penetrating stare bore through her flesh and bone.

"What are you really asking me?"

She shrugged. "I'm curious, is all."

He took his time before he answered. His hesitation gave her second thoughts about the way she phrased her question. But, to recant or attempt to reword would probably result in disaster. She'd dug a verbal hole and stepped in it. No need to pull the dirt in after her with an elaborate explanation.

"I'm a conceited bastard. I don't like being an also ran or second choice." His eyes started at her lips, traveled the length of her and back in sensual perusal. "You don't strike me as a mistress type and I'm a mistress kind of man. But, if you're asking me would I want you in that way, then I'd say..."

#

"Have you seen Miranda?" Ian poked his head into Kiki's office and asked. "I've been looking all over for her. We talked for quite awhile this morning. Then, she disappeared."

"Sorry, I haven't seen her either."

He looked down the corridor as though he expected Miranda to suddenly materialize. "I need to run an errand. If you see her and she asks, tell her I'll be back in an hour or so."

Ian considered mentioning Miranda's quiet mood the past couple of days. It crossed his mind, Kiki might have a clue. He didn't, believing it better to talk to the source. In the meantime, he run to Sound City and buy the Sarah Brightman CD's he wanted. Kiki told him Brightman was a favorite of Miranda's.

He stopped short of the store. There was a flower stand across the street. Why not get her a bunch as a surprise? He made a u-turn and darted into the road. Ignoring the driver's angry honking, he barely made it to the center divider ahead of the fast moving Royal Mail van. Four traffic lanes separated the flower stand from Sound City. He bounced on the balls of his feet for a second before making another honk inducing mad dash for the sidewalk.

He people watched, while the vendor wrapped the double bouquet in green tissue paper. Large, plate-glass windows lined the front of the store. A steady stream of customers came and went.

Ian's relaxed gaze drifted to the inside of the shop, to Alex and Miranda—the woman he loved and the best friend a man could have dancing. His hands flexed at his sides as he walked to the curb.

"Sir, your flowers."

The vendor handed him the arrangement. Ian took them without looking away. He thought about surprising the couple and then changed his mind. Instead, he sat at an outdoor table of a nearby Starbucks that gave him full view of the music store.

One cup of coffee grew cold as he kept his vigil. She said something to Alex that had him looking pensive and serious. Whatever he said back made her smile bigger than she had with Ian the past two days. After what seemed an eternity, their dancing ended and they left the store, stopping in front.

They appeared so happy.

In six hundred years it never occurred to Ian to strike Alex. There'd been arguments. There'd been rough sport in the lists, but never had he wanted to raise a hand in anger against the man he was closer to than any other. All of that changed in an instant.

Alex caressed her cheek and ran his hand along the curve of her jaw and kissed her. Ian shot up. He swore every expletive possible as his view was blocked by the red bus.

Moments later, the bus pulled into traffic.

Alex and Miranda were gone.

Ian searched the crowds across the road. Then, he saw her. She sat in the back of the bus, by the rear window of the upper deck on the bus. All Miranda had to do was look down and she'd see him. He kept pace with the bus for about ten yards, running along the curb, willing her to turn his way. Instead, she turned the other direction and waved. Ian stopped and followed her gaze. Alex stood a few feet from the bus stop, waving back.

Ian sat at the outdoor table, the flowers and coffee forgotten.

It wasn't supposed to be this way.

He sighed and thought back to the day he and Alex were given their new lives.

Chapter Fifty-Five

Basil and Guy leaned on the crenels of the ruined parapet. This was the seventh new century they saw. Celebrations had started early and were the liveliest welcome of a new century they'd seen.

"Are you terribly disappointed?" Guy asked.

"Not terribly, no. There've been worse disappointments. I had hoped to be reunited with Elinor by now. It's been over two plus decades since we parted...since her death."

Multiple explosions filled the sky in the distance with red, white, and green, star-shaped flashes. With a shrug, Basil added, "For such as we, that's the blink of an eye in time. Still, I expected to be among the living again by now."

"Maybe this decade."

Another explosion close to Badger Manor sounded and more fast burning starbursts lit the area.

In the corner, something moved in the shadows. Basil turned to look. A small-boned blonde sat on a pile of broken stones. The intruder wore a modern style blue suit and white silk shirt open at the collar.

Guy had also turned. "Who's this then?"

The stranger appeared without them hearing. Unusual for a mortal.

They walked over, unalarmed by the mysterious presence. No one had managed to surprise them since their demise. The possibility of frightening either was beyond comprehension also. As Basil once said, "how do you scare a ghost?"

The blonde stood. "Good evening."

Basil and Guy nodded and mumbled "evening" back as they drifted past. The stranger suddenly appeared in front of them. The knights exchanged glances. Mortals didn't move that fast.

Curious, Basil asked, "What are you and what do you want?"

"I am Gaby. The two of you are my assignment."

Guy moved closer to within arm's length of Gaby, eyeing the blonde carefully. In death as in life, Guy always wanted to know who he dealt with, friend or foe, man or woman. He picked up a lock of Gaby's shoulder length hair. The pale strands glistened in the full moon's light and reminded Basil of the wet threads of a spider's web.

The stranger stood quiet under the scrutiny.

"What is your given name? Gabriel? Gabrielle?" Guy asked and let go of the lock.

"Just Gaby."

Basil smiled.

"What are you thinking?" Guy asked, seeing his smile.

"I was remembering back to that first night at Elinor's. When I materialized, she mistook me for an angel. She was disconcerted by my physical appearance. She said she always believed angels were blonde and androgynous."

Basil's smile faded. "What do you mean we're your assignments?"

"You were promised another chance at life. I am here to show you some possibilities." The diminutive Gaby looked from one to the other, expressionless. "Come or don't come. I must know your decision. I have others to attend to this night."

"We'll come," Basil and Guy answered in unison.

#

They found themselves in the Sisters of Mercy, a country hospital near Cheltenham. The complex resembled a manor more than a medical facility. Every patient had a private room, even those on the national health. The busier, well known London hospitals sent their hopeless cases to the Sisters of Mercy.

"I would prefer to resolve the easier matter first," Gaby said.

Basil knew he should be ashamed, but he hoped the comment referred to him.

It didn't.

Gaby addressed Guy, "I have a young man to show you. I believe he will be satisfactory."

Basil and Guy followed the guide into a room where a male patient about twenty-five years old lay asleep. A metal stand held a bag of fluid connected to a needle inserted into the man's hand.

Guy's eyes widened. "He looks so much like me."

"He is your descendent over many generations through your sister. My superiors noticed the resemblance immediately and thought you might be interested."

Guy lingered by the foot of the bed. "What is wrong with him?"

"He is in a coma, the result of a motorcycle accident. Whether he recovers or not depends on you." For the first time since the meeting on the parapet, Gaby displayed a modest amount of emotion. "I see worry in your eyes. Let me put your mind at ease. Excluding this circumstance, he is healthy. There will be no permanent effects from the accident."

"Thank you. I did wonder." Guy stepped to the side of the bed and laid a hand on his descendant's arm. "My nephew," he whispered. "So few of my family survived the Civil War, I didn't think there were any more of us."

"Time grows short. You must choose," Gaby said, firmly.

Guy looked over at Basil. "What about you?"

"Go. Don't lose this opportunity. No matter what is in store for me, you must take this chance." Whatever the future held, the centuries old burden of guilt that weighed on Basil's soul would now be lifted. "Your fate is your own once more."

"I'll see you soon my friend." Guy turned and stared pointedly at Gaby. "I'd better."

Neither agreeing nor disagreeing, Gaby asked, "Are you ready?"

Guy smiled at Basil and with a single, small nod said, "Soon," then to Gaby, "I'm ready."

Wary, Basil stared at the now empty space where Guy had just stood. A mute Gaby offered no words of reassurance.

The man in the bed groaned and shifted. His eyes opened, and he looked at Basil. "I feel like I was hit by a lorry. And, this needle hurts like the devil. If there was a Frenchman here, I'd say stick it in his arm."

Gaby laid a hand on Guy's shoulder. "Welcome to your new life, Alex Lancaster. You should take things easy at first. You will need to learn how to work with two sets of memories but my superiors and I have every confidence in you."

"Shall we?" Gaby said to Basil and indicated the door with a sweeping gesture. As they left, Gaby glanced back and smiled, "For the record, you *were* hit by a lorry."

In the corridor, Gaby spoke in a serious tone. "Your options are not so easy. There are no distant relatives to present you. Instead, I will show you two young men. Both are the age you were when your mortal life ended. Ready?"

"Yes. Absolutely, yes." Basil flexed his fingers at his sides in nervous anticipation.

They entered a room where a ginger-haired fellow lay. Freckles blanketed the grey pallor of his face. His lips had a bluish hue and under his thin covers the man's body appeared wasted, almost emaciated.

Basil tried not to recoil. "What's wrong with him?"

"He overdosed on a narcotic cut with toxins."

Basil backed away and shook his head.

"Let me give you the details before you say no." Gaby brought a hand up in mock surrender. "This was his first time ingesting heroin. The concoction triggered a heart attack. Since this is his first time taking the combination there'll be no long term physical damage. Between modern medicine and healthier living, most of what has been done to his heart can be repaired. A normal life is more than possible."

"No. He is nothing like the man I was. I cannot do this, not with him." Basil hurried from the room.

Gaby joined him. "There is one more."

"Show me."

In the room across the hall lay the second man. Basil approached. The man in the bed was tall and broad shouldered, extremely pale, with dark hair, dark as Basil's. His features were similar to Basil's but different. His cheeks had sunken in, as though he'd lost interest in food, circles under his eyes gave them a bruised appearance.

"What is wrong with him?"

"There are extenuating circumstances with this one. They may make a difference to you." With those words, Gaby pulled the covers back to reveal thick bandages on each wrist. "He is a suicide or will be should you reject him. Some might find the taking of one's life unforgivable. I must warn you, as I did Guy, you will have mixed memories. Some of his sorrow will come to bear on you."

"It's not a matter of forgiving or not forgiving. That is between him and his God." Basil turned the man's wrist over and ran a finger down the length of the bandage. "He appears to have done a fine job. The cut is vertical and quite deep from the feel of the padding."

"A competent young man. He was thorough, even to the end."

Basil studied the face that may or may not become his. He stared hard at the man's nose.

"It is quite grand, I admit," Gaby said, eyes fixed on Basil's nose. "But, straight."

Basil touched a self-conscious finger to the bump on his crooked nose. "Mine was straight, once, a long time ago. As a young knight, I missed the target during a tilt. I took a solid blow in the face by the quintain." Basil shook his head. "The nose isn't important." Depressed, he stepped away. "I don't think he's suitable. I'm not sure I want any part of those memories."

Gaby looked thoughtful and sat on the corner of the bed, hands folded. "These are the only two I have to show you. I cannot guarantee when another opportunity will arise."

Basil shook his head no again.

"There's something else you should know," Gaby added. "Elinor lives. She no longer goes by that name, obviously. But, she lives."

"Where is she? Tell me." Basil reached out to grab Gaby by the suit's lapel, then dropped his hand to his side and tried to calm himself. "I must know. There are promises involved."

"I am Gaby, not Cupid. I have said all I can on the matter. I need your decision."

Basil opened his eyes a crack. He felt no pain from the cuts. He expected to. He'd been cut many times in his mortal life and in general most were grievous. He knew little of modern medicine but assumed this painlessness resulted from it. He opened his eyes completely.

"Welcome to your new life, Ian Cherlein." Gaby patted his leg.

"What about the scars? They are the mark of a coward. I would hate to have other people believe such of me."

"I can fix that. I am certain my superiors won't object."

Basil looked up to say thank you but Gaby was gone along with the scars.

#

Ian watched Alex walk back into Sound City. He stood, throwing down twice as much money as the bill required next to the untouched coffee.

It wasn't supposed to be this way.

Chapter Fifty-Six

Ian spent the rest of the day chastising himself for suspecting Alex. Miranda seemed genuinely pleased with the flowers. Her reaction helped him rein in his jealousy and concentrate on the details of his plan.

She hadn't come into his office except on business since his return. It was unusual. It would've seriously concerned him but she had agreed to give him the time he needed. He figured this was her way of doing that.

His plans came together fast. Today was the day.

"Julian, you've outdone yourself. I'm impressed with how accurately you duplicated these replicas," he said, when the set designer brought the requested props. "From a distance no one would know they're painted and not true tapestries. Really well done, thank you."

The normally cantankerous designer beamed. His crush on Ian was common knowledge. "Thank you for the opportunity. Are you sure there isn't anything else you need me to do?"

Ian didn't notice the adoration in Julian's eyes. "There is one more favor you could do for me. If you'll direct Symington's Transport to my office when they arrive, I'd appreciate it. They're delivering these someplace else this afternoon."

Julian agreed and lurched forward as Ian gave him a hard pat on the back. Alex nearly ran into the little man in the doorway as he worked to recover. A collision would've driven him back into Ian's chest. Julian mumbled a quiet curse in Alex's direction and made his way down the corridor with mincing steps.

"I'm glad you're here." Ian closed the door and laid the canvases out flat on the floor. "What do you think?"

"They're brilliant." Alex eyed the hangings and took a step back. "The old poof must be quite smitten with you," Alex sighed dramatically, patted his heart and plopped into a nearby chair. "So, I take it you've lined up a place to substitute for Ashenwyck?"

"I have." Ian rolled the canvases up and set them to the side. "Coffee?"

Alex nodded.

"You know Phillip Weymouth, don't you?" Ian went on as he poured two mugs of coffee. "His family still has an estate on the outskirts of Kenilworth. He's giving me the use of it over the weekend."

"You mean Weymouth Hall? I thought they gave the castle to the National Trust for tours."

"They did, but one wing is privately maintained by the family. It doesn't matter though, Phillip pulled some strings and the castle will be closed to the public for the weekend." Ian sat, confident in the soundness of his scheme.

"Let me see if I have this straight. You're going to hang copies of your old tapestries, move some other props in and recreate part of Ashenwyck's great hall?" Alex rested his forearms on his thighs and leaned forward, cradling his cup. "Then what? You bring Miranda in and hope the sight will trigger some distant memory?"

Ian didn't respond and braced. Alex's tone of voice carried an undesired negative taint.

"I see. Is this where you tell her she's your long lost Elinor? Please, don't answer yet. I assume you'll follow with an explanation of how much you and Elinor loved each other. Give Miranda the history of this past passion?"

Alex had twisted the intent and made it sound like something Miranda would hate.

"Is there some point you're trying to make here?

Alex gave his friend a long, hard look. "Ian, have you thought this through? Thoroughly? Because, I don't think you have. This scenario you're planning is not sharing the romance of the past with her. You're dragging her back to it. They're two different things and you don't see it. She's not Elinor, not the Elinor you knew."

"You're wrong. Just like Basil and I are the same, she and Elinor are the same."

Alex shook his head.

Ian slammed his palm down on the desk. "You shake your head no, but it's the truth. Our love has survived time. She needs to know. Look around you," He made a sweeping gesture with one arm. "In this day and age, it's considered remarkable for love to survive the honeymoon. There isn't a woman alive who wouldn't appreciate how incredibly romantic it is that Elinor and I shared a love so strong."

Alex quietly listened. "When you first told me about this scheme, I didn't say too much. I figured Ian's a clever fellow, lots of experience with women, he'll come to his senses." He set the coffee down. "Had I known you'd lost your wits, I'd have done more to discourage this lunacy."

Taken off guard by his friend's harsh judgment, Ian replied, "Why is this so hard for you to understand? I promised Elinor I'd always be there for her. I broke my promise which caused us both untold heartache. After her accident, I made another promise. This is the fulfillment of it. I let her down once. I won't do it again."

Neither man said anything and an uneasy minute passed.

"Ian, as your friend, I am telling you, don't do this. It's a disaster waiting to happen."

"You're wrong. She will remember. Except now, she'll remember the good, maybe not everything, but enough, and that's fine." Ian wasn't about to let Alex sway him. "Miranda deserves to know. It's her story, too."

"I swear you're the most obstinate fool I've ever met. If you follow this course, you will likely lose her. She's not the_same. We're not the same. You wanted my point, that's the point._We haven't been the same since that day at Poitiers. Open your eyes, Ian. We've all changed, and I, for one, am glad. Can't you love what you have?"

Ian didn't want this argument with Alex. Not now, not when he was so close to setting his plan in motion. He couldn't recall a time they'd argued so bitterly. If he were a superstitious man, he might consider this a bad omen.

"It's you who doesn't know. You've never been in love. You don't know what it is to love someone and lose them. I gave Elinor up. I had no other choice."

Angry with Alex's logic, Ian stood and moved to the window. He shoved his fists into his pockets, trying to keep his temper in check. He stared out at the grey-green dome of St. Paul's Cathedral on the distant skyline. After the 1666 London fire, he and Guy had come to see the rebuilt cathedral. Guy. How could Miranda recall him alone? Under his breath Ian said, "She remembers a connection to you."

"You're right," Alex said, "I've never been in love."

Ian's attention snapped back.

"But ignorant soul that I am, I always thought you loved someone for who they are, not who they were."

Jealous suspicions Ian had buried surfaced. "I guess that philosophy goes well with your personal agenda regarding Miranda."

Alex rose. "Meaning?"

Ian stepped around his desk to confront his friend.

"I'm not blind. I see how you are around Miranda. Oh, you try to hide behind humor and play comic relief to my serious suitor. You think I don't notice how you look at her or your gaze that lingers a bit too long."

"You accuse me of betraying you?" A expression of stunned disbelief came over Alex. He looked more pained than on the day he found himself earthbound along with Ian. "For the record, you're the last person I'd do that to. What would make you think so little of me, of our friendship?"

Ugly sound bites, Ian had said in anger. The words were out and couldn't be taken back. Remorse filled Ian but not absolute certainty he was wrong.

Alex walked towards the door. Stopping midway, he turned and shot Ian a nasty half-smile. "If I'm to be condemned, then let me give you reason. When this is over, I want Miranda."

Ian stiffened. "You've got some balls. Where do you come off asking that?"

"I want her. Although until now, I haven't done anything about it. I may not know what it's like to be in love. I do know I care about *Miranda*." Alex stressed each syllable in *Mir-an-da*. "Do you?"

He walked out.

Ian's grip tightened around the coffee cup. "Damn you Alex. Damn you for not understanding. And damn me, for forgetting what sort of man you are, what sort of friend."

Ian considered Alex's warning. In the years since their return, opportunities and good fortune came along nonstop. For Alex these last years were a romp, but in that entire time, Ian never stopped searching for Elinor. Now he found her in Miranda. No force on earth would to ruin it for him.

Miranda knocked softly and opened the door just wide enough to peek inside.

"Is everything all right? Alex stormed by my office. Did you quarrel?"

"It's nothing to worry about," Ian said and hoped at the end of the day that would be true. "We have some philosophical differences on how to handle a situation." He took a moment to study her, head to toe, no lusty intent, just a simple look. She was so winsome standing there. Intelligent, quick to laugh, charming...when she chose to be, and naturally sexy, Elinor couldn't have come better packaged. He should be more grateful. In that respect, he'd give Alex his due.

Ian took Miranda by the arm. "You brought your overnight case?" She nodded as they entered her office. "Good. Grab your bag. We're leaving for the castle."

"Now? I thought we weren't expected until later this afternoon. I haven't put my paperwork away or anything." Miranda began closing books and clearing her desk.

"Leave that stuff." Ian picked up her case and purse. "We're going now," he said and held the handbag out.

She slipped the purse strap over her shoulder. When she reached for a book on Norman castles, Ian intercepted her. He wrapped his hand around hers and tried to lead her away.

"Ian, stop." Miranda tugged against him. "I need the book. You said you wanted pictures to compare and see if Weymouth Hall was feasible for future location shoots."

"Pictures aren't necessary. Weymouth has everything I require."

Miranda resisted his pull, refusing to budge.

"What are you doing?" Ian asked, confused.

"If you know Weymouth has what you want, why are we going?"

"Because, I want you to see it. Your reaction is important to me." A host of disturbing emotions showed in her eyes. Wariness? Hurt? Suspicion? "God, not now," he whispered, as an ominous sense of foreboding nagged at him. She had to go. "You'll like it. I think you're going to be pleasantly surprised."

The emotions of a moment earlier disappeared. "No," she said, flatly.

"What do you mean no?"

"Just what I said, no. I'm not going."

"You already agreed. You have to come. It's important."

"Nonsense. You're saying that to get your way. You've just said Weymouth has all you need, so why is it so important for me to go?" she inquired in that same flat tone.

"Trust me, it is."

"I can't go."

Impatient with her obstinacy, he demanded, "Can't or won't?" He hadn't anticipated this situation, never even contemplated the possibility she'd refuse.

"Both. I can't let myself be hurt by you anymore. I'm done playing mouse to your cat."

If he thought himself confused before it was the tip of the iceberg compared to his current state. "Pray, go on," he said, sarcasm getting the better of him. "I'm afraid you have me at a disadvantage. I am utterly baffled as to your meaning."

"In the beginning--"

Miranda glared when he sighed aloud.

"Sorry, go on."

"In the beginning, I thought you were truly interested in me."

Ian opened his mouth to interject but didn't. Instead, he half-listened to her and half-questioned how a day that started off so good could turn to shit so fast.

"I wanted to think there was a chance for us. If you got to know me over the course of time, I'd come to mean something to you, not be some office fling."

Ian clenched his teeth to keep silent. He thought he'd made it clear she wasn't a fling. What triggered this sudden and unwarranted doubt?

She paused and took a deep breath, which Ian guessed was to screw up her courage for additional vitriol aimed at something he had or hadn't done. Ian wasn't sure at this point.

"The first time you began to seduce me, in the garage, I was embarrassed. I blamed myself for letting it go so far. I behaved like a tramp," she said with a cool, almost detached attitude that worried him more than tears or anger.

Miranda continued, "I haven't forgotten the disgusted look on your face. Then last weekend when you rejected me, I added ashamed and hurt to embarrassment.

"I'm not a complete fool, Ian. Twice, you've started to make love to me, and when I responded, you ended it. I spent the past few days trying to figure out why.

"Now, I realize it doesn't matter. I'm not good at these cat and mouse games. You are what you are, and I am what I am. Whatever that is, clearly it's not what you want."

He listened, stung by the cynical analysis.

"I'm your research assistant. It's better if we keep it that way," she said, with a hint of defiance, like Joan of Arc taunting the torchbearer.

The cutting speech wasn't spontaneous. She'd rehearsed and waited for the right time to deliver it. Ian cursed his blindness. All week, the evidence of her intent had been obvious. Her sparkle when they worked together had vanished, their easy repartee replaced by polite but reserved conversation. He'd been too absorbed with his own grand plans to question her behavior the way he should have.

Ian drew Miranda closer, anchoring her at the waist with his free hand. There'd be no tug of war, no battle of wills, no chance for her to do anything but listen.

"Everything you believe is wrong."

She opened her mouth to no doubt object.

"Don't say a word. It's my turn to talk. I listened while you crucified my character for the last few minutes and called me an insensitive s.o.b."

"I never said that. I didn't call you names."

"Didn't you?" Ian grunted, "Could have fooled me."

The corridor wasn't the best place for this conversation. He was afraid if he moved them to his office, he'd lose the advantage of time. The longer she had to think the more adamant she might become.

He bent low and spoke in a hushed tone. "I was not disgusted with you that night in the garage. I was disgusted with myself. I backed off because you deserved better than a quick seduction in a dirty car park. From the earful you just gave me, I see that courtesy was a mistake."

Miranda had the decency to look embarrassed.

"I've wanted you from the moment I saw you and not just physically. If I'd told you the truth then, you'd have misinterpreted my intentions. You'd have labeled my sincere feelings as self-serving flattery."

She remained stiff in his arms and refused to make eye contact.

"As to last weekend, I said all would be explained, which I plan to do today. What I have to say can't be said here." Ian lifted his lips to her temple and brushed a light kiss against a small blue vein that pulsed.

Miranda gave her head a little shake.

"I'm sorry Ian. I imagine you have a host of reasons to justify what's transpired. It doesn't make a difference."

Her voice broke and she cleared her throat. A small sign of how close to the surface her emotions were. He didn't know if that was a turn for the good or bad.

"I know with a certainty, you will break my heart. Better to remove myself from your crosshairs before I'm too shattered to recover."

"What makes you so sure?"

"I just know. It's as if it's stamped on my psyche, almost organic. I've...I've...sensed it in a way I can't describe."

She remembered...but, only the pain. Not the love.

His mind raced.

"Four hours, that's all I ask. There's so much you need to know."

"What can four hours do?"

"Everything you think you know will change."

"And if you're wrong?"

"I'm not."

An agonizing long minute passed in silence. He held her so tight it took him several seconds to realize she nodded yes.

With her in tow, he rushed to his car.

The Lotus's engine roared to life.

"Before we get to Weymouth, I've a story to tell you. It may be hard to believe, but it's true." He glanced over. Miranda sat straight, eyes forward. A horrible vision of her covering her ears by the end of the drive flared. He took a deep breath as he pulled out onto the ring road leading to the motorway.

"I used to be the ghost of a medieval knight named, Basil Manneville. You were a lovely young woman named Elinor Hawthorne. You owned the house I haunted—Badger Manor. We..."

Chapter Fifty-Seven

Weymouth Hall sat on a hill, its butter colored walls visible for several miles. An impressive structure from a distance, it was glorious up close. A winding, gravel drive snaked its way from the road to the front door.

The original gatehouse and curtain wall were destroyed long ago and the ruins removed. The surviving rectangular Keep had been restored in stages over the last three centuries along with the other buildings. Square towers rose high at each corner, all topped with grey stone and pointed spires. Rectangular windows gracefully positioned along the curve of each turret on the upper floors were offset by the medieval arrow loop windows scattered around the stronghold.

Miranda rolled the window down as Ian entered the castle road. "It's magnificent."

Ian waited, letting her take as much time as she wanted to look the castle over. No matter what went on inside her head about the two of them, the historian in her would be fascinated. If only for a few minutes, she'd put aside everything else.

"Some guide books call it one of the most beautiful castles in England," she said, "and it is."

"I thought you'd think so."

Quiet on the two hour drive, Miranda listened as Ian told her about his past and then, their past. He'd gone into great detail discussing how Basil and Elinor's love affair changed him. He left nothing out-all that was good and all that made them separate was retold.

When he related how he knew she was his Elinor the first time they met, she asked only a few questions. Her stillness chilled him. He assumed when she heard their story it would awaken some memories. Just a shred, the smallest acknowledgement, would be enough. Nothing. Not the tiniest reaction. Perversely, he'd welcome any emotion from her now, even if she called him delusional, or a liar. Anything was better than this silence.

The Weymouth family butler came out to greet them.

“Good afternoon, I hope your drive was pleasant." The butler dipped his head to Miranda and took their bags.

"Thank you Claude, the drive was fine. Did the delivery from Symington’s arrive?" At this point, Ian didn't really care if the tapestries came. He doubted they'd have the effect he'd sought.

"Yes, they were placed according to your request as was everything else. Did you wish to see them?"

"No, I'm confident they’re perfect." Hesitant, Ian laid a light palm on the small of her back and led Miranda into the elegant receiving hall of the castle's private quarters.

A fair-haired woman Miranda’s age in a simple black dress with white collar and cuffs stepped forward.

"I'm Hannah, your maid. I'll take your bag upstairs and unpack for you Miss Coltrane."

"Hannah, you needn't bother to un--" Miranda shot a hesitant glance in Ian's direction. "That will be fine, thank you."

As she started to follow the maid, Ian hooked Miranda’s elbow. She raised flat, firm palms to his chest. The response seemed defensive and his spirits sank lower.

"Talk to me, please. I can't let you walk away, not knowing what you think, what...," Ian stopped. He struggled to find the words to make her stay.

Miranda put a finger to his lips.

"Don't say anymore right now. Let me be alone with my thoughts for a bit. Give me a little time to sort out my feelings. We'll talk after."

Ian's arms folded around her in a tight embrace that went unreturned.

"Where will I find you?" she asked.

"Just past this room is an informal drawing room. Take as long as you need," he said and dropped his arms to his sides. He wanted to offer reassurance, as much for his sake as hers. The only words that came to him seemed inadequate and hollow.

He watched her climb the stairs and walk down the hall until she was out of sight. Never, had he been so unsure of himself. For the first time, in a long, long time, he said a silent prayer.

In the drawing room, Ian paced a relentless path over the Aubusson rug. He lifted a scotch he'd poured at the start of his vigil to his lips only to bring it back down untouched. An action he repeated numerous times as Miranda remained upstairs.

He stopped pacing as the scent of L'interdit drifted over to him. Ian started toward Miranda and then paused, uncertain what to do. For one interminable minute neither moved nor spoke.

"My room overlooks a giant garden maze," Miranda said at last.

"How apropos."

Her gaze bypassed the tapestries as she glanced around the room and settled on the one of several vases of pale roses.

"The roses are lovely. My favorite colors. Thank you."

"I wanted to impress you, can you tell?" Ian forced a smile as he surveyed the profusion of flowers. "Shall we talk?" He extended a hand and gestured to the sofa.

Miranda lingered in front of the leopard tapestry. '*Virtute et Armis*,' with courage and arms. It sounds like a king's motto, fearsome and regal."

She moved closer and inspected both hangings. "We used painted canvas for the backdrop when Hugh interviewed you."

Ian let her take time to scrutinize the replicas. "I remember. Do you like them?"

"Yes. They're very colorful, especially the leopard one," she said, fingering the edge of it.

"Do they seem familiar at all to you?"

"No, should they?" She watched him with an odd mixture of challenge and curiosity.

He tried not to let his disappointment show. There'd be no going back. He'd opened this particular Pandora's Box and would see it through to the end.

"'Virtute et Armis' was my family's motto. The leopard was our badge," he told her.

"I imagine Elinor would've known them," she said quietly and sat on the sofa.

"Yes."

She moved a bit farther away as he joined her. A subtle action, but not so subtle it went unheeded. They were like strangers sharing a park bench.

"I'd like to explain more about what I told you this afternoon."

She inclined her head and opened her mouth to speak, but he cut her off. "I know my story is the most far-fetched tale you've ever heard. You've every right to think me crazy and go running out of here. I've no physical proof I can offer you. I only hope somehow you will believe me."

She took his hand and a brief surge of optimism rippled through him.

"I believe you." Her soft fingers slid over his rough palm, but she made no effort to move closer. "Ian, from the first time we met, I've had strange, ethereal visions of you. Visions of you as a knight, or dressed in medieval clothing, never as you are now. Often they were flashes that disappeared as fast as they came, like the coming attractions of an action movie. Sometimes, I'd see a woman. I'd never see her face, not clearly anyway, but the man was always you. What you described were my imaginings in detail. I've never told anyone about them. You couldn't have known so much unless--well, unless in some way you shared the experience." Miranda slipped her hand from his. "I need a moment to collect my thoughts."

Somewhere a night owl screeched, followed by the high-pitched, plaintive squeal of its dinner. Ian never cared much for owls.

The silence between the two of them stretched.

Miranda inhaled and then blew the air out in a slow stream. "I'm trying to muster courage I'm not sure I have."

He reached to hold her hand again but she folded her fingers together.

"Tell me again about you and Elinor?"

Ian searched for the words to make her understand. "What...what Elinor and I had was the best thing that happened to me. In my old life," he clarified, "I had everything except love. After I lost all the mortal world had to offer, I gained something far more precious. I fell in love, and by some miracle, my love was returned. In death, when I had nothing to give her, she gifted me with her heart.

"Her love, our love, gave me my life back. It's an enormous present I never believed possible." Ian leaned in and clasped Miranda's hands between his. "I thought you'd want to know, want to remember, even if it was the tiniest of memories. When I saw Elinor again in you, I assumed what we shared would mean the same to you as it did to me."

Miranda looked away. A shiver moved from her shoulders along the length of her spine and arms. After a long pause, she straightened and faced him once more. His heart wrenched at the regret and anguish in her eyes. Hope faded.

"The relationship you've described sounds beautiful. On the other hand, I feel like I've been crushed under a steamroller, smashed into a million pieces." She took a deep breath, her shoulders sagging over a sad sigh as she let it out. "I'm sorry. Only a hideous, selfish person wouldn't be happy for you, for what the two of you had, but I'm not glad. That's awful of me, but it's the truth."

Ian's heart split apart.

Miranda explained. "Sometimes, when I'd have a vision I'd be overwhelmed with fear, fear you'd break my heart. I was never sure whether the feeling was a knee-jerk reaction to your reputation or not. In spite of that, I felt an attraction to you which surpassed anything else. Now, I wonder if it wasn't some lingering memory of Elinor's experience."

Ian knew it was. Why had only the hurt come through?

"I've always wanted to believe in reincarnation, although it was an abstraction to me, like Heaven and Hell."

At her comment about reincarnation, optimism briefly surged again.

Miranda went on, "Faced with the reality, the truth of its existence, I think I preferred it as an abstraction." She tilted her head, her focus fixed on a spot over his shoulder.

Emotions warred within him. A part of him wanted to know her thoughts, a part dreaded knowing.

Her gaze returned to him.

"I'm not Elinor. I'm Miranda. I have my own likes and dislikes, my own desires and dreams. Elinor is somebody I used to be and no longer am.

"I don't know Elinor, and I don't know Basil. I do know I love you...Ian. I love the way you bluster about when you're peeved." A faint smile touched the corners of her mouth.

"Miranda-"

"I love your mind and your wicked sense of humor. Mostly, I love the way you make me feel when I'm in your arms. When you hold me, there's only we two in the whole world."

She lifted a hand and combed his hair with her fingers. "I love you. The mortal man." She caressed his temples and the tender stroke of her fingertips tickled his cheek as she drew a path to his jaw. "And you love the memory of the woman I used to be." Several seconds passed before Miranda spoke again. "It appears we've come full circle, one still loving a mortal, and one still loving a ghost. Rather a bittersweet irony, don't you think?"

Her words cut deeper than any French blade.

Miranda bent, kissed him lightly on the lips, and rose.

Ian tried to stop her and make her stay. "No." His hand closed on air as she moved out of reach.

"My friend lives nearby and can pick me up." Miranda stayed out of his reach as she hurried for the door. "I'll talk to Kiki on Monday. She'll be a good assistant for you. Of course, I'll be available if she runs into any problems."

"Miranda." Ian closed the distance and seized her elbow. He didn't fight her when she pulled away. "Don't go, please."

She paused at the threshold. "I wish to my very bones it was me you loved." Without looking back, she walked out.

Chapter Fifty-Eight

Furious with himself, Ian launched his drink into the fireplace. Shards of glass covered the large stones of the hearth, the amber liquid rolled into the crevices. The violent act did nothing to ease his turmoil. He wandered the room aimlessly and found himself in front of the arched windows staring into a black night that reflected his mood.

A dismal picture of the future formed as he imagined the emptiness of his world without her. There'd be no Miranda to tease and make blush, just as she could make him laugh with a single look, or a few flirtatious words. She understood him, knew what ruffled his feathers and what didn't. They were simpatico in all ways. Until this week, a day didn't go by that they hadn't sat in long conversation, shared ideas, exchanged small confidences. They trusted each other, at least they used to.

The moon escaped the cloud cover and bathed the spacious garden in soft white. The evening breeze whipped fallen leaves into a swirling funnel. In the pale light, they seemed made of silver. In the bright sun, their rich colors would return. Tomorrow they'd change to green. Miranda's eyes changed from green to almost gold when excited and deepest of greens when passionate. *Miranda.*

Ian tried to envision Elinor, whose eyes were so similar, only to find the image fuzzy, vague. He pressed the heels of his hands to his eyes and pictured another. *Miranda.*

How could he be so blind? The time he wasted in nostalgic daze.

Claude entered from the servant's area and began to clean up the broken glass. Embarrassed, Ian apologized. "Sorry about the mess. I had a small accident."

The butler acknowledged with a slight incline of his head any personal thoughts shielded by his calm demeanor.

"I've taken the liberty, sir, to tell cook dinner will be later than requested."

"Thank you." Ian didn't want to say dinner might not be necessary at all, as though the words made it a certainty.

His work complete, under ordinary circumstances Claude would leave. The stately old butler did the unexpected. He remained. Then, he did the unthinkable for a servant, he ventured an opinion.

"May I offer an observation, sir?"

Ian nodded. "Of course."

"Sometimes the worst results come from our intentions to do what we think best for someone else. When in truth, it is what's best for us. It takes the worst happening for us to realize the difference. Talk to her, sir. I think your lady will understand." Claude added, "I've found most things can be salvaged with a clever wit and a heartfelt appeal. Oh, humility goes a long way, too."

Ian regarded the butler for a long moment while he considered the statement, a simple comment that carried a world of wisdom. Smiling for the first time in hours, Ian thought anthropologists should make a special classification for the English butler. Those dignified gentlemen who know more of what goes on in a household than the owners, capable of being everywhere and nowhere at the same time.

"You're right. If you'll excuse me, I have salvage work to do." He winked conspiratorially at Claude who returned it in kind. "Tell cook not to fret. We may enjoy her meal yet."

"Good luck young man."

Ian took the stairs two at a time and dashed into Miranda's room not bothering to knock. He glanced around the dark bedroom and waited for his eyes to adjust. The only light came from the bathroom, where the door stood open.

"Miranda?"

Silence.

Ian switched on a crystal table lamp and checked the bathroom. Empty. Alarmed, he made another visual sweep of the bedroom. Her purse sat on the dresser along with other personal items, her brush, and make up case.

"Miranda?" he called out again.

She sat in the shadow of the window embrasure, still and quiet. A sliver of moonlight lit the edge of the oriel window, enough to reveal part of her to him. She looked weary and forlorn. Long, dark streaks trailed from under her lower lashes to her chin. The faint light deepened the hollows of her cheeks. *The Lady of Shalott,* the famous painting by Waterhouse came to mind. Miranda wore the same haunted expression. A painful stab of guilt cut through him.

"We need to talk." Ian tugged her up from the stone seat.

She shook her head and tried to retreat back to the niche.

"Please go away, Ian. I don't want to talk right now. I'm tired. My mind is tired. My soul is tired. Leave me in peace."

"You promised me four hours. You owe me at least this one," Ian reminded her as he led her to the bed. "Sit. I'll be right back."

He went into the bathroom, ran the water and then came out a moment later with a warm washcloth.

Ian moved a chair and sat opposite her, a knee against the outside of each of her thighs. He cupped her chin and with gentle strokes wiped the stain of tears from her face.

"The clock is ticking. What do you want to talk about?" Miranda looked down her nose while he worked.

He laid the cloth on the carpet. He wrapped his hands around hers, preparing for the most important speech of his life. He ran his thumbs across her knuckles to memorize the feel of her fingers, their smoothness, and their warmth. He studied everything about her hands, how pale her skin looked against the bright red of her polish, the ridges and valleys the bones formed, the pink scar from an old burn.

"I'm a fool Miranda. The oldest fool you know," he said and raised his eyes to hers.

"The problem with old fools is we tend to hold onto what we're used to, what we're familiar with. We're so attached to the past we become oblivious to the present. I lived with the memory of Elinor for so long, it never occurred to me I could love someone else. I've discovered I love another even more."

Ian brought her fingers to his lips and kissed each in turn. "The past is done. I will always relish what was good. But this is our time. I want to embrace my new life and everything it has to offer, with you. I don't want to lose you, Miranda. I can't. You are my future."

He paused, desperate to see forgiveness in her eyes. Whatever she felt, she kept it on a tight rein. Ian pressed his case.

"All I ask is a chance to start over with you. Give me that chance. Give *us* a chance."

He'd broken her heart, twice. The first time, as Elinor was unavoidable. Whether or not, Miranda acknowledged the power of that distant memory, he was convinced it held great influence. He'd unintentionally broken her heart again in his tragic effort to compensate for the first hurt. Each action was explainable...fixable, he only needed the opportunity.

The verdict showed in her eyes. The skepticism he saw in their watery depths changed to condemnation. She dropped her gaze and eased her hands from his.

"What am I supposed to say?"

Before he could answer, Miranda said, "Loving you is like being in free fall without a net. I'm asked to trust you with another chance. You say it'll be different. Yet, not so long ago you told me you never lie. I trusted you."

The bitter recollection hardened her gentle features. The firm set of her jaw turned her soft, full mouth into a tight, thin line. The pallor he observed earlier was gone. Anger and hurt had heightened the color in her cheeks.

"Every kiss, every caress, every touch you gave me was meant for another woman. But you let me believe they were meant for me."

"You don't understand..."

"Don't, Ian. Don't insult me with some ridiculous lie."

"Am I not allowed to defend myself? The lowliest criminal is given the opportunity to state his side."

He took a moment to chose his words. If all she heard was frustration, she'd tune him out.

"How can I get you to understand? To me, you and Elinor were the same woman. Until today, all the things I hold dear about you, all the reasons my day is made brighter by your presence, I didn't see as unique to you. I only saw it when I realized I might lose you...you...*Miranda*, not Elinor."

All he saw were recriminations in her eyes. His explanation hadn't moved her, forgiveness as out of reach now as before.

Frustration returned.

"Tell me. What exactly is my crime? Being blind to what I had until I risked losing it? I agree. Guilty as charged. I doubt I'm the only person to make that mistake. Have you never spoken rashly and wished you could recant, never done something you regretted and wished you could undo?

"I'm human, Miranda. I make mistakes. Would you condemn me, condemn us, because of an unseeing fool's mistake? I've asked only for a chance. Is it so much to ask for when there's so much to gain?"

Maybe the spark of love she had for him would sway her to consider his plea.

"I don't know. I suspect the only real fool in this room is me. How can I believe you?" She sounded confused and unsure, but not indifferent. Ian feared her indifference the most.

"You don't have to believe me right now. All I ask for is the opportunity to convince you. I'm told I can be quite charming." He threw the last hoping she'd find it amusing. She said she liked his sense of humor and he needed every advantage.

"You might want to rethink that statement. Under the circumstances, charm is not your best selling point."

Ian gave himself a mental kick. In her current mood, of course she'd put a negative spin on the comment.

"One chance, please," he said in a more serious tone.

Her expression softened. A ghost of a smile touched the corners of her mouth as she studied him and then disappeared and she yanked her hands free. She knocked his knee aside and pushed past him.

"You're a conceited, bottom dwelling toad."

She was pissed, but he didn't think it meant he'd lost her yet. Pissed meant she still had strong feelings for him, even if they weren't taking a positive direction at the moment.

She paced four strides, pivoted and took four back and pivoted again.

Ian swung the chair around and calculated his next move, worried her hurt deepened with each step. He'd explained himself to the best of his ability. He was at a loss as to what more to do or say. He needed to distract her and said the first thing that came to mind. "Toads aren't bottom dwellers, by the way."

The feeble quip worked. She stopped, and a long, scarlet tipped finger pointed close to the end of his nose.

"Don't you dare get pedantic with me. You know very well what I meant."

Ian wrapped his hand around her finger and offered the only appeal he had left. "I've endured many losses in my time, both in life and death. The pain of those totaled up can't compare to the pain of losing you."

"Ian..."

She tugged her finger from his grasp. "You made me love you. Then, you made me weep for you. I've never been a crier. I hate it. Only the emptiest headed twit would give you another chance."

He didn't argue, pleased she mentioned a second chance. She was giving it consideration.

"What a wretched, pathetic wimp I am. You frustrate me, vex me beyond measure, I—oh!" her hands fisted as she turned the force of her fury on the heavy oak door. She slammed an open palm against it. "I don't want to love you anymore!" Open-handed, she pounded on the ancient wood. "I want to hate you."

She rested her forehead against the door and continued to beat a palm on it. Each strike grew less forceful until the storm finally passed.

"I'd have to stop loving you to hate you, and I can't." Her shoulders sagged as she hung her head. "Damn you Ian, and damn me too."

It was over.

He breathed a sigh of relief and took her in his arms. She laid her head on his shoulder, offering no resistance. Ian stroked her back, as little by little, the bunched muscles relaxed under his touch.

"Are you done being angry with me?" The slight nod of her head rubbed his collarbone. He brushed the hair back from her face and tilted her chin with his forefinger. "Are you done being angry with yourself?" She nodded again. He kissed her temples, her nose, her cheeks, all the places she was flush from exertion. "I haven't heard the word vexed used in a sentence in quite awhile."

"It was a first for me."

"Can we start over?"

“I’d like that,” Miranda said.

Ian stepped back and extended his hand. “Hello, I’m Ian Cherlein.”

“Hi, I’m Miranda Coltrane.”

She held her hand out as if to shake his, but the former knight kissed the back of her fingers. “Have I told you Ms. Coltrane how very happy I am you joined me today?”

“Sort of.” Smiling, she added, “Yes.”

Ian slipped her hand through his elbow. "Why don't we go downstairs? I've got a surprise for you."

"Another surprise?" Miranda froze; her eyes huge.

"Nothing earthshaking I promise," he reassured.

"God, I hope not."

Chapter Fifty-Nine

They entered the main drawing room where he walked them over to a bare area in front of the windows. "An old friend told me you like to dance." With an inward groan, he realized too late how she might interpret "old friend," as Elinor.

"Yes, I love to dance. Why?"

Relieved, Ian said, "I believe you'll like this CD. I thought we could dance to it." The music was his choice and he wanted to impress her with his selection.

"Ah...okay."

"You're hesitating."

"From your enthusiasm, I'm guessing you picked up a CD by one of my favorite rock bands." She stared at him like he'd grown another head. "To be honest, I never pictured you dancing to rock music. The image is almost surreal."

Ian wasn't sure if she'd insulted him or not. It didn't matter. "Dance with me." *With me, like you did with Alex.* He gathered her in his arms and hit the remote control.

The first few notes of Sarah Brightman's *Time to Say Goodbye* played. He'd never knowingly listened to the song before now. Kiki said Brightman was a favorite of Miranda's.

In the past, Alex would've gone with him to select the music, but Ian had chosen this particular CD on his own. Above Miranda's head, as he held her close, he smiled in silent self-congratulation.

Sarah Brightman opened with Italian lyrics then switched and sang the next line in English.

"Am I to get no breaks?" Ian released Miranda, hit the stop button on the remote, and stormed over to the player.

How could everything he planned go so wrong? Today, the most important day of his life, a day when the possibility of failure never entered his mind, was one debacle after another.

Miranda slammed into him with an, "oof."

He didn't notice. He glared at the player and ejected the disk.

"What are you doing?" She moved to his side, plucked the CD from his fingers and put it back in the tray. "I love that song."

"*Time to Say Goodbye*? *Time to Say Goodbye*? Do I need this right now?" Ian challenged back, incredulous she had to ask.

What she found redeeming about the song was a mystery. It took a minute for her protest to register in his brain.

"How can you like this song? It's about people leaving each other, as in, breaking up isn't so hard to do." He flipped the plastic holder over and read the song list. "I can't believe my luck. The first time I pick music and it's about goodbyes."

His grumbling continued. "What's so funny?" he asked, seeing Miranda's grin.

"You. You are so cute, all huffy and puffy." She pulled him down and kissed him on the cheek. "Ian, the title is on the front cover of the case."

"I didn't read the bloody thing. I grabbed a bunch of Sarah Brightman CD's and paid for them. I knew you liked her. I figured there'd be something to please you in the stack."

Her chest and shoulders vibrated with suppressed laughter. His best quelling look didn't faze her. "Go ahead; get it out of your system."

"Oh Ian, if you knew how adorable you look, you'd laugh too." Miranda played with the hair at his nape. "I think this is the most romantic CD on the planet."

"Truly?"

"Truly." She slid her arms down until her palms rested midway between his chest and abdomen. Her nails dragged back and forth along his ribcage. The tension evaporated as he envisioned all the other places those lovely hands could linger.

She ran her tongue along the exposed portion of his throat. "I thought you were going to dance with me," she said, her lips tickling the skin over his Adam's apple as she spoke.

"Your wish is my command, milady."

His hands rode low along the curve of her spine, the heat of her body warming his palms through her summer dress. She nestled her hips against his. With every intimate sway of Miranda's, Ian responded with the same effortless grace he'd demonstrated in the sword fight. Their two bodies moved as one.

The words of the song blended with the music. A pleasant but indistinguishable sound he listened to only so he wouldn't miss a beat.

"Will you answer some questions, even if you don't want to?" she asked in a soft voice.

The question surprised him. He revealed the most pertinent information. What remained?

"After what I've already told you about myself, you think there's something I'd hold back now? Whatever you want to know I'll tell you."

She took a moment seeming to gather her thoughts.

"I'm ready. I had to sort out what to ask first. You and Alex came back together, right? How? Was it some kind of...," Miranda hunched her shoulders and looked a little sheepish, "I'll apologize ahead of time here for any errors in verbiage, some kind of package deal?"

The language of the question didn't bother him. Ian contemplated how to answer. He hadn't discussed the details of their return when he talked to Miranda on the drive. He planned to explain everything later, after she found out about Elinor.

"I wouldn't have used that terminology, but yes, for lack of a better phrase."

For the next few minutes he described how Alex's destiny had become entwined with his. He didn't elaborate, feeling no pressing need to relive his centuries of guilt.

"How long had you known each other before Poitiers? I'm fascinated by a friendship so strong death couldn't affect it."

Maybe not death, but unwarranted mistrust and petty jealousy could, he thought, ashamed.

"Since we were nine years old."

Miranda stopped dancing and drew back. "Ian, the two of you didn't worship...I mean...you didn't make some kind of pact?"

"No. We never needed a pact."

"I don't mean with each other. With...um..."

"What? What are you trying to ask?"

"Did you sell your soul to the devil? Because, I don't know if I could handle that."

Miranda blurted the question out so fast, Ian wasn't sure he heard right. One look at her anxious expression confirmed he had. Ian's jaw dropped, appalled by the suggestion.

"No, I did not! Where would you get such an idea? Good God! I've been accused of many things in my life, but never of being one of Satan's minions."

"Think about it. One day you're both living, breathing jolly fellows then bam." Hand like a guillotine blade, she chopped the air. "You're dead, fini, sayonara, ciao-,"

"I get it. Dead."

"You're not just dead, though. Your fates wind up meshed. You roam the earth disembodied for centuries. Then poof, magically, everything is made right. I think it's a logical question."

He rolled is eyes at her bizarre rationale. "I told you, there was a life lesson involved or did you forget?"

"No, I'm only clarifying the facts. Sorry if I offended you. You said ask anything."

Ian started dancing again. Either that or shake her like a rag doll. His ego still smarted at the idea she could suspect something so outlandish. He pushed aside the uniqueness of the real truth.

"Since we've established I'm not Lucifer's vassal do you have any other questions?"

"Yes, but I'm trying to find a diplomatic way to phrase it."

"You weren't hampered by diplomatic concerns when you accused me of being a soulless bastard. Pardon me, if I find your timing regarding diplomacy less than sterling."

"You needn't be so testy. I never accused you of being a bastard. I figured you had to be legitimate to be an Earl."

"Thank you for that. You can forgo delicacy. Get on with your questions."

"You've been very successful since you've...how to say this...been back. How? You didn't fall from the sky. What about identification, legal paperwork, the documents people need to prove who they are?"

She watched him closely. Did she expect him to hedge on the details?

"I was offered two choices. One was unsuitable. The second was a young man, twenty-six, and an attempted suicide."

Miranda stopped dancing. As if seeing him for the first time, her gentle fingers smoothed his brows and trailed along his cheekbones down the bridge of his nose and the line of his jaw.

He didn't know what to make of her reaction. "Whatever you may think, I'm the same man inside I've always been."

Her hands dropped to his shoulders. "I wasn't thinking anything negative. I wondered what you looked like before. What changed? I wish I remembered Basil." She smiled. "I was thinking he couldn't have been more handsome."

"The resemblance is, or rather was, close. Until the time came, I hadn't realized how important it was to me. Not to sound ungrateful, but returning to mortal life after, well, after such a long time, is a difficult adjustment. I didn't want to see a stranger's face in the mirror too. You probably see that a silly vanity considering the opportunity."

"On the contrary, I can empathize." Her warm breath teased his ear as she pressed her cheek to his. "What a phenomenal experience, both unnerving and miraculous. Tell me about him."

The memory of the exchange washed over him. "He'd been a loner without family. Abandoned as a child by his father, his mother committed suicide while he was a teen. Afterward, he lived in an orphanage. No one at the university remembered him, but he'd gone to Cambridge on a history scholarship. Charity cases there are rarely befriended let alone remembered."

The young man's memory of how he was shunned spiked through Ian. It took a few seconds for him to shake off the dead man's bitterness.

"Between his education and my experience, I made a quick name for myself."

"Do you remember the entire process? Did your spirit erase his? I'm not sure if I'm saying this right."

"I know what you're driving at. In the beginning, I experienced a constant residual sadness. His depression surfaces on occasion in a crushing wave of melancholy. I've learned to recognize and relegate those emotions to another part of my mind. Not to oversimplify, but he chose to die. I chose to live."

"What happened to his spirit?"

"I don't know."

"Was he different in any other way besides the sadness?"

"Yes, in little things, odd things. He was allergic to berries, for one." Miranda's brows arched unsympathetically into a "so what" expression. "I suppose you think that's not problematic."

"I don't see how life without blueberry pie is a crisis."

"Maybe it's not traumatic. But, it would've been nice to know before I shared a bowl of strawberries and cream with the hostess from Designer Mine." Ian recalled the unpleasant night. "I wound up in the emergency room covered with itchy hives and ugly red blotches. My nose ran. My eyes watered. Not the most romantic of scenarios, I can tell you."

"Designer Mindless, that's what my girlfriend and I call her. Jeez Ian, she's dumb as a stone."

"I wasn't planning on doing calculus with her."

"Can we change the subject? I have more questions."

"You're the one who asked how he differed from me." Ian said with a pointed look. "Ask away, the more you know the better. It's important you're comfortable with my history." The music ended. "Would you rather sit and talk?"

"You read my mind. For the record, I'm fine with your history. I'm just curious."

Ian stretched out and propped his feet on the coffee table, his head rested against the sofa's cushion back.

Miranda curled next to him. "Tell me about Alex."

"You want to know about Alex?" Ian repeated and not so teasingly asked, "Should I be jealous?"

"Not in the least. I know Alex Lancaster really enjoys acting like he's The Big, Bad, Wolf."

"Don't kid yourself, darling. He's not that good an actor. What about me? You think I'm a big, bad wolf too?"

"You're just a big wolf. However, I think you can be domesticated. Not completely though." She surprised him with a kiss that left no part of Ian's mouth unexplored. "The sexy bit should stay wild."

"You know, I could get untamed all over you right now," Ian offered with a wink. "Say the word."

"We're supposed to be starting over. You're going to be contrite and charming, and I'm going to be magnanimous."

"Ahh, silly me, I forgot. Regarding Alex..." Ian said, "By a twist of fate his choice happened to be a distant descendent of his."

"Did he suffer the same qualms about a stranger's face as you?"

Ian draped an arm over her naked legs. "We never discussed the matter. The point was moot since they bore a strong resemblance. The young man was in a motorcycle accident and slipped into a coma. He wasn't destined to survive. When Alex picked him, relatives and hospital staff considered it a miraculous recovery."

Miranda scooted closer so more of her legs lay on Ian's thighs. He started slow with small circles first. As he talked, his hands journeyed higher to stop at the ultra sensitive area behind her knees.

"Since we're talking about Alex, I have a question for you. The day I gave you the bouquet, I saw the two of you at Sound City."

"What about it?"

"You seemed involved in an intense conversation. What were you talking about?"

"You."

"Go on."

"I asked if I was attractive enough for a man like him. He said, 'any man with eyes in his head would be proud to have a woman like you on his arm.' Even Ian? I asked. And Alex said, 'especially Ian.'"

"I should've known better."

"What?"

"Nothing. I need to make amends."

"Want to talk about it?"

"No."

She let the subject go and their easy conversation gave way to a casual intimacy. Relaxed, they touched and stroked each other in the idle way of longtime lovers.

"You told me once you don't believe in hell. If you don't believe in it, how could you accuse me of selling my soul?"

"Ian, because I don't believe in hell doesn't mean it doesn't exist."

"Interesting logic. Is it always going to be like this?"

"Like what?"

"Will your mind forever be a mysterious labyrinth of twists and turns I'll have to navigate?"

"Probably."

He kissed her and kissed her again, and again, from different angles. Little moans of pleasure guided him as he wended his way to a vulnerable spot under her jaw. One of many trips he planned to make there.

Epilogue

Ian and Miranda eloped to France the weekend they went to Weymouth Hall. The day they returned, he moved into Badger Manor. Alex was their first guest as a couple.

After dinner, Ian and Alex retired to the drawing room.

"I read your History Alive program is getting renewed." Alex bent to light a cigar.

"Yes, the ratings are excellent."

Miranda wiped her hands on a towel and joined the men but only half-listened as they talked. She had a plan to introduce Alex to her best friend, Shakira. She just needed the opportunity to present it.

Earlier in the week, she'd broached the subject with Ian over coffee while he read the London Times.

"Forget it. Alex has more women than a dog has fleas."

"I heard that same cliché about you."

"We're not talking about me."

The paper snapped to attention and Ian buried his nose in the financial section.

Miranda rejected the opinion. Men have no vision about some things. Shakira could use a knight in shining armor in her life, and Alex could stand to meet a nice girl, for once. She told Ian as much.

He lowered the paper long enough to laugh and inform her, "If there's one thing Alex has no use for, or interest in, it's a nice girl."

Ian was a lost cause. She didn't waste more breath trying to convince him. She schemed, knew the time had to be right. To succeed, Alex had to be in a receptive mood. Since he was a great lover of wine, women, and food, she waited until after dinner to execute her plan. A nice meal, then a good cognac, Miranda figured he'd be, at least, half way amenable.

The men nursed their brandies, puffing away.

"Alex," Miranda smiled the sweetest smile as he looked over, "why don't you come with us this weekend? A friend of mine is playing at a small club not far from here. She's interesting and a lot of fun. I think you'd enjoy meeting her. Miranda ignored Ian's disapproving look.

"What do you mean she's playing at a small club?" Alex nonchalantly flicked his ashes. "Is she an entertainer?"

"Yes, she's the second lead guitar in a weekend band. They perform at local clubs. Shake, my friend, is a barrister by profession." Before Miranda could describe Shakira in more detail, Alex shook his head and reached for his brandy.

"Absolutely not. I listen to grubby little rock bands all week long. I'm not spending my off time listening to yet another. It'll turn into a mini-audition." His steady, unblinking stare emphasized he'd brook no argument.

Miranda pretended not to notice and presented her friend's case. "I told you she's a barrister. The band is a hobby. Honestly."

"No. No way. She says the band is a hobby. They all say that until they meet me. Then dreams of being a rock star fill their heads." Alex picked Miranda's hand up and kissed the back of her fingers. "I appreciate the offer though. Please keep me in mind for any of your other friends who aren't musicians."

Ian interrupted as Miranda opened her mouth to make one more plea. "The subject is closed."

She glared at her husband and left to make herself a drink.

Alex cringed at the idea of another blind date. He'd gone on three in his life and that was three too many. He trusted Miranda's judgment up to a point. But he found out the hard way, women never see their girlfriends in the same way men do. Not to mention, her friend was called 'Shake.' What kind of name is that? Bouncers in sleazy Soho clubs are called, 'Shake.'

Ian met her friend and said she was pretty and smart. A good recommendation, Alex conceded. It wasn't enough to overlook her participation in some kind of garage band. He could imagine what the band was like. A bunch of chicks with silly New Age names...Karma, or Destiny, or Shake, who played bad cover versions of good songs. Alex downed the finger of brandy left in his glass and poured himself another.

#

The next morning, Alex drove back to Badger Manor. He and Ian left to join a mutual friend and some local riders for a game of polo. They played two matches and then went on to the Bird Cage pub for lunch before returning to Ian and Miranda's.

Ian hopped out of the car to manually open the gates of his curved drive.

A black Jaguar, classic early 1970's, V-12 model XKE, in mint condition sat farther up the driveway and caught Alex's appreciative interest.

Alex's attention switched when Miranda and another woman came out the front door carrying shopping bags. The two talked as the woman loaded the Jag's trunk and then went to the driver's door. Tall and long legged, she dressed in tight jeans and a little white tee shirt. Razor straight hair hung to the middle of her back. Large, movie star style sunglasses covered her eyes.

She looked familiar.

The blue-black hair, the shape of her face, the height, Alex removed his sunglasses, squinting, he tried to place where he knew her from. Then, he remembered. He hopped out and hurried up the gravel drive as she climbed into the car.

"Is something wrong?" Ian called after him.

"No." Alex spun as he answered and walked backwards a few steps. Behind him the Jag's engine started, followed by the crunch of stones. When he turned, the car had pulled away toward the far gate.

He caught up with Miranda.

"Who's your friend?" he asked.

Miranda continued toward the house, "My girlfriend, Shakira. You know, the one I tried to introduce you to."

"That's Shake?"

Miranda nodded.

"Shakira what?"

"Constantine."

Shakira Constantine. At last, he had a name for the mysterious lady he'd danced with at the charity ball, a brief dance which was regrettably interrupted. She disappeared from the event before he had the chance to speak with her.

"Why do you ask?" Miranda said in a sugary, sweet voice feigning ignorance.

Alex graced Miranda with his most charming grin. "Perhaps I was a bit hasty. When and where is her band playing next?"

"Tomorrow night, did you want to go?"

"Wouldn't miss it."

ABOUT THE AUTHOR

Chris is a retired police detective. She spent twenty-five years in the law enforcement with two different agencies.

The daughter of a history professor and a voracious reader, she grew up with a love for history and books.
She has traveled extensively throughout Europe, the Near East, and Northern Africa satisfying her passion for seeing the places she read about.

A Chicago native, Chris has lived in Paris, Los Angeles, and now resides with her husband, and five rescue dogs in the Pacific Northwest.

56033997R00239

Made in the USA
San Bernardino, CA
09 November 2017